To Kara,

"I am defenseless against you, Kara.
My will, my strength, my life are yours.
Command me as you will."

– Rune

OF CHAOS AND
DARKNESS SERIES

INVOKING
THE
BLOOD

BOOK ONE

KALISTA NEITH

KALISTA NEITH

INVOKING

THE

BLOOD

AMMEWNITION STUDIOS

ARTITHIA • ANARIA • NECROMIA • HELL • CHAOS

First published in the United States of America in August 2022 by
Ammewnition Studios
www.kalistaneith.com
ISBN 978-1-957303-00-0 (ebook)
ISBN 978-1-957303-01-7 (hardback)
ISBN 978-1-957303-02-4 (paperback)

Book cover design by Seventh Star Art
Character Art by Tonyviento

To be kept up with all things in the realms of Chaos and Darkness
please visit www.kalistaneith.com and sign up for our newsletter.

To my war horse,
til death baby.

Trigger Warnings

Attempted Murder
BDSM Bondage
BDSM Impact
Blood
Depression
Genocide (mentioned)
Kidnapping
Poisoning (mentioned)
Occult
Racism (of fantasy races)

Sexual Themes Throughout
Sexually Explicit Scenes
Slut Shaming
Suicidal Thoughts (no one dies)
Threat of Death
Torture
Vampires
Violence
Voyeurism

The Realms of Chaos and Darkness

Artithia
A series of floating continents serving as the capital of the five realms.

Necromia
Home to those both the immortal and short-lived who carry soul shards.

Anaria
Referred to as the commoner's lands, this realm is considered a territory of Necromia. Home to the short-lived who do not carry soul shards called Anarians.

Hell
A closed realm containing the souls who have yet to return to the Darkness.

Chaos
The mysterious realm of the Familiar, keepers and caretakers of Chaos and Fate.

Soul Shards

A small marquise cut crystal worn as jewelry, serving as an exterior indication of the power housed within an individual.

Day-Blood
The weaker of the soul shards, indicated by the white tendrils within the clear to grey mist surrounding the soul shard.

Dark-Blood
The stronger of the soul shards, indicated by the black tendrils within the gray to black mist surrounding the soul shard.

Shard of Darkness
A rare soul shard unmatched in strength, indicated when the black mist obscures the soul shard within it.

INVOKING

THE

BLOOD

One

The only thing worse than being surrounded by dark-bloods was being surrounded by noisy drunk idiots playing dress up. Every establishment would be like this tonight. Faye had no idea how this ridiculous Hunter's Moon tradition started, but she wanted to slap the moron who brought it about. Glancing over the crowded bar with a sigh, she picked at her dinner. The smell of cooked meats wafted through the air, interrupted by the scent of cheap cologne. Faye impatiently waited for the appropriate amount of time to pass so she could conclude her birthday celebration without her sister's objections.

Sparrow kicked her under the table, leaving Faye's shin stinging. "At least pretend to be having fun, bitch. You're spacing out over there."

"Do you see what we're surrounded by?" Lost and Found, a

popular pub in the merchant district, was full of people wearing glamoured fangs, elaborate costumes, and theater blood dripping from the corners of their mouths. Drunken masses decided it would be great fun to masquerade as vampires and prance beneath the glow of tonight's red moon.

Sparrow's eyes widened bringing her fingertips to her lips. "By the Darkness, people are having fun." She threw back her shot of whiskey, slamming it on the table. "You're having fun tonight even if I have to beat it into you."

She beamed, looking past Faye. Dark-blooded men were all the same with one exception, Vashien, her sister's beloved, coincidentally the only man to last more than a few months with her sister as well.

He was the only man who made Sparrow light up every time she saw him. Faye always thought he was kind and settled some of Sparrow's wild energy. Though she suspected Vashien's acceptance stemmed more from his relationship with her sister Sparrow than a liking for her.

Vashien moved through the crowd, shoving some of the more inebriated patrons with his green membranous reptilian wings. Artithians were a large, winged race, but even by their standards, he was big. Faye smiled at the colorful, glittering cake he held, looking tiny in his hands. A sparkler jabbed into it.

"Happy birthday," Vashien said, his smile warm and genuine. Giving Faye a squeeze with one arm, he set the cake down in front of her. Moving to Sparrow's side, he thumped her with his wing. "Are you behaving and keeping the birthday girl entertained?"

She snorted, shoving at him. "Faye doesn't want to be entertained."

He nodded, sliding his fingers under Sparrow's plate. "Are you done with this?"

Holding her fork like it was a weapon, she said, "Take my food, and I'll stab you."

Faye giggled as Vashien held his hand up in peace and leaned down for a kiss. Glancing at their drinks, he nodded to Faye. "I'll get you two topped off."

Sparrow leaned back in her chair, craning her neck to watch Vashien leave.

"What are you even staring at? You can't even see his ass when

2

his wings are folded like that."

Sparrow fluttered her hand at Faye. Sister code for *shut up, I'm busy.* "Get your own man to ogle." Turning back, she lifted her second shot glass while pointing at Faye's drink. "I think Vash only keeps that shit on hand for you."

Faye raised her glass of pomegranate juice, swirling the dark red liquid and smirked at her sister. "What about that shit? I can smell it from here."

"Touché," was her only reply before throwing back another shot. Sparrow's gaze fell to the decorated chocolate cake. She leaned forward. "Are you going to eat that?" Without waiting for a response, Sparrow stabbed her fork into Faye's cake, taking a bite. "Wow, that shit is good."

Faye pulled the extinguished sparkler free and set it on the side of the plate before nudging the rest toward her sister. She didn't understand how Sparrow ate so much and stayed so tiny.

Faye's gaze rose to the open dark wood beams along the high ceiling. The tavern was warm and welcoming. Clothed tables were arranged through the front of Lost and Found for those who wanted a hearty meal. The back and loft hosted three bars, two on the lower level and one above. She smiled when she spied a large sign on the railing above. *No flying.* That was new.

Faye could only imagine the drunken Artithian who thought it would be brilliant to fly to the lower level instead of taking the stairs. She would have paid a gold mark to see Vashien's face if anyone tried.

"It's your birthday so you get to pick. And these are the only options. Either we sneak into the Hunter's Moon Ball at the High Queen's castle, *orrrrr* we sneak into the Hunter's Moon Ball at the High Queen's castle? Great options, right?"

Faye's brow furrowed. Sparrow had been this way since they were children, wanting to shove every experience into her life. Insisting, *the consequences will be worth the memory.* But this was a bad idea even by Sparrow's standards. Vampires lusted during the Hunter's Moon. The High Queen of Necromia was a Pure Blood, one of the only two left. A born vampire. She held her annual celebration for all her kind at her estate while the pretend vamps partied in places like Lost and Found.

Faye frowned. "You've lost your shit."

Her long, wavy blonde hair fluffed as she bounced in her chair, whining, "Come on, I want to see the vampire orgy."

Of course, she did. "We're not going. There are two kinds of attendees at the ball, vampires and blood whores. And we're not vampires so are you offering up your blood and flesh for coin this evening?"

Sparrow rolled her eyes and plopped her chin in her hand, pouting as she looked away. "They don't know we're not vampires."

Even with the best disguise, their heartbeats would give them away to start. Lack of fangs. Revulsion to drinking blood.

"Excuse me, ladies," a man said, interrupting their argument, flashing his glamoured fangs.

Sparrow straightened, returning a smile as Faye glared at her for encouraging him.

"May I inquire what court you beauties belong to?" The man clasped his wrists in front of him.

Faye didn't need to look at him further. The dark-blooded shard on his index finger told her everything she needed to know. All magic was a gift from the Darkness, borrowed through life and returned in death. Soul shards served as an external indication of the depth of power housed within the individual, divided into two castes: the dark-bloods and the day-bloods. The tendrils within the swirling mist determined which caste they belonged to. White tendrils were day-bloods, black tendrils, dark. The darker the mist surrounding the shard, the stronger the individual. These small marquise-cut crystals dictated a person's worth and social standing, as though magic was all that mattered in life.

She glanced up at the stranger, the words of polite refusal frozen on her tongue. Faye studied his face. "Who are you dressed as?" The man wore cheap costume accessories like everyone else celebrating tonight, but veined misted shadows swayed beneath his eyes, brushing the tops of his cheekbones. The light caught Faye's ring as she sipped her juice.

"A Pure Blood." The man answered cheerily, looking down at her hand. The corner of Faye's mouth turned down, instantly souring her mood. He'd been polite because he thought she was one of them. She shoved it underneath the table. Faye's ring was a fake, displaying a soul shard Sparrow charged with her power to mirror her dark-blooded shard.

"You have the wrong hair if you're masquerading as the Shadow Prince," Sparrow interjected.

This man's dark mass of curls was all wrong. Rumor said his hair was long and white. From her seat, she could pick out a handful of the crowd dressed as him, but she'd never seen anyone pair bad eyeliner with the glamoured fangs. She answered dark-bloods in the same manner as their requests. He had been polite, so she returned the favor.

Plastering a false smile, Faye inclined her head. "I'm sorry. I must decline your advances." The words of protocol within the dark-blooded courts to tactfully decline romantic interest.

The man placed his hand to his chest. "Of course. I belong to the Court of Silver Leaves if you have a change of heart." He bowed and turned away from them, disappearing into the crowd.

As an Anarian, she was either propositioned or ignored. The ones who deigned to speak to her acted as though she should be grateful to catch a dark-blood's eye. Eyeing her ring again, Faye glanced from her hand to Sparrow's, comparing the two, unable to discern the difference. This simple fraudulent piece of jewelry allowed her to walk freely in Necromia. The energy Sparrow put into it would fade over time, seeping from a shard never meant to hold its power. It would be empty by morning.

Many Anarians dreamed of being chosen by a dark-blood, their life ambition to live within their lavish dark courts. As a pet. They would have material things and want for little, but it came at a cost Faye wasn't willing to pay. Being a pet meant someone owned you. A possession to be stroked and touched when they pleased.

Sparrow slouched in her chair. "You should give them a chance."

Faye narrowed her eyes at her sister. She'd given them chances in the beginning, hoping to be seen for who she was, instead of the soul shard she lacked. Experience taught her how young and naive she'd been. But looking back, it had been glaringly evident from the beginning. Sparrow had waited a month for Faye to turn twenty so they could invoke their blood together. They traveled to Necromia. Sparrow insisted on invoking her blood at the largest of the blood temples, deeming it good luck, but when she failed, she knew what fate lay ahead. That day the entire walk back no one had met Faye's gaze. She'd come there full of hope and left an Anarian, a shardless, powerless mortal.

"No," was her only reply as she looked down at her drink.

Sparrow tapped the table, pulling Faye from her pained memories. "Vampire orgy?" Sparrow's green eyes lit with excitement.

Faye fell back in her chair, looking upward. "You ask every year."

"And every year, I hope you grow some balls so we can go." Sparrow tilted her head, staring at her expectantly. As though she were asking for something normal, like going to the bakery. "I can't *not* know things. Please."

"Dark-bloods already surround me. Why would I agree to be surrounded by more dark-bloods? *Blood sucking* dark-bloods."

Sparrow slouched. "They're not all bad." Her sister, forever the optimist. They weren't bad to her. She was one of them.

"They are, and I can prove it," Faye said casually, inspecting her nails. They'd baited each other with those words since they were girls.

Sparrow leaned forward, her green eyes gleaming. "What are we betting?"

"We'll go to the Hunter's Moon ball. I'll give you five minutes to find me a day-blood among them. When you lose, we never go again. You stop trying to set me up on dates and let me die a virgin in peace."

Her sister narrowed her eyes, scrutinizing her. "If I win, you have to go on five dates and be *nice*. And we go to the Hunter's Moon ball every year. I need an hour to find a day-blood. Blood whores count, right? Anyone in attendance."

Faye nodded. "Ten minutes, unless one of them tries to bite me. Then you lose, and we leave."

Sparrow smiled, waving her hand. "They won't even see you. Thirty minutes."

"Fifteen."

"Deal." Sparrow beamed.

Vashien returned with their drinks. Sparrow took her glass of whiskey and swallowed the contents in one gulp.

She set the glass down and got to her feet. "Faye agreed to fun!" She swatted Vashien's ass as she happily made her way to the door.

Faye glanced at her pomegranate juice, feeling guilty for letting it go to waste. "I'm sorry."

Vashien smiled reassuringly at her. "I'll put it in the batch going to the cottage. What kind of fun did she talk you into?" Vashien stacked their dishes waiting for her answer.

"Sparrow said it was a surprise." Faye lied, knowing Vashien would stop them if he knew what they were about to do.

Vashien nodded, picking the dishes up. "Well, be safe. Don't let Sparrow make too many bad decisions."

Faye smiled and waved as she weaved through the crowded tavern, making her way to the door.

Sparrow already had their coats. Faye took hers, pulling it on. "In a hurry, hooker?"

Sparrow bumped the swinging oak door open with her hip, her winter coat half on. "I'm trying to get there before you change your mind." Pulling her coat on completely, she hopped in place, holding the door open. "Let's go. Let's go."

Faye stepped out into the night, the brisk chill biting her cheeks. She glanced up at the red moon hanging full in the night sky.

"This way." Sparrow took her wrist and led her through the city streets, lined with shops and tall buildings.

They crossed several blocks before Faye finally asked, "Do you know where you're going?"

"Darkness, walking sucks. Remind me to take phasing lessons next year."

Faye laughed. Sparrow would complain a few times every year but never learned the teleporting skill most dark-bloods used to travel anywhere they'd been previously.

"We're almost there." Sparrow pointed to a stone spire that rose above the shop buildings.

They stopped a block away, at the outskirts of the city.

Faye stared at the open courtyard. "I think we're underdressed."

Dozens of people were entering the courtyard, dressed in ornate gowns. Their hair arranged and pinned, some in beautiful curls and others wore strings of glittering jewels woven into their elaborate braids. The men accompanying them wore tailored suits. "This doesn't look like the vampire orgy you've been dreaming of." Faye stuffed her hands in her pockets to fight off the cold of the winter night. She looked on at the people entering suspiciously. How were they not cold? None of them had coats. Not even a shawl.

"They're probably blood whores." Sparrow shrugged. "Orgies won't happen outside where anyone could see them."

Sparrow squeezed her wrist, and warmth spread over her body. "Sight shield. We're invisible."

Faye skeptically glanced down at herself, then Sparrow. "I can still see you."

"That's because it's the same spell." Sparrow punched her in the arm.

Rubbing her arm, Faye looked at her sideways. "Are you sure?"

Sparrow shrugged. "New spell. Let's see."

Faye stood in shock for a moment as Sparrow bolted for the courtyard. Faye dashed after her, catching up as she waved a hand in front of a man in a gray suit. Faye mouthed, *What are you doing?*

"Relax, he's a baby dark-blood. You can talk. We're invisible, and they can't hear us." To the man, she yelled, "Can you?" Sparrow smiled at Faye triumphantly.

"Fifteen minutes," Faye whispered.

Sparrow waved her on, slipping further into the courtyard.

Faye followed cautiously and could scarcely believe what she saw.

The air carried a heavy floral scent. Twinkling lights laced intricate archways. Beautifully manicured plants and flowers surrounded grand fountains—pathways carved through the grounds with wrought iron benches scattered throughout. A string quartet played, setting the mood.

Beyond the hedged walls of the gardens rose a massive stone structure with several turrets arching high at different heights.

"I'm not burning my fifteen minutes here." Sparrow linked arms with Faye pulling her forward.

Faye followed, nearly tripping over Sparrow when they passed a woman seated on a male's lap on one of the benches. His mouth pressed to her throat as she clung to him. Her nails dug into the dark material of his suit jacket.

Faye could only watch, knowing she was invading the couple's intimate exchange but couldn't bring herself to look away. She abstained from sex, unwilling to surrender what little control she still had over her life. But this give and take between them appealed to her. Faye could see the woman led their exchange. Her vampire surrendered, receiving what she offered. An intoxicating dynamic Faye was nearly tempted to try.

The woman's moans of pleasure followed Faye as Sparrow led her further in. They snuck into the inner courtyard within the estate's towering stone walls. Sparrow followed the sounds of guttural groans and screams of pleasure. Faye knew vampires lusted tonight, but she expected them to have restraint. Or even modesty.

Vampires were no shy creatures. Couples and groups writhed in the darkened corners, a few even taking them on the benches for all to see. Another pair sat at the fountain's edge. This man had his hand up the woman's skirt as he drank from her—blood dripping along her bared skin.

Sparrow glanced back at her, her eyes gleaming with excitement. "This is amazing."

Amazing? Faye would have been shocked by such displays if Sparrow hadn't dragged her to several brothels, deeming it educational to watch when they reached eighteen and moved out on their own. "Drink it all in because you're about to lose in thirteen minutes."

Faye pulled her arm free from Sparrow when she got far too close to a woman being taken by two vampire men. "You don't have to be that close." Sparrow only fluttered her hand in response, and Faye rolled her eyes, stepping away from the trio.

Musk combined with the night-blooming flowers, scenting the air. It wasn't *entirely* unpleasant, though she could do without the overlapping sounds of bodies joining. Faye glanced over her surroundings, focusing on the more civilized vampires.

A large balcony overlooked the courtyard. Beneath it, dozens of vampires danced. Their gowns swayed with each sweeping step as they turned, circling the dance floor with their partners.

Faye watched, mesmerized.

A bell tolled, the single ring clear and crisp, reverberating through her chest. Faye swore under her breath, blinking her eyes as they began to burn.

"You okay?" Sparrow rubbed her back and led her away to a quieter area.

Faye rubbed her eyes. "I have a lash in my eye or something. We should go. It's one in the morning."

Sparrow snorted. "That wasn't the time." She tapped Faye's

wrist. "Let me see."

Faye opened her eyes wide, meeting Sparrow's gaze. "What is it then?"

"Their sacred moon is at its apex. They're supposed to do a ritual." She scrunched her face, leaning closer. "Your eyes are shimmering."

"It's just the lights here." Faye rubbed her eyes, beginning to feel better. She blinked, testing her vision, then focused on her sister. "I'm so proud of you, doing research."

"I wouldn't have to if you had the balls to go the first time I asked." Sparrow's eyes grew wide at something behind her. "Bitch they have food here."

Faye let Sparrow drag her to a towering, intricate display of tiny plates arranged with fresh-cut flowers. "Do vampires even eat?"

Sparrow shrugged. "Maybe it's for the blood whores." She picked up a flaky square.

"What are you doing?"

"Sampling the High Queen's menu." Sparrow popped the pastry in her mouth and leaned back, closing her eyes. "That is the best shit I've ever tasted. You need to try this." She stood on her toes, looking around the courtyard. "Do you see any other food stations?"

"No!"

"Stop worrying. They can't see us. Here, try this." Sparrow thrusted a pastry near Faye's mouth.

"Hooker, get off me." Faye pulled her head back, taking a retreating step. Her heel caught on a stone, and Faye lost her balance, falling against a hard, male body.

Sparrow snatched her by her coat and yanked her away before she broke into a run, laughing.

Faye's heart raced. She expected Sparrow to be the one to do something stupid like this. She glanced over her shoulder as they fled.

The man she fell into was tall with long white-blonde hair that looked silvery under the courtyard lights. He wore a tailored black suit like every other male here. He turned in their direction, and Faye's steps faltered.

A crimson so deep it looked black covered the entirety of his eye. Beneath his unnatural stare, shadows swayed, caressing the tops of his cheekbones, beckoning her. No, not shadows Faye realized, but the same mist that circled soul shards. The Darkness itself seemed to pour and dissipate beneath his dark gaze.

A wild sense of possession surged through her before leaving as quickly as it came. In those moments in between, she felt, *knew*, he belonged to her.

Faye mentally recoiled, unable to shake the lingering bone-deep instinct. She didn't want to own anyone. His dark gaze met hers, and Faye couldn't look away. Her lips parted as she exhaled a shaky breath, her skin heating in response to him.

He lifted his chin, taking a deep breath as his lids slid closed.

Faye remembered herself and turned away. What was wrong with her? "Sparrow, we need to leave."

Sparrow snorted, glancing back at her. "Fifteen minutes bitch."

"The guy I ran into is *sniffing*." They'd stopped at the opposite side of the courtyard near the ornate fountain, between two couples, feeding.

Sparrow's gaze bounced from the male, nuzzling a woman's throat to Faye. "But he's not *biting*, so we stay."

At her sister's words, Faye imagined she was seated on her vampire's lap. His long, elegant fingers traced circles on her thigh, inching higher with each rotation. Her nails scratched against the dark material of his jacket as his lips brushed the side of her neck.

"Figures, you would trip over the Shadow Prince." Sparrow glanced back at the man, who now walked to a more secluded corner of the courtyard.

He couldn't be. "How do you know who he is?"

"We're at the Hunter's Moon ball. Who else would dress like him.?"

"You think he's the only white-haired vampire?" Faye glanced back in his direction. She watched him, making sure he stayed on his side of the courtyard.

Sparrow hit Faye in the arm. "Look, it's the High Queen. Ritual time."

Faye followed Sparrow's gaze.

The High Queen stood at the center of the balcony, smiling at her guests. Her corseted gown tucked into every curve, accentuating her figure. Moonlight gleaming off the jeweled pins and combs in her shoulder-length rich brown hair tinged with bronze, she carried an effortlessly elegant air to herself.

The string quartet stopped playing as the guests silenced their chatter. Every attendee stood, focusing on their queen.

"Tonight, we give thanks to the Darkness," The High Queen's melodic voice carried through the courtyard.

Faye watched the High Queen raise a champagne flute. Her eyes darkened until they mirrored *his*. Faye's gaze snapped to the vampire she ran into earlier. The Shadow Prince. He watched the High Queen from a secluded alcove away from the crowd. A beautiful, dangerous male.

"For the wish granted that gave us life. Join me now as we cast our wishes to the Darkness." The High Queen continued.

Sparrow leaned closer to Faye. "This is not the vampire orgy I've dreamed of."

Faye glanced down at Sparrow and pouted her bottom lip. "Sad face."

"I'm stealing a plate of their food, and then we can go." Sparrow uncaringly walked around the vampires, who closed their eyes as they bowed their heads, making her way back to the food station.

The silence unnerved Faye. She crept around the solemn faces, her gaze wandering to the alcove. He bowed his head like the rest of them, clasping his wrist in front of him.

I wish for an equal.

Startled, Faye turned toward the voice, finding nothing. She heard a deep male voice; he spoke against her ear just behind her. Faye patted Sparrow's back. "Did you hear that?"

Sparrow turned, holding a plate piled with pastries. "Hear what?"

"Somebody wished for an equal."

Sparrow snorted. "Nope." She looked around at the motionless vampires. "I didn't spot any day-bloods. I would be upset about losing if they didn't get so boring. Let's go."

Faye followed Sparrow, taking one last look at the Hunter's Moon ball. At the rings housing their dark-blooded soul shards. They were all dark-bloods, Faye realized. She took a sweeping glance over the attendants. Not a day-blood among them.

Dark-bloods looked down on her kind. On anything weaker than them. They loved power, seeking out others they deemed equals.

Pain and anger whispered through her veins. She thought of all the times a dark-blood had dismissed her. Every dark-blood that wanted her, but only as a pet. She'd learned they couldn't hurt her if she rejected them first.

She thought of the deep male voice and willed all her seething frustration and hurt into a reply she cried in her mind. *I can hear you, but you're no equal to me.* A message to every dark-blood she'd met. Every dark-blood she had yet to meet. Her promise.

She would refuse them all.

Glad the night was over, Faye joined Sparrow on the street as they strolled away from the High Queen's estate back into the city.

"Did you have fun?" Sparrow linked arms with her and glanced in her direction, suddenly halting her steps. She leaned one way then the other, staring at her eyes. "Your eyes don't hurt?"

"What's wrong with them?"

"You're going to a healer." Sparrow grabbed her wrist and began leading her through the streets.

"I can't see a healer here." They were in Necromia, and she was wearing a fake dark-blooded soul shard.

The castes were more than just the soul shards. Dark-bloods didn't recognize her as a person. To them, she was nothing more than an animal. They refused to wait on her or let her purchase goods. The healers didn't waste their time on her kind.

"I'm dark-blooded, and I say they will." Being on the darker side of the spectrum among the dark-blooded, Sparrow always forced the issue.

"I feel fine. Let's just go home."

Sparrow pulled her up the stone stairs and pushed open a door. "Hello?"

The reception area of the clinic was small but well lit. The walls were painted in neutral earth tones. A middle-aged woman with a healer insignia on her chest came to the front desk. "How can we help you?"

"She needs to be seen. Her eyes are changing color."

Faye stiffened, apprehensive as the woman looked her up and down before she approached, pausing on her ring. She peered at her eyes, leaning closer. "That is peculiar."

Peculiar? What the hell did that mean? She smacked Sparrow,

staring straight ahead so the healer could continue her inspection. "What do you mean my eyes are changing color?"

The healer flattened her palm over Faye's eye, and warmth spread over the side of Faye's face.

Sparrow tried to bury her worry, but Faye could see it. "You have yellow streaks through your eyes."

"Well, the good news is I don't feel any damage." The healer flattened her palm over Faye's other eye.

The warmth covered the side of Faye's face and faded when the healer let her go.

"You should spend the night. If anything changes, we'll be here to heal you. I can recheck you in the morning." The healer motioned for them to follow her.

Faye glanced at Sparrow, who gave her a stern look and pointed after the healer. Defeated, Faye followed the healer to a small, furnished room with a single bed under a window.

As they entered, the healer asked, "Which court do you belong to?"

"Sparrow's Song," Sparrow answered.

The nurse nodded and closed the door.

"What are you doing?" Faye hissed, heading straight to the mirror over the dresser.

"Making sure you don't wake up blind."

Faye leaned closer, inspecting her eyes. Thin streaks of gold slashed through her black irises. She turned to face Sparrow. "You don't belong to a court." A fact the healer would find out in the morning when she invoiced a court that didn't exist. Or worse, it did, and Sparrow was sending them a bill.

"She doesn't know that." Sparrow settled in an overstuffed chair with her plate of stolen pastries. "If you don't get in that bed, I'm going to take it, and you can sleep in the chair."

"You can turn into a cat. We both fit on the bed." Neither of them knew their race, having grown up in an orphan home. Sparrow claimed Familiar, a race of secretive people who served the realm Chaos and worshiped fate, enabling them to see the future. Sparrow's chaotic nature and petite, voluptuous figure fit the race's characteristics. Her ability to turn into a small, fluffy, white cat when they were young girls was what convinced her. A trait only inherited by Familiar.

14

Sparrow rolled her eyes. "Last time I slept with you as a cat, you tried to suffocate me."

"We were seven."

"Which makes it worse now because I'm still the same size, and you have gotten much heavier."

Faye tucked into bed, glaring at Sparrow. "One time." She held the ring out at Sparrow. "Charge this."

"I'll do it in the morning before we leave."

Curling under the blankets, Faye debated on what worried her more—being dragged before the city's ruling court or the possibility of going blind.

Blindness won by a sliver.

Faye glanced out the window, looking up at the full moon that glowed blood red. She closed her eyes, enjoying the softness of the bed and how silky the sheets felt. Dark-bloods were spoiled things. Even the beds for their sick were fancy.

She took a last look at Sparrow, "Goodnight, hooker."

"Good night, bitch."

Two

Rune would never admit it aloud, but his existence was lonely. Leaning against the railing of the balcony, he glanced down at the masses who crowded the courtyard below him. The night garden was in full bloom, lending its sweet fragrance to the air. His gaze rose to the Hunter's Moon. It sang to a vampire's bloodlust, driving the desire to drink or for sex to a fever pitch.

Rune never experienced such a pull. Not once in over three thousand years. He dreamt of reaching his twentieth year in his youth, wanting to feel it. He heard stories of how blood tasted richer. Vampires warned when he drank beneath the Hunter's Moon. It would ruin him, that he'd crave it until the following year when he could once again drink under the sway of the moon.

They described sex in the same way. That he should find an accommodating female vampire, so on edge, a brush of his fingers in the right place would bring her off.

"I brought you fresh blood since you're obviously not partaking," a woman said. But Rune knew that voice anywhere. Her scent of honey and citrus, covered with perfume deemed popular by the nobles for the time being, filled the space they stood in now.

"Ignoring your guests?"

The string quartet below played an eerie and sensuous melody. It was a hypnotic trance lulling its prey to dance. Rune turned around, his eyes narrowing at her perfect appearance, taking the offered glass. He didn't participate in the showy preening for the houses and courts established in wealth or nobility. Lyssa seemingly thrived on it, relishing the opportunity to lord her status above others. From her silvery satin gown, tailored for this occasion, to her rich brown hair painstakingly pinned and styled. Despite her outward perfection, Lyssa's emotions tasted as they always did.

A lusting want soured with fear. He tasted a variation of this on every woman he'd come across. Some men as well.

Rune secretly longed for a woman who didn't fear him. But after century upon century of disappointment and embarrassment, he ceased looking. He was a Pure Blood, separated from the dancing fools below him as the turned vampires were from their originating species. They were vampires, turned who transitioned in death with vampiric blood in their system.

Pure Bloods were gifted with many abilities: strength, speed, heightened senses, and the ability to taste the emotions of those around them. But cursed with true bloodlust, far greater than the shadowed urges the turned felt.

The Ra'Voshnik was an entity separate from himself yet existing within him. The balance for his dark gifts tied him in a shared existence with a volatile creature he kept subdued.

"I think half of my guests only attend to catch a glimpse of you." Lyssa glanced in his direction momentarily before returning her attention to the masses.

He found crowds to be exhausting and lived a secluded, private life. When he was forced to attend a public gathering, the Ra'Voshnik picked up the scent of fear, fixating on what it considered prey. Which subsequently moved Rune to mentally hold its murderous urges at bay.

"I believe they are here in hopes of catching the attention of a darker court." Rune spared Lyssa a passing glance before teasing, "Or perhaps they wish to taste your wares." He could feel her glaring at him but continued to watch the vampires below. A bell tolled behind them, carrying across the courtyard.

"I should cut out your insolent tongue."

Rune knew he was undoubtedly a curiosity rarely seen in the flesh, but their presence at Lyssa's ball had nothing to do with him. This was a chance to see and be seen by other dark established courts.

Courts were a means of protection, typically forming around and led by a woman. Lyssa's mother, Belind, decreed a single law during her rule as High Queen of Necromia. Rape was punishable by death. The sentence was carried out by the ruler of the realm. Any other dispute, including murder, was to be resolved between the courts. Belonging to a strong court meant protection. Safety. Power.

The corner of his mouth lifted in a smirk. "You like my tongue when I care to use it."

He half expected another barb or a possible knife between his ribs. Lyssa quieted, folding her hands on the railing. "Will you see me tonight?"

Rune's gaze lifted to the Hunter's Moon. He took a deep breath and slowly exhaled. He'd been her consort once, over a dozen centuries ago. He tended to her now and again at her request, after he relinquished the title of consort.

More than a decade had passed since the last time he obliged her. She'd taken other lovers but always came back to him. His attempt to make light of their past prompted her to ask him to visit her bed.

"I think you should find a man who feels the same way toward you, that you feel toward him." He wasn't purposefully being unkind. This was for the best.

It didn't matter how well she masked her fear or schooled her expression. He could taste it on her. And with the taste of fear, his body refused to respond. The part of him she wanted most held no interest. He could service her with his hands and mouth, but she deserved more than that.

He deserved more than that.

"I am sorry." He brushed the back of his fingers over her arm.

"Thank you, Shadow Prince." She kept her eyes forward, standing tall. Regal. Dismissing him with his title.

Rune inclined his head. "High Queen."

Leaving the glass balanced on the railing, he phased away from Lyssa, materializing near the food station. This late in the evening, the blood whores would be engaged in—

Someone fell into him, elbowing him just under his ribs. His fangs lengthened with aggression as the Ra'Voshnik charged to the surface in a rush hungry for violence.

It bled through his eyes, coloring them a deep crimson as veined misted shadows crept from beneath his gaze, swaying over the tops of his cheekbones. A trait received when the original Pure Bloods drank the Darkness. It tore through their systems, transforming them.

Rune turned, seeing no one as a pair of footfalls retreated away from him. A scent carried to him, clean and subtle. A night breeze through plum blossoms. His fangs sharpened as an unfamiliar feeling settled over him.

Vsenia, the Ra'Voshnik purred deep in his mind.

His brow lowered in concern. Vsenia was High Tongue, loosely translated to *cherished beloved*. He'd grown used to the constant stream of aggression, the Ra'Voshnik whispering from the recesses of his mind he'd chained it to. Never in all his years had it behaved in this manner, thrashing wildly against his hold, urging him to find her. A loyal dog eager to get back to its master.

Rune leashed the Ra'Voshnik, cruelly tightening his hold until it fell silent. He listened, tracking the slowing footsteps until they stopped near the fountain he'd wager. He waited for the sight shields to drop, impatient for his first glance of the dark-blooded vampire who unwittingly brought the Ra'Voshnik's viciousness to heel.

He lifted his chin and inhaled as his lids slid shut. Her scent calmed his mind, sharpening his focus until she was all that remained. A long-forgotten feeling snaked through him. Rune opened his eyes, focusing on the place she stood, wrapped in a sight shield.

Movement caught his attention, and Rune cursed. Delilah stood within his line of sight, just beyond his true interest. She raised her glass at him and smiled coyly. The dark-haired queen made his skin crawl. She ruled over the Court of Lace and Bone, a ruthless court that had a reputation for their sadistic appetites when they warred and captured rival courts.

Rune ignored her invitation, uncaring if he offended her. She could send her court for him if she wished. He would send them back to her. In pieces.

He turned, heading to a quiet, darkened alcove and Lyssa's voice pulled him from his musings.

He looked toward the balcony as she used a spell to carry her voice over the courtyard. She held up the glass he left on the railing in salute, reciting pretty words Belind once used. The festivities concluded with a wish to the Darkness, a tradition honoring the creation of the Pure Bloods.

He'd been a fledgling eager for his first centuries of life the last time he participated in this ancient ritual. Rune bowed his head and closed his eyes, his mind descending within himself.

Possessing a soul shard tied the mind to a great psychic ravine, allowing individuals to turn inward and descend to the depths of their power, to a space beneath the physical world—a private intangible place within themselves where it was stored and drawn. Within the ravine that cradled the Darkness were a few shared spaces. The Pure Blood's birthplace being one of them.

His shoes sank into the fine white sand as he materialized in the small cove. A steep cliffside rose out of sight to his back, and before him, the Darkness ascended in a towering wall.

It raged and coiled in on itself. Black, pulsating mist. The outer wisps and tendrils lined in a deep glowing purple. Rune listened to the low roar as it coiled onto itself and took the subtle mental shift to stand at the depth of his power.

I wish for an equal.

Rune mentally projected the words as he did each year during his first few centuries, hoping to be answered by a dark-blooded vampire who would match him in strength. He ran his hand over his mouth, feeling the accumulation of his many years.

He'd made a choice long ago during his first century. As he matured into what he was and the power he wielded, he saw two clearly defined paths before him: embrace the lessons and training that forged him into a terrifying weapon for his court's arsenal or squander his gift and strength to prove he wasn't a threat. Live as every other man, building a life with a partner he would trust and be devoted to.

He'd chosen the former, becoming the deadliest soul to walk the realms.

He thought of the life he had forsaken from time to time. Envied people who'd found their partners. Useless thoughts that pained him when he let his mind dwell. Knowing if he had to choose again, his choice would remain the same.

His mind wandered to his night breeze and he found himself full of questions. What had she wished for? What court did she belong to? Would his interest fade as the Hunter's Moon set? Rune couldn't decide if he wanted the feelings she stirred in him to stay or fade with the night.

He ascended, returning to his physical body, and opened his eyes.

The balcony was empty, and the night concluded. Guests would linger for another hour or so before returning to their courts and estates. Rune scented the air for his night breeze.

A mental sending struck his mind hard enough to make him flinch.

I can hear you, but you're no equal to me.

The Ra'Voshnik tore from his hold the moment her voice filled his mind, urging him to find her.

The corners of his mouth curled of their own accord as black bled through his gaze. His night breeze had steel to her backbone. Perhaps this would carry past the night. She held a shard of Darkness if she heard his wish. Strong enough not to fear him. A young vampiress who could accept his nature and darker urges.

He purred through the mental communication tether she established to his mind. *Good evening, my Lady.*

Courting was a delicate dance among the dark-blooded. One the woman controlled. Rune needed to meet her and learn what court she belonged to. He would send a letter of intent, seeking permission to pursue her romantically, accompanied by a talisman connected to his mind. If she accepted his advances, she would use it to speak to him.

Rune waited for her reply as he strolled through Lyssa's private gardens away from the lingering crowd. He walked past manicured rose bushes, the blooming black roses' sweet scent carrying to him. He debated taking a flower for his night breeze. Who had yet to answer him.

She hadn't withdrawn her tether but remained silent. Rune slipped his power down the connection between them. The lick of force he used as a mental nudge touched an impressive mental shield. Withdrawing, Rune brushed his fingertips over an open bloom.

Rune was nothing if not patient. He bowed in the direction of the public courtyard to his unseen Lady and phased to his home in Hell.

The dark stone walls of his bedroom came into sharp focus. Hell's ever-twilight sky streamed into his room through tall narrow windows evenly spaced along the exterior wall. A simple desk was arranged beneath the windows, and a four-post bed made of dark wood dominated the opposite wall. Dark silk draped over the posts, matching his sheets.

The Ra'Voshnik stirred, growing restless as it realized the object of its affection was no longer in its proximity. The creature's urgings were easy enough to control. The twinge in his chest was another matter. Rune rubbed his thumb over his sternum at the strange sensation. Not pain, but something akin to sadness. He unfastened his cuffs, deciding to reevaluate himself after the night passed.

He stripped, showered, and retired to his bed. Tucking a hand behind his head and gazing at the vaulted ceiling. He would find out which court she belonged to tomorrow and write his letter of intent. His mind drifted, leading him to thoughts of her. Her scent captivated him. He wanted to hold her close, purring in contentment. Rune closed his eyes. His breathing became deep and even as he drifted to sleep.

He wasn't sure how much time passed when soft images surfaced in his mind.

A woman held his hand. His vision cleared enough to see her while everything else remained blurred and dark. She walked ahead of him. Her arm outstretched and fingers twined with his as he followed her lead. Her long black hair fell between a pair of delicately boned reptilian wings. The iridescent scales glimmered in the soft light.

Rune glanced upward as their surroundings took shape. He

followed her through a meadow in the moonlight. "Where are we headed this evening?" He asked, brushing his thumb over the back of her hand.

She turned her head slightly as she led him through the field. Not enough to glimpse her face, merely an acknowledgment she heard him. "You'll see."

The images faded as her words echoed, sounding far away. Rune's consciousness slipped once more, and he drifted back to sleep.

Hours later, Rune's lids fluttered as another dream softly drifted over his mind. He recognized the location through his slow, hazy awareness. Tall, dark wood bookshelves lined the walls, containing a number of tomes he studied out of in his youth. He comfortably sat lengthwise with his night breeze in his study on a settee before the fireplace. She curled against him between his legs, reading a book with her back to the fire. Its light danced over her smooth tanned skin.

"Good evening, my Lady."

She didn't respond. Rune couldn't see her face from his angle, only the tip of her nose and a teasing glimpse of her dark lips as she muttered to herself while she read.

"Are you enjoying your book?"

"I was."

Rune smiled at her teasing tone. She was warm. Having her in his arms felt so right. He ran his fingers through her hair, and she sighed, tilting her head to rest on his chest.

"Grant me your name."

He felt her shoulders slump. "You're ruining the mood, big guy."

Rune conceded to silence and let her read, content to be in her company. He parted his lips, taking a shallow breath, and tasted nothing. Not a hint of her emotions. Perhaps it was for the best. She already commanded too much of the Ra'Voshnik's attention. If it had her emotions to fixate on, he might never subdue it.

She turned her page, reading against him like he was a favorite chair. He was patient and would see her in the flesh soon enough. He ran the back of his fingers over her wing and was rewarded with her giggle.

"Stop that." She laughed; her wing snapped open, pushing his hand away before tucking it back into place.

Rune chuckled and resumed stroking her hair. The scene darkened and faded as sleep settled over Rune's mind.

A low roaring filled his ears as images that felt like memories floated through his mind. Rune sat with his back against something hard. He glanced at his surroundings, waiting for the puzzle pieces to arrange themselves.

Rune recognized his bed, but this wasn't his room. He was in the center of a circular hollow the size of a large room. The Darkness surrounding him, a mass of swirling dark mist making up the walls of this place. The mist constantly churned, curling and twisting onto itself. Tendrils curled through the swirling fog, edged in a sharp glowing purple.

Fine white sand covered the ground in this strange place. Next to him, his night breeze stirred, rustling his sheets. She slept in a plain white nightgown tucked under his sheets. Her dark hair fanned over her pillow.

At first glance, Rune thought he dreamt of Sadi, the Familiar King's daughter. While their similarities were uncanny, they also possessed glaring differences. His night breeze had wings, while Sadi did not.

The twinge he'd felt in his chest earlier in the night eased as he gazed at the woman sleeping beside him. Her presence comforted him. Easing down, Rune lied on his side, watching her.

She blinked after a few moments, gazing back at him. "Hi."

He'd never seen eyes like hers. Midnight streaked with gold, framed by thick black lashes. Her high cheekbones tapered to her narrow chin.

"Evening."

Her full dark lips turned up in a lazy smile as her sharp nails grazed over his side. She was gentle, careful not to break his skin, but her nails felt more like claws.

She scooted closer to him, ducking her head under his chin and muttered, "You smell nice."

Rune didn't have time to ponder her words as she curled up to him. Her lips pressed to the base of his throat, and Rune froze. He spoke several languages but couldn't think of a single word.

She began to fade along with his surroundings, dissipating to reveal the gray stone walls of his room. Rune sat up to find himself

in his room. Rested from a night's sleep.
Alone.

Three

"Get up."

Faye jerked awake, remembering where they were. Her hand rested on the pillow near her face, the soul shard crystal clear and lifeless. She hid her hand under the covers, sitting up as she tensed. She should have insisted Sparrow recharge the ring last night, but she hadn't expected the healer to barge into the room without warning.

A woman with an annoyed expression leaned in the doorway. Faye slowed her breathing, doing her best to act natural. She smiled at the woman, hoping they'd gotten lucky, and her empty soul shard went unnoticed. That the healer's expression was due to a long shift nearing its end.

The woman didn't return Faye's smile as she dried her hands on a towel. The swirling mist around her day-blood shard shimmered with her movements. "Get dressed and leave. We don't treat Anarians."

Faye's smile fell. She heard a variation of this statement countless times since her ritual failed. Time did nothing to dull the simmering rage that lived in her. She hated the social hierarchy that weighed a person's worth solely by the shard they carried. But this was the world they lived in, and Faye held no power.

Sparrow sprawled on the chair's seat cushion, still in cat form. She slowly blinked at the woman, regarding her upside down. Rolling to her feet, Sparrow stretched her back before leaping to the floor. A brilliant light consumed her form, reshaping as she rose a woman.

Sparrow took a threatening step toward the healer, the dark mist surrounding her soul shard gleaming with her emotions. "Check her eyes."

Faye got to her feet, thumping Sparrow in the back. "It's okay." To the healer, Faye inclined her head. "Thank you for taking me in last night."

The healer nervously looked between the two of them. Her gaze stopped on Sparrow. "You parading your pet as a dark-blood will be reported."

Sparrow closed the distance between herself and the healer. "I'm about to parade my foot in your ass."

The healer stared at Sparrow, eyes wide. Flinching when Sparrow stomped her foot, leaning toward her sharply. "Say something dayblood."

"Sparrow! You're just as bad as she is." Faye grabbed her arm, pulling her away from the healer. Her sister typically ignored a person's shards, a trait Faye once considered normal, believing it extended to the rest of the dark-bloods. Sparrow only leaned into the caste separation when Faye was mistreated, too eager to *return their energy,* as she put it.

"I'll leave, thank you." She glanced at the healer, then at the door, silently begging the woman to go.

Sparrow opened her mouth wide, hissing at the woman. The healer ran, her footsteps echoing down the hall.

Faye shoved Sparrow away from her, slapping her on the shoulder. "You need to calm down. I shouldn't be here." She shook her head, taking off the fake soul shard ring and slipping it into her pocket.

"Sit down before I beat your ass. I need to check your eyes."

Faye gathered her boots, pulling them on as she hopped on one foot. "I feel fine. Let's just go."

The last thing she needed was the healer returning with a dark-blood guard. Sparrow was too mouthy for her own good. They would end up before the court that ruled this city. And while Sparrow was a strong dark-blood, she wasn't trained. Wouldn't stand a chance against so many of them.

Faye didn't understand the court's internal workings or what would happen if they were arrested and taken before the court to answer to the city's queen. But she had the feeling Sparrow claiming her as a pet would explain why the two were in Necromia. However, it wouldn't excuse them from threatening a healer and offering a fake court name for billing. Not to mention Faye's false soul shard.

Sparrow shoved her as she dragged on her other boot, knocking her off balance. Faye fell on the bed, glaring at her sister.

"We don't have time for this. We need to go before they come back and arrest us." Faye glanced over the room as she spoke, focusing on things at different distances. She felt hungover, but she could see. Her vision wasn't obstructed or damaged. Her gaze returned to Sparrow as she hissed, "And you're not a healer."

"No shit." Sparrow covered Faye's eyes with her palms, splaying her fingers over her scalp. "But I can tell if you have some weird internal bleeding or blockage."

Warmth spread over Faye's eyes, into her skull. The tinges of pain eased, and Sparrow let her go.

"I don't feel anything wrong. Are you sure you're seeing fine?" Sparrow leaned forward, peering into Faye's eyes.

Faye pulled her head back, pushing Sparrow's face away. "You need to brush your teeth."

Snorting in response, Sparrow made a rude gesture.

Pulling her winter jacket on, she grabbed Sparrow's coat with one hand and her sister's wrist with the other. Faye managed to slip from the clinic before the healer returned. People bustled in the streets, going about their morning business. They walked with the crowd, blending into it.

"Want to stop and get breakfast?" Sparrow lifted her chin at a bakery down the street.

Men glanced at Faye as they walked, their smiles fading when they found her index finger empty.

Faye tucked her hair behind her ear, ignoring the crowd. As much as she claimed to not care, their dismissal hurt. "I want to get out of here. We can get breakfast in Anaria."

They made their way to the coach with quiet conversation. Faye preferred to travel manually. She couldn't phase, and Sparrow refused to dedicate the time to learn the skill. Faye had trouble trusting a stranger not to phase her to his dark court, where he could keep her as a pet.

After Sparrow purchased their tickets, the two of them entered the carriages designated for dark-bloods, which would take them to the main station. From there, they would phase to Anaria.

She leaned back in the plush seats. An ornate lantern hung from the ceiling, illuminating the cabin's dark interior. Sparrow immediately sat next to the large shelf affixed between the windows. She selected a square of dried meat from a platter of fruits, cheese, and cuts of dried meat. Faye took the pitcher next to the platter, pouring them both glasses of water.

"Do you think day-bloods get this in their carriages?" Faye took a small cluster of grapes sitting back in her seat.

Sparrow shrugged, picking through the cuts of meat. "Never been."

Faye watched the landscape pass by her window, wondering what her life would look like if Sparrow had left her to join a court.

After they'd invoked their blood, numerous courts sent invitations, requesting Sparrow to join their ranks. Faye accompanied Sparrow to a few in the beginning. Sparrow hadn't taken it well when they welcomed her and ignored Faye.

A man at one of the courts had approached them and asked, "Is this your pet, love?" Brushing Faye's hair back over her shoulder.

Sparrow had knocked him across the room with a blast of power, yelling, "Call my sister a pet again."

The court's guard advanced on them, and the interaction went downhill from there.

Faye had insisted that Sparrow should join a court. Her sister refused, claiming she would only join a court if they also took Faye and recognized her as a member. No court was willing to take an Anarian.

The sunlight beamed, warm on Faye's skin. She glanced at Sparrow, who kicked her feet, watching the scenery go by as she ate her fill.

A few years ago, after Sparrow stopped answering the court invitations, she thought it would be a brilliant idea to start their own court. Just the two of them.

Until she found out starting a court needed a minimum of five members, and it needed to be authorized by a ruler of one of the five realms. She'd snorted, proclaiming they were an unofficial court.

Faye glanced out over the rolling hills, her thoughts falling to the night before. She'd been dreaming of the man she ran into before the bitch healer woke her up.

He'd been lying on his side when she woke in the dream. He looked the way he did at the Hunter's Moon ball. Crimson so dark it looked black covered his eyes. Veined misted shadows swayed beneath them. His eyes didn't unnerve her. They were expressive, held such yearning as he gazed at her.

Faye tapped Sparrow's boot with her own. "Do you think the guy I ran into was really the Shadow Prince?"

Sparrow tilted her head. "Probably, who else would masquerade as him at the Hunter's Moon ball?"

She was probably right. The attendants didn't glamor fangs. They had them. She imagined the Pure Bloods frowned on normal vampires masquerading as them as much as the dark-bloods hated Anarians wearing dark-blooded rings.

"Why?" Sparrow widened her eyes, silently demanding more details.

Faye glanced out her window again. "I was dreaming about his bad eyeliner."

Sparrow's squeal pulled Faye's attention. "Wait, are you talking about the Shadow Prince or the guy at the Court of Silver Leaves? Because you have a shot with Silver Leaves. Did you like him?"

Faye was definitely not dreaming of Silver Leaves. He would forget she existed the instant he found out she didn't carry a soul shard. But the Shadow Prince was worse.

He embodied everything she hated about the social hierarchy. He belonged to the darkest court. He ruled Hell. The only redeeming quality he possessed was he lumped day-bloods and Anarians together, seeing them both as little more than animals.

Which wasn't right, but it amused Faye that the day-bloods received the same ill-treatment they passed on to Anarians.

"No. I just dreamt of eyes like that."

"Pure Blood eyes? Kinky."

She curled up to him during the dream. Faye imagined him leaning down, bringing his lips a moment from hers. Waiting for a touch that would serve as an invitation to her body.

And for the first time in her life, she was tempted to offer it.

Faye shook the feeling, refusing to allow anyone that close. All a dark-blood saw when they looked at her was a pleasant evening. She understood. A life with her would diminish their social standing. The family she once dreamed of could only happen if she found a man willing to weaken his line by tying it with hers. She'd taken that pain, soothed it the only way she knew how. By covering it with an anger that constantly burned in her.

She would offer herself to no man. Her body was the only thing they wanted, the only thing she had left to give after fate stripped her of everything else. She wouldn't offer it up like a doe-eyed fool and leave herself with nothing. She wielded their desire like a weapon, letting them choke on their want.

This was the only choice fate left to her, and she defended it viciously.

"So. What were you doing with Pure Blood eyes?" Sparrow grinned.

"Nothing," Faye answered too quickly.

"That's so boring. Were his eyes up here?" Sparrow held her hand near her face. "Down here." Sparrow lowered her hand to her breasts. "Was he down here?" Sparrow moved her hand lower, spreading her legs.

Faye shook her head, turning to look out the window.

"I've heard vampires purr. It's supposed to feel amazing. You need to ride that guy's face and report back." Sparrow crossed her arms, giving Faye a stern look.

"You can research that for yourself."

Sparrow brought her hand to her chest, gasping dramatically. "I'm with Vash, you harlot." Her expression returned to normal as she raised her eyebrows. "And I know how much you love blue balling every dark-blood that happens to stumble across you. Think of riding his face as taking it to the next level."

Faye laughed. "No." She couldn't imagine straddling a man's mouth, but the logistics of it needled her. "How does he breathe?"

Sparrow snorted. "Beauty of dating immortals, it doesn't matter. Just sit. If he dies, he dies. He'll wake up in a couple hours after he regenerates."

"You haven't done that to Vash, have you?" Faye managed between giggles.

Sparrow winked. "I try to kill him anytime he gives me the opportunity."

They both broke out in laughter. When they calmed, Faye glanced out her window once more.

"I'm sure Silver Leaf would love to dress up like the Shadow Prince for you." Sparrow teased. "He'd probably be more than willing to go to his knees for you too."

Faye's smile faded. "He was only nice because he thought I was dark-blooded." Silver Leaf didn't see her.

She was a body to him. One he'd like to warm his bed with.

The coach came to a stop, and the door clicked. They exited, and Sparrow dropped her head back dramatically.

"Look at that line." She turned to Faye. "Carry me."

A brilliant light consumed Sparrow's form and reshaped smaller before fading. A fluffy white cat with Sparrow's green eyes looked up at her.

Sparrow squatted down and wiggled on her haunches.

Faye pointed at her. "Don't you fucking miss and scratch me."

The small white cat leaped, landing on Faye's shoulder.

Faye shifted her shoulder. "Get off me, hooker."

Sparrow swatted the side of Faye's head.

Faye pointed at her, and Sparrow froze with her paw up, poised to swat her again. "Do it again, and I'll stuff you in a bag."

The white cat narrowed her eyes but lowered her paw.

Faye got in line with Sparrow on her shoulder. It looked long but went quickly as each traveler went to the next available cashier. There were a dozen of them separated by low dividers along a long counter. It didn't take long before Faye stood before the cashier. "Two tickets to Anaria, please."

The young woman was a day-blood. She eyed Faye's index finger

32

as Faye slid silver marks across the counter to pay their fare.

"Where's your owner?"

Faye plastered on her fake smile and gestured at Sparrow.

"Looks like a cat." The young woman slid the silver marks back to Faye.

Sparrow leaped to the counter, scratching the woman's hand hard enough to draw blood. A flash of light enveloped her, reshaping and faded as quickly as it came. Sparrow now crouched in front of the cashier. "The fuck did you call me?"

The cashier held her hand with a look of terror.

An older woman came to stand in front of the cashier. "So sorry for the misunderstanding." She held out two ticket stubs to Sparrow as the cashier retreated out of sight to a back room.

Sparrow took the tickets. "Thanks." She bit off the word, standing to her full height, and turned. Hopping down from the counter, she linked arms with Faye.

Faye leaned toward Sparrow as they walked, speaking in a low tone. "You didn't have to scratch her."

Sparrow snorted, "And she didn't have to be a bitch, but here we are."

"You don't have to act like them because of me."

Sparrow snorted, closing the subject. She was technically in the right since the cashier insulted her and refused her pet's payment. But just because she could, didn't make it right.

They entered a small platform where a man collected their tickets. "Which village are we going to this morning?"

"Alexander," Sparrow answered, taking the man's offered hand.

Faye closed her eyes as they phased. It was done in an instant, but the dizziness lasted for a few moments after. They stood on the small landing platform at the outskirts of their village.

The man inclined his head at them. "Ladies." Then vanished.

Travelers to their little village were rare, so they didn't have to hurry off the platform out of fear of getting knocked over by the next set of people.

"You coming home or going to Vash's?" Faye asked, stepping off the platform.

"I need to clean up, so he doesn't think I'm a complete heathen."

"It's too late for that hooker."

They walked to their home, a small cottage twenty minutes outside town.

"I'm starving, so don't take forever in the shower." Sparrow bounded through the front door, disappearing into her room at the end of the hall.

"You just ate," Faye called down the hall as she closed the front door standing in the room that doubled as their kitchen and dining room. She took off her coat, laying it over the closest chair at the small wooden kitchen table. She went to her room halfway down the hall. She had a simple bed beneath the large window with a view of the forest. Picking out what to wear, she crossed the hall to her bathroom. She showered quickly and dressed after drying off. Faye leaned closer to her bathroom mirror, inspecting the golden streaks through her irises. They shimmered, reflecting the light differently than the black of her eye. She could only hope the streaks would heal in time and her eyes would return to their original color.

"Bitch."

Faye backed away from the mirror and yelled, "Hooker." A game of echolocation she and Sparrow used since childhood.

"Come on. I'm starving," Sparrow whined.

It sounded like Sparrow was already outside. Faye headed down the hall to the kitchen. The petite blonde stood outside. Her wavy golden hair gleamed in the sunlight. Throwing on her boots, Faye shouldered the large backpack she'd set out for herself the night before. Meeting Sparrow outside, the two began walking back to the village.

"Cough up some details, bitch. You've had that stupid grin on your face all morning." Sparrow snorted at her and did her little hop before trying to hook Faye's ankle with her foot.

Faye took a longer step avoiding Sparrow's efforts. "I don't have details. I don't remember."

"Did he bite you?"

"No. At least I don't think so."

"You don't remember?" Sparrow deepened her voice and lifted her hand at Faye, pressing her fingers together, opening and closing her hand to mimic talking. "Faye, I love you." Then she made kissing noises biting at Faye's neck with her fingers. Laughing, Faye shoved Sparrow away.

"You have to remember something. Just tell me. I need to know." Sparrow pleaded as they walked.

Faye turned toward Sparrow and sighed. "I remember his eyes. He has fangs. They're just flashes."

A mischievous glint lit in Sparrow's eyes. "Does he have good lips?"

What were good lips? Faye remembered his mouth. His lips looked smooth and firm. His bottom lip was fuller than the top. No facial hair. "They're guy lips."

"But do you want to kiss them?"

"Is that the measure for good lips?"

Sparrow nodded, quirking her lip.

Exhaling, Faye conceded. "He has good lips."

Sparrow squeaked, hugging Faye's arm. "What you need is to get laid. There are brothels with vampires. You could pretend he's your dream guy."

At Faye's silence, Sparrow made a rude noise, waving her hand dismissively. "You can borrow my ring. They won't even know."

"No, thank you."

"It would be an early birthday present." Sparrow insisted.

Faye narrowed her eyes. "My birthday was literally yesterday."

"Fine, a second gift. A late present! Me and Vash could get you a nice looking one. They must have ones with long white hair. I think they're ones that glamor up too. He could look just like your Shadow Prince."

"One, he's not the Shadow Prince. Two, you're talking about a person, not a dress."

Sparrow dropped Faye's arm. "One, I'm talking about a well-paid *whore* who does this for a living. Two, there are two Pure Bloods. The High Queen and the Shadow Prince. You are dreaming of the male variety, and that's the Shadow Prince, bitch."

Faye didn't respond.

They walked in silence as the buildings of their small village came into view.

Sparrow turned toward her. "You going to Aunty Clara's house to give the little beasties candy?"

Faye grinned. Sparrow rarely went back to the orphanage they were raised in, while Faye went back at least once a month. Bringing supplies to the old woman who'd been like a mother to her and treats for the Anarian children. Ones she knew were rarely adopted.

"We were little beasties once."

"And did anyone bring our asses candy?"

"Didn't you want someone to bring you candy?" Faye laughed as Sparrow split off to the coach that would take her back to the main station.

"I'll tell Vash you said hi. See you at home bitch." Sparrow raised her arm as she yelled over her shoulder.

Faye turned and made her way to the altar in the middle of the village. A small stone pedestal held a brazier lit with hellfire. A magical flame that burned blue and extinguished when the spell ran its course.

She purchased a prayer from the nearby stand taking the small, folded paper with beautiful script to the brazier. The prayers were to The Creator, a man who lived long ago and shaped the realms. People still worshiped him as a god even after his death eight hundred years ago. His daughter, the High Queen, now ruled Necromia.

The Crumbling occurred long before Faye was ever born. It was a force that manifested after The Creator died. Many believed The Creator's magic faded with his death, undoing the realms he created.

Faye bowed her head as expected. She didn't believe magic faded or that these prayers to The Creator would save them. He was long dead. She purchased the prayer to help the young family who sold them. It allowed them to keep their dignity instead of asking for handouts.

She opened her eyes, tossing the prayer into the hellfire, hoping they reached someone among the living who could stop The Crumbling.

Leaving the altar, Faye leisurely walked along small window displays in the open market. Alexander was a meager village, even for Anaria. There was no extravagance here.

Faye turned into the shops that purchased the potions and ointments she made, collecting their orders for next month.

Purchasing a bag of caramels and hard candies, she made her way to the far side of town to a place she and Sparrow once called home. It had an official name but would always be Aunty Clara's house to them. Named for the elderly woman who ran the place.

The age of the house began to show. The screens ripped in some of the windows. Instead of replacing them, they were shut tight. The small green yard gave way to dirt over the years, and the few plants that grew out of the corners of the property were wildly overgrown. Faye frowned. The house seemed so much bigger when she played here as a child.

The smaller children squeaked and called for others as she approached. She came here every month for the past seven years. All the little ones crowded around her as she sat on the creaking swing set in the front yard. She held the bag of candy out for the children.

Echoes of "Thank you, Faye" came as they all took their piece and moved away so the rest could get their treat as well. After they moved away to different parts of the yard with their snacks, some of the older children approached her.

Movement caught Faye's attention. Aunty Clara stood on the porch. The plump white-haired woman waved her arm over her head for Faye to come inside.

Faye hurried up the stairs, smiling brightly. She kissed the elderly woman's cheek. "How are you doing?" Faye gently rubbed Aunty Clara's hands. "Are your hands still bothering you?"

The old woman huffed, pulling her hands away. "Don't worry about me. I'm old, you know." She reached into her pocket, removing a small red envelope. "Happy birthday." The old woman pressed it to Faye's palm, curling her fingers around it.

Faye's brows came up. Aunty Clara had enough to worry about without giving her marks as a gift. "I don't need this. You should buy something for the kids." She tried to put the envelope back in the old woman's pocket.

She slapped her hand like she did when she was a child. "That's good luck marks. You keep it." She gave Faye a stern look and walked into the house.

Faye smiled and followed Aunty Clara in the house, slipping the gift into her back pocket. She would buy something nice for the kids with whatever she gave her.

The floor creaked as Faye entered the kitchen. Halls branched off the large room leading to the many bedrooms. The white walls began to peel, blisters of paint pulling away from the wall exposing the wood beneath it. It was old but filled with love. Faye's memories with Aunty Clara were what made this place her home.

Faye loved her and how she never looked at her as less than because she didn't carry a shard. She brushed her fingers over the large
dining table that had been a fixture as long as she could remember. It
was worn and scratched, showing its age. Sparrow carved their names
in one of the legs when they were girls. Something Aunty Clara didn't
know about until after they'd moved out and one of the younger
children saw it while playing hide and seek.

Smiling, Faye moved to the cabinets and restocked the supply
of potions and ointments. After Faye was satisfied, she pulled a chair,
sitting at the table.

"Sparrow still with the wing boy?" Aunty Clara asked over her
cup of tea, her day-blood shard always gleaming as she gossiped.

"She's still with Vashien." Faye laughed, wondering when she
would learn his name. Sparrow did go through a lot of men, but
she'd been with Vash for a couple years now.

Aunty Clara nodded to herself. "He's a good boy if he can get
that one to settle down. She's so wild. You should get married too.
You're pretty, you know. Don't wait until you're old like me."

Faye smiled at the elderly woman. She was always trying to
marry her off, claiming it was so she didn't have to worry about her.
When Faye would explain she didn't want to be married, Aunty Clara
would argue with her that she was too headstrong. Faye stopped
insisting she would never marry and just nodded to save the ten minutes of lecturing.

Faye listened to Aunty Clara tell her about the children and the
trouble they were getting into. Talking through the day as Faye helped
her prepare the evening meal.

Aunty Clara pulled back the curtain peering at the sky. "The sun
is going down; you should go home before it gets dark. It's not good
to walk in the dark by yourself, you know."

Faye stood, giving the old woman another hug. "I'll see you next
month. Send one of the older ones if you need me sooner."

Aunty Clara waved at her. "I'm okay. Stop worrying. And take
some food home. You're so skinny. It's not good to be too skinny,
you know."

The children followed her to the gate of the property before
running back to the house to wash their hands for dinner. Aunty

Clara stood on the porch watching her until she was past the bend in the road, out of sight. Faye smiled, making her way back to her cottage.

She would set out her herbs on the drying rack and turn in early tonight. The sun began to set over the forest, casting long shadows as Faye walked.

The breeze shifted the treetops making the shadows sway at her feet. Memory of his dark gaze and different shadows filled her mind. He saw her, cherished her in spite of what she lacked.

Faye pushed the image away, ignoring the soft feelings that bloomed in her. She wouldn't allow herself to linger on useless fantasies. Not when reality dug its claws into her day after day. Reminding her of the pain that awaited her if she continued down this path.

Men like him didn't exist, not for women like her.

Four

A restless emotion he hadn't felt since his fledgling years rose in his chest. The corner of his mouth lifted. He was anxious to meet his night breeze. Longed to wake up next to her. Rune glanced at the undisturbed sheets on the empty side of his bed. He found himself curious if she would curl to him in her sleep as she had in the dreams. Or would he wake to find her sleeping on her side, with his sheets low on her waist?

He imagined brushing the backs of his fingers over her bare back, already missing the feel of her soft skin. Rune thought back to the dreams that weren't dreams at all. Her mental tether connected their minds, allowing her to visit him while he slept. He eased his senses over it, not wanting to disturb her if she was still asleep. He withdrew at the first touch of her mental barriers.

The Ra'Voshnik was strangely calm, satisfied for the time being.

Or until it roused enough to realize she was now gone. Spending time with her pacified the creature, but his body didn't fare as well. He was strung too tight. Taut and anxious for… he didn't know. He had no words for what he felt. The strain, while not entirely unpleasant, was certainly uncomfortable.

Rune rose, making his way to the shower.

He stepped under the water, letting the hot water sluice over his back. His thoughts seemed to always circle back to her. Questions one after the other. What was she doing now? Did his queen have a court of her own or belong to an established one.

He imagined her speaking to her queen, requesting permission to invite him to court. Would her queen believe her when she confessed, she snared the Shadow Prince? He had much to discuss with his secretive night breeze. What court they occupied mattered little to him; he would follow her lead.

Rune finished showering and dressed in a tailored black suit.

He straightened the lapels of his jacket in the mirror. He had a meeting with the High Council at midday he would attend begrudgingly. He sent his monthly reports, but the mortal Artithian King pestered him constantly, summoning him at least twice a month.

Jha'ant was a mere decade into his rule, and Rune already looked forward to the next king's appointment.

Rune should have seen to The Crumbling yesterday, but he'd attended the Hunter's Moon ball instead. *And found his night breeze.* He needed to send her court a letter of intent, asking permission to pursue her romantically. She seemed tight-lipped about her court. Perhaps she contemplated leaving them and starting her own court with him.

The Ra'Voshnik purred its agreement and Rune paused a moment. He'd subdued the creature ages ago. Confining it to the recesses of his mind. It remained dormant for the most part, silent unless Rune tasted the emotions of fear. The Ra'Voshnik roused for his night breeze, struggling against its confines as it had in Rune's youth.

He ignored the creature and straightened his cufflinks. He would deal with it after he found his dark queen. She refused to speak with him across the mental tether she tied to his mind, but he could locate her court another way. Address the letter to her instead of her queen. She answered the wish he'd made at the depth of his power. A wish that would only be heard by a shard as dark or darker than he was. She carried a shard of Darkness, which should be relatively easy to find.

With luck, he would locate his night breeze and have his letter sent before his meeting.

Rune phased to the grand library housed within the Artithian palace. It extensively cataloged information from each realm in a centralized source.

This gaudy, multi-level palace, in its gilded whites and golds, served as the capital of the five realms. Rune walked through the familiar halls; ornate bookshelves lined in matching rows on either side of him. He'd spent much of his first two centuries here, researching spells and techniques to hone his power. The library stood ten stories high, each floor dedicated to a specific area of study or information.

Rune arrived on the third floor, the leather-bound books dedicated to courts and shard registries. Several of the darker courts requested listings of the dark-blooded shards who were not associated with a court. They would send invitations attempting to fold them into their ranks with offers of wealth or position.

He could have asked the librarians that served here to assist him. He'd decided against it. Their assistance would draw unwanted attention to her and himself. He valued his privacy and was not in the habit of explaining himself. His search for a woman would invite too many questions he had no desire to answer.

The books were organized chronologically. Rune strolled to the end of the hall, where the most recent volumes were stored. He selected the dark-blooded shard registries covering the current century. He narrowed his eyes, reading the spines of the adjacent leather-bound books. Court appointments may prove useful. Newly formed courts. He could narrow his search by race. Though he wasn't sure what she was.

The only winged race was Artithians. The race was divided in two. The Artithians with feathery wings were short-lived mortals, existing for less than a century. Her wings thankfully were reptilian, the immortal variety. Only Artithians didn't possess her physical characteristics. Their wings ranged from green to black. Her iridescent scales didn't fit, and neither did her claws.

Her soul shard would be the most efficient means to locate her.

She carried a shard of Darkness, must have recently come into her power. Another shard of Darkness would set Necromia a buzz with gossip. Lyssa and every other dark court would offer her wealth and privilege, anything within their means to bring her into their ranks. Males would flock to her—moths drawn to a flame.

Rune frowned. Was he not drawn to her as well? Another moth.

He concluded she was twenty, just invoked her blood. She may very well have come to the ball to seek him out. He and Morbid were the only males who carried a shard of Darkness. Did she mean to ask him to see her through her Ceremony of Blood and lose her nerve?

After a woman invoked her blood, she could see what was necessary to survive her ceremony. If she survived, the woman would raise with a tendril, capable of healing or injuring as she chose. During the ritual, women surrendered their virginity and plummeted toward the Darkness. The darker her shard, the harder she fell. A trusted court member or a blood priest or priestess performing the ritual would breach her and keep her from falling until the danger passed.

He'd seen to one ceremony more than twenty centuries ago. Lyssa requested their court see her through her ritual. The duty would fall to the darkest unattached court member. Belind brewed a concoction that roused his body to comply, but Lyssa had been ritual. He did what was needed and left her bed when the danger passed.

His night breeze would be different. He would worship and honor her. The brewed concoction he'd once taken to rouse his body would be unnecessary with her.

Rune phased to his research suite within the palace. His surroundings faded in the blink of an eye, and his suite came into sharp focus. He stood in a large well-lit room with tall arching ceilings. Large ornately carved double doors swept up the wall. The carved railings and bookshelves both matched the door's design.

A long, gilded table was the dominating piece of furniture here, near a few steps leading to a raised platform. A carved banister separated it from the ground level. Against the wall of the platform were floor-to-ceiling bookshelves containing the tomes Rune selected himself or requested from the librarians.

While considered fashionable to Artithians, Rune found the architecture garish. Preferring his keep with its gray stone walls. He sat at the head of the table, neatly arranging the books beside him.

He leased this suite from the reigning Artithian house. Over the twenty centuries he kept this room, he'd seen the ruling house change a number of times. Some had been peaceful, an old king without heirs abdicating his throne for a strong relative to take his place. Others were bloody.

Rune paid little attention to the affairs of mortals. They aged and died within a minuscule amount of time. No different than animals.

He opened the shard registry, reading over the entries. Reviewing every entry dating back the last two weeks, he noticed she wasn't listed. He'd read it again to be sure.

Her family could have bribed the archivists to keep her from ending up on the lists dark courts purchased for recruitment, but she would still be recorded. Rune phased back to the bookshelf holding the most recent shard registries. He brushed his fingertips along the spines, searching for the shard registries specific to Artithia.

Rune pulled the book when he found it and leaned back on the carved railing behind him. He flipped the pages open, reviewing the Artithian entries. She had to be here.

Hours passed as he poured over every entry made during the past three months. His fingers grazed over the pages as he read. Rune rolled his stiff neck. How could she be this strong and not be documented?

Lancing pain shot through his skull and Rune's fangs lengthened.

The Ra'Voshnik broke from its confines to circle Rune's mind, growling its displeasure. *Tear the bird king's wings from his back, it* grated.

Be silent, Rune growled at the creature as a second stabbing pain seared his mind. The High Council was led by the short-lived. A safeguard Belind put in place. *They help keep perspective.* She decreed.

Rune lost track of time looking for his night breeze. His meeting with the High Council was overdue. Be damned if the Artithian King ever learned to communicate through Rune's talisman instead of channeling power through it. Spelling it to share the pain he caused could prove to be a motivational tool. *Or an act of war depending on the bird king's mood.*

Rune sent a warning growl to silence the bird king and returned to his research suite. He reached across the tether to his night breeze and withdrew when he felt her metal shielding remained in place. That she kept a tether to his mind but refused to communicate with him perplexed him. If she visited him again tonight, he would learn her name.

He debated asking for a listing of all dark-bloods from the past week and decided against it. That he intended to court a woman would provide Necromia with ample gossip. He didn't need that fire lit before he had a chance to pen a letter of intent to her.

Rune ran his hand through his hair, reminding himself she recently came into her power. He needed patience. The newly documented dark-blooded entries would update tomorrow. The scribes were typically a week behind. Recording the backlist into a spelled tome, then updating each copy linked to it. Rune vanished the heavy leather-bound book so it would travel with him unseen.

He phased, materializing at the center of an airy building separate from the Artithian palace. The open-air, domed structure served as the meeting place for the High Council.

The white and gold constant throughout Artithian architecture gleamed in the sunlight. Rune inherited his mother and father's blood. He was a Pure Blood like his mother, but his father's blood laced him to Hell and allowed him to walk in the sun. While uncomfortable, Rune didn't burn like others of his kind.

He knelt in protocol on the raised, circular platform called The Eyes. A long, narrow table followed the platform bending in a half-circle. Rows of seats provided space for anyone who wished to witness court announcements, bindings, or blood debts.

Today the large domed building held no audience. A private meeting between Rune and the High Council. Rulers of each realm made up the committee, seated at their table at the edge of The Eyes. Rune assumed his father's mantle as Hell's ruler but held no interest in serving on the High Council. As a compromise, Rune's younger brother Jareth served in his stead.

"Shadow Prince." Jha'ant, the Artithian King, spoke his title in protocol.

Rune rose, canting his head and said, "Apologies for my tardiness."

Jha'ant cleared his throat and shifted in his chair. "I've grown concerned. There has been no progress against The Crumbling."

Rune never cared for explaining himself, never tolerated the opinion of a short-lived creature. He obeyed the High Council Belind created so long ago because honoring the way they ruled was all he had left of them. "I exhaust myself on the matter." Rune said, thinning his lips as he pinned Jha'ant with his gaze. "Destroying a realm would be a less daunting task."

The Artithian King averted his gaze and turned to Morbid. "You assigned him to the task. Is it beyond his capability?"

Kill the talking bird, the Ra'Voshnik growled through his mind.

Be silent. Rune hiss, ready to silence the creature if it continued with its outbursts.

The Familiar King tilted his chair to balance precariously on its two back legs, resting his booted feet on the table as he laced his fingers behind his head. "I said it would be in Rune's best interest to look into The Crumbling." Morbid corrected, staring up at the intricately designed ceiling.

Rune smiled at Jha'ant, a cold flash of his fangs. "Did you have another in mind to take my place? A rest would be welcome."

"I meant no disrespect," Jha'ant said as he paled before clasping his hands. "I'm not as strong as the rest of you. The shields are getting more difficult to maintain."

The Crumbling gained strength with each passing day, building into a terrifying force over the last eight hundred years. The High Council decided each ruler would shield their realms when The Crumbling began. Within the first half-century, shielding both Necromia and Anaria strained Lyssa. Rune took Anaria from Lyssa in secret, shielding it along with Hell, allowing the realms to believe their High Queen protected them.

"We thank you for your efforts, Prince." Morbid's deep purring voice pulled Rune's attention. The Familiar smiled then winked at him.

Rune turned back to Jha'ant. He'd given up his attempts to understand Familiar lifetimes ago. They worshiped Chaos and fate. Could see the past and future. Their perspective would always be skewed from reason. He inclined his head at Jha'ant. "If there is nothing else."

"Thank you, Shadow Prince." Jha'ant's words closed the meeting.

Rune phased and reappeared at the far end of his crystalline realm. The loose crystal grinding under his steps as though he walked on broken glass.

The Crumbling rose before him. A mass of blackened clouds constantly rolled over each other, twisting sinisterly. Lightning arching within it, illuminating different depths in blacks, grays, and purples. Rune would have found the sight pleasing had it not been devouring his realm along with the rest.

Within its destructive clouds was something else. Something vast Rune's senses couldn't encompass. He tested it against the other realms. Found changes made in one realm carried to the rest. A single entity caused the slow destruction of the realms. Rune sought to overpower The Crumbling and break it under his will during his early attempts.

Force proved to be a fruitless effort leaving him with a single alternative. Rune needed to untangle the spell manifesting The Crumbling, dismantling it layer by layer.

Rune spent a millennia honing his power until he wielded it at will. The complexity of this shield was more advanced and intricate than any spell he'd created. He'd thought with time and patience he would unravel it. Mastering this as well.

It became a fascinating frustration. The spell changed as he manipulated it. Seemingly adapting to him as he learned it.

Rune shielded himself and stepped into The Crumbling's rolling clouds. It enveloped him. Crushing pressure bore down on the layer of his power that protected his mind and body from being consumed and destroyed.

What he did was precarious. His protective barrier was spelled to regenerate as The Crumbling consumed it. In doing this, Rune perceived the burning pain of the steady pressure grinding against his mind and body. He focused through the pain and monitored the steady drain on his power. Rune would need to retreat from this place before his strength gave out and he was destroyed. Rune mentally reached for The Crumbling, pulling the spell that maintained it before him. Glowing green threads surfaced. The lines crisscrossed, tightly woven together. Rune selected the first strand, beginning the task of unraveling the spell.

His agile fingers picked up the threads, holding them apart as he unraveled the overlapping pattern. As he pulled up the last string, the first layer vanished. Rune worked quickly, untangling the strands as they slid to various positions. Rune adjusted his grip, trading filaments to other fingers as the pattern moved to avoid the silken lines pulling in the wrong order and snapping. Forcing Rune to start the process once more.

Rune reached the sixth layer. His reserves significantly drained in the ten short minutes he stood within The Crumbling. He swapped a line to his thumb, but three strands shifted, cutting the thread and shattering all the ones he held. The lines glowed, pulsating. Taunting him. Rune phased out of The Crumbling and would need a day and a half to recover before he could make another attempt.

Exhausted, Rune phased back to his home, appearing next to the desk in his room. He recalled the soul shard registry and set it down, impatient to review the new listings it would contain tomorrow.

He would slumber and recover his strength. Stripping off his suit, he lied in bed staring up at his ceiling. The next seven days would be the longest of his life. Darkness willing, his night breeze would be among the entries listed tomorrow.

Rune closed his eyes, and sleep soon followed.

His mysterious female's scent drifted to him, teasing closer as Rune's vision adjusted and cleared. They were seated on the settee as they had been the previous night. She wore a light gray backless shirt, this time with fawn-colored leggings.

"Is that the same book?" Rune asked the woman curled on her side, leaning against his chest.

She didn't reply. Simply turned the page and continued reading.

Minx. Rune slid his finger down the inside of her wing, where it connected to her back.

The Ra'Voshnik seized on the breathy sound she made, focusing on her. *Pull her closer and ask for her throat.*

Rune dismissed the creature as it prowled his mind. His night breeze shifted her wing, but her movements did little to move his hand. Stroking the same spot, he continued to stare. She flattened her book to his chest and straddled his hips, knocking his hand away. "You're being an ass today."

"I promise to be better behaved in person." He smirked up at her.

She pouted at him for a moment, letting the expression drop as she opened her book to begin reading again. She muttered, "I like it better here," before turning a page.

Rune gently closed her book, and she reluctantly let him take it. "I'm reading that."

"Grant me your name, and you can have it back." He raised a brow at her and held her book behind his shoulder.

She pressed a hand to his chest and stood on her knees, leaning closer to retrieve her book.

Rune's fangs lengthened. The slender column of her neck so close to his lips he could perceive her warmth.

Take what is offered. The Ra'Voshnik growled, growing aroused. *She is not offering you anything. Be silent.*

He turned his head toward hers as she fought to pry her book free from his grasp. He fanned his breath over the shell of her ear. "Grant me your name, and I will let you read *uninterrupted* for the rest of the evening."

Rune stilled when she turned to meet his gaze, still holding the book. Her full dark lips a moment from his. He swallowed, worried if he made a wrong move, she would reject his advances.

Her lightning-streaked midnight eyes twinkled with mischief. "We renamed you fangs."

We? Rune laughed softly. "Fangs?"

She nodded, her gaze dipping to his mouth.

His eyes slid closed as she pressed her lips to the corner of his mouth.

Five

Faye woke up with a start, jerking upright and glancing around her. She ran her hand over the front of her throat, to her collar bone. Her heart pounded as she took deep breaths to calm herself.

She climbed out of bed feeling like she didn't sleep.

Sparrow spelled their cottage, keeping it warm as the colder months approached. Faye peeked into the hall dressed in her white nightgown. Sparrow sat at the kitchen table with toast and eggs.

"Dream of fangs again?" Sparrow asked around a mouthful of food.

Faye joined her, making a plate of fruits and cheese. "Yeah, but it was a weird dream."

"Sexual depravity weird, or you two riding a unicorn weird." Sparrow pointed her fork to one side then the other.

Faye gave Sparrow an impressed look as she took her seat.

"Look at you, using your big words like you know what they mean and shit."

Sparrow smirked. "I'm all about sexual depravity. So, spill." She tapped the table at Faye twice before going back to her breakfast.

"We were curled up on a couch thing in this big, fancy room." Faye glanced around their kitchen-dining room. "The room was the size of our cottage, and it had a fireplace I could walk into."

Sparrow nodded, chewing her toast. "Typical dark court. Get to the naked part."

"There is no naked part."

Sparrow exhaled dramatically. "Why are your dreams so boring?"

Faye fluttered her hand at Sparrow. "I'm in his lap."

"Less boring." Sparrow looked thoughtful for a moment. "Does he have the bad eyeliner on in your dreams?"

"I like his eyeliner." Faye paused. "Is that weird?"

Sparrow shrugged. "Usually, it's a precursor to being eaten. But I heard their bites are almost as good as their purrs."

Faye widened her eyes, finishing a bite of fruit. "He purred!"

"Riding his face is naked time bitch. Even if you left your panties on."

"I wasn't doing that, hooker."

In the dream, she'd brushed her lips from the corner of his mouth to his jaw. He lifted his chin as she trailed kisses down his throat. She ran her hand up the back of his neck into his hair, trying to distract him enough to loosen his hold on her book.

"I bit him." *Then he pulled me closer.*

The rumble from his purr startled her, and she tensed, biting down hard and yanking his hair.

"Is that it?"

"When he purred, I felt the vibrations." Faye waved her hand at herself. "On my non-dreaming body."

Sparrow quirked her lip. Her expression turned uncharacteristically serious. "Are you sure Silver Leaf isn't poaching you in these dreams? He could be a Familiar."

The thought made Faye recoil. Poaching was a term used to describe a person who had a beacon cast on them without their knowledge. Beacons were Familiar magic that tethered a connection from the Familiar to an unsuspecting mind. The Familiar could shape their dreams, pull secrets, even leave marks on their body.

She would have dismissed Sparrow's wild notions if the vibrations of his purr hadn't woken her up.

There was no reason for her to be targeted for a beacon. As soon as a Familiar stepped into her mind, they would see she held no power.

No, this was a momentary attraction she felt in a place she and Sparrow should never have been. The excitement of it was still fresh in her mind, working out of her system. Nothing more.

"My brain is just working through all the nonsense you made me witness." Faye insisted

Sparrow shrugged. "The Shadow Prince might be poaching you. You said he was sniffing for you."

Faye nearly choked. She thought of him standing there after they'd run from him. The way his lids lowered as he breathed in the night air. The small act made her feel desirable. Which was idiotic.

She shoved the memory away. But a tiny part of her wanted him to come find her that night. Which was the reason she was having these dreams. *He's a passing fantasy.*

Faye finished her plate and got up to set it in the sink. "He's not even a Familiar."

Sparrow shrugged, and thankfully changed the subject. "Got any plans?"

"Thinking about spending the day at the hot spring." Faye spent the majority of her time there during the colder months.

"I'll go with you for a bit. I'm meeting Vash for a late lunch. I'll come find you when I come back if you're still reading."

Faye smiled walking down the hall returning to her room. She changed into her bathing suit. A simple black bikini made of leather and string spelled to stay dry. She put her boots on then slid her thick fluffy robe on.

She returned to the kitchen to find Sparrow gone. Faye took a basket from the kitchen counter, packing it with dried meats, cheese, fruits, and some hard bread.

"Hooker." Faye called.

"Bitch." Sparrow's voice came from down the hall.

Faye tossed the latest romance book Sparrow brought back from Necromia for her in the basket as Sparrow came down the hall dressed in a slinky silver one piece.

"Carry me!" Sparrow shifted into a small white cat. Faye held still as Sparrow climbed up her robe and crawled into the furred hood at her back.

"If you learned to phase, we would already be there."

Sparrow purred, wiggling around in the hood.

Faye left their home, closing the door behind her. She made her way across the open field toward the forest, following the path she marked with painted rocks. The short hike along the mountain branched off, leading to a clearing.

The change in humidity hit Faye before reaching the spring.

Two lounge chairs were placed next to the spring. Faye and Sparrow arranged the larger rocks to border the spring, and Vash even built seating for them in the water.

Faye untied her robe, dropping it in a pile along with Sparrow on one of the lounge chairs.

Steam rose from the clear blue water. The plants and small trees surrounding the spring were green year round. Even on the coldest winter day, this little clearing stayed warm and comfortable.

Sparrow, still a cat, crouched at the edge of the spring dipping her paw into it. She backed up and took a running start before leaping into the water. She turned into a woman mid-air and cannonballed into the water. At the last moment, Faye grabbed her book, holding it to her chest as she turned her back to Sparrow's splash.

Standing, Sparrow pushed her hair out of her face. "This water is so nice."

"You're splashing the food and my book hooker."

Sparrow fluttered her hand at her as she made her way to the seating area in the spring. "I'll still eat it."

Faye tucked her book safely under her robe before she pulled off her boots. She tied her hair up in a bun and waded into the water. The heat seeped into her as she ran her fingers over the surface of the water.

Faye sat next to Sparrow, laying her head back on a smooth stone. Listening to the wind rustling the leaves far above them.

Sparrow elbowed her, and Faye gave her a sideways glance, not wanting to move.

"Have you seen his," Sparrow gave a short whistle and stuck out her index and middle finger, "Yet?"

"No."

Sparrow eyed her suspiciously. "Do you close your eyes the whole time?"

Faye lifted her hand out of the water to make a rude gesture. "No."

"They're supposed to be trained in pleasing women when they serve in the dark courts. And your Shadow Prince belongs to a really dark court. I bet he got some really nice training."

Faye laughed, sitting up. She rolled her neck, popping a crick. "I'm surprised you haven't volunteered."

"I would. Vashien won't give me the details."

"Vash served in a dark court?" Faye thought he'd always owned his tavern, Lost and Found.

Sparrow waved her hand. "Long time ago, centuries before us."

Vash looked to be in his early thirties. It was easy to forget he lived for hundreds of years.

Faye stared at the steam rising from the water. "Do you ever get worried?"

Sparrow raised her eyebrows.

Faye turned toward her then. "That Vash will leave when you age?"

Sparrow crossed her legs, leaning forward. "First, we're only twenty-five. We might still be immortal. I just haven't aged to my most beautiful yet." Sparrow flicked her hair, turning her head to the side. "And second, I can't control Vash. If he leaves me, it's his loss, and my memories will haunt him for the rest of his undying life."

Faye couldn't imagine being in Sparrow's place. She pretended the rejections and dismissals didn't matter to her, but in truth, they stung, cutting deep.

She had no emotional investment with the men who dismissed her after a single glance—actually giving her heart away? Out of the question. She would be too vulnerable. The potential for pain was more than she could bear.

Love meant giving another person the tools to destroy you and hoping they don't. A gamble Faye wasn't willing to take. Especially with an immortal. She would age, and they would leave.

While Sparrow, through her memory, would haunt the men she left. Faye was an Anarian. There was no reason to stay with her. If

Faye gave her heart away, she would be the one haunted.

Bits of water struck Faye's face.

"Bitch, I don't know what you're thinking about but stop it." Sparrow flicked more water at her.

Faye leaned her head back again, gazing up at the forest canopy.

"So fangs hasn't bitten you. You haven't seen his dick. What the hell do you dream about?"

"It's stupid."

Sparrow snorted but stayed silent.

Faye's mind drifted back to her dreams of him. Sitting with him in front of the fire was nice. Faye smiled, even if he was an ass, and tickled her back. Flirting was fun, but if she had to pick, she would take the dreams where he held her until she fell asleep.

"He holds me. He pets my hair." In her dreams, he laid on his back, and she curled up to him, resting her head on his chest. He covered her hand with his, brushing his thumb over her index finger to the back of her hand and back again.

Faye turned to face Sparrow. "He doesn't look for a shard I don't have." Faye lifted her right hand out of the water, looking at her bare index finger as she turned her hand. She could almost feel his caress, the scent of him teasing her memories. Amber and sandalwood.

"He doesn't ask me what court I belong to." *He sees me.*

"You're just sick." Sparrow linked arms with her. "Fucking dreaming about affection. That's what does it for you?"

Faye flicked water at her, not wanting to admit how close to the truth her sister was.

Sparrow leaned her head back on the stone, looking up with Faye. "Well, tell your subconscious when you get to the naked part. I am expecting you to have a three-finger killer."

Faye turned her head. "A what?"

Sparrow lifted her hand over head, holding three fingers together, and tapped across the middle joint of her fingers. "If he's not this wide, you throw his ass back."

Faye glanced at her hand, holding three fingers together. "I feel like this would hurt."

Sparrow snorted and stood up, climbing out of the spring. "Not if he knows how to use it."

"You heading back?"

"Need to get ready for my hot date. Where's your book?"

Faye turned, leaning on the stone. "Under the robe."

Sparrow handed the book in front of Faye. "Make sure you come home before dark. It's not good to go home in the dark, you know."

"I'm going to tell Aunty Clara you're talking shit." Faye took her book and turned in time to see Sparrow as a cat, running on air through the forest. She yelled, knowing Sparrow would hear her.

"You'd be home already if you learned to phase."

Six

With a sharp intake of breath, Rune sat up, his muscular arms circling no one. He blinked, glancing at his surroundings. He placed his hands on either side of him and leaned his head back.

The minx bit him, sending the Ra'Voshnik to frenzy. *She wants us to give chase,* the creature growled as it prowled the edges of his mind. *And you do nothing. You will lose her to another male if you don't act, polished fool.*

Rune exhaled. *Be silent.*

It'd been an age since the Ra'Voshnik spoke to him. The creature began as whispered thoughts in the awkward stage between boy and man. In less than a season the Ra'Voshnik had taken root in his mind, struggling against him for dominion over the body they shared.

Mastering Saith's lessons required absolute control of his mind and will. The Ra'Voshnik hindered his progression, fighting him at every turn. Rune imprisoned it in the depths of his mind, unable to truly kill it. And now after thirty centuries of rage and impulse, the creature rose from its confines to fight against him once more. All because the minx bit him.

He brought his fingers to her bite low on his throat. He felt indentions, the spot tender. He rose and headed to his bathroom mirror. Rune brushed his hair behind his shoulder, inspecting the side of his neck. A dark oval of teeth marks marred his pale skin. Leading a dream was one thing, marking his body when they had yet to meet quite another.

Rune thinned his lips as he stepped back into his room.

He rolled his neck. Her mark was superficial, not hindering his movement, though quite forward. Her disregard of protocol allowed him to follow suit.

Rune focused his mind and felt for her mental tether. Brushing his mind to hers, he felt her shields still in place. He gripped her tether, focusing his power along it, directing an offensive spell he created to track targets that fled from his court.

Rune cut the connection, initiating his spell. His brow knit together. It held, unscathed. Welling his power, he made a second attempt, and still it held fast.

The inability to cut his mind free of her concerned him. Rune reached for the Familiar King's mind next, *Morbid*.

Shadow Prince, Morbid's deep purring voice answered in Rune's mind.

I require your assistance on a matter.

I'll see you after I've tended to Angelique. I'll send Sadi ahead.

Rune's thoughts drifted to Morbid's wife and queen. Angelique became ill during her pregnancy with Sadi. She was poisoned, narrowly surviving it. The ordeal left her weakened. Angelique rarely left Chaos, spending her time hidden away in Morbid's sprawling mansion.

Morbid carried a shard of Darkness and was gifted with Sight, the Familiar's ability to see the future. With all he was, he couldn't save his wife. There was no retaliation. The Court of the Black Rose didn't go to war. He didn't call on any of them. Morbid himself was formidable, yet he chose to do nothing.

The Familiar King was a far better man than him. Had Rune been in Morbid's place he would have reduced the realms to ash.

Sadi phased into his realm minutes later as he dressed. His father was a Shadowman created as a caretaker to Hell. Rune, like his father, had Hell stitched into his being. Could feel anyone entering or leaving his realm.

All but other Shadowmen.

When the court was still whole, his father and brothers could feel when Rune entered or left the realm. His vampiric blood gave him away.

Rune made his way to his study. Sadi sat on his desk, the outline of her features lit by Hell's twilight sky streaming in through the intricately designed iron trimmed glass that encompassed the entire back wall.

She wore a black leather under bust corset over a lace halter. Crossing her legs, the high slit in her skirt exposed the length of her leg. Practically a twin to his night breeze. The same dainty features. Same wine-colored lush lips. But Rune's body didn't respond to Sadi. The Ra'Voshnik remained silent in her presence.

Sadi's midnight eyes glinted with excitement as she hopped to her feet. "Are we hunting?"

The corner of Rune's mouth lifted. Hunting. A term Sadi used when their court went to war with another. Or when Rune was sent to deliver retribution on behalf of his court. She'd joined him on several occasions.

"No. I am having trouble severing a mental tether. If you could track the line back and give me her location, it would be appreciated."

Sadi stood nearly as tall as Rune in her exaggerated heeled boots that covered her legs to mid-thigh. Her brow raised as she sauntered to him. "Her?"

Rune said nothing and stared straight ahead as Sadi tilted her head. He had no knowledge of how Familiar magic worked. Only that it worked within an entirely different mental plane, he had no access to.

She seemingly peered into his head, brushing her fingertips over the side of his face. Tracing behind his ear and following down his neck. Her finger slid beneath the collar of his shirt, pulling it open. "She bit you."

Amusement lit Rune's eyes. "I would like her location to repay her kindness."

Sadi's expression grew serious. "This is a beacon. But I've never seen one like this."

"Are you certain?" It couldn't be a beacon. Familiar magic wasn't felt. Rune could feel it, had felt it when it struck his mind.

Sadi nodded. "The anchors are deep in your mind. When did this happen?"

"The Hunter's Moon ball. I believed it to be a mental sending. Is she a Familiar then?"

Sadi pulled at his collar, examining her bite mark. "We have fangs, not as pronounced as yours, but a bite like this would have drawn blood."

"Can you remove her beacon?"

Sadi stepped back. "My father should look at it first. It feels like Familiar magic, but it's not constructed the way we would use it."

Rune took his seat behind his desk. "How do you mean?"

Sadi followed, taking a seat on Rune's desk to his left, resting her booted foot on his armrest. "Beacons are meant to be used as a back-door into a person's mind. We offer a distracting dream, sift through their mind, steal our information, and slip away.

"She constructed a beacon with impressive anchors. Anchors pierce the mind, snaring it to the fantasy we offer. Like when we war and I call out *love and defend me,* those are anchors. The minds I snare, butcher their brothers in arms to protect me." Sadi tilted her head as she sighed, gazing over Hell's jagged landscape as though she were recalling a fond memory.

The information sickened Rune. He'd waited lifetimes for his dark queen. Was any of it real? Did he actually desire his night breeze? Rune met Sadi's gaze and forced the words past his lips, "What delusion did she anchor in my mind?"

Sadi held his gaze, going still. Rune waited agonizing minutes. "I don't see a command woven into the anchors." Sadi squinted, tilting her head like she was peering at something. Studying it. "I think she's using the anchors to hold the beacon in place."

Relief flooded Rune. His dark queen was real.

Morbid appeared in the chair across Rune's desk. The Familiar King slouched in his chair, wearing leather pants, a trench without a shirt, and a magenta scarf that matched the patch of color under his midnight eyes. He set his heavy boots on Rune's desk, crossing his ankles.

Inclining his head, Morbid asked, "Prince?"

"I have a beacon that is anchored to my mind. I would like it removed and her location."

Morbid laced his fingers, setting them on his lap as his brow drew down. He blew out a slow breath. "Such things you plan to do to your mate."

Rune stilled, meeting the Ra'Voshnik as it surged forward. It thrashed beneath his hold. *Release me! We must find her.*

Rune ignored its furious cries, tightening his hold until it fell silent. He calmly turned his attention back to Morbid. Only a fool discarded a Familiar's words, and that went twice for their king. "My what, now?"

"You've asked for a queen for a very long time. Fate has finally given her to you." Morbid examined his painted black nails.

Our dark queen. The Ra'Voshnik purred at Morbid's words, seizing on them the same moment Sadi said, "How can he have a mate?"

Familiar thought themselves blessed, receiving predetermined mates as a reward for serving Chaos and worshiping fate.

Rune wasn't a Familiar, didn't serve Chaos, and he certainly didn't worship fate. Why would fate tie a Familiar to him? "Familiar call to other Familiar."

Morbid shrugged his broad shoulders, fiddling with the shard of Darkness embedded in the silvery chain that hung around his neck. "I can't say. I did chase your mother for centuries. Maybe all the thinking I did of her made you part Familiar."

Rune exhaled. "That is not amusing."

Morbid laughed, holding his thumb and index finger together. "What's amusing is I was this close to being your father." He dropped his hand to his lap. "But then Julian spoiled my chances by stealing a shard of Darkness for himself."

Rune sighed, glancing upward for patience. He was never truly sure if Morbid fawned for his mother as a way to get under his father's skin or if he truly harbored feelings for Michelle. He glanced at Sadi to assist him in redirecting her father's focus, but her features chilled him. She looked... afraid. Rune thinned his lips. "What is the significance? I do not worship fate as you."

"Being fated ties your life to the other. Death in either will claim you both."

Rune heard that Familiar saying over the centuries, believing it to be an expression of devotion among their kind. Alarmed, he turned his attention to Morbid. "My life is *tied* to another?"

Morbid didn't answer.

The Ra'Voshnik broke free, circling his mind as hot fury roiled in him. He was into his thirtieth century. Had survived wars. Torture. Only to have his life held by a woman he didn't know. He silently thanked the Darkness. She at least matched him in strength. But being so young, she would be reckless. Not yet aged into her immortal body. Too young. Vulnerable.

Shield our dark queen.

For once Rune agreed with the Ra'Voshnik. He would need to protect her to safeguard his life. Join her court. "Where can I find her?" Rune bit off the words. Every moment she spent away from him was an unnecessary risk.

"Let your Ra'Voshnik free," Morbid answered.

I will give chase if you won't, the Ra'Voshnik purred as Rune said, "I want to find her, not devour her."

A dark chuckle slid through his mind. *So afraid she will prefer me to you.*

My queen will tolerate you as I do, Rune growled.

The Ra'Voshnik prowled the edges of his mind. *Our queen will purr under my touch. Submit to my bite.*

Rune ruthlessly dragged it deep within his mind. *You will never touch my dark queen, debase creature.*

Whose face do you think she sees in her dreams, polished fool, it hissed.

Rune tightened his hold silencing the Ra'Voshnik and found Morbid arching a brow at him.

"Come now, Prince, we both know the Ra'Voshnik doesn't want to devour her." Morbid paused, looking thoughtful for a moment. "Unless that's what they're calling it these days."

Rune exhaled. "Do you know her location?"

Morbid gave him an apologetic look. "My words fall on the ears that need to hear them."

A growl slipped from Rune at Morbid's non-answer. "There must be a Familiar binding that will allow me to speak to her the next time she calls me to dream."

"I could offer a binding that would sever your beacon, offer up your queen's location, and let you speak with her during your next dream." Morbid counted off on his fingers, then his gaze raised to meet Rune's. "But I need something from you."

"What do you require?" They were of the same court. If Morbid needed something of Rune, he had only to ask.

"A blood debt."

Rune was not in the habit of offering blood debts. They were binding, permanent. There was no escaping or twisting the debt. The bargain compelled you to comply. They carried through the centuries, concluding in one of four outcomes. The owner relinquished the blood debt, the death of the owner, the death of the one in debt, or the blood debt's completion.

He'd accepted a single blood debt during his long life. One that haunted him. Casting a shadow over his young would-be queen. Rune steepled his fingers, knowing he had no alternative. "The price?"

"A favor." Morbid shrugged.

Vague. But what choice did he have? "Done."

The Familiar King stood, cutting into his palm with his thumbnail, offering it to Rune. "I offer a blood debt, in exchange for fashioning a Familiar binding, the Shadow Prince will owe me a favor."

Had it been anyone else, Rune would have required more specific wording. He'd known Morbid his entire life. Trusted him. Rune stood, grasping Morbid's fingers lightly. "I accept." He bent, running his tongue over Morbid's palm. Straightening, he swallowed the blood, sealing the debt.

Morbid stood, pulling off his magenta scarf to wipe the remaining blood as he healed the cut. Then reached into his pocket, removing a simple obelisk made of lepidolite, and set it on Rune's desk. Only a few inches tall, it looked insignificant.

Morbid inclined his head at Rune. "Your blood will initiate the binding."

"Tell me when you find her." Sadi slid her hand down his back as she stood to join her father.

The Familiar vanished, phasing out of his realm.

Rune took the obelisk and returned to his room. He placed it on the nightstand beside his bed and allowed the Ra'Voshnik to surface. Black flooded his gaze, and his nails became black tipped claws. He dragged a claw over his wrist, his blood forming a thin red line. Turning his wrist down over the obelisk, Rune made a fist as drops of blood fell over the crystal.

It pulsed, coming to life. Rune hissed as Familiar magic stabbed into his mind, hooking deep. The painful sensation, reminiscent of a mental snare. One he couldn't escape.

Rune scarcely made it onto his bed before the spell overtook him. His final thought as he closed his eyes were of his brother Alister and the eight-hundred-year-old blood debt that hung between them.

Darkness help Alister if his brother proved foolish enough to oppose him.

Seven

Faye leaned her head back on the smooth rocks. She closed her book using her finger to hold her page as she stretched her arms overhead. She'd been soaking for more than an hour. Standing, Faye abandoned her spring for a lounge chair. After drying off, she draped her fluffy robe over her as a makeshift blanket.

She set the book down, splayed open on her lap to hold her page. The sound of running water and the birdsong overhead lulled her. It was still early afternoon. Faye yawned, covering her mouth. She could afford a catnap. She closed her eyes, listening to the forest.

Falling asleep before she realized.

A dream arose. This wasn't like her usual dreams that took shape softly. This was jarring, snatching her to another place. A steady, low roar seemed to come from all around her.

She grabbed at the ground to steady herself. No, not ground.

This was too soft. Faye blinked, realizing she lay on her stomach in a large bed covered in a heavy blanket. The dark silk sheets snagged on her nails.

She pulled her hand free, tearing the silk. Faye examined her nails in disbelief. They were thicker and curled, ending in sharp points. Claws?

Her vision adjusted slowly as she looked over the room. She could see the walls were dark but couldn't make them out yet. She glanced over the large four post bed, draped in dark silk. She knew this bed. This was fang's bed.

Even her perfect dark-blooded man was still a typical dark-blood underneath. Excessive and wasteful. This bed could fit four people easily. No one needed this much room. And silk? The sheets alone would cost more than she made each month selling her potions and ointments.

Faye thought back, remembering she decided to take a nap at the hot spring. But she felt awake here. Faye could hear Sparrow's teasing voice. *Maybe the Shadow Prince is poaching you.*

The thought sent a chill up her spine. She cast it away. She wasn't being poached. She was an Anarian, nothing worth poaching. And even if they did want something, they wouldn't leave her aware. She would be dreaming of fangs right now, not alone in his bed.

Faye sat up on her heels. Dressed in her swimsuit, but she wasn't cold. The weight on her back didn't slide off. Shifting her shoulders, her eyes widened.

She had wings. Real wings. They were like Vashien's but smaller, and the scales shimmered in whites, greens, and purples. Faye bounced on the bed, pumping her wings. She disturbed the air around her, tossing her hair wildly. She had to tell Sparrow about this.

Faye's vision cleared enough to see the rest of the room. The curved walls were made of a swirling mist that churned constantly. Tendrils of sharp, glowing purple twisted inside it, illuminating its depths.

She remembered this place. Faye crawled to the edge of the bed, spotting white sand that covered the floor. This was one of her dreams. She slept as he held her in his arms. She could almost feel him running his fingers through her hair while she rested her head on his chest. His heartbeat lulling her to sleep. The simple act meant so much to her. He cherished her.

She wouldn't mind curling up to him now.

Faye half expected him to appear in bed next to her. Wasn't that how lucid dreams worked?

She glanced at the empty side of the bed, running her fingertips along the sheets. Her claws snagged the material, lifting it as she pulled her hand away.

Faye tested the points of her claws and straightened.

A man stood inches from her, beside the bed.

She gasped, stopping short of swiping her new claws at him.

He glanced at her hand before pinning her with his gaze. "Apologies."

Darkness, his voice. It was deep with an accent she couldn't place. This lucid dreaming was amazing. These weren't flashes of moments or glimpses of him. She could actually see him. He was tall, dressed in a tailored black suit. His long white-blonde hair hung loosely around him.

His eyes were different, a clear, piercing blue. No trace of the black crimson that covered his eyes during the other dreams or the shadows that swayed beneath them. He was still nice to look at. His sharp jawline, straight nose, and those kissable lips.

Without his bad eyeliner, he seemed… tame.

His gaze lowered over her body for a moment. The corner of his mouth lifted as he met her gaze. He didn't stop at her bare index finger or ask her what court she belonged to. He didn't see what she lacked. He saw her.

Wanted her.

She pulled him to her by his jacket. Her lips met his in an urgent kiss. In those first moments, he didn't respond. His rejection stung her, cutting deeper than she expected.

Faye pulled away, but he followed, moving with her in a fluid motion. She stared at him as he leaned closer. His lids slid closed, and their lips touched. He met her with a slower, soft kiss. Pulling her in, holding her against the hard planes of his body. His fingertips traced over her lower back. She parted her lips for him as he kissed her with short, languid strokes.

Darkness, he felt so right. His scent of amber and sandalwood caressed her senses. He was made for her. Her perfect, dark-blooded man. Faye closed her eyes, losing herself in the feel of him.

She'd kissed a handful of boys and a few men before she invoked her blood. None of them compared. They'd all wanted something from her, something she could offer. Faye never gave in, knowing once they took what they wanted, they would discard the rest.

When fangs held her, she felt their connection, a tangible bond between them. She was all he saw, and for once, she wasn't lacking. With him, she was enough.

A small part of her knew the only reason he looked at her with such reverie was because she made him up. Men like him didn't exist. Faye shoved the nagging voice down. She was dreaming. This was real enough.

He slowed, sliding his hand into her hair as his thumb traced her jaw. "Tell me your name." He rasped between kisses.

Faye pulled him closer, deepening the kiss as she rolled her hips. "You're overdressed fangs."

He chuckled, smiling against her lips. "Am I?"

She brushed her hand down the front of his throat, petting his chest. His muscles tightened and flexed as he pulled off his jacket. She fought the urge to sink her claws into those hard muscles and pull him to her. She wanted him closer. Needed more of him.

"And you talk too much." Faye sighed against his lips.

"Minx."

Faye flicked her tongue to his bottom lip, giving it a playful lick while she held his gaze. Crimson spread through the whites of his eyes. The same way dye would when poured into water. But it dissipated, his ice blue gaze returning.

Faye bit the inside of her lip. Maybe fangs wasn't so tame.

She kissed the corner of his mouth, his jaw. He lifted his chin and purred as she trailed kisses down his neck.

"Plan on biting me again?"

Faye unbuttoned his shirt and found her dark oval of teeth marks. She pressed a soothing kiss to it. "I'm sorry, I didn't mean to." She pressed her hand against his chest, the vibrations of his purr reverberating through him. "This startled me."

His lips brushed her ear. "I may ask you to do it again." He brushed the side of his face along hers. "If you allow me to reciprocate."

Faye parted her lips, spreading her hand over his chest. "I'll think about it." She pressed her hands higher, feeling his purr. At his chest, the vibrations were weak, but as she moved higher, they inten-sified. Fangs smirked as she brushed her fingertips over his mouth. She gasped when he bit her index finger, holding her with his teeth.

His purr reverberated through his mouth, tickling the tip of her finger.

Faye pulled her hand back, needing more of him. "Touch me." She pulled him down with her as she laid on her back, her wings outstretched above her.

Her vampire guided her legs around his waist. He kissed her collarbone, the side of her neck. At her ear, he purred, "Tell me your name."

Frustration mounted in her, she wanted his mouth on her, but he wouldn't shut up about her name. Without thinking, she gripped the front of his throat and immediately dropped her hand. What was wrong with her? "I'm sorry." Faye lowered her gaze. Shame burned her. She was taking what she wanted from him. Behaving no better than the dark-blooded men she despised.

He brushed her hair from her face. His purr softened as he coaxed her to meet his gaze. This close, she could see flecks of yel-low in the blue of his eyes.

"You have nothing to apologize for." He gave her a dazzling smile. "Vampires appreciate aggression." A crimson so dark it was nearly black bled through his gaze. Those lovely shadows crept from beneath his eyes, swaying over his cheekbones. He lowered his head, nuzzling her throat. His lips brushed her ear as he whispered, "I crave it."

She drew him in. Faye knew she shouldn't, but she preferred him this way. His dark gaze felt right, his eyes holding so much more emotion like this. She could see his yearning. How much he needed her.

He lifted his chin, a lock of his long white-blonde hair falling forward. "I am yours to command."

Faye swallowed. She ran her fingers over the front of his throat before gripping him lightly.

He lowered his head, his lips meeting hers. Light and slow. A savoring kiss.

He pulled back after Faye was breathless and whispered in her ear, "Now grab my neck like you mean it."

Faye tightened her grip, and he obeyed as she guided him. She brought his lips a moment from hers. Arching up to him. The power she wielded over him was intoxicating.

But she was still unsure how to proceed. "Now what?"

"Command me."

Command? Faye didn't know where to start. There were so many things Sparrow told her about she wanted to try.

Her mind went back to the Hunter's Moon ball. The first night she glimpsed him. How she imagined sitting in his lap. Her nails scratched over the material of his suit with his mouth pressed to her neck. The moans he would elicit from her as he drank.

Wicked thoughts arose in her mind, scenes of him taking her body and drinking from her at the same time. Faye tightened her grip, meeting his heated gaze. "Drink me."

Faye released him. If this was her fantasy, she should have all of it. "And touch me if you can do more than one thing at a time."

His mouth lifted in a sexy grin, flashing a fang as he spoke. "Seeking a demonstration before you accept me?"

His words made her chest tighten. He wanted her acceptance. Hers. This wasn't real. Fangs was her dream. Something she desperately wanted but didn't exist.

Faye returned his smile, playing with a length of his hair. "You talk an awful lot."

"And still, you withhold your name."

"Does it really matter?"

He studied her and seemed to come to some decision. "Offer me your throat."

Faye turned her head to the side, baring the slender column of her neck. She sighed at his first touch. His mouth was hot. He nibbled and licked, not piercing her with his fangs.

Faye's breaths turned shallow as she parted her lips.

He caressed the swell of her breast and trailed his hand lower. Over her navel. Tracing his fingers along her hip and down her thigh.

"What court do you belong to?"

Faye's fantasy shattered. Years of resentment burned her desire to cinders. *This poaching bitch.*

Faye gripped the front of his throat, digging her claws in deep, so he knew she meant it. Darkness, she hoped he felt it. Hoped it carried to his actual body. She dragged him up to meet her fury.

Suddenly her lungs burned. Faye choked as her dream ended.

Her surroundings snapped to blurred streaks of blue. She felt rocks and gravel.

She was underwater.

Eight

Water broke over Faye, cascading down and pulling hair across her face. Hot needles burned her lungs, as she spasmed for breath. She lurched forward, coughing up the water she inhaled before she could right herself. Faye blew out a breath as she searched her surroundings for that poaching dick to appear and drown her until she managed to wake up.

Her sister hunched over her toppled lounge chair. Her blonde curls obscuring her face.

"Did you throw me in the water?" Which admittingly was better than being drowned by fangs, but did she have to overreact so much? Faye splashed her sister when she continued to ignore her.

Faye's lips parted. "Hooker?"

Her sister's feet swayed, turning in her direction. She wore a blank expression, staring off in the distance. A thin trickle of blood ran from her nose, past her lips.

"Sparrow!" Faye screamed, lifting herself out of the hot spring. Her heartbeat drummed in her ears as she grabbed Sparrow's face, searching for her gaze. "Hey. Look at me. Come on."

The Familiar magic controlling Faye's dream wouldn't have hurt Sparrow. Was fangs here while she slept, and Sparrow chased him off?

Faye's brow came down when she touched something wet and tacky. She dragged a red smear with her thumb. The source of the blood still trickling from her sister's ear.

No, no, no. Faye's hands shook as she wiped it away. "Sparrow, come on. Please."

Sparrow's lethargic gaze shifted. Lowering her brow with a grimace, she said, "You just gave me the worst. Fucking. Hangover."

Faye threw her arms around her sister, squeezing her tight, fisting her hair as tears welled. "Are you okay? Does anything hurt?"

"Just you bitch." Sparrow squirmed, but Faye wouldn't let go. "Get your wet ass off me." She wrinkled her nose. "Are you…" Sparrow slapped her hands away. "Are you fucking crying?"

Faye took a calming breath and wiped her eyes. "You need a healer. Tell Vash to get here now."

Her sister snorted at her. "*Your* ass needs the healer."

"You're bleeding." Faye swiped her finger across the trickle now on Sparrow's chin, showing her proof with widened eyes.

Sparrow frowned as she wiped her hand beneath her nose, but after several swipes it still refused to come back clean. "It's fine," Sparrow muttered, wiping her hands on her pants. "When I came back to check on you, black mist was rolling off you. It was fuck-you level magic. I had to wake you up before you melted my brain."

"You're bleeding, I'm not. Tell Vash to poof his ass over here. Now."

Sparrow fluttered her hand at Faye.

Faye pulled on her robe and roughly tugged on her boots, not bothering to dry off. Her sister made a series of facial expressions while talking with her hands. All of which, Faye guessed, matched whatever she was saying telepathically to Vash.

Sparrow shifted her weight to her back foot and faintly quirked her lip. "He's coming, now spill. What happened? I couldn't wake you up. I tried to use my power to throw your ass in the pool. It didn't work so I had to magic your chair instead, bitch."

Faye's cheeks flamed in a burning rush as the memory of her dream surfaced— She should have seen through him. He was too good to be true. She let herself get caught up in the moment, and now she felt like a fucking idiot. How could she put Sparrow in danger like that?

Faye lowered her gaze, unable to look her sister in the eyes. "Fangs is real. He's poaching me. You must have felt his magic bleeding over, past the dream."

"Fangs the Shadow Prince?"

"It had to be a glamour. Some Familiar's idea of a sick joke." *One that hurt her sister.* "Why is Vash taking so long?" Faye needed to know for certain Sparrow was okay. She would never forgive herself if Sparrow was hurt because she had stupidly let her guard down.

"Darkness, the man is running a business. Give him a fucking minute— He said he's coming. If anything, we need to take your stubborn ass to get a mental shield put in. If Silver Leaves is poaching you, I'm about to fuck his life," Sparrow said, cracking her knuckles.

Faye rolled her eyes. "He can't poach me unless I'm sleeping. Your *face* is bleeding. You're going to the healer first."

A figure appeared in the corner of Faye's vision. "Vash, I need you to—"

Faye's breath seized, and her eyes widened. A man stood beside them. His long white-blonde hair shifted with the breeze, a stark contrast against his black garments. Every muscle in her body tensed when her gaze fell to his throat at the trail of blood on either side.

Where I dug in my claws.

Faye stepped between him and her sister. "Sparrow run."

"Fuck that," Sparrow said from behind her as the man stepped closer.

He stood more than half a foot taller than her. The expensive cut of his clothes molded over his impressive frame. A flood of black swept through his pale blue gaze for a moment, like ink in water. Then it was gone, revealing a mask of indifference.

He grasped her arm, parting his lips. Faye glimpsed his canines seemingly lengthening before her eyes. This wasn't a glamour. Her heart pounded as she twisted away from him, but he held fast.

"Sparrow run!" Faye's cry became a shriek.

Sparrow ignored her, stalking toward her captor. Her dark shard blazing to life. "Fuck this poaching ass bitch."

Sparrow raised her hand, in a sharp motion. The dark mist surrounding her shard coated her hands. A ball of dark swirling mist swelled between her palms before firing into the man's chest.

The sizzling crack of magic struck, filling the clearing. Sparrow's ball crashed against a black light that covered the man. Faye's hair whipped in the backlash of power as Sparrow's magic failed to crack his shielding and dissipated.

Sparrow had thrown multiple men across rooms with the same flare of power. Faye stared up at the man who seemed completely unconcerned her sister had attacked him.

He glanced down at her, arching a brow. "Is she your pet Familiar? It explains much."

His accented words that had been kind in her dreams were now harsh and biting. His pale blue gaze bore into hers. Challenging her.

Faye jerked frightened by his sudden movement. His hand shot out in a blur, catching Sparrow by the neck. The corner of his mouth tilted up as he lifted Sparrow to his height. Her sister choked. Legs kicking for purchase

"No. I'm sorry!" Faye frantically grabbed at his arm trying to lower it. Sparrow's face reddened as ugly wet choking sounds filled the space between them.

"I'm sorry. Please, don't hurt her." Tears spilled over Faye's cheeks. She gazed up at him, cupping the side of his face. "Please."

A crimson so dark it looked black poured through his gaze, covering the entirety of his eye. Veined misted shadows crept from beneath his eyes and swayed over the tops of his cheekbones.

His expression softened as he leaned into her touch, closing his eyes. She smoothed her thumb over the edge of his cheekbone. "Let her go. I'll accept your advances."

A muscle ticked in his jaw, and the shadows receded. He pulled away from her touch, glaring down at her with clear blue eyes.

Faye glanced at her sister, who was running out of time. Faye stepped into him, pressing her body into his as she met his gaze. "You can have me, just put her down." Faye glanced at her sister. Her choking sounds were slowing, and she wasn't kicking anymore. Faye stared up at him, eyes pleading. "Please."

He said nothing. Holding her gaze for a heartbeat. He then shifted his attention to Sparrow. Her sister went limp, arms and legs dangling lifelessly.

"Sparrow? Sparrow!" Faye yanked viciously against his hold, screaming, "What did you do to her!"

The man splayed his fingers wide, and the little blonde collapsed in a heap.

Faye fell to her knees, reaching for her sister. "Sparrow! Sparrow!" Her fingertips inches from her.

The man canted his head at her a fraction. "Why do you not use your power?" His free hand slid to her wrist, pulling her hand up. "Where is your shard?"

Faye twisted in his hold, desperate to reach her sister.

Vashien materialized across the spring. He paled as his mouth went slack.

"Sparrow," Vash said in a desperate whisper.

Faye met his gaze. The anguished shadows in his eyes cut into her heart. This was her fault. She mouthed, *I'm sorry.*

He took a shaking breath, and his eyes hardened as he focused on the man. A long wicked looking curved blade appeared in his hand. He lunged over the pool with a hard beat of his wings, charging them.

Faye's vision blackened and Sparrow faded.

Her clearing once filled with lush grass and pebbled rocks was replaced with a wide hallway. Faye's heart hammered too hard as tall gray stones rose up like a prison cell all around her.

She couldn't breathe as the colorless walls closed in, trapping her with the man that murdered her sister.

Nine

Pain shot through her shoulder as Faye was hauled from the
ground. Her feet dragged along the gray stones as she dangled
from his forceful hand, staring at the space her sister once occupied.
Silent tears slipped from her unblinking eyes. She felt as though she'd
been gutted and hollowed out.

The man exhaled when she didn't bother to get her legs under
her. "Stand up."

Faye closed her eyes, tuning her captor out. Sparrow had been
so sure she would be immortal since they were girls. As certain as she
was, she would carry dark shards. He jostled her, but Faye hung limp.
She couldn't bring herself to care about anything.

Dizziness overtook her, and Faye opened her eyes. The gray
stoned hall refocused to reveal a lavish room. Faye was falling the
next moment, and she landed hard as she took a small narrow table

with her. Pens and loose pages scattered around her, but it was the letter opener that caught her attention.

Faye fisted her newly found weapon and swung at him straight armed, driving several inches of it into his thigh.

He didn't scream like she expected. He exhaled, glancing at her hand still holding the handle. Faye's weapon slipped from her hand as he stepped back out of her reach. He pulled the inches of metal from his leg, letting the letter opener fall and bounce on the thick carpet, staining the plush fibers red. Just like Sparrow had been before they vanished. Discarded and alone.

He strolled out of the room, glancing back at her over his shoulder. Black flooded through his gaze and cleared a moment later. Turning away from her, he closed the door behind him. A moment later, a black light flashed over the double doors and faded.

Faye sobbed and curled forward, hugging her knees. Her body shook with each short shuddering breath. Her pride had costed her. She played with fire, but it was her sister who was burned. Her hatred for dark-bloods made her lose the person she loved most. How long would it take for her to share the same fate? Hugging her knees tighter, she tried to push the image out of her mind. Her sister was dead, and she was a pet. Faye's gaze fell to the letter opener once more.

Crawling forward to retrieve it, she twirled it. The blood staining the silver ran on either side and dripped over the carpet until it gleamed.

Pain would be better than the guilt that ate her. Sparrow crumpled on the ground was a sight that wouldn't leave her mind. Vash's look of anguish. All because she was proud and wanted to prove dark-bloods weren't better than her because they carried a shard.

Faye gripped her makeshift knife in both hands, the tip pointed at her neck. Sparrow would be waiting for her in Hell, and they could return to the Darkness together.

Why are you so boring? Make him pay, bitch.

The dull blade slipped from her hands as Sparrow's voice circled her mind. Her tears came faster, obstructing her vision.

"Hooker?" Faye said aloud, anxious for her sister's reply.

Minutes passed, and Faye's brush of hope distilled her despair into something darker and broken. She wasn't sure how long she cried before she curled on her side, or how much time passed until she had no tears left to shed. Faye's head pounded, her eyes were swollen and aching until she noticed a pair of weighty-looking metal candle holders the length of her forearm. *Make him pay.*

Faye got to her feet, picking the closer of the two. She tossed the candle on the floor, taking a practice swing to test its weight. Satisfied, she wiped her face. "Let's go fuck his life, hooker."

Faye approached the fancy, dark-blood double doors. The black light flickered, stopping her from touching the door handle. Faye pushed harder, and thin glowing purple cracks began spiderwebbing away from her.

It shattered. Faye pulled back as the shards fell. Examining her uninjured hand, she wiggled her fingers. Hmm…It didn't seem to hurt her.

Faye went for the door handle again and opened it without interference. She stepped into the hall and found fang face silently strolling toward her. Faye matched his steps letting the candle holder slip from her grasp, catching the end of it.

He tilted his head slightly before acknowledging her weapon. "Go back to your room, minx. We would not want you injuring yourself," he said as the corner of his mouth lifted.

A hysterical fury rushed through Faye. This fucker was smirking. Faye clenched her jaw and tightened her hold on her weapon until her knuckles went white. If this dark-blooded asshole found this amusing, *then buckle up big guy, I'm about to be hilarious.*

Faye bared her teeth, swinging for his arrogant fang face. An invisible force rushed her, tossing her hair as it passed through her. Black light flickered and shattered as Faye's blow landed across his cheek.

Ten

Pain exploded as Rune snapped his head to one side. The Ra'Voshnik surfaced in a rush, bleeding through his gaze. *She wants us,* it purred, the creature's excitement thrumming through his mind. It urged him to pin her beneath him, certain she would offer him her throat once he asserted dominance over her. The violence of her actions only fed into its desires.

Be silent. Rune dragged the Ra'Voshnik into the recesses of his mind, as the fiery minx swung the candle stick. Rune caught it by its base, ripping it from her hands and throwing it behind him. The metal clattered as it tumbled down the hall.

The hot-tempered harpy broke through his shield with little effort as waves of unharnessed power radiated off her. He searched her body for another piece of jewelry that would display her shard, while dodging her inept attempts to strike him. When he found her bare, he demanded, "What game are you playing? Where is your shard?"

"Kill me!" She hit at him blindly, following him each time he stepped out of reach. New tears fell from her red, puffy eyes. Seeing her like this twisted something unfamiliar in his chest. The Ra'Voshnik echoed the sentiment wanting to take her in his arms and comfort her.

Rune ignored the urgings. She toyed with him during their dreams. Her Familiar lover attacked him. And now she incessantly wailed to join her lover in death. If he wanted the petite blonde dead, he would have liberated her head from her body.

"Kill me!" She shrieked, flailing at him.

Rune phased partially, becoming incorporeal as her fist passed through him. It was painfully evident his so-called mate received no combat training. She lacked any evidence of being raised within a dark court.

She could be from a lesser family. It occurred rarely, but she may even have been born in a day-blood court. So many details were wrong. The rags she wore screamed peasant. Her hair was an unkept tangled mess. This unsophisticated female could not possibly be what fate chose for him.

Darkness, if this was some elaborate hoax contrived for the Familiar King's amusement, Rune would have several choice words for him. Catching her wrists in one hand, he grated, "Calm yourself. I know you carry a shard of Darkness. What court do you belong to?"

"I don't have a shard!" She raised her knee.

Her movements were no match for his reflexes, and Rune caught it before she could land the debilitating blow. "That was unkind of you."

His minx straightened her leg, struggling against his hold. When she couldn't break free, she stood on her toes, leaning up as far as she could. "Kill me before I kill you!"

She promptly bit down on his hand with enough force to draw blood. The Ra'Voshnik snapped his hold. *Pin her and take her throat. Show her who will master her.*

This is not foreplay. She is not trying to fuck you. It growled in disagreement and whispered through his mind, growing aroused.

Rune released her, pulling his hand away from her mouth.

"Kill me!" She sobbed swinging and scratching at him. "What are you waiting for?"

Rune cursed in High Tongue, avoiding her attacks. The minx would end up hurting herself at this rate. He whipped a lash of power at her mind. A mental attack meant to knock her unconscious. When she remained upright, he blinked before striking again harder.

He couldn't touch her mind or cut himself free of her mental tether earlier in the day. While concerning, he had more pressing issues at hand. He would have snapped her neck and waited for her to regenerate if she were immortal. He couldn't be certain she'd aged into her immortality. A risk he wouldn't take with his life in the balance.

Rune phased behind her and moved in a blur, sliding his arm beneath her chin. He tucked her windpipe in the crook of his elbow and gripped his bicep, pushing her head forward with his other hand. He squeezed as she struggled, clawing at him.

Her nails raked over the material of his jacket as the moments ticked by. She would be unconscious soon. Rune narrowed his eyes at the sound of cloth tearing and sucked in a breath as razor-sharp claws dug into his forearm.

Rune held fast, counting his heartbeats.

One.

She raked her claws across his arm. By the white-hot lick of pain that followed, he was sure she'd cut to bone.

Two.

Her struggles slowed, growing sluggish.

Three.

Pain tore through his chest as his arms were forced apart. She fell to her hands and knees, a pair of iridescent reptilian wings sweeping around her. They ripped through her robe and his suit, leaving deep gouges across his chest.

She stood and lunged at him, swiping at him with her claws.

Rune leapt back narrowly avoiding her swing. "Calm yourself, harpy."

His words didn't reach the woman. She kept going.

He reached for Sadi's mind. *I need your assistance. Wrap yourself in a sight shield.*

Rune felt Sadi phase into Hell a moment later. *What are you doing?*

Distracting her. Can you slip beneath her shields and knock her unconscious? Rune recalled the candle holder and tossed it to the minx. "Care for another swing?"

She caught it and bared her teeth running toward him. Rune dodged her blows as she struck the gray stone wall. Black swirling mist exploded, raining dust and pebbles over her.

Rune's mouth went slack at the decent-sized hole she left in his wall, one she seemingly didn't notice. Perhaps returning her toy was a poor decision. He phased, avoiding her next swing.

I can't get past her shields. Sadi's panicked voice called through his mind.

Before he decided his next move the harpy swayed on her feet. Her wings darkened until they became swirling black mist holding the shape of her wings. It thinned and dissipated, fading from sight. Rune narrowed his eyes at her transformation and lurched forward to catch her as she fell.

Revulsion etched over her dainty features as she glared up at him. A snake coiled ready to strike. "What did you do to me?"

What did he do to her? A bitter grin spread over his lips. *She poached him with her lover and played offended.* Rune lifted her into his arms and phased to the room adjoining his. The spiteful creature in his arms clawed to consciousness, returning his gaze with her own seething glare. "I did nothing to you."

Her lids slid closed even as she demanded in a hushed whisper, "Kill me."

Rune cradled her to his chest as her breaths became deep and even. It maddened him that he found touching her pleasant. He even had an errant urge to brush the hair from her face and tuck her under the blankets. Rune exhaled. This wasn't fate. This was a spell. One geared to cause him to feel affection to the very thing that would kill him. This was a brilliant spell, he decided.

He brushed his mind against hers, determined to break the tie binding them and be done with her. Rune cursed in High Tongue. The same damned mental shielding barricaded her mind— As she slept. He gently lowered her to the bed, hating he pulled the blankets over her before he'd made a conscious decision to do so.

Thinning his lips, Rune forcibly dragged himself from his captive. "You're injured." Sadi splayed her hands over his chest.

Heat spread over the wound tingling as his flesh knit together. When his court was whole, Sadi served as their healer seeing to their wounds and injuries after wars and skirmishes.

"I am well." Rune remained still as Sadi moved her hands lower, mending one arm then the other.

"She attacked you." Not a question. Sadi fingered the tattered remains of his suit. A fierceness crossing her features, a glimmering promise of violence reflected in her midnight eyes.

Rune shrugged, "She believes I killed her lover."

"I'm going to kill her lover in front of her," Sadi said, turning toward the bed and stopping short. After a moment she approached the sleeping minx, leaning in close and poking her cheek. Rune canted his head as she inhaled deeply over the minx's mouth.

Sadi straightened, turned to Rune, and asked, "Why does she have my face?"

By the sound of it, she was deeply offended she and the minx could be twins. "I do not know." Rune kept the laughter from his voice lest he invite Familiar steel between his ribs. "I am unable to breach her mental defenses. Is it Familiar magic?"

Sadi moved to the peasant's bedside and pushed her hair to one side, before turning to Rune. "You won't win her by letting her believe you killed her lover."

"I have no want for a female that toys with men for sport."

"Rune she's yours," she said.

"That remains to be seen."

She sighed at him and stared off into the distance. Rune strolled into his adjoining room, giving Sadi time to navigate the minx's mind. He stripped off his rags, selecting another suit from his closet. After dressing, he returned to the minx.

Long moments passed before Sadi finally said, "I can't get past her shields."

Unfortunate. "Can you look into her? Tell me what she is."

Sadi narrowed her eyes at his words.

"You witnessed her wings and claws. Those are not characteristics of any living race."

Sadi stilled, her consciousness drifted to a place only Familiar could access. Those of her kind, who worshiped fate, could touch the life threads of every living being.

She explained it to him once when she'd first come to court. She would spend hours with him in Saith's study. While he actively refined his terrifying powers, perfecting them, she sat in a chair staring off into the distance.

When he'd asked her what she did while he honed his craft, she replied that she did the same. Each life's thread was constructed of hundreds of lives. The individual's thread remained at the heart of the cord, but every life they encountered entwined and spun with theirs, creating the tightly woven braided cord.

A Familiar needed to master pulling these strands apart without breaking them. Snapping the fragile filaments ended lives, cutting them short. Altering fate.

After they mastered handling the threads, Familiar could witness the individual's life. Watching it play before their eyes, spying on a person's deeds and actions.

Rune scrutinized the two women identical to each other and loosened his hold on the Ra'Voshnik a fraction. *Why do you prefer one and not the other? They are practically twins.*

If you can't recognize the difference, you're a bigger fool than I take you for.

Rune drove the Ra'Voshnik down, silencing it.

Sadi stood suddenly, drawing Rune from his inward thoughts. Worry flickered through her gaze as she began pacing the room. "You're bound to her."

"Your father said as much," Rune stated dryly.

Sadi stole glances at the sleeping woman. "I've never seen a thread like hers. She's lived for the past eight hundred years."

"The minx is immortal then?"

"She lives, ages, and dies a mortal life. Over and over. This is the ninth life she's lived back-to-back. Before then, her line was dormant. Your fate tie is its only company. You've been tied to her your entire life."

Rune glanced at the bed. She would age and fade in less than a century. The thought of her inevitable absence from his life left him with a gnawing hollow feeling. Rune pressed his fingers over his sternum as though the pressure could subdue the ache. "If she has been fated to me my entire life, why do I only feel her now?"

Sadi shook her head. "I don't know."

The minx stretched her arms over her head in her sleep, and the

Ra'Voshnik fought him viciously. *Lay beside her. She will curl to us and sleep in our arms,* it purred.

With a growl he dragged his gaze from his captive. Nothing about her made sense.

Rune glared at the sleeping minx, subduing the Ra'Voshnik. This wasn't fate. He was the Shadow Prince. Immortal. He wore a shard of Darkness. Fate would not be so cruel, slighting him with a mortal that would age and die. A death that would seep into him through their fated bond.

"The fated tie is a spell which likely runs my entire life because it needs to tie to me. That is why I have not felt it before. Her lives are iterations of a spell being perfected." One he would break, freeing himself of her sway over him.

Sadi hugged her arms close to herself. "What if my father is right, and she is yours?"

Her words didn't surprise him. Familiar worshiped fate. Honoring it first, above all others. Including their lives. Rune was no Familiar.

She is not mine.

Eleven

Warmth and comfort surrounded Faye as she happily cocooned in blankets nestled in the softest bed she'd ever felt. She pulled the blankets tighter around her, tucking her arms under her chin.

She recalled the Shadow Prince. The way he cradled her against his chest and sweetly tucked her into bed. She breathed in deeply, surrounded by a light floral scent instead of his amber and sandalwood. She reached her arm out for him and remembered closing her hand over a weapon. Holding it as the length of metal jutted from his leg.

Faye scrambled up, and her memories returned.

The gravity of her situation threatened to crush her. Sparrow was gone, and she was the newest acquisition of her murderer. A pet he would expect to stroke and touch, caged in this opulent room of wealth and finery.

The scent of roasted meat wafted to her, and Faye's mouth

watered. A woman who could be her twin sat on the window ledge. Soft light shined past her into the room. She held a small plate, eating small cuts of meat— with a knife? Glancing up, meeting Faye's gaze.

Faye felt embarrassed for her, being forced to wear such a demeaning outfit. A corset squeezed her frame, pushing her breasts up. It was fitted over what looked like a man's white collared shirt. Her skirt had obscenely high-cut slits in the front. Her belted thigh-high leather boots completed her outfit. Was this how fang face expected his pet concubines to dress?

Faye recoiled, imagining the Shadow Prince demand she wear a similar outfit.

An articulated metal ring covered the woman's index finger, hellfire gleaming off it with her movements. Cold prickles of fear slid down Faye's spine as she stiffened. She was in a room with a real Familiar. Dark mist twisted over the woman's soul shard, but Faye was too far to see exactly how strong she was. The Familiar woman smiled at her, heightening Faye's suspicion.

"Are you a pet too?" If she wasn't too crazed, they could escape together.

The woman laughed. "Darkness, no. You're not a pet either. Are you hungry?"

Was the Familiar sane enough to know the difference? The glamour she wore to mirror her was unsettling, but she had no time to navigate what Familiars deemed acceptable. "I'm being kept against my will. What else would you call it?"

She narrowed her eyes and glanced up, tapping the clawed point of her articulated ring against her bottom lip. "Political prisoner?" The Familiar gave her an expectant look. A silent question poised in the Familiar's addled mind, *Is my answer acceptable?*

The woman frowned when Faye remained silent. She glanced down at her meal and smiled brightly, before offering her plate, and tilting it back and forth.

Faye didn't move. Mildly insulted her look-alike tried to entice her the same way you would a nervous animal. Faye looked down at her hands, bunching the white blanket. "The Shadow Prince killed my sister."

Moments passed in silence, and Faye glanced up. The woman was peering down the hall, wiggling her fingers in greeting. "Looks like the High Queen is paying Rune a visit."

Faye threw the blankets back, rushing out of bed. Vashien must have brought a petition to the High Queen. She would free Faye and bring her sister's murderer to justice. She hurried to the only opened door and the woman caught her wrist pulling her to a stop. "You should wait until Lyssa leaves to speak with him."

"I want to see the High Queen, not him." Faye yanked her hand out of the woman's grasp and turned toward the hall in time to see a black satin skirt enter a room halfway down the hall.

Faye slowed as their voices carried toward her, near the door.

"A woman knocked out three of my guards before she was subdued. She claims you kidnapped her sister." The High Queen's melodic voice was bright with laughter. "An Anarian."

Tears pricked Faye's eyes. Sparrow was alive? Faye dashed into the room.

"Are you here on her behalf?" The Shadow Prince asked a moment before his pale blue gaze landed on her.

He moved a finger in a subtle motion for her to return to her room as the High Queen said, "Darkness, no. The woman is delusional."

Faye ignored him turning to the High Queen. "The woman that attacked your guards. Was she blonde?"

The High Queen sneered at Faye, scrutinizing her from head to toe.

Faye's heart beat faster. Why was she just staring at her? "Is she blonde?" Faye blurted, louder.

The High Queen turned from her to glance at the Shadow Prince. "Honestly Rune, I see the accusation is true."

Her sister was alive. He didn't kill her. Faye brought her hand to the bottom of her throat. The void in her chest filled, lifting a stabbing weight off her. Sparrow was alive. And beating up guards. Faye wasn't sure if she would laugh or cry. She smiled, teary-eyed, but the High Queen was already walking away from her.

"High Queen." Faye ran to her, taking her hand and bowing her head. "I'm being held here against my will. Please tell the Shadow Prince to release me."

The High Queen tore her hand from her grasp. Faye flushed unsure how to address her properly. Faye glanced up, and the High Queen turned her back to her, holding her hand open as though she touched something foul. A handkerchief appeared in her other hand,

and she meticulously wiped each place Faye touched.

The High Queen glanced back at the Shadow Prince and exhaled sharply. "Your pet hasn't learned her place?"

Faye's chest tightened. "Please, I don't want to be a pet. If you could just take me to Anaria, I'm from Alexander."

"Go back to your room." The Shadow Prince stated calmly from his seat behind a large dark wooden desk.

Faye could only stare at him. He watched her suffering. He knew. "Why didn't you tell me you didn't kill her?"

"It matters not."

The High Queen stepped closer to her, pinching her chin. Inspecting her as she turned her head one way then the other. "Her likeness to your pet Familiar is remarkable." She turned her gaze to him. "Does she spread her legs for you?"

Faye flushed deeply as the tops of her ears heated.

The High Queen leaned toward her and parted her lips, taking in a breath. Faye held still, growing more uncomfortable with each passing moment. She'd never seen dark-bloods behave this way. Were these vampiric customs? Faye lowered her gaze, afraid of insulting the High Queen.

She straightened, glancing at the Shadow Prince. "I can't taste her emotions. Are you camouflaging her?"

"I require her for a spell," was all he said, returning to his documents.

The High Queen flicked her hand in Faye's face, dismissing her. "High Queen. Please, I don't want to be here." Faye begged.

"You have no choice in the matter. Go back to your room. Sadi if you would escort her, it would be appreciated."

Faye glanced behind her at the Familiar woman and turned to the High Queen, silently pleading to be saved. The High Queen turned toward her, and her face lit. She would take her back. Faye could go home to her sister.

"You're in his realm dear. Feel free to call your court to war against the Shadow Prince."

The peasant blanched and her arms went limp. Her pained, defeated look twisted something in Rune's chest. It hurt him to see her distressed. The Ra'Voshnik circled his mind. *Go to her*, it growled, demanding he comfort and soothe her.

Rune drove it down, ignoring the ache. The sooner he was free of this spell, the better. It must be tied to the Ra'Voshnik, which would explain why it acted so strangely toward her.

The mortal left the room with her head down, and it took all of Rune's self-control not to go after her.

"I've never seen you take a pet before." Lyssa stood beside him, leaning closer to scent him. "I can smell her on you. You refused my offer but took an Anarian to your bed?"

The Ra'Voshnik purred from the recesses of his mind. *Yes, bring her to our bed.*

Rune schooled his expression and lifted his gaze to meet Lyssa's. He didn't need to taste her emotions to know the rotten taste of jealousy covered her. "You know no one has ever received an invitation to my bed." *My queen will be the only woman I offered that to.*

Lyssa clicked her tongue at him. "I'll leave you to train your pet."

She phased out of his realm leaving him in his study. Rune exhaled, frustrated with his inability to control the Ra'Voshnik, and its incessant want for her. The mortal clouded his mind, impairing his judgment. Twisting something in him each time he glanced her way.

Rune dragged his hand through his hair before closing his eyes. He took a deep breath in and released it slowly, centering his mind. Assuring himself what he felt was no different than what every other male experienced. The driving desires were new, and he was untested in this regard. But Darkness, the learning curve for his minx was far steeper than any of the magic he dedicated his life to.

Not his. Rune thought bitterly, pinching the bridge of his nose. Even as every instinct within him screamed she was.

Twelve

The gray, colorless walls closed in on her with each step. Faye was a fool to think the High Queen loved her people. She was a dark-blood like the rest of them. Faye straightened her back as they passed a closed door along the hall a few feet from hers. Taking a deep cleansing breath, Faye focused her mind. She didn't need the high bitch. She would escape on her own.

From her doorway, Faye glimpsed the sky through the window beside her bed. She could see the sun was setting. Or was it dawn, how long had she slept? She strolled to the window hoping to find a landmark. Anything that would identify her surroundings and aid her plot to escape. Faye's breath caught as she stood before the window.

The ground glimmered, stretching as far as she could see, blending into the horizon. Mountains and jagged spikes rose from the ground in chaotic bursts. The entire landscape was made up of the same beautiful shimmering crystal. The sun dipped just below the horizon. The stars beginning to emerge as the last of the colors gave way to the darkness sweeping over the sky.

"Where are we?" Faye asked absently. She could hear the High Queen's voice laughing through her mind. *You're in his realm, dear.*

Sadi came to stand beside her, fingering the white gauzy material draping either side of the window. "This is Hell."

Faye's hope of escape shattered before it began. Her stomach knotted, and Faye thought she would be sick. Her breaths came in short pants as she fixed her gaze on the window ledge. It's just a realm, she told herself. A closed realm he had stolen her to.

His realm.

Faye forced several deep breaths, steadying herself. Sparrow was alive. She clung to that knowledge with strangled desperation as tears pricked her eyes. Her queen abandoned her. She couldn't phase and was held captive in Hell. There would be no escaping him. Faye blinked the tears back grasping at what little choices she had left. He held her hostage but she would never break.

Sadi tugged the sleeve of her robe. "We can talk over a meal. You must be famished."

She was starved but remained silent. The Familiar woman wearing her face, took a seat at a square table and crossed her legs, waiting for Faye to join her. Faye remained at the window glancing over the luxurious room that dwarfed her cottage. Was Sparrow at their kitchen table now? Worried sick. "Can I write a letter? Send word to my sister and tell her I'm alright?"

"I'm sure…"

The Shadow Prince appeared in the room, glaring at her. "No."

Sadi exhaled, and her shoulders slumped. "Rune, be reasonable."

He ignored her and silently stalked toward Faye. "If you disrupt my dealings a second time, I will revisit your lover and return with the piece I carve from her."

Faye drew a shaking breath, squeezing closer to the wall at her back. She stared up at him into his cold, pale blue gaze. "Please don't hurt my sister."

The hard set of his eyes eased a touch, and he took a step back. "Sister."

Faye nodded, squeezing her arms to her side. "The blonde I was with when you found me. She's my sister."

Rune glanced Sadi's way, grating, "See that she eats," before vanishing from the room.

Sadi sighed, resting her chin on her hand. "You're handling your stay poorly."

Faye observed her, she seemed decent if not sane. "I don't want to stay here."

Sadi smiled at her, patting the table for Faye to sit across from her. "You're a guest in our dark court."

Faye straightened her robe and took her seat, surrounded by carved expensive furniture arranged with rugs to define the space. A large bed, plain in comparison to the other room she'd been in, was covered in thick ivory blankets. Blue and gray pillows decorated it. Faye turned her attention back to Sadi. "Your court is beautiful, but I would like to go home."

Sadi placed a black stone on the table and touched her finger to it. "Please bring us a selection." Faye schooled her expression as the Familiar spoke to the air before slipping the stone into her corset between her breasts. She smiled brightly at Faye, leaning back in her chair. "You'll enjoy your stay once you understand court protocol. Court life is very simple. Touch is an invitation. A strike allows him to engage you physically. Using magic allows him to do the same. A romantic touch is an invitation to your body."

"He touched me without invitation and brought me here." Faye hoped using her own words would help her understand the Shadow Prince wronged her.

The Familiar drummed her long nails on the table. "That was rude of him."

Faye bit the inside of her lip. *Kidnapping* was rude. A chime sounded startling Faye, and several dishes appeared on the table. Meats, breads, and vegetables were arranged beautifully. A three-tiered plate setting was filled with the same pastries Sparrow had stolen from the ball. Faye's mouth watered at the feast before her. She swallowed, making no move for it.

Sadi poured herself a flute of dark liquid and held the bottle out to Faye. "Sweet wine?"

"No, thank you." Faye leaned forward, adding softly, "Can I ask you something?" Sadi nodded, sipping her wine. "Why are you glamoured to look like me?"

Sadi dragged the pointed claw of her ring down the side of her cheek. "I've never worn a glamour in my life."

"We must be related." Faye studied her with new eyes. She never imagined she would be part Familiar. Maybe more than a part, it would explain why her ceremony failed. Their altar was in Chaos—though that was the extent of Faye's knowledge.

"I've bore no young, but Familiar trade partners often. My father shared many beds."

Sadi spoke so easily about her father's infidelity as though it were an idle conversation. "This doesn't upset your mother?"

"Why would it? She joins when the mood strikes her."

Faye flushed. Familiar were strange, but she knew promiscuity wasn't isolated to a race. The darker the court, the more debauch they became. Faye pushed the thoughts away, focusing on her bubbling excitement at the prospect of a family, or at least a part of one. "Who's your father? Do you have any other family?" They could be more distant relatives.

"Morbid is my father."

Faye's mouth slacked. "The Familiar King?" At her nod Faye began piecing the Shadow Prince's court together. She should have seen it sooner but was too blind with grief. Three houses made up his court, each ruling a realm. Faye didn't dare to hope to have a tie to the Benevolence house, but why else would they be so similar. "Could you look into me and see if I'm tied to your father?"

Sadi hesitated.

"I don't want his riches. I've never known my family. I can't tell you what it would mean to have a tie." A family to belong to.

"There is a simpler way to see if you're a Familiar." Her gaze dropped toward Faye's bare index finger. "You invoked your blood in Necromia, and it failed. You could invoke your blood at our altar. If it fires, you'll have your answer."

The answer to her possible race, but not if they were related. Faye hoped with time they may become friends and she could revisit the subject. "My sister is Familiar. She invoked her blood in Necromia."

"If her blood fired in Necromia her dominant line belongs to that altar."

That would mark Sparrow as part Familiar. Faye didn't shift into a cat like Sparrow. She grew claws and wings. Being mostly Familiar was the only thing that made sense, but she lacked their most prevalent trait.

Faye stilled. Was she inadvertently poaching the Shadow Prince? Her stomach knotted and she thought she might be ill. "Why is he holding me here? If I was poaching him, it was unintentional. I'll learn to control it."

"I will speak with him and see if my father would allow you to come to our altar." Sadi took her glass and stood. "I would recommend the choice cuts," she said, pointing at a small plate of roasted meat with a long thin knife placed across it. She sauntered out of the room saying over her shoulder as she left, "I'll see if I can have Rune make your stay more comfortable as well."

Once she was gone Faye left the table. She paced the room nervously. Not allowing herself to hope she found where she belonged. She passed the table, and her mouth watered.

The Shadow Prince wanted her to eat, and she wouldn't be doing *anything* that asshole wanted. Maybe he wouldn't be such a dick if he found out she belonged to the Benevolence house. She glanced over her prison, tilting her head at the two doors next to each other. One led to the hall, and the other was closed. There was a third door on the same wall at the opposite end of the room and a fourth to her left.

Faye went to the closed door near the hall first. Maybe it was a coat closet. Faye turned the handle opening it.

She immediately recognized the large four post bed draped in dark silk. Her cheeks flamed, and she closed the door, resting her forehead on it. Memories flooded her mind. She'd slept in that bed, curled in his arms. Looking forward to the dreams that were now a walking nightmare.

She tightened her grip on the handle until her knuckles turned white. Dragging her lip through her teeth, she eased the door open again, scrutinizing his space and searching for anything she could exploit.

His furniture was sparse compared to the other rooms. The desk under the windows looked expensive, but the designs carved into it were far simpler. Leather bound books and loose papers topped it. There was nothing else. No personal effects, no art, no portraits. Even the scones holding the licks of hellfire illuminating his room were the same design found in every other part of his... castle?

Sparrow would say you're boring, she thought, closing the door.

Two doors left. Faye chose the closer of the two. She turned the handle and peeked in. It opened into a large walk-in closet. It was empty but free of dust. A small black crystal chandelier hung at its center, alone. Faye shook her head, closing the door.

Only a dark-blood would need a chandelier for their closet.

She approached the last door across the room and found a huge bathroom suite. A large soaking tub made of what looked like white marble with glittering silver licks through it rested lengthwise against the wall, facing an enclosed shower that took up the width of the room.

Faye stepped through the space, brushing her fingers across the lip of the tub. She turned to the counters, looking for bathing oils. Wanting something strong to offend fang face's heightened senses.

Every drawer was bare. No soaps, not even a toothbrush. Faye supposed she should be grateful for the folded black towels tucked into the floor to ceiling built in cabinets.

Faye jumped at two sharp knocks made in quick succession. She poked her head back into her room and found the Shadow Prince strolling in like he owned the place. He peered over the table and glanced her way. "You have not eaten."

Faye kept her distance, "I'm not hungry."

"You have not eaten in a day. Is the meal not to your liking?"

Faye glanced at the food and back at him, weighing her options. Sadi breezed into the room, saving her from having to respond. Faye's eyes widened at the loose pages the Familiar held. She started toward her in rushed steps, and the pages promptly vanished.

Faye stopped, leaning back on her heels. She'd been too eager, showing her hand. A mistake she wouldn't make again. Both she and Sadi looked to Rune and the corner of his mouth lifted. "I will supply you with the stationary of your choosing after you have eaten."

"What do you want?"

"For you to nourish yourself."

Faye shifted on her feet. "I'm sorry if I was poaching you. Don't you think this is a little drastic?"

He scowled at her. "Admitting to your games?"

"Is this a punishment?" When he didn't answer, Faye clenched her teeth and sat on the edge of her bed. She gazed at the twilight sky through the window, determined to ignore him.

Dishes clattered, and Faye dug her nails into her palm, hidden beneath the sleeve of her robe. A bowl of soup entered her line of vision. Faye glanced up at Sadi. "Eat this, and I'll take the letter to your sister."

Faye leaned to the side, peering around Sadi at Rune. "What do you want?"

"Eat."

"You have me in a nice room, trying to get me to eat. Why am I here?"

"I need you for a task."

Darkness, could this guy be any more vague. "What task do you need me for?"

"I need to look into your mind," Rune answered simply.

Faye glanced between Sadi and Rune. "What are you looking for?" Now Rune glanced at Sadi. "You don't get challenged much, do you?"

He took a slow breath staring at her. "It would seem you are making up for my many years."

"Is this part of your touch invitation? You need me to cooperate?"

Rune canted his head at her. "Are you requesting I tear through your mind until I find what I need? Your suggestion is a painful alternative I can arrange."

Faye looked him up and down. "You're a dark-blood. I'm betting if you could, you would have done whatever you're planning by now. So, I think you need me more than I need you."

The two dark-bloods exchanged a glance, and Faye got the feeling they were speaking telepathically, which solidified her assumption. They wanted something from her and needed it *badly*. "Just tell me what you're looking for."

Rune glared at her, and said, "It does not concern you."

Faye waved at her surroundings. "You holding me here begs otherwise." She lifted her chin and walked to the other end of the room to sit on the far window ledge and stare off into the crystalline landscape.

Rune took the bowl of soup from Sadi and placed it back on the table. "Leave her. She will eat when she becomes hungry enough."

Faye drew her feet up on the ledge when they left and leaned on the window frame.

No, I won't.

Thirteen

Rune scanned the tomes that lined the bookcases in his study. His clarity left him when he stood in her presence. He wanted her close to safeguard her and placed her in the only other room in his wing. Rune reminded himself it mattered not. She was unfamiliar with court and wouldn't understand the significance. He would be rid of her in a few days at most.

Rune selected the volumes he needed and sat behind his desk. The pages creaked as he opened the first tome. Delicately tracing his fingertips over the page as he read.

Sadi appeared beside him, leaned back, and ran a long red nail over the book spines stacked beside him. "What are you doing?"

"Reading."

She tugged on a length of his hair. When he glanced up at her unamused, she said, "With her."

"Containing my liability until I can free myself." Rune turned the pages of a journal containing the races his father destroyed.

His father hunted each race that sided against him during the Great War to extinction. But Julian lacked focus. Discipline. He slaughtered a great many of them. But a few surfaced now and again through the ages.

"Do you think she's a descendant?"

Such a simple word fired horrific memories through him, a filth that coated his mind.

"We purged Sadira's court," Sadi laid her hand over his wrist. "She's no longer a threat."

Sadira hailed from a race Julian massacred. She'd captured him thinking he was his father and kept him to suffer for his father's deeds. Centuries separated him from his time in her court, allowing him to push the memories away.

Rune took Sadi's hand, returning it to her. "I am well. I am reviewing the shifting races my father thought to exterminate. Her wings and claws are not a characteristic of any living race. To be reborn as you say she is, she would need to be linked by blood. Likely the same bloodline of the coward behind this spell."

"Like calls to like."

He nodded absently. "It troubles me that she was in Anaria." It was a brilliant hiding place. "If I invested this much time into a weapon, I would keep it near. Protect it." Rune glanced toward her room again. "Perhaps fate smiled on me, and it takes time for the spell to bind. I found her before her keeper." Or the Familiar sister is her guard. It mattered not. She was in his possession now. They would need to come through him to wield her against him.

"You're treating her badly."

Rune raised an eyebrow. "I am holding her as I would anyone who posed a danger to my court."

Sadi folded her arms. "She's unhappy."

Rune exhaled before saying, "Willfully so."

Sadi sat on his desk and closed his tome. "What if she's yours?"

"She is not."

"My father's Sight is never wrong."

Rune opened the heavy leather-bound book once more, giving Sadi a pointed stare. She only gazed at him, her midnight eyes pleading.

Believing he proceeded in error. He placed his hand over hers, giving her a reassuring squeeze. "I am not Familiar. Shadowmen were not created with mates. Neither were Pure Bloods. Magic binds me to her. Her mortality to me."

Sadi looked away, staring over his realm. Hell's ever-twilight sky reflected in her gaze. "She thinks she's related to me."

"Did you tell her?"

Sadi shook her head. "You should hire a staff."

Rune thinned his lips. "The Keep is empty. I do not require staff."

"Your captive doesn't drink blood. She will need meals. Maybe get her some clothes."

Rune leaned back in his chair and exhaled.

"She's in a torn bathrobe."

"Her torn bathrobe was caused by her sprouting wings." But perhaps Sadi had a point. She was a dark-blood and deserved to be treated as such.

"I'll go to the Hall of Empty Eyes after she's settled. Having a double doesn't sit well with me." Sadi stood and dragged her fingers through his hair, pulling the long white-blonde strands through her grasp.

Darkness, why was he surrounded by women that frayed his temper. Rune glanced up at her. She gave him a coy smile. "We need her cooperation to get past her shield so maybe play nice?"

Fourteen

Faye sat at the window ledge until her leg went numb. She gingerly rose taking small steps as pins and needles climbed up her thigh. She moved to the table, glancing over the food that somehow stayed hot. Wasteful dark-bloods and their magic. This could have fed half her village. Faye poured a glass of water and drank deeply, gazing out of her cage.

She'd waited for the sun to set. For some sense of time to pass. The sky remained unmoved, caught forever in twilight. Faye set her glass down and ran her fingers through her hair. It had dried into an unruly mess after she slept on it wet.

She turned to peer down the long hall. The end of it opened into a larger room with polished black floors. Faye was tempted to close her door and lock it. She didn't bother since the Shadow Prince could just poof into places out of thin air.

Faye shrugged out of her robe and set it over the foot of her bed. She glanced down at her leather bikini. He couldn't have chosen to kidnap her on another day. No, she was trapped in Hell dressed in little more than underwear.

She pulled the blankets and got into bed, clutching a pillow to her side. A hot bath sounded wonderful, but the Shadow Prince might interrupt her. She could soak in her bathing suit and not be exposed. Faye kicked around the idea snuggling further into the bedding.

The sharp sound of metal clanging on metal startled her. Faye sat up, holding the blankets over her front, glancing over the room. She studied the space. Nothing was a miss

The faint rhythmic sound continued, and Faye pulled herself out of bed and dragged her robe back on. She followed the sound to the chandelier closet. Her hand closed over the handle as she slowly pulled it open.

Clothing swung from their hangers as though someone roughly set them. Shirts, pants, and jackets now filled the closet. Faye flipped through the clothing and pulled out something leather with long ribbons hanging from it. "Is this a fucking corset?" Faye said, stuffing it back in place. What's this guy's deal? He kidnapped her and bought her clothes to make up for it?

Faye exited and movement caught her eye. The arrogant jackass was walking toward her room. She turned her back to him, taking a seat in her window ledge, hoping he was going to his room and not planning to bother her further.

Rune knocked once against the doorframe before entering. The peasant sat in the window staring out over his realm. He wondered what she thought of it. If she found the ever-twilight sky as soothing as he did and immediately growled at himself. He cared not if she found his realm pleasing.

Her torn robe offered him a view of the smooth skin of her back. The Ra'Voshnik rose, frantically circling his mind. *Our queen is upset with you. Mend things with her.* Rune dragged it down, silencing it.

The fool creature would invite his death to his bed if he allowed it.

She watched his reflection. A defiant mask settled over her features as she straightened her back. "Are you going to keep me in this room forever?"

The Ra'Voshnik seized on her word. *Ours forever,* it feverishly whispered from the depths of his mind. Rune muttered a curse in High Tongue. The way the creature fawned over this mortal was unacceptable. "Cooperate, so I can be rid of you."

She turned towards him then. The lightening in her midnight eyes flared, prepared to strike. "You do need me."

"I do not need you." The Ra'Voshnik fought him viciously, struggling to surface. It purred its desire, wanting her splayed beneath him. The misted veined shadows crept from beneath his eyes as he clenched his jaw, drawing it back. Rune thinned his lips. "You try my patience."

She raised her chin as though to claim she'd won and turned to stare out the window once more.

"What is your name?" When she refused to reply, he added, "Would you rather I keep calling you mortal? Or perhaps pet?"

Her attention snapped to him. Her lovely lightning-streaked midnight gaze met his. She remained silent, likely debating her reply. Scheming minx. After long moments, she reluctantly answered, "Faye."

Faye, the Ra'Voshnik purred her name, savoring the feel of it on its tongue.

"You need to eat."

She glanced at the food then back at him. "I'm not hungry."

"If you are attempting to wait me out, you will find I am quite the patient man."

Her eyes narrowed at his remark. "You're not a man."

'No," he supposed he wasn't. "Not in your sense of the word." He glanced over the untouched food spread over the table, aware she watched his reflection. "Nothing offered appeals to you?"

"I don't eat any of that."

"Finish a meal, and I will allow you to pen a letter to your sister."

"I'll eat when I'm at my kitchen table."

His gaze flicked upward for a moment before settling on her again. "You will eat here. You have no choice in the matter."

She squared her shoulders and the corner of Rune's mouth lifted. Such a proud thing for having so little.

"You need me more than I need you."

Rune bristled. "I do not *need* you."

Faye leaned forward. "Then let me go."

"You shall be freed after my task is completed."

"What is the task?" His lips thinned at her question.

"You will eat when you are hungry." Rune turned. "I've arranged clothing and essentials to be brought in for you."

"I don't want it."

Rune spoke over his shoulder as he left her room. "You will wear the clothing I purchased because I need to look upon you."

Her spiteful words followed him into the hall. "No, I won't."

Fifteen

Rune stalked down the hall, away from the mortal. The Ra'Voshnik thrashed, infuriated to be out of her company. Tension filled him, his body taut and aching. Betraying him for her. Darkness help the person who wove this spell. He would spend weeks drawing their death out.

He ignored the aching need gnawing at him. The desire to coax the fiery minx to bed and learn every inch of her. He wanted to blame his desires on the Ra'Voshnik he'd dragged into the depths of his subconscious. In truth, she affected him just as strongly.

Rune sat at his desk pouring through tome after tome long into the night. He closed the last book and rolled his neck, no closer to finding a race with her unique characteristics. He phased into his room, and his body went rigid.

Her clean, subtle scent intoxicated him. A night breeze through plum blossoms tempted him past reason. His fangs lengthened, sharpening for her. He closed his eyes and inhaled, resisting the urge to purr his contentment. He opened his eyes and exhaled, hating his body's reaction to her.

Rune couldn't help but wonder if he would miss it when she was gone? A foolish question. Her scent would be like every other after he freed himself of her. He stripped and got in bed. Tucking his hand behind his head, Rune stared up at the ceiling. He grew more restless and taut with each breath. Her scent lingered too near. Too familiar.

You long for her as I do. The Ra'Voshnik crept through his mind, prowling slowly, seemingly searching for the object of its lust. *Give her the sister. Ask forgiveness.*

You are too simple to see her for the death she is. This is artificial. A spell bound her to me. Rune closed his eyes, descending into himself. Meeting the Ra'Voshnik in his mind. Rune had not conversed with the creature in this manner since his youth. It unnerved him, now as it did then, to speak with the Ra'Voshnik separate from himself yet shaped and mirrored in his image. Their gazes were the only discernable difference. Where Rune's eyes were a pale blue, the Ra'Voshnik peered at him with its veined, misted shadowy gaze.

The Ra'Voshnik prowled closer. "Your pride and jealousy turned her away from us. You squander our gift. I will ask her forgiveness if you're too proud."

"You will do nothing." Rune would never surrender dominion over his body to it.

"You blame me, but at least admit the truth. We both grow hard, wanting our dark queen. I see your thoughts just as you see mine."

"You are depraved."

"I'm honest." It shrugged. "If you returned her sister, we could have our mouths on her soft flesh. Bring her into our mind." It smirked before continuing, "I would share her with you."

Rune's fangs sharpened. "You will not touch her."

It parted its lips and leaned closer, inhaling. "You taste of jealousy. Hardly an emotion dignified of the great Shadow Prince."

"Be silent," Rune grated. It laughed as he returned to his physical body. Whispering even after he confined it to the recesses of his mind.

We are halves of the same whole. You will never be rid of me. It would be best if you learned to share, polished fool, because I will be taking our queen.

The thought of Faye beneath the Ra'Voshnik set him with a heated tension without an outlet. He may not be able to destroy the Ra'Voshnik living within him, but he caged it for thirty centuries and had no intention of allowing it near the young mortal.

He glanced to his side, remembering the dreams of how she curled to him in her sleep. Rune pulled his gaze from the empty place in his bed and closed his eyes. She could not be his. He couldn't have such an ill-suited pairing.

Fate would not slight him so badly.

Sixteen

Time bled together during Faye's stay in Hell. For two days the
table in her room changed her selection of freshly prepared
meals every few hours— and for two days she didn't eat a bite of it.
Lightheaded and weak, she stayed in bed. Her heartbeat became a
constant pulse driving a pounding headache that wouldn't ease.

Sadi had come to see her this time. She pulled a chair beside
Faye's bed and set a tray over her. "You need to eat to regain your
strength. Did you want something else? I can have anything brought
in."

Faye scooted from beneath the tray, sitting up. She would be
tempted to eat if Morbid allowed her to attempt her ceremony in
Chaos, but Morbid told Sadi he would think on the matter.

Which left her the Shadow Prince's captive.

"What does he want? Why am I here?" Faye asked.

"I need you to eat something. Anything. Take a few bites." Sadi moved the bowl of soup closer to her.

The creamy white broth smelled divine. Faye set her jaw, steeling herself for their same conversation to play out. They would ask her to eat, and she would refuse until they told her what they wanted. Caught in an endless stalemate, Faye was determined to win.

Two of the strongest people in the realms held her captive in a luxurious room. They needed her for something. Badly and apparently alive.

Faye took a labored breath, stirring the soup she had no intention of eating before turning to Sadi— the kinder of her two jailers. "I can't give him what he wants if I don't know what it is. Tell me what it is so I can go home." Darkness, she was so tired. "Just tell me what he wants."

Sadi lowered her gaze, petting the soul shard embedded in her articulated ring that looked more like armor. Faye bit the inside of her lip, keeping perfectly still. The Familiar was wavering.

Her gaze flicked up, meeting Faye's. She parted her lips but said nothing before glancing back down. She muttered words too low for Faye to hear. It sounded like a prayer, something about walking the twisted path of madness.

Sadi met her gaze once more, clasping her hands in her lap before saying, "You're fated to him."

Rune stood, phasing out of his study the moment he heard Sadi's damning words. He materialized beside her and glared coldly at Faye. The mortal refused to eat, or don the clothing he'd acquired for her, or even bathe. He glanced at Sadi who greeted him with a weak smile.

"If you would leave us," he said, planning on exchanging words with her at a later time. Sadi stood and vanished as Rune turned his attention to Faye. "A spell has tied a fated bond between us. That is the reason you are here."

The minx met his gaze and visibly recoiled, dropping her spoon. "Fated? As in your mate?"

The peasant deemed *him* ill-suited for her. "I assure you. The feeling is mutual."

If you don't want her, get out of the way. The Ra'Voshnik circled the edges of his mind. It disagreed with his methods, constantly demanding he return Faye's sister. Rune dragged it away, cruelly sinking his claws into it until its cries were silenced while the minx stammered, "But *you're* not a Familiar."

"I am aware. This is a spell tying me to you, blessing me with your mortality. I mean to break it and be free of you." She flinched, dropping his gaze. Her pain intensified the bothersome twinge in his chest. It gnawed deeper, leaving him feeling hollow.

"What if you really are fated to me?" Faye asked quietly, lifting the blanket to cover her chest.

"Impossible. You are mortal."

Her gaze shot to him. "I'm twenty-five. I could still be immortal."

Rune shook his head once. "Sadi investigated your line. We have confirmed your mortality."

The minx pulled her knees to her chest, curling forward. "I want to go home."

The Ra'Voshnik roared from its confines, pressing him to comfort his mate. To sit beside her and take her in his arms. Soothe her and brush her hurt away. While the rational mind that kept him among the living for thirty centuries demanded he distance himself from her. His thoughts and emotions stood in conflict, paining something deep within him. He moved her tray closer, grating, "Eat."

Her back straightened, and she glared at him with glassy eyes. "Death in one will claim you both." Surprise momentarily crossed his features and the minx smiled bitterly. "Sparrow taught me that. You need me alive. Take me to my sister, or I will escort us both to the Darkness."

"I will escort you to Anaria to see your sister, but you will remain with me under my protection until I break the tie between us."

"I won't eat as long as you keep me here."

Rune took Sadi's seat and leaned forward, propping his elbows on his knees. At her level, he held her gaze. "Understand me. I have lived for a very long time. I will not surrender my life to your care."

The minx shifted her shoulders, looking him up and down before saying, "You have no choice in the matter."

"I have attempted to allow you dignity since you are a dark-blood."

112

"I'm not a dark-blood," she hissed.

A growl rumbled from his throat and Faye stilled. She hid it well, but he could hear the increasing rhythm of her heart. "You are a dark-blood. It is time you acted like one."

"If you don't let me go home, we will return to the Darkness together."

"Do not push me. I am more than capable of keeping you alive. It will be unpleasant, and you will never see your sister again." Her complexion blanched, but she stubbornly stared at him, remaining silent. "Do we understand each other?"

The minx nodded and looked away. "I want to spend a few hours each day in Anaria."

"We can discuss a schedule after you have eaten."

"I'll eat in Anaria." Rune leaned back in his chair, and the minx slumped her shoulders. "You've kept me from my sister for four days. Please, I promise I'll eat there."

"I will take you back to Anaria after I look into your mind."

"You can poke around my head all you want after you take me home."

"If I find what I need, you can return permanently."

The minx wet her bottom lip, apparently something she did when she was thinking or sought to drive the Ra'Voshnik to frenzy. "One minute, and then you take me home."

Her demand was far from ideal, but Rune hoped if he gave a little the minx would follow suit. "One minute, once I am in your mind."

Faye nodded, watching him carefully, as though she'd agreed to do something depraved. "What do I do?"

"Relax."

You can do this, it's just a minute, and then we go home and see Sparrow. Faye crossed her legs under the blanket and cleared her mind, unsure of what to do. Moments passed, and a strange sensation touched her mind. Like a shadow at the edge of her vision that vanished when she turned toward it.

113

"Your mind is closed off."

His tone was gentle, so Faye responded in kind. "I don't know how to open it."

"Take deep breaths and bring yourself to rest."

Faye sighed. "I don't know what that means. I don't speak dark-blood."

He looked away for a moment, drumming his fingers over his knee. When his attention returned to her, he said, "What do you do when you go to sleep?"

"You want me to take a nap?" She wasn't following his logic.

"You will naturally bring yourself to rest when you prepare to sleep."

Okay, Faye thought as she touched the tray. "Can you take this away please." Rune took the tray and Faye laid down pulling the blankets to her chin. She clutched a pillow to her side and wiggled until she was comfortable. This was the stupidest thing she'd ever heard of, but if it brought her closer to seeing her sister, she'd do it.

Faye closed her eyes, relaxing her body and letting her mind drift. The smell of roses lingering in her sheets mixed with the faint scent of amber and sandalwood. It reminded her of the dreams where she slept in his arms. Faye let her mind wander where it wished, deciding it counterintuitive to steer her thoughts. "When does your minute start?"

"You will know."

Minutes passed in silence and Faye breathed easy, shifting into a more comfortable spot. She felt something then. An easy pressure into her awareness. Faye lowered her brow.

"Shh. I almost have it."

A strange sensation brushed up against her mind. It warmed the edge of Faye's consciousness, growing more persistent with each tantalizing stroke. The resistance snapped all at once, and Faye winced as a presence flooded her senses. Aggression and sexual heat thrummed against her mind, volatile and distinctly male. Faye's breaths accelerated with her heartbeat. She held still, focusing on relaxing the tension in her body, but this presence wanted to claim her for its own.

A familiar purr vibrated through her, beneath the compulsive hostility, was a soul deep yearning. Faye helplessly turned toward it.

It must have sensed her. A flash of excitement pulsed through her mind as it turned its focus on her. The wild aggression surging forward.

Faye gasped, her eyes snapping open as she jerked back. A wet snap sounded, and Faye's gaze shot to Rune. Blood ran freely from his nose. "I'm sorry."

He stood, waving a hand at her. "Apologies. The Ra'Voshnik slipped my hold." He silently strolled to the bathroom, turning on the faucet.

The what slipped his hold? Some part of him that saw her and didn't care if she had a shard or not. Faye stared at Rune's back, realizing two things.

They were fate tied, and this Ra'Voshnik was her fangs.

Seventeen

Faye got out of bed while Rune was occupied. She hurried to the wall, where he couldn't see her dressed in so little and pulled her robe on. As she finished tying it, the water turned off. Faye turned to find Rune standing in the doorway with an outstretched hand. "Shall we?"

She stepped closer, studying his pristine shirt. She was sure he bled on it, but he stood before her, a perfectly arranged, polished dark-blood. She nodded and placed her hand in his. The moment she touched his hand, her surroundings faded into inky blackness, sweeping away just as fast. Faye squinted against the harsh light. He phased them on the road in front of her cottage. Faye snatched her hand away and ran for her door, screaming, "Sparrow!"

"Bitch?"

Faye threw the door open and found Sparrow and Vashien

sitting in the kitchen. Her sister stood bleary eyed. Faye ran to her, nearly taking her to the ground as she threw her arms around her.

Sparrow squeezed her, just holding her for long moments.

"How did you get back? I was so worried." Sparrow pulled back and grabbed Faye's face between her hands, searching her eyes before pulling her into a tight embrace.

Faye held her, smoothing her hair. Sparrow looked awful. Her eyes were swollen, and her cheeks were red and splotchy.

Chairs dragged and Faye was shoved by strong dark green membranous wings. Her sister released her, pushing her behind her as well. Past Vashien's outspread wings Faye glimpsed a tailored black suit.

A long, wicked blade appeared in Vashien's hand. The next moment it ripped from his grasp and embedded halfway into the wall.

"Stop!" Faye shoved past her friends to get in front of Rune. She touched his chest, meeting his chilling blue gaze. Turning to her friends she repeated, "Stop."

Rune canted his head and the corner of his mouth lifted. "Attack me and I will retaliate."

Sparrow yanked her away from Rune. "Are you returning her?" To Faye she said, "I petitioned for your release, but the High Queen denied it."

Feel free to call your court to war against the Shadow Prince. The High Queen's parting words filled Faye with fury. "She came. She's a bitch."

Vashien stood between them, fanning his wings out. "She won't stand against him. He was her consort. The High Queen favors him."

Rune arched his brow. "Are you court born or just a gossip?"

Faye glanced Rune's way. "Can I have some privacy?"

"That was not part of our bargain." Rune brushed past Vashien's wing and pulled out the closest chair at her kitchen table, taking a seat.

Sparrow turned toward her, widening her eyes. The word bargain formed silently on her lips.

"He's still holding me hostage. We're working out a schedule."

"Honey, why is your robe ripped? And you're so skinny. Is he starving you?" Sparrow turned to Rune. "You can't just keep her."

His smile was humorless. "I assure you I can."

Faye schooled her expression as his cruel words replayed in her mind.

I am more than capable of keeping you alive. It will be unpleasant, and you will never see your sister again.

Faye went along with the *dignity* he granted her, wondering how long it would take the arrogant Shadow Prince to admit this was fate and not a spell. "His Familiar called me a political prisoner."

"It's customary to host her court if you are requiring her presence." Vashien volunteered the information.

Sparrow snorted. "Requiring her presence. Is that dark court talk for kidnapping?"

Faye eyed Rune. He didn't deny it. "You keep telling me to act like a dark-blood. I want my court with me."

He glanced up at her, his expression bored. "No."

"You need me." Rune thinned his lips. "And I help with the orphanage in town." When Rune narrowed his eyes at her, Faye continued. "You'll have it repaired and staffed like a Necromian orphanage."

"You try the extent of my benevolence."

"Do these things, and I will cooperate."

Rune exhaled and turned to her friends. "If you join her, you will remain in Hell until my task is completed."

Sparrow snorted. "We're a package deal."

"And I want my garden." Faye blurted out, her mind racing with what else she would need from here. Rune's gaze shot up before he glanced her way once more. She could almost hear his deep voice slipping through her mind. *Truly?* "I make potions for the people in town. You need to let me come back every month."

"She brings candy for the beasties," Sparrow added.

Eighteen

Rune awaited the next demeaning task she would demand as payment for her cooperation. Hating that he needed it, sharpening his temper. He felt no pull to Sadi, and the two were identical. This was a spell. Each pull and attraction, manufactured. He would break this spell within a week and be rid of her.

"Agreed." Rune schooled his expression. The minx blinked at him before she lifted her chin.

She is pleased with us. Kiss her. The Ra'Voshnik urged him to fist the hair at the base of her skull and kiss her until she begged for his touch.

Be silent.

Rune stood moving toward the door. "Where is your garden?"

Faye pointed. "Other side of that wall, you'll see it."

They quieted as Rune stepped outside. Did they truly believe he couldn't hear them simply because they whispered?

"I need to pack. What's the weather like in Hell bitch?" The blonde harpy's voice.

"You don't have to come. I can ask him to bring me back a few hours a day."

One of them snorted, then Faye's sister said, "And miss the chance to see a closed realm? We're going together."

"Only you would want to go to Hell." The male's voice.

"Closed realm, *aaaaand* we'll be staying at a dark court. *The* dark court. Is it fancy? Wait don't tell me. I want to see it."

He stood at Faye's garden while she and her ilk conversed while packing their belongings. The corner of his mouth lifted as he carved out the earth around her small garden. He wondered if his mother tormented his father half as much as Faye did him.

Michelle had raged, destroying half of Julian's castle when he came for her. To appease her temper, he tore a piece of Necromia out, bringing it to Hell. Replacing it with a piece of Hell. Belind had that part of her estate in Necromia sealed, not pleased with Hell's landscape.

Carving out the minx's garden he would soon add to his estate, Rune listened to their conversation.

"Are you sure you can leave your tavern?" Faye voiced.

The male answered. "I've already sent word to my managers. I can't leave my best girls alone in Hell."

Rune caught the sound of rustling fabric. Was that male touching her? *Rip his wings from his back!* The Ra'Voshnik surged forward, bleeding through his gaze.

Calm yourself. Rune focused on his task. This is part of the spell. He carved away enough earth to keep the roots intact. Rune vanished the paltry number of plants he would transplant into his mother's gardens.

Rune glanced behind him at the field. Faye had led him through this meadow in his dreams. He expected his night breeze to be his dark queen, at his side for eternity. Bitterness washed through him. There was no queen for him. A self-inflicted pain he would suffer if he was fool enough to hope for an equal to share his life with.

We have our dark queen. The Ra'Voshnik offered him a scene. He sat at the edge of his bed. Gray lace covered her, revealing more than it hid. The minx sauntered toward him to stand between his legs. Fingertips grazing his neck teasingly before she gripped the front of his throat.

And he smiled in answer. Hiking her leg up his body and pinning her back to his dark sheets.

No! Rune viciously shoved the fantasy away. His bed was reserved for his queen. Not a peasant.

The front door opened, pulling his attention as the Ra'Voshnik prowled the edges of his mind. Faye came out with a large backpack and a suitcase. The blonde carried nothing followed by the male. They'd vanished their luggage to travel with them and left Faye to carry her things.

The stubborn creature likely refused their help.

Sparrow turned to glare at him. "Are you arranging a coach, your dark highness?"

This one had an unhealthy lack of fear. The male hid it well, but fear rolled off him in waves. Surprisingly the Ra'Voshnik wasn't demanding to make a massacre of him, too focused on Faye. At least the peasant served in that small comfort.

"No. Stand close." Rune approached the trio. His surroundings faded and refocused in Hell a moment later. Faye swayed on her feet. He and the male both reached for her. The winged male paled but placed his hand at the small of Faye's back

Peel the flesh from his body. Slowly. The Ra'Voshnik purred through his mind.

Perhaps this spell would prove useful after he broke it. The Ra'Voshnik didn't compulsively fixate on every notion of fear it scented or tasted. He could repurpose it to calm the Ra'Voshnik. Let it be fixated with a charm he could carry with him rather than the problematic minx at his side.

"Why is the High Queen's estate in Hell?" Sparrow asked, tipping her head back as she gawked over his home.

The corner of Rune's mouth lifted. *Because my mother's temper was a thing of legend.*

"Before Lyssa, Belind was High Queen, and Michelle was Queen. Michelle was his mother, and they shared time between Hell and Necromia," the male answered.

Rune arched his brow. Not the story, but he wasn't about to volunteer information.

"There were two queens?" At Vashien's nod, Sparrow glanced over her surroundings. "What the fuck is that?" Sparrow asked, pointing off into the distance.

Rune glanced at the winged male, waiting for his explanation of Julian's palace. At his silence, Rune said, "Unimportant," and made his way to the tall bloodroot double doors of his towering estate.

They followed him into the great room. The large open space held two ornate staircases on either side of the room. Black marble made up the floor, reflecting the twinkling lights of two enormous three-tiered black crystal chandeliers.

"Faye's room is at the end of this hall." Rune pointed to the left and continued walking up the staircase on the same side.

The group followed him up the stairs, through a hall that opened to a large ballroom. Rune proceeded through it without comment and led them down another wide hallway. He stopped as the hall turned the corner.

"This is the south wing." Rune gave Faye a pointed look. "My study and rooms are off limits."

Sparrow peered around Faye to stare at Rune. "We're not here for you, in case you didn't get that." A growl emanated from Rune as he took a step toward the mouthy blonde. Faye took a matching step toward him to stand between them. To Rune's disbelief, the blonde continued as though nothing had happened.

"Where's your kitchen?" The male touched her shoulder, and she paid him no mind. Perhaps she was touched with madness. Sparrow came to stand next to Faye, hugging her arm to the side of her body. "Listen, I know we just met. But I eat a lot. So where do you keep the food?"

Rune narrowed his eyes. Definitely insane.

Sparrow's gaze lowered to his ring, and she snorted. "Am I supposed to be afraid of you?" She met his gaze unphased. "Lots of people wear a darker shard than me. You're not that special."

Darkness, he could only hope to find and break this spell tomorrow. He called his talisman to Obsidian and held the ornate stone encased in intricate metal work out to the winged male. "I take it, you know how to use this?"

"I know how to use that," Sparrow all but yelled, snatching it out of his grasp. "Is this to Obsidian? The Obsidian?"

Faye pulled her sister away from him and hissed, "What are you doing?"

The blonde harpy beamed at her. "Obsidian, *the* most exclusive restaurant in Necromia. You have to be nobility to get in."

Rune got the sinking suspicion he made an error allowing her his talisman. It mattered not. They would be out of his home and life soon enough. "My realm is closed. You will find it unpleasant if you attempt to phase out. I have some business I must attend to if you would excuse me." Rune vanished, leaving them in his home.

Nineteen

Faye threw her arms around Sparrow as soon as Rune vanished. "I'm so sorry you're here." Faye looked up at Vashien. "Both of you."

Sparrow snorted and thumped her backpack before pulling away. "Where's your room bitch?"

"Next to his."

"Douche in the black suit is making you room next to him?" Sparrow stuck the tip of her tongue out of the corner of her mouth. "Gross."

Faye started walking back the way they came. "He put me in another room before I ended up in the one next to his. I heard you took out three guards at the High Queen's court.

"My greatest moment." Sparrow linked arms with her, leaning her head on her shoulder as they walked.

They entered what Faye imagined was a ballroom, the dark wood floors polished beautifully. Pillars lined the walls housing arched windows looking out over Hell's crystalline landscape. "I'm so hungry."

"You've dropped a lot of weight. Was he starving you?" Vashien asked as they walked into the next hall.

"No, I did that to myself. There's food in my room." Faye squeezed Sparrow's arm to her side. "The day he kidnapped me, I thought he killed you."

"That bitch ass can't kill me."

"Darkness, save me," Vashien muttered behind them.

Sparrow leaned back, still holding Faye's arm. "What? Tell me I'm lying."

Vashien grumbled, and Faye elbowed Sparrow in the ribs, getting her attention. "I thought you were dead, and I wanted to hurt him."

"Darkness, tell me slowly," she said in a breathy voice. "Did you knock his fangs out of his face?"

"I hit him with a candle holder." Faye looked away as the color drained from Vashien's face. "And stabbed him with a letter opener."

"You stabbed him and didn't tell me? Where!"

Vashien held his hand up at Sparrow.

"Darkness." Sparrow leaned on her hard, wrapping her arms around her shoulder and neck. "Tell me he screamed like a bitch."

"I shifted but not like you. I had wings and claws. I haven't been able to do it again."

"What?" Sparrow hopped, jarring her shoulder. "Bitch you lead with that. My Familiar senses were right. I knew you would be on my level when we were little. And you wanted me to abandon you for a court. Those courts will be *wishing* they took us now."

They entered the great room again, and Sparrow broke away, running to the stairs. She jumped up, sitting sideways on the railing.

Vashien dove over the railing after her.

Faye could only hold her breath as Sparrow laughed sliding down the banister, her hand trailing behind her. She twisted, landing on her feet on the bottom.

"Are you serious?" Faye hurried down the stairs.

Sparrow snorted. "I always wanted to do that. Doing it in Hell is just a bonus."

"What if you fell? You made Vash jump over the railing." Faye reached the bottom of the stairs and punched her in the arm.

Sparrow fluttered her hand in Faye's face starting toward the hall on the right. "I'm a cat. I always land on my feet."

Faye exchanged a look with Vashien and followed Sparrow.

Her sister backstepped to link arms with Faye again before asking, "So, you have powers now?"

"I don't know how to use them," Faye said as Sparrow jerked her to a stop in front of Rune's study.

"No." Vashien's voice boomed from behind them.

Sparrow stomped her foot, glancing back at him "I just want to mix all his books up and put them back with the pages pointed out instead of the spines." Sparrow pouted at Vashien, who remained unmoved. "Okay I'll just do one bookshelf. Look in there, he has at least ten of them." She outstretched her hand and hit an invisible force at the threshold. Sparrow narrowed her eyes. "This motherfucker." She flicked her hand, striking it with a lash of power.

Faye pulled Sparrow away. "Are you fucking crazy? It's probably tied to him."

"I'm getting in there," Sparrow grumbled as Faye pulled her along.

After a handful of steps, Sparrow stopped pulling against her. They approached the end of the hall. Faye opened the door. "This is huge." Sparrow ran into the room and immediately flopped on the bed.

Faye turned back to Vashien. His expression pinched as he surveyed the room. "What's the matter? I mean, besides the obvious."

He immediately went to the door separating her room from Rune's. He opened it, peering in, and reached out tentatively until he touched the shield barring him entry. He shut the door, turning back to Faye. "What cooperation did you promise? Is he trying to force you into his bed?" Faye hesitated for a moment. "What cooperation does he want? This is a consort's room. Does he know you haven't gone through your Ceremony of Blood?"

"No, he's not— This is a what?" Faye looked over the room again.

"Adjoining rooms are for a queen and their consort. The larger room is the queen's, and this is the consort's."

"So, can I call him Shadow Queen?" Sparrow gave Vashien a toothy smile.

Vashien frowned at her and said, "Stay here. Stay together. I'm going to get a feel for the place. I'll phase back when I'm done."

"Tell me when you find the kitchen," Sparrow yelled after Vashien as he disappeared down the hall. Sparrow set the talisman on the table.

"Should we all stick together?" Faye asked.

"No. He used to serve as a guard, he's just doing his dark court stuff. Being able to phase all over is important." Sparrow rolled her eyes.

Faye picked up the bowl of soup from earlier and a hunk of bread. She dug into her meal, wondering if Rune meant to put her in the consort's room.

Sparrow touched two fingers to the obsidian talisman. "Take all this shit away. I need two of the most expensive things you have. Your best dessert and a bottle of whatever your best vodka is. Oh, and pomegranate juice. Make a batch of it and tie it to a craft I can keep here, please. Thank you."

"What are you doing?" Faye hissed.

Sparrow snorted at her taking her bowl of soup and setting it on the table. Everything promptly vanished. "Payback for picking me up by my neck."

"I was eating that."

"You're about to be eating better shit." Sparrow inspected her room and walked into Faye's closet. She examined a few articles of clothing before turning to her. "Did fangs buy these for you?"

"He said my clothes were ill-suited."

"Well, I mean they are." Sparrow opened the drawer in the back of the closet and held out a lacey thong, pinching it between her two fingers. "I think he fancies you a little. He still poaching you or have you seen his—" Sparrow held her three fingers together and raised her eyebrows.

"I don't want to see his dick, and he says I was poaching him."

Sparrow fluttered her hand at Faye. "He's a lying bitch."

A pleasant chime sounded and a large, covered tray appeared on the table. Well, that's fancy. She turned to her sister. "Food hooker."

Sparrow danced her way to the table and lifted the metal cover in a flourish.

The plates were arranged beautifully. Two of them had medallions of steak over mashed potatoes shaped into a triangle. A slash of red and golden sauce followed the curve of the plate.

A chocolate cake was topped with candied fruits and had straws of chocolate lanced into it. Faye took a fork and stabbed a raspberry. She bit into it, pleasantly surprised. There was no tartness to it. It was sweet. Perfectly ripe.

Sparrow cut into the steak as Faye picked up the craft of dark red liquid. She filled a glass and poured water for herself and Sparrow as well.

"Bitch, you need to try this. Best meat I've ever had in my mouth." Sparrow held a bite of her steak out at Faye.

Faye bit the meat off Sparrow's fork. It was buttery and tender, melting in her mouth. "What is that?"

"What I'm ordering as every meal for the extent of our stay." Sparrow scooped up another bite of steak with potato this time. She threw her head back, closed her eyes, and moaned.

Faye ate the candied fruits. Before she started her entrée, Sparrow pushed her empty plate away.

She stretched, leaning back in her chair. "I hope shadow dick is rich because your court is expensive." Faye giggled while eating her meal as Sparrow opened a bottle of vodka and poured a shot.

Faye dragged her fork through the sauce on her plate. "He's convinced himself our fated tie is a spell."

Sparrow turned uncharacteristically serious. "You can't fake that. You're fated to the Shadow Prince?"

Rejection sliced her deep, cutting to the bone. "But I'm mortal. He doesn't want me."

"We could still be immortal."

Faye shook her head. "His Familiar looked into me." She was still trying to process that she was mortal. She hadn't felt immortal, but she'd hoped. And now, it was just another thing that slipped away from her. Faye's eyes widened as she pictured Sadi. "His Familiar looks just like me."

"Lots of people have black hair."

"No, she has my face. We could be twins."

"I'm sure we'll see her, and I'll tell you, you look nothing alike." Sparrow stabbed the cake with her fork and chocolate pooled from its center. "That's fancy."

Faye leaned forward. "Is it cooked all the way?"

Sparrow dipped her fork in it and tasted it. "It's chocolate." She

128

gave an approving glance and took another bite of cake.

Faye found herself looking at the door separating her room from Rune's. Her heart stung. She had power but not immortality. Forever lacking something.

Sparrow scooted her seat closer and leaned against her. "He's fated to you. Fuck him and make him your bitch."

"I think a part of him likes me. His bloodlust." Faye smiled at the memory of the male viciousness enveloping her. Purring. *Fangs accepts me.*

Sparrow poured herself another shot. "If by likes, you mean wants to eat you and not in the good way, then yeah."

"He looks at me like he did in the dreams."

Sparrow straightened. "He's been all bad eyeliner while you're here?"

"No."

"You need to rile his bloodlust up. Show some neck. He's fated to you. He'll be hard up wanting you."

Vashien materialized in the room, interrupting them, and peered at their dinner disapprovingly.

Sparrow skewered a piece of Faye's steak and held it out to Vashien. "Want a bite, baby?"

Faye pushed her plate away. "How do they know when we finish eating?"

"Cover the tray. They'll call it back after some time," Vashien said, surveying the room again.

Sparrow ate Vash's bite and took her vodka, and Faye's juice off the tray. She picked up the lid, giving it a shake. "We all done?"

Vashien glanced between the two of them, then asked Sparrow, "Are you sleeping in here or am I taking another room so you two can share one?"

"All three of us fit in these giant ass beds," Faye answered.

"Sparrow just said there's a fated bond between you and the Shadow Prince. I'm not sleeping in the same room, let alone bed as you. I like my wings firmly attached to my back."

"Pussy," Sparrow said with a laugh, covering the tray.

"Be nice." Faye took her glass and her juice. Sparrow opened the door leading to Rune's room. "Leave it," Faye said, widening her eyes when Sparrow turned toward her. Faye pointed at the door leading to

129

the hall. "Let's go."

Sparrow sighed and slumped her shoulders. "Fine."

Faye headed back to Sparrow and Vashien's room.

Twenty

Rune materialized in the lobby of the library in Artithia. The grand room was lit with small balls of hellfire seated in their fixtures. The room gleamed in its whites and golds, reflecting the light shining through the tall glass double doors.

An aging Artithian stood behind a podium. He folded his weathered hands. "Shadow Prince. How may we be of assistance to you?"

Rune strolled to the podium. He parted his lips taking a breath. He tasted nervousness and fear on the man. Yet Ra'Voshnik didn't react, too preoccupied with Faye's absence. After he broke the enchantment he was under, repurposing it would be his first priority.

The corner of his mouth lifted. Perhaps he should be grateful to the minx. Rune's gaze lifted to the Artithian's. "I would like any documents you have predating Saith taken to my research suite."

The man rustled his white feathered wings. He scratched a pen over a small piece of parchment. "We will bring you everything we find." The librarian lifted the parchment between his two fingers, and it blazed before vanishing.

"It is appreciated," Rune said and phased to his private suite. He took a seat, pleased to see a few documents already waiting for him.

Sadi materialized next to him, hugging herself. "You need to be careful with her."

Rune nodded. "What did you see?"

Sadi ran her hand through her black hair. "My visions say one of us is death and the other is maddened darkness. Chaos and madness go hand in hand. Rune this girl is death."

"I am aware. I need to break the tie linking my life to hers."

Her gaze fixed on him. "Not just your death. When I asked whose death, they said all. If she kills you and you can't stop The Crumbling, everything dies."

"Calm yourself. I will untie myself from her. Your father assigned me this task. I will see it done." He'd seen her like this from time to time. Erratic, still half in her visions.

Sadi paced back and forth in small steps, rubbing her arms. "Something is wrong. I just can't see it."

He stood, catching her against his chest, and she stilled. "Be easy." He murmured. "You are too deep in your visions. Let your mind quiet."

She clutched at his shirt, bunching it in her hands as she leaned closer to him. Her eyes darted wildly around the room, witnessing things he could not. He murmured comforting sounds to her as he stroked her hair.

Her grip loosened as time passed. After several minutes Sadi seemed calm, her midnight gaze focusing on him.

"You should rest."

Sadi nodded, stepping away from him. She muttered, "Be careful. You may be able to avoid death, but pain will be inevitable with her."

She vanished before Rune could ask if that was part of her vision as well.

He pushed the Familiar's riddles from his mind and turned back to his table. A tattered book appeared on the loose pages. He took his seat, opening it.

He read, carefully turning the pages. Nearly three hours passed as he closed the book. Useless information on the first incarnation of Pure Bloods. Rune leaned back in his chair and rubbed his forehead. No other books appeared. Was this book and a handful of loose documents all they possessed? He'd return tomorrow.

Rune phased to his room and was met with the door separating his room and Faye's ajar.

The Ra'Voshnik raged to the surface, bleeding through his gaze. *She offers invitation.*

Fool creature. *She is not from court. This is not an invitation to her bed.*

Rune peered into her room to find it empty. The Ra'Voshnik growled its disappointment. He turned and pushed his senses over his estate, feeling for Faye and her entourage.

Rune withdrew his senses. She was in his south wing. The male in a separate room further up the hall than the women. He felt a perimeter set at the beginning of the hallway. Nothing that could keep him out, but it would alert the male of his presence. Court born who served as a guard perhaps?

The male thinks to keep her from us. Strangle him with his own wings!

Rune slammed the door and took a step toward the hall before he regained control of his body. A chill ran through him. He'd never lost control to the Ra'Voshnik. The creature didn't seem to notice, frantically circling his mind.

Invite her to our bed, it insisted. *She will curl to us in her sleep.*

Be silent, Rune growled, dragging it beneath the surface.

Twenty-One

Faye woke, remembering where she was the moment her gaze lifted to three arched windows. Hell's haunting sky gently lit the room through sheer white panel curtains.

Sparrow sprawled gracelessly next to her, snoring with her arms over her head. Her mess of golden curls strewn over the pillows and around her arms. Faye got out of bed and pulled a robe over her nightgown. Rubbing her eyes, she went to the bathroom suite and paused. There were no toiletries in this room.

Great housekeeping fang face.

Faye quietly walked back into the room. She emptied her backpack's contents on the narrow table beneath the windows and started off to her old room. And if he took all the toiletries from her bath, she would break into his room and steal his.

Faye stepped into the hall making her way back to Rune's side of the— She didn't know what to call it. House seemed inadequate. It was a ridiculous amount of space for one person.

She searched the walls as she went, studying her surroundings. Searching for insight into her host. What she gleaned was depressing. The halls, while spelled to be comfortable, were detached and cold. Like his room there was no art, no personal effects. Nothing to reflect his interests or personality. Nothing that made this massive structure a home.

Faye went through the ballroom. The large open space empty and unused. Faye couldn't imagine living in this sprawling shell of a home. With nothing but silence for company.

She reached the great room without incident. Faye peeked into the corridor leading to her room, hoping Rune would be elsewhere. The passageway was clear, and Faye hurried down the hall.

Slipping past his study, Faye made the mistake of looking in. The Shadow Prince sat behind his desk, Hell's ever-twilight sky serving as his backdrop through the ornate window spanning the wall behind him. Faye didn't slow her steps, hoping he was too busy reading his papers to notice her.

"Minx," his voice called into the hall.

Faye froze her steps and cursed under her breath. She turned back to stand in the doorway. "Yes fangs?" She grinned with feigned politeness. Rune arched his brow at her. Faye dropped her grin with an exaggerated look of surprise. "Oh, were we not doing nicknames?" He exhaled at her, and Faye pouted at him.

"We should arrange a schedule."

Faye entered Rune's study, mentally noting the room. Floor to ceiling bookshelves took up the entire left wall. Leather bound books of various sizes filled every shelf. Tables and chairs defined small areas to sit and read. She was surprised to see a bar cart stacked with glasses and decanters filled with liquids of varying hues.

Sparrow would make quick work of that. Faye glanced to her right and her back went rigid. The last time she was here she'd been too focused on the High Queen to notice the black marble fireplace dominating the wall and before it a settee. She'd curled against him there, reading during their dreams. Had straddled him during her last dream. Her lips trailing down his neck.

With more effort than Faye cared to admit, she dragged her

gaze away feigning boredom. Rune's impassive gaze shifted from her to the settee and back. His expression revealing nothing. No hint of shadows. Nothing lingered in his gaze to tell her he remembered the dreams.

If he wanted to pretend he was unaffected by their dreams, she could too.

She took the chair across his desk, adjusting her robe tighter around herself.

"I'll give you one hour if you admit you are not superior to an Anarian."

"Like it or not, you are a dark-blood."

"I'm an Anarian."

The corner of his mouth lifted. "What good would a lie do between us? Four hours and you may split them into two, two-hour sessions."

"I'll agree to *a* two-hour session."

"Done." He glanced back down at his papers. "Noon to two daily." Faye rose from her chair and turned to leave. "You should also learn court etiquette," he said to her back.

Faye dug her nails into her palm and turned to lean against her chair, not bothering to suppress the roiling fury eating at her. He flipped through pages covered in elegant sweeping script, not even looking at her. With all the venom she could muster she said, "I have no interest in being like you."

He looked up at her then. "You were never meant for Anaria." His voice held a hint of sorrow, though the emotion didn't lend to his features.

The only thing she detested more than the dark-bloods who looked down on her were the ones who pitied her. "You'll just have to endure my ignorance." Faye lifted her chin and turned on her heel.

"Your ignorance left the door ajar between our rooms."

Was he serious? Faye's brow knit together as she turned. "Was it too much of a bother to close it yourself?"

Rune canted his head at her. "It serves as an invitation to your bed."

His words caught her off guard, dousing her anger. Faye paled, an apology forming on her lips. Before Faye could utter the words, the corner of that bastard's mouth lifted. He lifted his wine glass, swirling the red liquid as he studied it. He glanced back at her, pinning her with his gaze. "An offer I will not be taking."

Hot fury surged up in her, catching fire in her veins as it burned away any awkward embarrassment she felt. She held onto it, clutching it close. "If I want court training, I'll ask Vashien."

She turned and marched out of his study.

Twenty-Two

An offer I will not be taking. Faye mouthed the words as she roughly shoved the soaps and oils into her backpack. The vials clinked as she tossed in another handful. The nerve of that man. After collecting every last vial, Faye stole a few large black towels for good measure and made her way back to Sparrow's room. She glided past Rune's study, not sparing him a glance.

When Faye returned to her sister's room, Sparrow was crawling out of bed and trudging to the bathroom. "Wait, there's nothing in there. I went to my room to get you shampoo and stuff."

Sparrow leaned into the bathroom and looked back at Faye, squinting and bleary eyed. "What are you talking about?" Faye leaned over Sparrow's shoulder, looking into the bath suite to find it stocked identically to hers. Fang face could have saved her a trip. Faye set her backpack on the bed.

Sparrow rubbed her eyes and called the obsidian talisman. She walked over to the table in the sitting area near the door. She set the stone down and held two fingers to it. "Your really expensive steak with eggs." Sparrow glanced at Faye, pinching her fingers together and brought it to her mouth.

"Fruits," Faye answered in a hushed whisper.

"Cut fruit and a platter of meat and cheese. Orange juice and water. Thanks." Sparrow dusted off her hands and returned to the bathroom to brush her hair.

"You're having way too much fun with that."

"Approach determines response." Sparrow shrugged. "And grabbing my neck before you buy me dinner or shiny things?" Sparrow rolled her eyes and lifted her hand. "Wrong fucking approach."

Faye smiled as she leaned in the doorway. "I have a schedule now. He gets to try to break the tie between us for two hours every day."

Sparrow met her gaze in the mirror. "You should wear that cute lingerie he bought you and drive him insane."

"He probably just bought the whole collection." She couldn't imagine him going to a store let alone selecting each piece hanging in her closet.

"Lingerie and tie your hair away from your neck," Sparrow ordered.

"I'm not doing that."

Sparrow's shoulders slumped. "Don't be so boring. The man is fated to you. *Use it.*"

"For what?"

Sparrow shrugged. "Jewels. Houses. Revenge for not appreciating you. Make him your bitch."

A pleasant chime sounded, and Faye turned. "Hooker, that is so much food."

A large, covered tray dominated the table. Sparrow glanced past her and skipped toward the food, lifting the cover with a squeal. The platter Sparrow ordered took up half the table. It was beautifully layered with several cubes of dried meats and diced cheeses, fanning out in a colorful display.

Faye recognized the medallions of beef from yesterday. Faye took her fork, spearing a piece of fruit. She stood near Sparrow waiting for her to cut into the steak. When Sparrow cut the bite of meat free, Faye stabbed it off Sparrow's fork and ran with her prize. With the bed between them, Faye stopped laughing long enough to eat the bite of meat she'd stolen.

"I will stab the shit out of you," Sparrow said before returning to her meal.

Vashien strolled in shirtless, and Sparrow gave him a low whistle. "You, my tall, dark, and sexy man, can wash my hair." He grunted in answer but scratched her back before bending for a kiss. Sparrow beamed up at him. "If you do a really good job, I might let you do other things."

"Really." Vashien took a handful of the dried meat cubes and glanced around the room.

Sparrow rubbed his thigh. "What are you looking for, baby?"

"A chair without a back. These chairs aren't meant for wings."

Faye searched the room and spotted a padded stool under its accompanying vanity. She brought it to Vashien.

"Thank you."

Faye smiled. "Vampires have a good sense of smell, right?"

"Yes," Vashien answered hesitantly.

Sparrow fluttered her hand at Vashien. "If you want to fuck with him, go to your meeting naked."

Vashien caught Sparrow's hand, his expression one of shock. "Don't play with him, he's dangerous." Faye could feel the stern look Vashien was giving her through his tone.

Sparrow snorted, snatching her hand away. "Bathe in perfume, and I'll help you pick out an outfit from your new wardrobe."

Twenty-Three

Faye drew herself a bubble bath while Sparrow and Vashien had breakfast. She sniffed several vials before emptying an entire bottle of sweet-smelling floral oil. She tied her hair in a high bun and sank into the water. She balanced her breakfast on the edge of the oversized tub and let the hot water seep into her bones.

The swirls of silver gleamed against the white marble. She traced one with her nail before closing her eyes. She'd never seen any of her would-be suitors after they found out she was an Anarian. The ones who asked her to be their pet fled after she knocked some manners into them.

Faye thought back to her first night here. The force rushing past her when she'd swung her candle holder. She'd thought the dark-bloods who propositioned her were untrained idiots with bad aim.

The Shadow Prince wouldn't have missed. He needed her cooperation because she was unaffected by his power. By any power apparently.

Faye leaned her head back, resting on the lip of the tub. A book would be nice. This would be nice if she wasn't trapped here. He could have just explained his situation and asked her here. Given her a choice in the matter. Things would have been different. Faye glowered. But he was a dark-blood. Power was all they cared about. He might be fated to her, but she felt no pull for him. He was attractive, but so were a lot of men. Her man would be kind and accept her.

Faye took her time finishing her breakfast and enjoying her bath. After washing her hair at a lazy pace, she finished cleaning herself up before draining the water and getting out of the oversized tub. She dried off and dressed returning to her friends. Sparrow was sprawled over the bed watching her upside down. She scrunched her nose before saying, "You're wearing that?"

Faye glanced down at herself. "What?"

Sparrow closed one eye and pointed at her. Faye's hair dried and untangled, falling down her back in smooth waves. "Thanks," Faye said as Sparrow rolled to her feet and hopped off the bed.

Her sister grabbed her wrist, "You're going to wear some of the nice clothes he got you for your meeting."

"My clothes are fine." Faye dug in her heels and shook her wrist free before saying, "I need you to do something." Her sister turned, staring at her expectantly. "I need you to try and move me with your magic."

"What?"

"I'm testing something."

"Are you serious?"

"Yes. Come on." Faye held her hand out and Sparrow glanced between her and her hand. "Use your magic and push my hand."

Sparrow dropped her head back and sighed heavily. "Fine. Go stand by the bed in case I knock you over." Faye stood by the bed and nodded. Sparrow grimaced. "This is such a bad idea." The dark mist around her shard coated her hand. She softly motioned at Faye and an easy force swept past her.

Faye laughed the same moment Sparrow said, "What the fuck?"

"Do it harder."

Sparrow widened her stance and flicked her wrist a little harder.

She tilted her head when Faye's hair flicked. "This is some bullshit." Sparrow shoved her hand at Faye and the bed groaned, sliding a few inches.

Faye laughed, glancing behind her. "You missed."

"I didn't miss. My magic won't stick to you."

Faye's smile widened. "I felt the same force rush past me when I was fighting with Rune. His magic doesn't work on me either. I think I'm immune."

"Don't get too cocky I can still stab your ass just fine." Sparrow shook her hand, and the mist dissipated. "Come on, it's almost time for your meeting with his shadowy highness."

They hurried through the halls, dashing past Rune's study. Sparrow went straight for her closet, sliding over several pieces of clothing before pulling out a white silk shirt and a black skirt. Faye leaned in the doorway as her sister went to the back of the closet and rummaged through the drawers holding up a red thong and a black one. "What color do you think his shadowiness would like?"

When Faye didn't answer, Sparrow kept the black one and pulled out a matching lace bra. She walked back to Faye grinning like an idiot and shoved the clothes in her hands. "Wear these."

Faye glanced down at the clothes. "I'm not wearing this."

"Fiiiiine," Sparrow whined. She took the skirt, replacing it with a pair of black pants. "There. Change. I won't let him in." Sparrow exited her closet and shoved her in, closing the door.

Faye glowered at the door. "Not funny."

"Put it on! I did the thing you asked."

"Fine." Faye walked to the back of the closet setting the clothes on the dresser. She changed, folding her clothes. She opened the door, and Sparrow clapped her hands together, beaming.

"It's a little scary how he knew your size."

"I'm sure it's magic," Faye grumbled.

"But you look so pretty bitch. Now tie your hair up. Give me some neck."

A sharp knock startled Faye. "Did you forget our arrangement?" Rune asked, entering the room.

"It's just a couple minutes past noon Runey." He arched a brow at her but didn't respond. Sparrow stood up sipping her glass of water as she walked over to Faye. "And look I got her to wear nice clothes."

Faye shrieked when her sister dumped her glass of water down the front of her shirt. It wasn't enough that her white silk shirt now clung to her, showing the black lace that didn't quite cover her breast, but that bitch had to use ice water. Faye covered herself with her arms, staring at her sister, speechless.

"Got something around your eye there," Sparrow said, patting Rune's arm as she left the room.

Black flooded his gaze as the veined misted shadows swayed beneath his eyes. She met his gaze, and for the briefest moment he looked like the man from her dreams. Faye turned her back to him, recalling the feel of his lips on hers. Ashamed that she longed to feel them again.

Rune outstretched his arm into her field of vision, remaining behind her. Faye took the folded black towel he offered and covered herself with it. She glanced behind her and said, "Thank you."

"I will be in my study when you are ready." He turned and silently walked down the hall.

Faye retreated into her closet and pealed the shirt off, followed by her bra. She toweled herself off, deciding to change her pants too. Faye's gaze lifted to the dresser, and her clothes were missing. *Darkness, I'm going to kill her.* Faye had no choice but to pick out something else to wear or go to her meeting with Rune naked.

She dug through the drawers until she found undergarments that weren't all lace and string. Then dressed in a gray sweater to take the chill off with black leggings. She went to his study and found him seated behind his desk. He looked up as she entered his space.

She stood behind the chair in front of his desk. "I'm sorry about Sparrow."

He canted his head at her. "The harpy should be apologizing to you, yet you apologize to me?"

Faye shifted on her feet. "She's not a harpy."

"Noted."

She drummed her fingers on the chair. *Not much for small talk, big guy.* "Did you want to look through my mind here?"

"We can begin in any location you are comfortable with."

Faye eyed him suspiciously, curious if his sudden development of manners stemmed from a genuine kindness or guilt over being an unwilling participant in her sister's schemes. She glanced down at the chair, doubting it would work. She needed a place she could lay down. A bed worked but felt too personal. Faye glanced behind her, spotting the settee in front of the fireplace. Faye bit the inside of her lip. Both options were uncomfortable, and she didn't want to ask for something else to lay down on and have to answer when he asked why. "I'll lay down on the settee," Faye said, choosing the lesser of two evils.

Faye stretched out over the settee, purposefully positioning herself so there wasn't enough room for him to sit at her head or her feet. He casually leaned forward, resting his arms over the curved back of the settee and peered down at her. Faye met his gaze, realizing this was worse that if she allowed him sit at her feet.

Her cheeks heated as she remembered his face when Sparrow drenched her shirt. How the black swept through his gaze. It was only an instant, but when his gaze met hers, she could almost see the way he looked at her during their dreams. The yearning that left her feeling cherished.

Faye reached for a subject, needing a distraction. "Is the touch invitation in all courts or just yours?"

"It is protocol in all courts. Dark-bloods are intimidating. What we are makes us inherently dangerous. Rules and protocols keep the pursued comfortable until they come to a decision. Different rules apply after a pairing has occurred. Protocol maintains a balance, so we know our advances are welcomed."

It sounded good in theory, Faye thought as she closed her eyes. "The touching thing, does that extend to pets?"

"Were you planning on keeping a pet or becoming one?"

Faye cracked her lids. He peered down at her with a hint of a smile. "I've been propositioned to be a pet. Do you have to wait for a pet to touch you before you touch them?"

He remained silent for a moment before saying, "Pet is a position in court. It is given to those who are beneath its standing. A dark-blooded court would consider a day-blood a pet. Pets are protected by their courts, and the court member keeping them is responsible for their actions. They are treated with the same courtesy all court members are."

Faye's brows came together. The courts that would have taken Sparrow and let her be Sparrow's pet had accepted her in their own way. She was accepted but as less than.

Rune gave a soft laugh, and Faye's gaze snapped to him. His pale blue eyes glinted. "You think us savages."

They are. "Dark bloods steal Anarians. They practice their magic on them."

Rune nodded. "Many do."

"Did you?" How many Anarians suffered because of him?

Rune smiled, flashing a fang. "I am immortal. We train on our own bodies." When Faye only stared at him, he continued, "When your magic is depleted, you can still draw power at the cost of your body. Being able to focus through pain can mean the difference between victory and defeat. Causing pain for sport is not a taste I acquired."

"But some dark-bloods do." Far outnumbering those who did not.

"Cruelty is not exclusive to the dark-blooded," Rune stated simply.

"Does it matter when you've destroyed courts and decimated armies? Not killing for the pleasure of it makes little difference when you still kill."

"We should speak of more pleasant things."

Faye felt the strange pressure on the edge of her awareness. She took slow breaths, deep and even, trying to ignore it. "Do you see what I'm thinking when you're in my head?"

The side of that smug bastard's mouth lifted. "What are you afraid of me finding?"

Faye held his gaze and smiled genuinely. "Chopping your head off with a hatchet is my happy place."

He chuckled, the corners of his eyes crinkling. "And here I thought you were fond of candle holders."

A ghost of a smile touched her lips, but she stayed silent and closed her eyes.

"I can feel your emotions. Pulling memories without damaging them is Familiar magic."

Faye nodded. "What are you looking for?"

"A spell laced in your mind."

"What if it's in your mind, and I'm just an innocent bystander?"

He laughed softly at that. "That is not how magic and balance work."

Faye felt the same pressure on her mind. The growing tension pressing harder.

"Be easy. I almost have it."

A compulsive aggression washed over her. She was prepared for it this time as it flooded her mind. Beneath its violence, she could feel it yearning for her. It rushed in her direction, its presence circling her before it enveloped her, settling over her senses. She smiled as it purred its contentment against her. Rune exhaled and Faye opened her eyes to see him looking off in the distance. His bad eyeliner pulsing beneath his eyes. She felt his Ra'Voshnik thrashing against his hold, fighting to stay with her.

He was taking fangs from her.

Faye closed her eyes, not trusting her expression. "It's okay. Your Ra'Voshnik can stay. He just spooked me the first time."

It wound around her tighter, seemingly growling at Rune. Faye bit back her smile. His Ra'Voshnik wanted to be near her, to touch her mind. She imagined running her fingers through its presence, hoping it could feel it. *I would keep you, big guy, but you're attached to an asshole.*

Twenty-Four

Rune's fangs dropped, lengthening to sharp points. With her on the settee, all he could think of was her thighs straddling him when she bit down on his throat. Marking him. He needed to break this connection bewitching the Ra'Voshnik.

Darkness, he hated she affected him so deeply with little effort. Staring down at her filled him with tension as he grew hard. He wanted to lean close, bringing his lips a moment from hers. She needed only to touch him, and he would have her screaming his name.

Rune tore his gaze from her, tightening his hold on the carved wooden frame. He stared into the fireplace, assuring himself his thoughts and feelings were an aftereffect of the spell tying him to her. He searched her mind, and in a few short minutes, he found himself captivated by her intoxicating scent.

No, Rune mentally shook himself. This spell was no different than being drugged. Old memories fanned over the edges of his mind, extinguishing his want of her. Rune glared down at the source of his torment.

"Tell me about magic. Balance. Why does this have to be in my head."

Rune's mind calmed. Magic was his comfort. He'd dedicated two millennia to his craft. His tension ease as he recalled lessons of his youth. "Balance is needed to invoke your will successfully. In our instance, your mortality has been tied to me. A spell alone could not render me mortal. A living mortal is required. You have been tied to me through a fated bond. In this balance, your life is the trade. Killing you will destroy me." Apprehension rippled through her, and Rune frowned. "Be easy. I will not allow anything to happen to you."

He'd expected to feel relief in her mind or a kind of comfort. A wave of anger filled her followed by sadness. Her loneliness clawed at his chest, a deep ache unsettling him.

"You will carry the Darkness as I do," he assured her. She stared up at him, her eyes like a storming night sky that called him into their depths. He mentally shook himself, remarking, "Another phrase for carrying a shard of Darkness."

She blinked a few times and looked away before closing her eyes again.

"You should reconsider receiving court training." She tensed, blistering anger stirring in her. "Why do you refuse? You would be accepted into the mortal court of your choosing when you have your shard." Courts would offer her anything within their means to secure her. She would want for nothing living out her days in luxury and comfort. His fangs sharpened once more at the thought of court born males fluttering to her. Each too eager to pleasure her in an attempt to win her favor.

Rune was pulled from his thoughts as hurt and fury crystalized, sharp and piercing, through her mind. And through it, the minx seemed to cling to the Ra'Voshnik. This female perplexed him. "We should speak of other things."

"You think?" Venom edged her voice, cutting.

Rune glanced up for patience. Silence stretched between them as Rune searched her mind. She didn't speak for several minutes, the set of her jaw growing more and more tense with each passing moment.

"I want books. We're just locked in here without anything to do. And where's my garden?"

He exhaled. "What type of books?"

"Take me to a bookstore."

Darkness, she dug her claws in for no other reason than to spite him. "That would cause unwanted attention."

She opened her eyes, the fury storming within her palpable. "Sparrow made a scene at the high bitch's court. You don't think people are already talking?"

Likely. "Adding to the gossip is unwise."

"Romance and fantasy books."

Rune stifled a curse, finding nothing in her mind. "We will continue this tomorrow," he said as he straightened, returning to his desk.

Faye remained silent as the presence that enveloped her faded to nothing. She stood, glancing his way. She wasn't sure what she expected to find but she felt like a fool hoping some shred of what she felt in her mind would reflect in him. He wanted her, she'd felt it, but the man didn't even bother looking up from his papers. Faye turned leaving his study.

Dark courts weren't in her future. She wanted love and acceptance not wealth and power. The things she desired didn't exist in their world.

Faye made her way back to her sister's room and found it empty. She followed the hall further in, peaking into each room. The hall turned and opened into a large den. Faye spied blonde curls hanging over the armrest of an oversized chair beside the fire.

"What the fuck, hooker?" Faye yanked her sister's hair.

"I'm sorry! Let me go." Sparrow cried, holding Faye's fisted hand.

"You threw water at me." Faye pulled tighter, shaking her with each word. "Cold. Ass. Water."

Sparrow wailed, "Vash help me."

"Nope." His voice sounded from behind her. "Sister business. What'd she do this time?"

Faye released her, turning around to rest her hip on the back of Sparrow's chair. "She thought it would be a good idea to make me flash the Shadow Prince."

Vashien paled. "Please. Tell me you're joking."

"You had a bra on." Sparrow got to her feet rubbing her scalp.

"Lace. See through." Faye snapped, motioning to her breasts.

Sparrow gave her a toothy grin. "But did it work?"

Faye turned to glare at her sister. "Pissing me off?"

Vashien's voice rose over theirs. "Don't toy with him. He's dangerous."

Sparrow snorted, walking to Vashien before taking a seat next to him at the table. "He's fated to her." To Faye she said, "Make him your bitch."

"You're not doing anything to him, you're doing it to me." Sparrow regularly dragged her along with her wild ideas, but this was the first time her sister disrespected her.

Her sister drooped in her chair. "Don't be boring."

"Don't treat me like a blood whore!"

"Sparrow." Vashien bit out. Faye quieted. He rarely spoke a harsh word. Her sister folded her arms and laid her head down, giving Vash her best pair of sad eyes. "You can't play with him like a drunk dark-blood at my bar."

Sparrow huffed and Vashien stroked her hair, glancing at Faye. "Are you okay? He didn't touch you, did he?"

Faye shook her head. "He brought me a towel and left. He seems very big on the touch invitation thing."

"That's a good thing," Vashien said.

Sparrow rolled her eyes. "It's a boring thing."

Faye glared at the top of her sister's head then returned her attention to Vashien. "He seems hung up really hard on it."

"He's court born. He was raised with their protocols. It's all he knows."

Sparrow picked herself up off the table and leaned on Vashien's shoulder. "You're from a dark court."

"Our court experiences are nothing alike. I joined and served in a court. I wasn't born into one."

"Thank the Darkness." Sparrow fluffed her hair and peered past Faye. "It's only one. He cut you loose early?"

Faye shrugged. "I guess."

Sparrow's toothy grin returned. "Maybe it did work." Faye kicked her under the table and missed. "I'm sorry. Don't be mad." Faye glared at her unmoved. "I found your garden and a hot spring."

"Shut up." There was a hot spring in Hell? Faye's mood brightened.

"You want to go for a soak or water your plants. They're right next to each other."

"When did you find them?"

"I went exploring. What, you think I just sit in my room waiting for Runey to get done with you?" Faye giggled as Sparrow stood. "Come on. I know you want to see your leafy babies."

Sparrow linked arms with Faye as she stood, and Vashien gave her a pointed look. "Behave."

Her sister drew an *X* over her heart and Faye followed her back to the great room. They went through the hall on the right lower level, and it opened to the balcony and gardens she'd seen at the Hunter's Moon ball. Instead of gardens, crystals stuck out of the ground imitating trees and shrubs.

The same ornate fountains filled the space with the soft sound of flowing water. Faye stared at the benches and pathways. It was all here. Sparrow pulled her along as they walked through what had been the dance floor at the High Queen's estate. Faye couldn't help but glance at the spot the food display would have been where she first ran into Rune.

Faye wondered if it was all identical and the archway ahead of them would lead out. Sparrow led her further back into the gardens. The loose crystal scratching the sole of her boots. "His realm is beautiful, but it's not what I expected."

"I thought there would be souls here or something," Sparrow said, kicking a chunk of crystal down the path. They turned a corner and Faye stilled. A stone archway rose before them. A lush green gardened appeared beneath the clear open skies, bathed in sunlight.

"How is this here?" Faye stood at the threshold and reached forward. The moment her hand crossed over, she felt the warmth of the sun beaming down. She stepped into the gardens and her attention was immediately stolen by the immaculate black rose bushes.

The satiny petals drew in every bit of sunlight beaming down on Faye's head and shoulders, returning none of it. She brushed her fingertips over the dark bloom. The faintest sheen of blue outlined each petal. A shame these beauties were stuffed away in Hell with fang face where no one could see them.

"Don't know." Sparrow plucked a black rose, bringing it to her nose.

"What are you doing?"

Sparrow snorted and followed the path. "It's a plant. You pick its flowers." Her sister shoved the flower to her nose. "They smell really pretty, but they die in a couple hours."

"They need blood and water."

Her sister curled her lip at its black pedals. "Figures, his shadowiness would have vampire roses."

Faye gave a soft laugh as they approached a second archway holding double doors made of wrought iron. Bars rose through the frame, and over them, cherry blossom branches stretched in beautiful metal detail.

Sparrow pushed the gate open, stepping in, and Faye could only stare. Steam rose from a large pool surrounded by tall willows. Small flowering plants dotted the edges. Her sister elbowed her ribs. "He might be a dick, but he has good taste."

Faye nodded her agreement, admiring the space, and smiled. To the left, tucked near the towering gray stone wall, was her garden. Her watering can was placed near a small, simple half-moon fountain attached to the wall.

"Just think, this will all be yours after he's your bitch."

Faye dragged her hand through her hair, sitting beside her garden. Her sister talked about the Shadow Prince like they were a foredrawn conclusion. Which they weren't. "He's a dark-blood and immortal." *And an arrogant asshole.*

"Bitch, you bagged *the* dark-blood."

Faye's mouth fell open as she turned to her sister. "I didn't bag shit. I'm trapped here." Her sister quirked her lip and fluttered her hand at her. Faye shook her head going back to her garden. "You can chase him if you like him so much."

"I like my men big, dark, and winged— Not tall, pale, and scary."

"But you want me with tall, pale, and scary."

"I saw the way you looked when you were dreaming of fangs. It's not my fault you have questionable taste in men."

153

Faye drew her knees up and didn't respond. Her sister had a way of knifing wounds too close to her heart. She hugged her knees, telling herself Sparrow didn't do it purposefully.

Her sister took a seat across from her, bumping her with her legs. Faye reluctantly met her gaze, muttering, "He doesn't want me."

Sparrow snorted. "I don't care what that lying bitch says. He's yours, so go own his ass. Did he get a," Sparrow whistled, holding two of her fingers together, "when he saw the girls?"

Faye shoved her sister with her foot. She wobbled but sat up again, staring at her expectantly. Faye sighed. "I don't know. He gave me a towel."

"You didn't look." Sparrow sagged forward, clearly disappointed.

Faye backhanded her sister's thigh. "I was busy covering myself."

"Why are you so shy. You changed in front of plenty of people at Aunty Clara's house."

"They were girls we shared a room with." Faye couldn't grasp why her sister's kitty brain couldn't see the difference between that and exposing her to Rune.

"Naked is naked."

Of course, it was. "I'm not having this discussion with you."

"Fine." Sparrow fell back against the grass. "Be boring."

Twenty-Five

Sparrow left Faye in the gardens. Spending the afternoon with the sun on her back soothing her. Hell's sky was beautiful, but it didn't compare to the sun's comforting warmth.

The rest of the day passed quietly. Faye searched for Sadi, curious if her father made a decision on whether to allow her into Chaos. Her search came up empty, and she didn't bother asking Rune. His earlier dismissal still stung.

Faye had the bed to herself last night, Sparrow stayed with Vashien, which suited her. Her sister restlessly tossed and turned in her sleep, kicking Faye, or laying an arm over her. She stayed in bed staring out over the twilight sky through the sheer gauzy window panels turning the events over in her mind that landed her in this situation. It was a comfortable, polished cage, but a cage no less.

"Bitch," Sparrow's voice carried from the hall.

"Hooker," Faye answered. Her sister flounced into her room moments later and flopped on her bed.

"Are you still mad?" Sparrow crawled up next to Faye and sat cross-legged. "Don't be upset. I'm doing this for you."

"No, you're not. You're doing this for you, like everything else."

"You have so much power you refuse to acknowledge. I don't like seeing him have an upper hand on you. You don't have to fuck him. Just use what you've got to make him squirm. Because right now, you're his bitch." Sparrow took her hand, squeezing it. "I don't like it."

Faye glanced at her misguided sister. Her intentions were in the right place even if her execution was completely deranged. "We've always been a team. When you did that, it didn't feel like you were on my side anymore."

"I know," Sparrow said, pulling the blankets up and laid down beside Faye. "We can team up against his shadowy highness." She linked arms with Faye. "Together."

Faye smiled. They spent countless nights like this as they grew up. Plotting out what they would do when they were adults and could move out. Sparrow's plans regularly veered while Faye imagined a quiet life. She hugged her sister's arm to her side. "I'm not going to our meetings naked."

"Baby steps," Sparrow assured her. "Do you remember how I showed you to call a bartender."

"I'm not pushing my tits in his face."

"That's too advanced for your ass, but we'll get there. Do this," Sparrow pushed the blanket down to her waist and fingered the seam of her tank. "Or option two if you don't want to show cleavage." She fiddled with a lock of hair in the same place.

Faye played with her hair, mimicking her sister. "What's the goal? We aren't buying shots from him."

"The goal is to blue ball him."

Faye turned toward her sister with a pinched expression. "Darkness, you're serious. He doesn't even like me."

Sparrow dropped her hands turning her way. "He doesn't need to like you, to want you."

"You're demented." Faye stared up at the vaulted ceilings. Her sister's words hurt her heart. He wanted her on some level but consistently rejected her. She always lacked something.

Sparrow jerked Faye to the side, hugging her arm. "Make him climb the walls until he asks to tend to you."

Faye's brow lowered. "I'm afraid to ask what that means."

"Tending? Worshiping at your altar?"

Faye imagined Rune kneeling between her spread legs. His long white-blonde hair brushed her inner thigh with his movements. She flushed, shoving the image away. "You've lost your damned mind. I'm not letting a vampire *with fangs* put his mouth there."

"Dark courts train the males who serve. I bet the Shadow Prince got some top-shelf training. His tongue was good enough for the High Queen. You should totally take a ride on it."

Now Faye's traitorous mind imagined him with the high bitch. Possessive fury fired through her, and Faye stilled. Dismissing her imaginings and the feelings they roused, she said, "No. Hard pass. I'm not into biting."

Sparrow wagged a finger at her. "You *think* you're not into biting, and they purr."

"Why don't you go to a vampire brothel and stop trying to live vicariously through me."

"Oh bitch, I was going to, but then I met Vash." Sparrow stared up at nothing in particular. "Think it'll spook him if I want to go with him to a brothel?"

"Like all together?" Faye asked. At Sparrow's nod, she glanced up, mulling over the idea. "I think its midrange on the Sparrow meter. I'm surprised you didn't drag him to the brothel like you did to me."

"I like him. I don't want to make him feel..."

"Inadequate?" Faye volunteered.

"Yes. I don't want him to feel like I don't love him. But I also want to try every flavor of cake in the bakery. You can't know you like lemon cake until you try it."

Faye laughed at Sparrow's euphemism for everything. "You could also hate it." Her sister shrugged in answer. "Maybe it would be best to ask Vashien how he feels about lemon cake? See if he has a taste for similar things, like lemon tarts."

"He makes really good lemon macaroons."

"I'm afraid to ask."

"The cookies, get your mind out of the gutter." Sparrow gave her a sidelong glance.

"Depraved sicko," Faye said, laughing.

Twenty-Six

Rune arched a brow at Sadi, who sat on his desk to his right with her booted feet perched on the edge of his armrest. "Get rid of her," she repeated.

The Ra'Voshnik growled through his mind, offended by the panel of Sadi's skirt that fell between her legs, exposing the length of her belted thigh-high boots. *Get her legs away from us.* Rune ignored it, glancing up at Sadi. "My life is tied to hers."

"Entomb her in Standing Shadows."

Kill her. She threatens our queen. The Ra'Voshnik prowled closer, eyeing Sadi's throat. *A simple twist, and her head would fall at our feet.*

Rune dragged the creature deeper into his mind, away from Sadi. "Have you forgotten neither of us were able to subdue her? It is unlikely the crystal will hold. She would likely destroy my father's castle if I attempted it, which I will not." He couldn't bear the thought of entombing his night breeze, making her a permanent fixture in the macabre crystalline palace he inherited.

Sadi tapped the metal claw at the end of her articulated ring against his desk. "She's death Rune, on a catastrophic scale."

"Be easy. She is in my care, and I am quite difficult to kill."

She leapt gracefully to her feet, crossing her arms as she stared over his realm. "Damian and I will take my rooms in the north wing. You need someone watching your back."

Hardly necessary, but Rune replied, "As you wish."

A pair of footsteps heading up the hall pulled his attention. Faye and her harpy sister stopped in the doorway of his study.

"She does look like you." Sparrow stood shocked in the doorway while Faye entered, smiling at Sadi.

"I wanted to introduce you to my sister, Sparrow." Her smile faded when Sadi leaned back on her hip and crossed her arms. Faye hesitated for a moment glancing to him as if to ask what happened. Her attention returned to Sadi, and she asked, "Has your father decided if he'll let me invoke my blood in Chaos?"

Sadi leaned forward, pulling her shoulders back. Her mouth was wide, hissing at Faye. The minx's eyes widened, and she took a step back, pulling her arms tight to her sides as her sister stepped in front of her and hissed back.

Rune glared at Sadi as Sparrow yelled, "What the fuck is your problem?"

"You are not of my line." Sadi's feet lifted a few inches off the ground, her hair and garments swayed around her as though she were submerged in deep water. The telltale sign of Familiar magic.

"Enough," Rune growled at Sadi. When she returned to the ground, and her hair and clothes oriented normally once more, he turned to Faye. The damage had already been done. Her dark eyes took a glassy look with unshed tears. She took another step backward, out of his study and hurried back the way she came. Her sister a step behind her.

He turned his attention to Sadi. "That was most unhelpful."

She leaned forward, baring her teeth. "She is a danger to you. Get rid of her."

Faye blinked back her tears as she rushed up the stairs. Her family abandoned her, the one person who must have some familial tie to her didn't want her. The glimmer of hope that seeded when she thought she finally found her place rotted in her chest.

Sparrow called her name, but she kept moving, needing to get away. She was a fool to let her guard down with Sadi. She'd been kind, and her kindness blinded her to the simple truth. Sadi was a dark-blood, and Faye wasn't one of them. They would only ever see her as a shiny trinket to be discarded when her novelty wore off.

"Bitch, stop." Sparrow caught her wrist pulling her to stop in the empty ballroom.

"I want to be alone." Faye jerked her arm, but Sparrow held fast.

"No, you don't."

Faye pulled away, continuing down the hall. An angry yowl sounded from behind her and something small hit just under Faye's shoulder. It suddenly grew much heavier. Her sister hung on to her back, her arms circling her neck and her legs around her waist.

"Get off me," Faye said, shifting her shoulders.

"Not until you calm down and we talk some serious shit about your evil twin."

"I was stupid. I thought she was my friend. That we might even be related." A tear slipped down Faye's cheek. She'd hoped something good came from Rune kidnapping her. That fate finally smiled on her, and she found some lost family. A place to belong. But even her twin didn't want her.

"Fuck her." Sparrow slid down Faye's back, linking arms with her and pulling it to her side. "She's jealous."

Faye gave Sparrow a sidelong glance as they walked back to their room. "She's not jealous of me."

"She's totally on his dick and upset you're the focus of his attention."

"It's two hours."

"I'm just telling you what I see." Faye nodded, not agreeing at all. "You're all tense. We should soak in his hot spring."

That did sound appealing, and she had an hour to kill before noon.

"I'll have you back before your meeting, and I'll help you pick out something nice and respectable." When Faye glared at her she added, "Promise."

They returned to the room they shared, and Faye changed into her leather bikini. Her sister donned a matching bathing suit in red. Faye pulled her fluffy robe from her closet, pulling it on.

Sparrow snorted loudly, and Faye stilled waiting for her sisters opinion. "That's torn. Throw that away."

"It's my only robe," Faye said, pulling it tighter around herself.

"Darkness save me. You have a whole wardrobe of shit, and you're wearing your torn robe." Sparrow plucked a long black silk robe out of the air and handed it to her. "Here."

Faye shrugged out of her robe and wrapped herself in the silk. "When did you get this?"

"I liberated it from your closet yesterday," Sparrow snorted. "Someone should be using them." Sparrow recalled a matching robe in white. Faye assumed her sister procured it the same way.

She walked with Sparrow slowing when they approached the great room. Her sister linked arms with her and pulled her forward. "Do not tell me you're afraid of seeing Runey's stray cat."

Afraid was a strong word, but Faye wouldn't be upset if she never saw her again. When Faye didn't answer Sparrow said, "Fuck that bitch."

"Stop. She might hear you." Faye pulled her sister to the left, toward the hall that would lead to the gardens.

Her sister twisted as she dragged her along and yelled toward the hall leaning to Rune's study. "Fuck you bitch!"

Faye laughed pulling her forward. "You're so bad."

"You love me," Sparrow replied.

They entered the gardens, and Sparrow picked a few black roses before they reached the hot spring. Sparrow stood at the ledge, peering into the steaming water. "He has carved stone seating. Your man is fancy." Sparrow said, dropping the white robe in a pile at her feet and jumping into the pool.

He's not my man. Faye untied her robe, letting the subject go. Sparrow would only dig her demented heels in harder if she argued. She folded her robe, placing it on the ground before joining Sparrow.

The hot water was absolute bliss. Faye sighed leaning her head back on the smooth rocks bordering the spring. Her tension and muscle aches seemed to melt away.

"I think his hot spring is spelled." Sparrow twisted her back one way then the other.

"What?"

Sparrow leaned forward, shifting again before saying, "It is. I tweaked my back with Vash last night. It's all better now."

"Really?" Faye said, rolling her eyes. "So many visuals I didn't want in my head."

"We'll be trading war stories soon enough. His shadowiness probably wants to hold your ankles next to your ears."

Faye curled her lip. "I don't even bend like that."

"Better get to stretching then," Sparrow snickered.

"How are you always so sure of everything."

Sparrow fluffed her hair, turning her head up and doing her best to look regal. "Fate speaks to me. I have a feeling."

Faye splashed her and her sister splashed her back.

The gate creaked and Faye jerked forward, looking behind them. Rune stepped into the garden, closing the gate behind him.

"No boys allowed," Sparrow yelled as she turned on her knees and folded her arms over the stone boarder.

"I came for a word with Faye," Rune said.

"You can have your words at noon. Begone."

Sparrow vanished, the water swallowing the space she occupied. Faye met his gaze, demanding, "What did you do?"

Rune exhaled and said, "Your sister is unharmed. I phased her to her room."

"You can't do that," Faye hissed.

The corner of his mouth lifted at her remark. He strolled closer, and Faye lowered herself into the water to her chin. "Enjoying my spring?"

"I was." Faye retorted before she realized she was parroting their dreams. She flushed remembering the hard feel of his chest when she curled against him reading in front of the fire.

He stood at the edge of the spring, looking toward her garden. "I came to apologize for Sadi's behavior."

Faye tucked her legs under her. Bringing up her evil twin did nothing for her mood. "Is she still here?"

"She has taken up her rooms in the north wing," Rune said, glancing down at her.

"Why are you apologizing for her?" Faye peered up at him, not daring to hope he cared she left his study upset.

"Why did you apologize for your sister?"

"She's my family."

"My court is mine."

Sadi was part of his family. The information stung, and Faye covered her hurt with the only emotion that quieted her pain. Rancor, her constant companion since her failed ceremony. "And the High Queen, is she your family too?"

A yowl sounded from the outer garden as a small fluffy white cat ran toward them with its fur puffed out. Faye's eyes widened as she screamed, "Sparrow no!"

Rune chuckled, canting his head at her sister. She leaped at him, shifting back into a woman, slamming her shoulder into his chest, knocking Rune off balance. They fell back together, splashing into the pool.

They surfaced at the same time, her sister swimming toward her. Faye could only stare at him with parted lips. The water droplets slid over him in a tantalizing display. Dripping from his lips, trailing down his neck. His long white-blonde hair and suit clung to his body.

She bit the inside of her lip, shifting in her seat.

"I win, fuck you." Sparrow proclaimed, sitting next to Faye.

He scrubbed his hand over his face, glowering at her, then vanished. Her sister turned to her, pouting. "He's a sore loser."

"I can't believe you did that." Faye pulled herself out of the pool, pulling on her silk robe.

"He started it," Sparrow whined, following her. "Where are you going?" She called, chasing after Faye.

Faye hurried through the gardens back into the great room. "I need to talk to him before he evicts you from Hell, and I'm stuck here alone."

"If he didn't start shit, there wouldn't be shit."

Faye ignored her sister, looking into Rune's study as she passed it. He wasn't there. She just hoped he was in his room, and he didn't poof somewhere completely different. She entered her room and went to their shared door.

"Rune?" She knocked and slowly opened the door.

Faye's mouth slacked as she froze. Rune stood beside his bed with his back to her, peeling off his soaked black dress shirt. His muscles rippled with his movement as Faye's gaze roamed from his broad shoulders to his lean waist.

Sparrow leaned her head on Faye's shoulder and whistled low. "You didn't tell me he was hiding all that under his boring suit."

Rune pulled his arm out of the sleeve and discarded his still dripping shirt to the ground. He turned toward them then, and Faye's mind blanked. The chiseled hard planes of his body brought back memories of their last dream and the lingering whispers of the kisses they shared.

Sparrow's weight suddenly vanished from her shoulder. Faye looked down to find her sister gone. "What'd you do with her now?"

Rune leaned in the doorframe so close she could perceive his scent of amber and sandalwood. He reached out, gripping the door and Faye pulled her hand from the door handle. The corner of his mouth lifted and black swept through the entirety of his eyes, until his dark gaze stared down at her. Seeming to peer into her.

"I confined her to her wing. I did not appreciate her gaze." He crooned, leaning closer but not crossing over the threshold into her room.

Faye's heart pounded in her ears as he gazed into her eyes the way he had during their dreams. Their fathomless depths filled with longing and desire. Her gaze lowered to his sensual mouth, wanting to feel his lips on hers.

"Is there a reason you are at this door, vsenia?" Mischief glinted in his eyes before the shadows receded, and he took a step back as tension set in his jaw. "You should change unless you intend to wear that to our meeting." His pale blue gaze lowered over her body momentarily and rose to meet her eyes again. The longing and desire she'd seen earlier gone.

Faye couldn't tell if his mood swings were malicious or if he was touched in the head after living so long. And what the hell did vsenia mean? She turned on her heel, deciding she didn't care and left the room.

Twenty-Seven

Rune's thoughts seized as the minx turned on her heel and left. The black material of her floor length silk robe billowing behind her.

Our queen wants to be chased, the Ra'Voshnik purred, urging him to follow her.

Rune had enough of the creature's mouth. He dug his claws into it as he shut the door. Descending into himself, dragging it with him to meet the Ra'Voshnik at the depth of his power.

It stood before him a perfect reflection, mirroring everything but his eyes.

"Take control of my body ag—"

"Our body." It grinned.

Rune stepped toward it, baring his fangs. "Attempt to control my body once more, and I will bury you so deep you will perceive nothing. You will exist in darkness and shadow."

It canted its head, and Rune drew a slow breath past his lips, sampling its emotions. The creature tasted of wanton desire, the flavor of spiced honey thick on his tongue.

"Careful with your threats," it said, leaning forward breathing in to taste his emotions as well. "We draw from the same strength. What's to stop me from burying you?" It stepped closer, patting his chest as it walked past him. "I'm not unreasonable, I'll share her with you."

Rune turned, grating, "You will not touch her."

It glanced at him over its shoulder. "She'll crave my hands on her body." Rune glowered as it turned to face him, slipping its hands into its pockets. "And offer me her throat."

"You are a fool fixated on a spell meant to kill us."

"You are the polished fool if you don't recognize our queen." It raised its eyebrows and glanced upward for a moment before exhaling in a dramatic sigh. "But you've proven that kneeling for Lyssa. Our mate will taste much sweeter. Tell me you don't dream of having your mouth between her thighs." It smiled knowingly. "I do. Often."

"She is mortal. You will injure her."

"I'm hers to command. If she wishes me to be gentle, I will be." The Ra'Voshnik dissipated into shadow and smoke, its incorporeal presence gliding through his mind.

Rune returned to his physical body, tension still riddling him. He took a calming breath before stripping out of his wet slacks. The mortal commanded the Ra'Voshnik and the fool creature embraced her leash. Longing for it.

He strolled to his bathroom, retrieved a towel, and paused before the mirror. He arched his brow, noticing a stray hair. He had canceled his monthly appointment to trim his hair and clean his brow. The minx reduced the entirety of his life into chaos.

Rune dried off and dressed before returning to his study. He took his seat behind his desk and opened a tattered, aged tome, glancing over the page as he listened for the minx's returning footsteps.

Rune read the passage for the sixth time, unable to concentrate on his research. He glanced at the grandfather clock near the black marble fireplace, distracted by the litany of positions the Ra'Voshnik fantasized about coaxing the mortal into.

Rune's jaw slacked as the Ra'Voshnik dwelled on a scene. He was in his bed, sitting back on his heels. Breathy cries escaped the minx's parted lips as he held her against him. Thrusting up into her as he drank from her throat. Her thighs tightened over his waist.

Pushing the heavy leather-bound book away, Rune leaned back in his chair, glancing up for patience.

Faye's footsteps carried to him as she descended the stairs and stopped at the bottom for long moments. Rune glanced in her direction, curious as to why she stopped. Minutes passed before she resumed her march.

She lingered in the doorway wearing a gray sweater that swallowed her slight frame. It hung off one of her shoulders, exposing the black tank she wore beneath it. Rune clenched his teeth at the slender display of her neck.

Go to her. Tell her she looks beautiful, the Ra'Voshnik commanded while it frantically prowled his mind, needing to close the distance between them. Rune didn't dignify it with a response and confined it to the recesses of his mind.

Faye approached him, taking a seat across his desk. "Can we try it in a chair today, and if it doesn't work, I can lay down." She swept the stray strands behind her shoulder, leaving him a tantalizing view of her pulse point.

He stared at the rhythmic, fluttering beat as his lips parted. Rune swallowed, tearing his gaze from her throat to meet her gold lashed eyes. "Of course."

Rune descended into himself, gathering his power as he took the mental step to stand before the edge of her mind. Most barriers manifested as a wall of stone or metal. Hers manifested as the Darkness itself. The black mist rolled ominously.

He reached forward, pressing his hand into it. She tensed, taking a sharp breath as he met resistance of the shield barricading her mind. "Be easy." He crooned, spreading his fingers wide.

The swirling mist protecting her mind climbed past his wrist as he pushed. The wall opened a sliver, slow moving as though it was a door rusted shut. Rune wedged his power into it and pushed until he could pass through the opening.

His magic welled in the doorway he created, fighting to hold the opening that wanted to snap shut and viciously throw him from her mind. He hadn't taken this precaution the first time he entered her mind. It snapped shut on him, snapping the bridge of his nose in its backlash of power.

The Ra'Voshnik surged for Faye, breaking free from its mental confines. It sank into the depths of her mind, searching for her. Happiness laced with sorrow stirred within her as the Ra'Voshnik curled around her. A dog at its master's feet.

If she truly understood what it was, she would not welcome its embrace. Rune turned away from the pair and pushed his awareness over her mind, feeling for something that didn't belong. The foreign spell that wouldn't resonate with the rest of her mind.

"Where are you from?"

Rune divided his attention between her mind and the physical world. She studied him and the doorway he'd created into her mind wasn't actively trying to close on him. Perhaps he underestimated the mortal's mental capabilities. He indulged her curiosity and answered, "My court spent time between Necromia and Hell."

She spared him an unimpressed look. "Where's your *accent* from? The high bitch doesn't talk like you."

A low laugh escaped him. "Lyssa would skin you for such words."

"Lucky me, you need me alive." Faye crossed her legs, leaning onto her armrest.

A hint of jealousy caressed the edges of her mind, then receded as she gazed past him at his realm. The corner of Rune's mouth lifted as he combed through her mind. She seemed to hold tighter to the Ra'Voshnik, and the creature purred its contentment.

"I spoke High Tongue first. It has colored the subsequent languages I have learned."

Her brow pinched faintly as her gaze returned to him. "How many languages do you know?"

"More than a dozen."

The young mortal narrowed her eyes. "You know more than twelve languages?"

"Understanding what is said around you proves advantageous."

Faye sighed, leaning into the part of him she named fangs, its affectionate presence soothed her. The information she gleaned about dark courts only solidified her want to avoid them entirely. Learning more than twelve languages, not because they appreciated the culture and lived among its people, but because distrust was engrained so deeply, they could only see the worst in each other. It left a bitter, disappointing taste in her mouth.

She dropped her shoulder, lengthening the exposed strip of her neck while smoothing a lock of hair from the other side. She began braiding it, brushing her fingers over her collar bone as she went.

His gaze shifted to her hands and trailed up her throat, and Faye suppressed a smile. She tilted her head, and his gaze rose to meet hers. Her lips curved into a ghost of a smile as she asked, "Was that part of your formal training? Learn every language."

"It is common among immortal nobility."

His gaze swept over her, lingering on the thrum of her pulse, and Faye wondered if he was thinking of biting her. Images of the woman she'd seen at the Hunter's moon ball entered her mind. She was seated on her vampire's lap with his mouth pressed to her neck. The way her nails scratched over the dark material of his suit as he drank.

Faye averted her gaze to stare at the twilight sky as her cheeks heated. "It sounds like you were kept very busy," she said in a rush, grasping for a safer subject to cool her blush. She focused on her new information. Faye only spoke common tongue; she couldn't imagine how long it would take her to learn so many languages.

When her gaze returned to him, Faye found him observing her. A whisper of darkening shadow crept from the corner of his eyes. "My upbringing differed from a typical dark court."

Because he belonged to the darkest court in history. Did he even have a childhood? "And you would subject your children to the same training you received?"

He exhaled. A thing she noticed he did when frustrated. "Any young I sire will be none of your concern."

Faye recoiled at the word. He considered Anarians animals but referred to children as young. She pushed the thought away. They couldn't be more at odds. "Why did you learn High Tongue first? Is there a listed order of languages the immortal nobles learn?"

"It was my mother's native tongue."

Faye's chest tightened at how sadness tinged his words. She bit the inside of her lip, repressing the urge to comfort him. This arrogant dick kidnapped her. Actively searched her mind so he could be rid of her. He didn't deserve her comfort.

She turned to his bookshelves, smoothing her hand over the side of her neck. Refusing the soft feelings in her that wanted to curl up to him.

Silence stretched between them, and Faye settled into the longing he only offered her when he was in her mind. This other part of him that desired her. It didn't look for the shard she lacked or begrudge her mortality. It accepted her without hesitation.

The man left her conflicted. He longed for her during these short moments, a yearning so deep it made her heart bleed. But in the flesh, nothing remained. She would have thought she imagined it, but the intensity of his desire was undeniable.

Faye silently wondered if he was a jailor to the part of him that desired her. Locking it away the same way he sequestered her until he found a way to break the bond between them.

How would the Shadow Prince react when he finally realized he couldn't find the spell binding him to her because the thread connecting them was fate.

Twenty-Eight

The days passed quickly, and Faye adhered to her schedule, spending two hours with Rune each day. But the man never fully used his time. He'd leave seemingly frustrated after an hour. Which worked for her. It gave her more time to read.

Faye curled under a blanket on a chaise, reading her latest romance book. Her sister sprawled in an oversized chair. Her head and legs laid over the armrests with a book of her own

"I thought it would take you longer to get him to eat out of your hand," Sparrow remarked, turning her page.

Faye closed her book on her finger and turned toward her sister. "He's not eating out of my hand." In the last week, Faye graduated from playing with her hair to draw his attention to giving Rune a glimpse of the very tops of her breasts with square neckline shirts.

She smiled to herself. Every time she fidgeted with the top seam his veined misted shadows crept from beneath his eyes. Affecting him gave her a heady feeling of power she hated to admit was as thrilling as it was addictive.

Sparrow arched up, pulling the pillow she'd been laying on free. "He bought you a fucking library," she said, hurling the cushion at her.

Faye tucked her head behind her arms with a laugh. "He didn't buy it," Faye insisted, returning to her book. "This room was already here."

"Filled with books you like." Sparrow mumbled.

He did restock it. "He said it was overdue for an update."

"You're overdue to make out with him."

Faye returned to her book, saying quietly, "He hasn't tried to kiss me."

"What?" Her sister swung her legs and sat up. "I thought I heard you say something, not boring." Faye could feel her sister's gaze burning into the side of her face. "Do you want him to try to kiss you because that's a whole other game."

"He won't."

"I bet his ass will."

Faye lowered her book and stared up at the ceiling. He seemed to forget himself at times. She still thought of him wet, and shirtless, standing in the doorway as he leaned closer to her.

Is there a reason you are at this door, vsenia.

She'd forgotten the door between their rooms meant something to dark-bloods. Opening it was an invitation to her bed. He'd teased her, desire clear in his dark gaze. Then he pulled it all back to look down at her with his unfeeling pale blue eyes. She wanted to crack his control and bring those dark eyes out of him.

Faye glanced at her sister, and she immediately jumped to her feet with a squeal. "You've finally decided not to be boring," Sparrow said in a rush, flopping down beside Faye and shoving her back into the chair.

"Get your fat ass off me." Faye twisted to lay on her side.

Her sister paid her no mind wiggling to take up more space. "You'll need to get closer to him." Sparrow snapped her fingers and widened her eyes, saying, "That settee you dreamed with him on, sit there. It'll help jog his memory."

Faye rapped her nails on the book cover. "Maybe we should work on getting his eyes all black first."

"Their eyes change with strong emotion. Do this and you'll have the Pure Blood eyes you like so much. Sit next to him." Sparrow glanced down at her and stood. "Get up, it'll be easier to show you."

Faye got up, stuffing her blanket to the side and laying her book on it. "I feel like I'm going to regret this," she said, peering up at her sister.

"He's yours. You're allowed to kiss him if you want. We are going to remind fangs he's fated to you. Pull on the leash you have on him a little bit."

At the word leash, a scene rose in Faye's mind. Rune was in his bed, lying on his back. His wrists were bound and secured over his head. His white-blonde hair askew over his dark sheets. A few stray locks of his hair over his hard, chiseled chest. She straddled his hips, holding a leather strap that wound around his throat. She pulled it taut, and the corner of his mouth lifted.

Faye flushed, banishing the thought, and Sparrow elbowed her side. "Don't blush yet. You're just sitting next to him. He's going to get his panties in a bunch if you sit next to him like this." Her sister scooted closer to her, pressing the side of her body against hers. "This works in a bar, by the way, but your Shadow Prince is too stuck up for that."

Sparrow moved a few inches away and angled herself so her knees pointed toward Faye. "Be close enough that your knees almost touch, but," she patted the triangle of space their legs created, saying, "But have enough space here to fit both your hands."

Faye played along and set her hand down beside her.

"When you're talking to him, lean forward a little. Play with your shirt or your hair to get his attention, but don't move that hand." Sparrow pointed to Faye's hand between them. "He'll move his hand closer to yours, like brushing your fingertips or some shit."

Faye curled her fingers inward when Sparrow brushed her pinky. Her sister dropped her head back and slumped her shoulders saying, "Bitch, don't do that. You want him to kiss you."

Faye slouched, leaning back. "This feels so awkward."

"It will be fine when you're with him. Come on," Sparrow said, slapping her thigh.

"Fine." Faye sat up, positioning herself the way Sparrow said.

"He's going to touch your hand. When he does lean toward him and look at his mouth."

Faye wrinkled her nose. "Are you serious?"

"Works every time. And he's a boring dark-blood so you'll have to kiss him first."

"How do I know when I'm supposed to kiss him."

"Because he'll be this close to your face," Sparrow said, holding her hand in front of her nose.

"I don't know."

"Just do it. You'll thank me later." Sparrow got to her feet. "We'll pick out something cute for you to wear to your date with him."

"It's not a date."

"Only because your ass isn't treating it like a date." Her sister pulled her along. "He's fated to you. The man is destined to be your bitch."

"I don't want to make him my bitch." *I want him to look at me the way he did during our dreams.*

"The fucker bought you a library. A whole ass library. He has it bad whether he wants to admit it or not."

Faye wanted him to feel something but was afraid to hope. Voices drew her attention as they approached the great room. She peered over the railing to see a long dining table placed near the back of the room between the two staircases. Sadi and a man sat across from each other sharing a meal.

She hadn't seen the Familiar since she hissed at her in Rune's study. He told her she'd taken rooms here but when Faye hadn't seen her, she hoped Sadi decided to just leave.

The male looked up at her as she descended the stairs. His silver eyes were bright, gleaming as though honed from metal. "Rune's dove does look like you, kitten," he said, interlacing his fingers and resting them over his waist as he gazed up at them.

His clothing was as strange as Sadi's. He wore a black leather trench without a shirt, but a bright blue scarf coiled around his neck. Partially hidden by the colorful material was a thick chain that looked more like an animal collar. His dark shard embedded in the bottom link, glowing against his bare chest.

"Who are you stripes?" Sparrow remarked on the blood red streaks coloring the man's long dark hair.

He held out one arm and bowed his head in a flourish, answering, "Damian. And what are your names, my lovelies?"

"Sparrow, and this is Faye."

"Rune's mortal death and her sister," Sadi added, twirling the knife she used to eat with.

Sparrow leaned over the railing to hiss at Sadi, and she braced both of her hands on the table to hiss back.

"Easy," Damian crooned, glancing between Sadi and her sister. "No need to be rude."

Sparrow linked arms with Faye and continued down the stairs. "Faye will be sure to tell Rune you said hi while they are on their date."

"Don't antagonize her," Faye grated as they turned the corner and headed down the hall.

Her sister snorted as they made their way to her room. "She started it."

Twenty-Nine

Faye watched her sister flip through the clothing in her closet. She folded her arms already regretting whatever her sister was planning. Rune wasn't going to kiss her. How was leaning forward and staring at his mouth supposed to do anything?

Sparrow held out a pink shirt as she flipped through more hangers.

"I don't trust you with light colors," Faye said, hanging the shirt back up.

"I promise I'm not planning to throw water on you," Sparrow replied, handing her another top. A lace halter with billowing sleeves.

Faye curled her lip, positive she saw Sadi wear something similar. "No," she said, stuffing it with the rest of the clothes.

Sparrow shook a soft cotton sweater in front of her. Faye took it, eyeing her sister. "This neckline is too high."

Her sister fluttered her hand at her. "It's fine for what we're planning." She handed her a dark set of pants and exited Faye's closet, closing the door behind her.

Faye studied the clothes she would have selected herself. Her nerves were already frayed, she wouldn't be able to function if sparrow tried to strap her into a corset. She changed and stepped back into her room. Her sister beamed as Faye went to the full-length mirror, assessing her reflection.

"We don't want him staring at your neck this time so leave your hair down. Here cover it up for good measure." Sparrow said, holding out an ornate black and silver lace choker.

Faye took the bit of lace and clipped it around her neck. She adjusted its edges, admiring it in the mirror. The baroque lace covered her entire throat. "This is pretty, when did you get this?"

"Vash bought it for me. I haven't gotten to wear it yet, make sure fang boy doesn't ruin it."

Faye giggled and smoothed her hands over her sweater. Faye bit the inside of her lip before turning to her sister. "How do I get him on the settee."

"Just sit there, he'll follow you." Faye didn't reply, worrying her lip. "Stop being so scared. That man is your belonging."

Faye exhaled through her nose. She wasn't brave with men the way Sparrow was. Her sister was a dark-blood, their equal. And Faye wasn't. She never let them close, knowing she would be invisible the moment they found her index finger bare. Faye chose to go without rather than suffer their dismissal.

Now she tried to convince herself to reach for the Shadow Prince because they shared a handful of dreams.

"This is a mistake," Faye muttered as she reached beneath her hair to unlatch the choker.

Her sister took her hands. "No, it's not. He won't shut up about court etiquette, right? Ask him to explain what a romantic touch is." Sparrow squeezed her hands. "He belongs to you. I'll help you bag him." When Faye remained silent her sister added, "What's the worst that can happen. He doesn't kiss you. It'll be fine."

He was already trying to break the bond between them. Their situation couldn't get any worse. Faye nodded and her sister hugged her, rubbing her palms over her back.

"He'll be groveling at your feet in no time, trust me."

Our queen wants us. The Ra'Voshnik rose through his mind, impatiently awaiting the object of its affection. *Do not offend her.*

Offend her? He would be doing nothing with her. *Be silent,* he warned. Rune heard their conversations in the great room and Faye's bedroom. The minx could not possibly view their meetings as dates. The harpy only encouraged her to obtain a kiss. From him.

You desire her as I do.

Be silent, Rune grated as the harpy in question left Faye's room. Skipping by the sound of her steps. She stilled in the doorway of his study to wave at him before continuing on her way.

Rune shook his head, returning to his documents and tomes. *Go to her. Our queen awaits us,* the Ra'Voshnik insisted.

Calm yourself, she will arrive shortly, Rune growled through his mind as he set aside another tome that shed no light on what his night breeze was.

His gaze rose as her shy steps reached his ears. *She wants us to sit before the fire.*

Faye sat at the opposite side of his desk during each of their sessions. He would remain here.

The minx entered his study, sliding her hand across the door-frame as she entered. "I'm a little early."

Rune nodded in greeting, and she didn't come to his desk. The minx went to the settee instead. *Join her!* The Ra'Voshnik prowled his mind growing more agitated by the second. Rune pulled it away from the surface, silencing the creature as he stood.

Faye walked around the settee and took a seat. Glancing back at him, she said, "This is a little more comfortable than the chair."

The Ra'Voshnik thrashed under his hold as he approached her. The minx was mistaken if she thought to seduce him. He recognized her for the danger she was even as the Ra'Voshnik clung to the illusion of fate with a heated desperation.

Rune sat beside her. "There are many other rooms available if you are seeking a change in scenery."

"You spend a lot of time in here." She leaned forward, positioning herself toward him.

"I do."

"What are all the papers and books on your desk?"

"I am researching your race."

She looked surprised by his answer and scooted closer to him. "Have you found anything?"

Rune glanced down as her fingertips brushed the side of his hand. He hesitated before answering, "Nothing with your wings or claws yet."

She glanced at their hands, seemingly realizing she touched him. Rune waited for her to pull away. To his surprise she didn't. She ran the pad of her finger over his nail. "How do you control it?"

Rune remained still. His body betrayed him at her simple touch. His fangs lengthened as his muscles went taut. "Control what?"

Faye lifted her other hand and flexed her fingers. "I can't get my claws to come out. Or my wings. I always wanted to fly."

"My shift is unlike yours. Pure Bloods have a Ra'Voshnik living within us. The changes you see are when the urges are close to the surface."

She peered at him and Rune felt like an animal in a zoo. "So, you struggle to keep it down and it shows when you slip. While mine is sleeping and won't come to the surface at all."

He supposed that was an accurate description. She touched his hand again and Rune glanced between them, returning her touch with a feather light stroke over her nail.

She didn't react as he expected. With her eyes downcast she slid two fingers along his index at an agonizing pace. *Darkness save him.* It was all he could do to hold still.

She stroked his shard, and Rune realized he'd moved in error, underestimating her hold over him. She glanced up at him then, but her gold-streaked gaze didn't meet his. She looked at his mouth.

Lost, Rune leaned forward, wanting the soft brush of her lips that would serve as invitation for his touch. His eyes slid closed the same moment the minx gasped, pulling away from him. Rune's eyes snapped open, and the sight of her had the Ra'Voshnik surfacing in an instant.

Take what is offered, it growled as black flooded his eyes. The shadows stretched to sway beneath his dark gaze as his fangs sharpened, aching for her throat.

She wore the same choker but was now dressed in a negligee made of the same material. Ribbon and lace covered her body, hugging and accentuating her curves, enticing him and the Ra'Voshnik.

Rune shook himself, by her shriek and the way she drew her legs up to cover herself, Rune could see this was her sister's schemes and not Faye's doing.

She is not offering anything, you fool. Rune stood and removed his suit jacket. He held it out to her, staring through his window over his realm.

Faye took his jacket and he listened to the rustle of fabric as she pulled it on. She sniffled, the sound a knife to his heart.

"I can phase you to your room to change if you wish." He offered.

She sniffled again. "No, this is fine. You can turn around." Rune tentatively glanced over his shoulder. His jacket swallowed her but concealed everything the lace and ribbons displayed. "Can we take a break? I need to kill my sister." She said, wiping her eyes.

"Apologies. I did not intend to upset you."

"You didn't upset me," Faye said, taking a shaking breath before holding her arm out toward the south wing. "Sparrow is upsetting me. She said she wouldn't do this. She promised." She wiped his sleeve over her eyes, before muttering, "I need to go."

She turned and stormed out of his study. Rune followed her, unsure of what to say to soothe her pain.

Faye turned into the great room and hurried up the stairs past Sadi and her mate. Sadi gave him a pointed look but said nothing. Damian lacked Sadi's good sense. "Your dove upset with you?" He pushed his chair back to face Rune. "The jacket looks better on her." He glanced back at Faye as she disappeared down the hall.

Tensions set Rune's jaw. "Do not antagonize her," he warned.

"Lovers spat then?" Damian stood, strolling to Sadi before running his hand through her hair. "We'll leave you to it," he said before they vanished.

Thirty

Faye found her sister with Vashien in the den. Sparrow lied to her, betrayed her trust, and lounged in a chair reading a book like it was nothing. Trussing her up in lace and throwing her to the Shadow Prince was nothing.

Her hands shook as tears fell from her eyes. She marched to Vashien, snatching his drink and hurled it at her sister. It struck the wall across the room and shattered.

"Hey, not cool! You can't throw hard objects." Sparrow peered over the armrest at the glass and liquid surrounding her chair.

"I told you not to dress me up like a fucking whore! You promised." Faye screamed, digging her nails under the choker.

"No, don't do that," Sparrow said, holding her hand out the same moment Faye ripped the choker off her neck. Her sister's arm dropped, as she muttered, "Because now you're naked under Runey's jacket."

"What did you do?" Vashien's voice sounded from behind her. Something settled over Faye's shoulders. She pulled it around her thinking it was a blanket before she realized it was Vashien's robe. It dragged on the ground around her as Faye hugged it over her body.

"She magicked me into lingerie in front of him." Faye snapped, not taking her eyes off her sister.

Sparrow rolled her eyes and sighed dramatically. "You were completely covered. I dug through all my chokers looking for one that wasn't see through."

"You did what?" Vashien said.

Sparrow snorted, returning to her book. "It wouldn't have even fired unless you wanted to be naked with him."

She thought this was her fault. Anger blistered in Faye. She stiffened with tension stalking toward her sister and stopped to yell, "You shouldn't have put that thing on me!"

Her sister slammed her book closed. "I'm helping you!"

Faye straightened her back as her hand curled into a fist. "You're not helping me. You're doing what *Sparrow* wants to do and not giving a fuck about anyone else."

"I am helping you. You could have gone to your meeting naked, and he wouldn't notice you. You're too busy crying over yourself and overthinking everything. You're so pathetic that when you finally have the *one* guy in all the realms fate specifically designed *for* you. You can't land him. Because you're boring."

Faye took a step back, covering her mouth. Sparrow's words hit her harder than any strike and left a much deeper scar. Tears spilled down her cheeks.

"I'm sorry, I didn't mean it." Sparrow hopped down from her chair and sucked a breath as she stepped in glass. Faye turned and ran as her sister yelled her name behind her.

She ran aimlessly needing to get away from Sparrow. She found herself in her room, out of breath. Her sister limped into view at the end of the hall. "Faye."

Faye slammed the door, locking it as a broken sob escaped her. She turned in a circle at a loss of what to do. She wanted to curl into a ball and disappear. No one wanted her. Rune denied their fated bond. Sadi refused to acknowledge they were related despite their identical appearances. And the person she loved most saw her as a boring inconvenience.

She dropped Vashien's robe and crawled into bed. She tucked herself under the blankets, letting herself cry.

A knock sounded at her door. Too calm to be her sister. Faye ignored it, wiping her eyes on the sleeve of Rune's suit jacket. She pulled it higher, laying the side of her face against the lining. The knock sounded again, and Faye glanced at the door before saying, "I'm fine, Vash."

"May I come in?" That deep accented voice didn't belong to Vashien.

Faye glared at the door. If he was here for his jacket he could fuck off. Long moments passed as silence followed, filling the room. When Faye thought he'd left, Rune materialized on the other side of the door.

"If you're here for your jacket I'll return it later."

"I did not come for that," he said as he brought a chair to the edge of her bed.

Faye wiped her eyes on the blanket, before saying, "I'm not in the mood for you to poke around my head."

"I did not come for that either."

Faye didn't look up at him. She was tired and upset and pushed way past her tolerance for bullshit. "Why are you here? You don't even like me."

"Who told you I do not like you."

She peered up at him. It was strange seeing him in a dress shirt rather than his usual suit. She fingered the lapel of his jacket still wrapped around her under the blankets. "You don't want to be fated to me," she all but whispered. Surprised by how much the words hurt her when she spoke them aloud.

Rune exhaled and laid his hand next to hers, palm up. Faye only stared for long moments, before tentatively reaching for him. She couldn't decern if what he offered was out of affection or pity. She might care later when her hurt faded, but in this moment, she would take either.

Faye touched the edge of his palm. At her contact he slid his hand beneath hers, his fingers circling hers. "This is not fate between us," he said gently as he wiped her tears with his other hand. "What you feel is artificial."

Faye tried to pull her hand away and he didn't let go. Tears blurred Faye's vision. She whispered, "its not artificial. I feel you. A small part of you wants me."

"What you feel is the Ra'Voshnik. The Ra'Voshnik that lives within me." He brushed her tears away and stroked her hair. "I am not breaking the bond between us to be cruel. See this from my perspective. I am immortal, I have lived for more than thirty centuries. I do not wish for this one to be my last."

Her anger melted to sorrow as a hollow pain seeped through her. How could she ask him to choose her and die? Faye pulled his hand closer and rested her forehead against it. She would always be lacking. Close enough to see the life she longed for but missing the integral piece needed to obtain it.

He swept the moisture from her eyes. "Once you have your shard you will have the life of your choosing. This ordeal will be a fleeting memory. I doubt I cross your mind in a few years."

She sighed against his hand as he stroked her hair. He felt so much like her dreams, but he wouldn't shut up about courts. "You're ruining the mood big guy."

"Why do you reject the dark courts so venomously?"

Faye had the urge to bite his wrist for annoying her. She dismissed the strange impulse and said instead, "You were doing so good. Stop offending me."

He chuckled, running his fingers through her hair. "Offended? I am the one who should be offended in our exchange." Faye tilted her head up to squint at him. "You, my Lady, poached me, bit me, and dug your claws into my throat."

She did do all that. Faye sat up and scooted to the edge of the bed. She leaned on him, resting her head on his shoulder. His jacket smelled like him, but it didn't compare to breathing in his scent of amber and sandalwood when he was close to her. She glanced up at him, still holding his hand. "You forgot one, I hit you with a candle holder."

He turned toward her, bringing his lips a moment from hers. "That occurred after I kidnapped you. Turnabout is fair play."

Faye swallowed, waiting for him to turn away, but he lingered. Waiting for her to make a decision while he brushed his thumb over the back of her hand.

Her sister's taunt sounded in her mind. *You can't land him. Because you're boring.*

Determination set in her. She wasn't boring and she was going to land him. Fate wouldn't tie them together just to kill him. He wasn't a Familiar. Fate had taken enough from her, cutting away things she wanted. He was her fate and she meant to claim him.

Faye leaned up and brushed her lips against his. A moment between them, soft and chaste. She closed her eyes wanting the part of him that chose her to surface. Desperately needing to feel it to soothe the pain that ran too deep in her soul, carving chasms of hurt.

He moved with her, and Faye's heart leapt. He chose her. Wanted her.

The next moment he flinched, breaking their kiss and Faye instinctively pulled away. She withdrew her hand and Faye could only stare.

He let her go.

Faye clenched her jaw, fighting the tears that threatened to start anew. He didn't want her. She was a fool mistaking pity for affection. Faye pressed her arms to her side.

"Apologies, the High Council is requesting my presence. Did you want me to unseal this wing and allow your sister entry?"

Faye glanced up meeting his gaze, desperately needing his dark gaze to stare back at her with the longing she felt each time he touched her mind.

Nothing reflected in the flesh.

Faye looked away pulling the blankets up to cover her chest. "No. I want to be alone."

He didn't respond. Faye wiped the sleeve of his jacket over her eyes and turned back toward him. Her empty room stared back at her.

He left her. Alone.

Thirty-One

The Ra'Voshnik raged through Rune's mind as he materialized in The Eyes. *What are you doing? Return to our queen immediately!* Rune knelt in protocol, ignoring the enraged screams echoing through his mind.

Raw, undiluted desire sang through his veins from the gentle touch of her lips. Darkness, he still felt her and worse he had no way to conceal the stark evidence of his want. The scent of the winged male covered her. Rune had been a moment from phasing her to his shower. Needing to scrub the scent off her before covering her with his own.

Jha'ant's summons interrupted him. Rune found himself torn between thanking Jha'ant or tearing his head from his shoulders after he snapped every other appendage from his body.

You left our queen! The Ra'Voshnik roared and Rune's body flickered as the creature attempted to phase and return to Faye. *You rejected her invitation!*

Rune sank his claws into the Ra'Voshnik's frantic presence, dragging it down. And for the first time it took hold of him as well, dragging his consciousness into the depths of his mind with it.

Rune's surroundings changed and a crushing pressure solidified on the front of his throat. He stood face to face with the Ra'Voshnik, their claws sinking into the other's throat.

The Ra'Voshnik dragged him closer, baring its fangs, screaming, "Return to her and beg her forgiveness!"

"Do not think to order me," Rune grated. "You forget my will is greater than yours." The Ra'Voshnik's hold faded as Rune drove it from its physical form. Reducing it to smoke and shadow.

"Brother." Rune perceived Jareth's voice from far above him. Rune cursed in High Tongue as he confined the Ra'Voshnik to the recesses of his mind. The fool creature had thrown its tantrum before the High Council.

Rune returned to his body, blinking as the physical world came into focus.

"Are you well?" His brother asked.

Red stained his fingertips and blood trickled from either side of his neck. Rune met his brother's gaze not wishing to explain himself.

"Shadow Prince." Jha'ant's voice shook as he spoke the words that began their meeting.

Rune turned to the bird king as he rose, fear turning Jha'ant's eyes glassy. The bird king looked as though he now regretted summoning him. Rune could only be thankful the hard edge of anger cooled his desperate want of the minx.

"I have sent my monthly account of The Crumbling. What do you need that is not already outlined in my report?" Rune asked coldly.

Jha'ant ruffled his wings and crinkled the pages he held. A boy with a security blanket playing king to his betters. "I'm growing concerned. Your report didn't include an attempt on The Crumbling."

"The Shadow Prince is too busy licking his Anarian's slit." Lyssa answered for him.

Kill her, she insults our queen, the Ra'Voshnik whispered from its confines.

Lyssa leaned forward, propping her chin on her hand. Her gaze flitted lower, lingering between his legs before returning to his eyes. "I would say you were too busy with your cock in her mouth," she smiled and continued in a lower tone, "But we both know you can't get it up."

The Ra'Voshnik chuckled from the depths of his mind. *We didn't get hard because the noisy female wasn't worth breeding with.*

Rune remained silent, there was not a reply he could offer Lyssa she would find satisfactory. He turned his attention to Jha'ant. "You have the same access I do to The Crumbling. Attend to it yourself if you find my actions lacking. Do not summon me again."

He phased to his bathroom, materializing before the mirror. He listened for the minx and was met with her steady slow breaths. There would be nothing he could do to ease her hurt while she slept.

He lifted his chin to inspect the damage the Ra'Voshnik had done. Rune frowned and reached for Sadi's mind.

You will not *go to her while our queen is upset with you.*

Rune exhaled. It would likely upset his queen... The Ra'Voshnik's dark laughter echoed through his mind. *It's about time you admitted it.*

She is not my queen. It is a spell, fool creature.

And is it the spell that makes you hard with a touch of her lips? Careful not to embarrass us. I wouldn't want you coming the instant she touches your cock. Give her to me, I'll be sure to set her expectations.

Rune ignored the Ra'Voshnik, washing away what blood he could. The Ra'Voshnik sank its claws too deep for him to heal it himself. Rune pushed his senses over his home, searching for the blonde harpy. He located her and phased to the den in his south wing.

The Ra'Voshnik instantly fixated on the large Artithian male. *Kill him.*

Be silent.

His scent covered her!

The male paled as though he somehow sensed a predator sought his demise, but to his credit he stood between him and his harpy. Rune couldn't help but to develop a begrudging inkling of respect for the man.

"I would like a word with the blonde harpy," Rune said, and the male spread his wings, blocking Sparrow from view. Bravery that bordered on stupidity, but Rune respected loyalty. He met the man's gaze and asked, "What is your name."

The harpy answered, "His name is Vashien, you shadowy asshole. Did Faye not beat your ass enough? Come closer and I'll leave more claw marks on your face."

The large male paled further, and Rune resisted the urge to smile at his terrible choice in women. "Vashien," Rune said, taking a step closer, "it would be in your best interest to keep your scent off Faye." The large male nodded but didn't step aside. "I have not come to harm your female."

Vashien folded his wings and moved to Sparrow's side. The blonde harpy sat in a chair picking glass out of her foot before mending the lacerations.

Rune took a seat across from them and said, "A word harpy."

"That's three words, douche."

"Sparrow," Vashien said, giving her a pointed look.

The blonde snorted, glancing up from her task. "What?"

"You are able to mend flesh?"

"Obviously," Sparrow said, returning to her foot. She flicked away a piece of glass and pressed her thumb to the tiny cut.

"Would you mind terribly, if I requested you mend my throat?"

She stood with a huff and trudged to him. She pushed his chin up roughly, peering at the wounds. "Your stray cat too busy to heal you?"

"I would like to avoid prodding your sister's anger."

Sparrow jabbed her fingers over his neck. "Darkness, these are deep. You really pissed her off."

"Faye is not responsible for my injuries, and I believe you pissed her off." The blonde remained silent as she pressed her thumb to the first wound. Her magic was slow and clumsy, taking long moments to seal the puncture. "You will likely be immortal. You need to learn our most dangerous weapons are our words."

She moved to the next injury, pressing harder than was necessary. "I would have told her I was sorry if you didn't block off the hallway with your stupid shield."

"You must learn restraint," Rune said, glancing down at her.

She was bent forward peering at his throat as she worked. "Faye and I are fine, fang boy."

"I am speaking of you. Your sister is mortal. You will carry her memory for centuries. You should be wary of your mouth. A moment spoken in haste can echo for centuries."

Sparrow covered the last puncture with her thumb, pulling back to look him in the eye as she healed it. "And do you have echoing moments, Shadow Prince?"

Rune held her gaze after she finished healing him and stepped back.

Every immortal has many such moments.

Thirty-Two

Faye's bed shifted suddenly jarring her from sleep. She groaned narrowing her eyes to peer up at blonde curls. "Go away," she muttered, rolling away from her sister. Her head pounded and she didn't have the mental fortitude to deal with Sparrow right now.

The brief kiss she shared with Rune left her hollow and lonely. She thought she'd finally reached him, and he couldn't get away from her fast enough.

"I'm sorry," her sister said to her back.

Faye closed her eyes, wanting to be alone. The bed shifted with her sister's movements. Sparrow rubbed her hand over her back like she did when they were girls. Faye leaned her shoulder away, saying, "It doesn't mean anything if you keep doing it."

Her sister leaned back, whispering, "I won't." When Faye didn't reply she blurted out, "I say things I don't mean when I'm mad. You know that."

Anger coiled through Faye, burning away her sad feelings. She sat up and turned to her sister. "To everyone else," Faye yelled, stabbing her finger into the blankets between them. "You never did it to me. But I don't know why I thought I was special. This is how you treat everyone. It was a matter of time before you turned on me too."

Sparrow looked like she's struck her. Her lips parted and her brow pinched. "I didn't turn on you."

Was she fucking kidding? "You wrapped me in lace and threw me at his feet."

Sparrow's green eyes hardened as she pulled her shoulders back. "He saw you in your bikini. What I put you in covered way more of you. Nothing was see-through. He didn't get a peek at anything."

A bitter laugh escaped Faye as she glanced away. "You still can't take responsibility for what you did." Her gaze shot back to Sparrow as she said, "You think this is fine and I overreacted. This is not fine— *We* are not fine. What you did was bullshit. Get out."

Sparrow's shoulder slumped as she sighed. "Bitch, come on."

"Don't bitch me."

"Can you just punch me in the face and we call it even?"

Faye could only blink at her sister. "You just— This isn't about getting even."

"I'm sorry. I'll let you pick all your own clothes." Sparrow took her hands and made her best pair of sad eyes.

Faye pulled her hand away. "That face works on Vash not me."

Sparrow crawled over to her and hugged her arm to her side. "I'm sorry I upset you. I'm sorry I got mad and lashed out. I'm a bad influence and a worse sister."

"You're a terrible influence," Faye glared at her. She was still angry, but they were family. Faye took a deep breath and exhaled before saying, "You're not a bad sister. I can't think of anyone else who would come to Hell with me."

"And I crashed the High Queen's open court." Sparrow laughed, pausing long enough to say, "Vash was so mad."

Faye had two people willing to come to Hell for her. Having people who cared that much about her was a blessing.

Sparrow tugged on Rune's jacket. "You sleeping in his clothes now?" Faye jerked the sleeve out of Sparrow's grasp. Her sister raised her hand in a peaceful gesture. "I mean it's a fancy jacket, but did you want to put some clothes on under it?"

"It's your fault I'm naked under this," Faye grumbled.

"You're the—" Sparrow fell silent with a huff. "I'm going to be a better sister and shut my fucking mouth."

Faye smiled, leaning on Sparrow. "I appreciate you trying."

"You're lucky I love you. I don't do this for anyone."

Now that her anger was subsiding, her headache came raging back in with a vengeance. "I need to make some tea. My head is killing me." Faye patted Sparrow's thigh, signaling her to get out of the way.

Sparrow got out of bed and turned back to Faye. She leaned forward and rocked back on her heels before asking, "Can I ask you something and you not get mad?"

"Probably since you're asking and not doing," Faye said getting out of bed and stretching her back.

"What happened? Did you just get too excited grabbing his neck?"

Faye spared her sister a quizzical glance as she headed for her closet. "I didn't grab his neck."

Sparrow trailed behind her. "The man asked me to heal finger holes in his neck. You're the only one with claws."

"He said the High Council summoned him. I thought he was making an excuse to get away from me. Maybe he got frisky with someone there." *Like the high bitch.* Faye didn't want to be jealous but the emotion sank into her bones. She changed, pulling on her clothes roughly trying not to imagine the High Queen gripping the front of his throat. His words during their last dream rose in her mind.

Vampires appreciate aggression. I crave it.

Her sister's voice pulled her from her own thoughts. "Men don't usually want to get away from half-naked women. Just saying."

"Why were you healing him instead of Sadi?" Would Sadi know what those marks meant and be upset with him?

"Because he likes you," Sparrow said. Faye cut her sister a glance and pulled her shirt on. "I asked him the same thing. He said he didn't want to prod your anger." Sparrow spoke the last, lowering her voice and mimicking his accent.

"Did he kiss you?" Her sister's eyes widened as heat rose to her cheeks. "Darkness, is he a good kisser? Did he pull you in? I'm sorry. I'll be quiet." Sparrow's eyes gleamed as she pressed her hands together bringing her fingertips to her lips.

Her sister stood on her toes and squealed as Faye eyed her. "It wasn't that exciting."

Sparrow leaned forward to whisper, "But you did kiss."

Faye looked away. "I kissed him, but I don't think he kissed me back."

Her sister's arms dropped to her sides. "What do you mean you don't think he kissed you back?"

Faye dusted her pristine shirt, unable to meet her sister's gaze. "He saw me after we had our fight. I think he came out of pity. After I kissed him, he left."

"Well, he came to me to heal him, and he scolded me about my mouth. I'm voting he likes you."

Thirty-Three

Faye stared up at the ceiling, drumming her fingers over the knuckles of her other hand, lost in her thoughts. The Shadow Prince was fated to her, not the high bitch or her evil twin. Her, and she wanted him but she couldn't idly sit by. She needed to pull his attention.

Which meant she needed to be bolder. Not walk-into-his-study-naked bold. Less drastic. Less Sparrow. She couldn't sit and wait for him to accept what tied them was fate. Faye got to her feet and left the south wing to make her way to her room. She smiled as she went down the stairs. Her room, she hadn't slept there since her sister arrived.

But maybe she should.

Faye turned the idea over as she started down the hall. She didn't look into Rune's study, heading straight to her chandelier closet. Faye shut the door behind her and browsed the clothing he provided.

She sifted through the shirts stopping on the corset. She hesitated for the briefest moment before shoving it to the side. She wasn't going to dress up like a Familiar. Sadi's blatant sexuality wasn't something she was comfortable with.

Faye rummaged through her closet and settled on a backless gray top and black trousers. She dressed and exited the closet to examine her reflection in the full-length mirror. Her vampire would like her neck, wouldn't he? She pulled her hair into a high ponytail and coiled it into a bun. She used her favorite hair stick to keep her hair up. A polished piece of teak with two metal cherry blossoms dangling from delicate chains.

She took a breath to settle her nerves blowing it slowly through pursed lips. If vampires appreciated aggression, maybe she should just stab him. Faye laughed to herself as she turned to face the hall. A few feet separated her from her query. She just needed to keep her nerves from ruining her plan.

Don't be boring. Don't be boring. Faye closed her eyes, taking a final breath before taking fate into her own hands.

She entered his study and Rune was in his usual spot behind his desk. He didn't look like the man who sat next to her yesterday. He was polished. Controlled. He glanced up at her then, his pale blue gaze pinning her in place.

"A moment," was all he said, as he lowered his gaze to the documents before him. Flipping through the loose pages.

Faye swallowed, making her way to his desk. She crossed in front of it to stand beside him. Darkness, she felt so awkward. She leaned back on his desk. He didn't look up at her. Faye gripped the edge of his desk out of his view.

"Can we talk about court etiquette while you look through my mind today?" Faye stiffened as he looked up at her, but thankfully her cheeks didn't heat under his gaze.

He leaned back in his chair, resting his hand on the arm rest. "What would you like to discuss?"

His features gave nothing away, locked in a polite mask of courtesy. Faye glanced away, picking up one of the documents he'd been reading. Faye couldn't read the harsh script scrawled over the page.

"You said once I have my shard I could join the court of my choosing. I want to make an educated decision before I shun the prospect." Faye placed the parchment on its rightful pile and turned her attention back to Rune. *Now or never*, she thought as she said, "Tell me about a romantic touch. The one that invites a man to my body."

His gaze flooded black in a rush and Faye instantly felt more at ease. He watched her for long moments as those shadows swayed over the tops of his cheekbones. He canted his head at her, brows lowering a fraction. "The Ra'Voshnik calms you."

Faye shrugged one shoulder at him. "Did you want it to have another effect?" She took a step closer to him. In truth she preferred him this way. His dark gaze was more expressive. The yearning she felt when he was in her mind plain for her to see.

"A romantic touch is typically a kiss. The pursuer will lean close and the romantic interest will kiss or brush their lips over the pursuer's. We are taught to wait for an invitation before moving further. A kiss invites a kiss, nothing more until the pursued moves further. They lead the dance."

Faye remembered his leaning close to her while she laid her head on his shoulder. He waited. Lingering. Was that his invitation? Faye reached for conversation to keep the blush from her cheeks. "Dark-bloods have strange customs," she said inching closer to him.

"Court protocols." Rune corrected. "Civilized society practices them."

"What else would be a romantic touch?" Faye bit the inside of her lip and traced her finger over his shoulder. She met his gaze and asked, "Is this a romantic touch?"

He grinned up at her, and Faye's heart beat faster. Darkness, his fangs were sexy.

"No. On a male it is a touch to the lips, groin, or buttock."

Faye gripped his shoulder and sat on his thigh before she could overthink herself out of it. He parted his lips, leaning closer, and Faye nearly faltered. She forced herself not to squirm and said with all the bravado she could manage, "So, this means nothing?"

The corner of his mouth lifted as he leaned back in his chair once more. "It would carry weight if done in public. In private, this would be an invitation to a neutral touch."

Rune ran the back of his fingers up her bare back, sending shivers through her. Faye forced herself still even as her nipples harden to tight peaks.

He was toying with her. Faye leaned closer to him determined to play the same game. "This is all neutral?" Faye ran her fingers from just above his belt to his neck, making sure to run her nails over his throat. The way his muscles flexed as she touched him exhilarated her.

He nodded watching her lips.

She leaned closer, getting caught up in her game. A kiss would only lead to a kiss. He wouldn't do more. Her lips parted as her breaths grew shallow.

No, she played this game with him and lost. She would tempt him until he asked for her invitation. Faye pulled back and he watched her, tracing circles on her back with something cool and hard.

Her gaze lowered to his other hand. She took it, studying his black tipped claws. They were like hers, but bigger, ending in curved points. She pressed the pad of her thumb to the point.

"Careful." Rune lifted his fingers away.

A bead of red rose on her thumb. They were sharp. She didn't even feel it.

Rune pressed his thumb over hers and warmth spread over it. When he let her go Faye squeezed her thumb to her forefinger. It was healed.

Faye glanced at him before saying, "I didn't think vampires wasted blood."

"I was not aware you were offering," Rune said, his voice was rough. His accent thicker. Faye glanced down between them and immediately met his gaze again and flushed deeply. The corner of his mouth lifted. "I assure you my will is stronger than my flesh."

She took a deep breath and willed the heat from her face. If he was embarrassed, he didn't show it. Faye's mood soured. If she had this much of his attention and he wasn't leaning in to ask for a kiss he wasn't going to. Fine. She'd have to wear him down more tomorrow.

Faye pushed off his chest and stood. She did her best to saunter to the wrought iron glass wall. "Why is Hell glittery? Where are the souls that don't want to return to the Darkness?" It was pretty but not what she expected when she was taught about Hell.

His voice sounded from behind her, startling her with his closeness. "This was my father's realm before I inherited it." Faye watched him in the glass as he spoke. "I keep the realm as he shaped it, maintaining Hell's floor."

Faye's gaze swept over his reflection. If he could stand there and pretend he didn't have a clearly visible erection, so could she. Her gaze shifted to the glittering horizon as she said, "And the souls? It looks pretty empty here."

Rune canted his head. "They are the shimmering you see. Purging the souls back to the Darkness proves tedious. They are trapped beneath Hell's floor and fade in time."

Faye's mouth slacked as she turned to him. "You trap people underneath that?"

"Not people." Rune lifted his hand and tapped his soul shard. "Errant energy that has yet to return to the Darkness. The romantic notion that a lover will wait in Hell for their partner to join them before returning to the Darkness is fictional."

His words crumpled something in her. Faye's gaze lowered to the shimmering crystal below them. She loved reading stories of love everlasting. Knowing all of it was a romantic fantasy left her feeling empty.

Faye turned away from the window and moved past Rune. "Did you want to sit at your desk or in front of the fire?"

"Which ever you prefer."

Faye nodded and strolled to the settee.

Thirty-Four

A pillow landed next to Faye. She was still in bed and glanced at
Sparrow who continued to abuse the talisman they'd gotten. She
wondered if Rune was so obscenely rich he didn't care or if some
part of him felt guilty for holding them hostage. Or hosting her court
as the dark-blooded would say.

"When is his shadowiness going to admit he can't find the spell
because there isn't one? I mean the food is great, but I miss shopping
a little."

That was a good question. His options were either she was his
or he couldn't find the spell tying her to him. Neither of which he
was willing to admit to.

"You should get more out of him."

Faye rolled over. "Did you want a talisman for another fancy
restaurant?"

"Maybe for a distillery. But no, not for me. He doesn't think this is fate. He thinks this is a spell, and you make him weak. In his head, he's mortal as long as he's tied to you. So, you playing along with him is giving his immortality back, which is invaluable. You should think of something you want of equal value."

"What would be equal to immortality?" The only way she could have immortality was to be turned, but the transition wasn't guaranteed. Needing to die was a huge risk on a maybe.

"How many times a day do you think he strokes off to you?"

Faye laughed. She never considered what he did after she left him yesterday. The thought of him stroking himself thinking of her had her biting the inside of her lip. "Once?"

Sparrow snorted. "You're doing a terrible job if it's just once."

Faye laughed, rolling out of bed. "I should go find my tall, pale, and scary."

Sparrow leaned back in her chair, widening her eyes, and blinking at her. "Oh, he's yours now?"

"If I wait for him, I'll be an old woman before he decides this is fate," Faye said, holding her hands up as she shrugged.

Her sister quirked her lip, nodding to herself. "So you're going to help him along? I like it. Tell me every detail when you get back."

Faye laughed, wiggling her fingers at Sparrow as she made her way to Rune's side of the house. The halls were quiet. Faye entered Rune's study and stopped.

Her vampire wasn't in his usual spot. Faye walked to his desk, glancing at the loose pages organized in small piles. They looked old, yellowed and weather worn. Faye moved one gently to see the page below it.

Everything was written in a language she didn't recognize. High Tongue if she had to guess. Faye carefully put the page back, arranging them as they were.

Faye left the study and went back to her room. She stared at the adjoining door. Would Rune be dressing again? The memory of the hard, chiseled plains of his body made her smile. Maybe he overslept.

Faye rapt her nails on the door before pushing it open slowly.

The Shadow Prince wasn't here either. Faye peaked into his room and rolled her eyes at his perfectly made bed. She never made her bed. What was the point when she was just going to crawl back under her blankets later that evening?

Faye left the adjoining door open to tease him and stepped back into the hall. She walked down the corridor glancing into his study again as she passed.

Disappointment weighed on her. He never missed a day before.

Faye made her way back to Sparrow, wondering what to do with her time. She could harvest from her garden and start her potions and ointments. He could find her if he wanted to poke through her head for a non-existent spell. Faye returned to her sister's room and retrieved her basket and preening knife.

Her sister eyed her as she walked back into the room. "Shouldn't you be making Rune's life extra hard right now?"

"He's not in his study."

"So, what are you going to do?"

Faye collected her basket and preening knife. She never realized how much she looked forward to seeing him until he stood her up. "Gather my herbs to dry."

Faye headed back to the great room to follow the pathway to the gardens. Faye sighed as she walked into the sunlight. The sweet floral scent of the black roses filled the air. She stepped through the second archway and stopped. Her vampire was in the hot spring, reclined against the stones. His white-blonde hair spread over the grass out of the water.

Faye didn't move. Rune sat up, lifting one arm out of the steaming spring. Water fell from his pale, muscular shoulder as he laid his arm along its border. He turned in her direction, his other hand pulling his hair away from his face.

"We will pick up our meetings again tomorrow." His deep voice sounded… tired.

Faye walked toward him. "Long night?"

He didn't answer.

The man wasn't wearing a shirt. She wondered if he wore anything at all while soaking. As she crossed in front of him, she saw he was nude. The water didn't give her a good view, and he didn't seem to be bothered by his state of undress.

His eyes were closed, with his chin tilted upward. Faye admired his too perfect face, her gaze lingering over his high cheekbones, the sharp line of his jaw. She watched a bead of water slide from under his chin, down the front of his neck to collect at the hollow at the base of his throat. He was always clean shaven; no hair covered his broad chest. The hard planes of his body rose and fell with his breaths.

"You know Sparrow or Vash could stumble in on your skinny dipping."

He exhaled deeply. "I am in my realm, my home, and my pool. If my guests don't appreciate my presence, they may find another location." He rubbed his fingertips over his forehead and opened his eyes to squint at her.

"Does the sun bother you?" Faye asked as she took a seat at the edge of the pool. Setting her basket and pruning knife down beside her.

"The sun does not affect me in the same manner it does the others," he said, closing his eyes once more.

"Why?"

"I inherited lineage from both of my parents."

Faye leaned back on her hands and looked up at the clouds. "I've never seen you anywhere but your room and study."

"My study is where I spend the majority of my time. Today I looked into The Crumbling. I stayed too long, tapped too far into my reserves." He cracked his lids to peer at her.

Faye turned back toward him, crossing her legs. "What are you doing to The Crumbling?"

He gave her a curious glance before answering, "Unraveling it before it consumes the realms."

He did that? "What's unraveling?"

He closed his eyes again, leaning back on the smooth rocks. "You are full of questions this day."

"I'm broadening my horizons," Faye remarked.

He took a deep breath and exhaled. "Unraveling is what must be done if you are not strong enough to break magic with sheer force."

"Is it hard?"

He sat up, running his hand over his face, before saying, "Spells are woven, constructed pieces of magic. Unraveling it is exactly as it sounds. I deconstruct the layers of magic that created the spell by pulling its threads in the correct order."

The man sounded like he was reciting a lesson. Faye thought about his words, turning them over in her head. "So, it's like a cat's cradle game, layered on top of each other?"

His brow lowered. "I suppose that would be an accurate depiction, if the strings in the children's game also moved."

She looked at him more appreciatively. "So, to break up your day, you try to save the realms."

"Have you reconsidered joining a court when our time is concluded."

Change of subject much. "I'm not convinced."

He studied her for a moment, then said, "You would find the life your power afforded you pleasant."

Faye absently picked blades of grass. "Is your life pleasant?" She asked turning toward him.

The corner of his mouth lifted. "I am male. Women are seen to within their courts. Has a man never worshiped at your altar?"

Warmth spread over Faye as she flushed at his words. Images of him kneeling before her rose in her mind. She pushed them away and said, "Sounds like the courts are just an excuse to have gratuitous sex, like your vampire orgies."

He laughed and relaxed into a smile. "A single benefit to an intricate society. You would enjoy it."

"Doubtful," Faye answered too quickly.

He arched a brow at her. "I could show you." Faye blushed feverishly and he raised his hand out of the water. "You misunderstand my words. I would be willing to take you to witness how dark-blooded men are trained to please women."

Faye's brow came together, and he smirked at her expression before saying, "It is part of formal court training. A single aspect among many duties." She bit the inside of her lip and he grinned. "You look curious."

Faye turned away from him. "Not enough to want to see another vampire orgy, in your bed."

"I received my training long ago. I would take you to the same brothel I was trained at so you can witness it. It would behoove you to broaden your horizons. Move to the circles you were meant for. Know what to expect of men at court and not swing metal objects at them."

Faye straightened her back, refusing to back down. "I guess I can go see how you've learned to fumble through things. Can I bring Sparrow so we can share a laugh?"

Rune's smile didn't quite meet his eyes. "No. My offer extends to you."

"I can't leave here but you can take me to a whore house?"

"It is a high-end brothel that caters to the darker courts, not a whore house as you so eloquently put it. They are used to operating with discretion."

"Do you have to take a refresher course every fifty years or so?" He thinned his lips at her and Faye smiled. Fangs cared if she thought he was bad in bed. "Well," Faye said, as she stood, collecting her basket and knife. "I'll harvest my herbs and come back later to soak when the pool isn't occupied."

Faye glanced at him over her shoulder and smiled as the misted shadows peaked out from under his eyes. "When did you want to visit your fancy brothel?"

"When would you like to go?"

"You look a little long in the tooth today. Tomorrow? Noon to two?" She asked, walking to her gardens.

"Do you wish to witness a novice, a male midway through instruction, or one who nears completion of his formal training?" He asked.

Faye heard water movement and ignored him as she continued picking her herbs. "A novice and an intermediate," she said to her garden.

She heard him step out of the pool. Imagined his hair sticking to his wet body and wondered if he would be hard again? Her nails bit into her palms when she imagined licking the droplets of water off him.

"I will have it arranged and have a meal catered for you. Any requests?"

Faye couldn't have a nice ordinary man who would take her to dinner and the theater. No, instead, she got lunch and a live sex show. "Only that they write *blood* on your glass in big red letters."

He gave a small laugh. "Of course."

Thirty-Five

Sparrow came out of the bathroom in a robe, drying her hair, and stopped when she saw Faye. "You're back early."

Faye fluttered her hand at her sister. "He's taking the day off from poking around in my head. Did you know he's trying to stop The Crumbling?"

Sparrow shrugged. "He's the strongest, makes sense. So, you get the day off when he needs to poke around The Crumbling instead?"

Faye sifted through the leaves she collected, before quietly asking, "Do you ever worry about it?"

"The Crumbling?" Her sister asked. At Faye's nod she snorted, "I don't waste my energy on things out of my control."

It slipped her mind when she wasn't in front of the brazier at the center of her village. She'd seen the destructive force threatening the realms once. Sparrow insisted on the trip as their first adventure.

The Crumbling began more than eight hundred years ago after The Creator, Saith, returned to the Darkness. The Crumbling was a menacing wall made of storm clouds complete with lightning, stretching endlessly into the sky.

The sight filled her with dread, the wrongness of its existence sliding over her. Coating her in an unnatural, dirty film as though she'd been splashed with cloudy stagnant water that reeked of death.

Sparrow had been unbothered, throwing rocks into it and calling them back to see if they really disintegrated. Nothing her sister threw into the clouds returned.

Faye rubbed her hand over her arm, needing to think of anything else. "I'm going on a field trip tomorrow," she said, turning to her sister as she leaned back on the table. "I asked him if you could come, but he said no."

Sparrow rolled her eyes and asked, "Where are you going?"

"He's going to take me to the place he received his training."

Sparrow's arms slumped to her side and the towel fell from her hair. "Are we talking about *training*, training?" Faye giggled and nodded. "And he said I couldn't go?" Sparrow flopped on the bed to stare at Faye upside down. "That man is just evil."

Faye smiled and laid next to Sparrow. "He does rule Hell."

"But does he actually rule anything? He's more like Hell's babysitter."

She supposed her sister was right. Faye flicked a length of Sparrow's damp hair in her face. "Vash never told you about his training?"

Sparrow snorted, brushing the strand away before saying, "He's very hush-hush about it."

Faye wrinkled her nose. "Are you sure he had any?"

"He's really good at it. Why do you think I kept him for so long?"

Faye shoved Sparrow's shoulder. "Because you love him."

"I do love him, but it makes him much easier to love," Sparrow said, bumping her leg against Faye's.

Faye stared at the ceiling thinking of the life she could have. She wouldn't be passing on a life of rejection to her children. She could have the family she dreamed of. A little girl and boy. She turned to her sister. "Do you ever want kids?" Faye asked, glancing at Sparrow.

Sparrow waved her hand in a flourish above them. "Fuck. No. You're the one who wants babies between us."

Would Rune want children? If they were mortal like her, he would be forced to watch them age and die as she would age and die. Faye sat up and cupped her hand over the side of her neck. "I feel selfish... wanting him."

"Are you serious?" Her sister asked, sitting up beside her.

Faye lowered her head. "He's fated to me but I'm still mortal. What happens when I pass my mortality to my children?"

"You're overthinking this, he's fated to you—"

"But fated to what?" Faye whispered. *To watch her age and suffer after she's gone.*

Sparrow linked arms with her. "Let's say you both decide to ignore fate. Tell me you won't think about him for the rest of your life. I know he'll think about you for the rest of his. Is that any better?"

Faye leaned on her sister, wondering which path would inflict the least amount of pain.

"There's a reason he's tied to you. Trust the path fate set before you," Sparrow said quietly.

Faye glanced at her sister. "How are you so sure this is the right path?"

Sparrow beamed and said, "Because I know, I feel it, the same way I knew we would be dark-bloods living a fancy life."

Faye let out a breath. When Rune accepted what was between them was fate, she would let him decide which pain he'd rather endure. She drew a shaking breath. And she would take the steps needed to have a life without him. But when she pictured the simple life she once wanted, standing in the doorway of her cottage with her children, was Rune.

Selfishly she hoped he chose her, but if he didn't, she wasn't going to have some half-life missing him. She would find her own Vashien. A kind day-blood she'd share her life with. "I've been think-ing about what you said, about asking him for something."

"You're not asking— Trade. Same time, I don't know you."

Faye laughed. "I could ask him to find my altar, so I have a soul shard." It would allow her freedom, a future.

Sparrow gave her an approving glance. "That sounds like an even trade."

"But I would still need someone to take me through my ceremony of blood," Faye muttered to herself. He needed her cooperation because she was as strong as he was. Which meant she needed someone as strong as him to perform her rite.

Sparrow's grin widened into a toothy smile. Her green eyes gleaming as she asked, "You want the Shadow Prince to take your virginity?"

Faye flushed, imagining herself beneath him. Her legs tight around his waist as he moved, thrusting into her. "It's a ceremony," she insisted more to convince herself than her sister.

Sparrow hummed her disagreement. "He's pretty. A decent first lay. Have you seen his dick yet?" Faye shook her head. "He's got to have something under that suit." Sparrow elbowed her. "Don't fall in love when he sticks it all the way in."

Faye brushed her hair looking over her reflection. She wore high waisted slacks, a tank top, and topped it off with a soft sweater that hung off one shoulder. Her heeled boots giving her a few more inches of height.

She stepped back into her room and laughed. Her sister growled in cat form as she tried to stuff herself into Faye's too-small purse. A bright light consumed her form and faded as Sparrow sat as a woman on her bed. "That purse is tiny. Why are you even taking it?"

Faye snatched her purse away. "So, I can steal a business card if I see one and bring it back so you can go there later."

Sparrow looked thoughtful for a minute then called her own larger purse. "Take this one. I fit in it, *and* you can shove a business card in it." She shifted back into a small white cat and jumped into the purse, hunkering down as low as she could get. When Faye didn't cover her with the flap, Sparrow poked her head out and pulled it over herself.

A knock startled Faye as she whirled around. Rune stood in her doorway. Faye smiled and picked up the purse Sparrow hid in, slinging it over her shoulder.

His gaze roamed over her and stopped at the bag. He arched an eyebrow at Faye. "The blonde harpy is not coming."

Sparrow poked her head out of the flap and hissed at him.

"How did you know?" Faye asked, putting Sparrow's bag down.

The corner of his mouth lifted. "I have been around Familiar my entire life."

Sparrow wiped her back feet at him and jumped up on the bed to lay down staring at Rune upside down.

He offered his hand. "Shall we?"

Faye took a last look at her sister, offering an apologetic glance. She stepped closer to Rune, placing her hand in his. Dizziness came and dissipated quickly, and Faye found herself in a luxurious room. Similar to the ones in Rune's home. This one was decorated in every shade of red, complete with a four-post bed draped in flowing silk.

A beautiful woman in an antique gold corseted gown curtsied with an effortless grace before Rune. "Shadow Prince," she said and turned to Faye, "Lady."

Rune inclined his head at the woman, and Faye returned her bow. Her beautiful rich brown skin gleamed with a strategic dusting of gold powder. Her hair was arranged in an ethereal cloud of black curls. Rune made their introductions, "Faye, this is Kayla. Kayla, the Lady Faye."

Faye smiled. "It's nice to meet you."

"A pleasure, my Lady." Kayla held her hand out at two ornate chairs arranged on either side of a circular, clothed table covered in various dishes. Candied fruits, cubes of dried meats and cheese, the expensive steak Sparrow ordered with each meal, and her pomegranate juice was neatly arranged among fresh-cut flowers. A small square table beside the further chair held a lone metal wine glass. Faye smiled to herself. It wasn't big red letters, but it would do.

Rune guided her to the closer chair, releasing her hand. Faye took her seat as Rune moved to his. She frowned, how was she supposed to get him to lean in for a kiss sitting across a table. Faye stood and strolled to Rune. He glanced up at her remaining silent, allowing her to take a seat on his thigh. Kayla's eyes widened as her expression turned to a mixture of shock and surprise. Faye noted the woman's reaction, curious if she and Rune had history.

Her mind blanked when Rune stroked her hair, his fingertips brushing across her back. Tingles cascaded over her body with each stroke. Faye smiled at Kayla, staking her claim and she lowered her gaze before leaving the room.

"Do you come here a lot?" Faye wondered how many of these discreet women enjoyed his company. The bite of jealousy stung her when she imagined Kayla with him. Faye shoved that feeling down, smothering it.

"No," he answered simply.

"Oh?" Faye didn't believe him. He lived for thousands of years. He was gorgeous, powerful, and wealthy. His list of lovers was probably as long as she was tall. Faye skewered a candied fruit with a metal stick. "Why did she look at you like that?"

Rune raised a brow, studying her for a moment in silence. "She looked to you. Through your actions, which I am sure were not your intent, you have informed Kayla that you are my whore."

Faye smiled around the candied fruit, sensuously sliding it off the metal pick. She flicked the long piece of metal, pointing it at his eye. "Call me that again and I'll stab you in front of your friends." The corner of his mouth lifted at her remark. That sexy smirk made her heart race.

"I am court born. If I had a romantic interest in a partner, they would be announced before the High Council. To behave this way in public projects the impression I have already," Rune glanced at her metal skewer, then met her gaze. Amusement lit his pale blue eyes. "Had you."

Faye turned away from him to scrutinize the extravagant room as she said, "Well, it's a good thing we're in a whore house." She could feel his disapproving gaze and fought the smile that pulled on her lips.

"This is an exclusive, high-end brothel."

Feigning boredom Faye skewered another piece of fruit as Rune stroked her hair. "You haven't shown me anything that makes me want to join a court."

The door opened, drawing Faye's attention. Kayla returned, leading a tall brunette by the hand. Her eyes made Faye pause. They were entirely white. She leaned closer to Rune, asking in a hushed whisper, "She's blind?"

"You may speak. I have us concealed."

Faye turned toward him and asked, "An invisibility spell?"

"Similar but more complicated. I could still scent you when you and the harpy trespassed into Lyssa's ball."

Faye nodded, studying the brunette. She wore a satin robe matching the antique gold of Kayla's gown. Kayla led her to a plush chaise, where she took a seat.

"She is spelled with temporary blindness," Rune explained. "This is where the darker courts receive training. The women are not entitled to know the identity of those who service them. Kayla is the madame, she and her managers are the only ones privy to the identity of their clients."

Faye hid her shock as Rune explained this like it was commonplace. Dark courts and their sex games. Her eyes widened as Kayla called in a black leather riding crop. "What's that for?" Faye shifted in Rune's lap, resting her hand on his muscular thigh.

A man entered the room wearing a tailored suit much like Rune's.

"Motivation should he not listen. This is the novice beginning his training." Rune's hand left her back as his other hand rested on her knee. His thumb was tracing small circles.

The man's dark shard glowed as he ran his hand through his copper-colored short hair. His pallor complexion wasn't unattractive. Faye watched as he stripped off his jacket and shirt revealing lean, hard muscle. Not as chiseled as Rune, but still appealing.

The male knelt before the woman, taking her hand to press a kiss to the back of it. She brushed her hands over his face, her thumb sliding over his bottom lip. "My name is Erin. What are you?"

"Vampire," the male said and grinned at her answering smile.

Faye glanced at Rune's hand on her knee. The slow lazy circles he traced. She wondered if the vampire was coincidence or if Rune requested one of his kind.

Erin bent forward, giving him a soft kiss before saying, "No fangs."

"As you command," he answered, purring as he nuzzled her palm.

Rune purred for her during their last dream. Catching her finger between his teeth. Faye pushed the memory away, but it remained, teasing at the edge of her mind.

"More and rougher," Erin said. Faye's breath caught as the vampire's purr deepened, the sound humming through the room. She stroked the side of his face. "Good."

Faye wet her lips watching them. Her nipples hardened as the man slowly pulled the sash of the woman's robe. Kayla stood close observing while not obstructing their view of the couple.

She'd seen live sex shows with Sparrow but being here with Rune was different. The way he stroked her hair and the damned circles he traced just above her knee made her too aware of his closeness. Faye shifted her hips. Her breath stilled as she caught friction on Rune's hard thigh beneath her.

"You like to watch." Rune wasn't asking. It was a statement.

One Faye wouldn't dignify with a response. The vampire spread Erin's legs, lowering his head between them and Faye unwittingly tightened her grip on Rune's thigh. He was going to lick her there while he purred. She bit the inside of her lip wondering if Rune would have done the same if she didn't stop him. Their dream would have played out differently if he didn't ask what court she belonged to. If she didn't dig her claws into his throat.

A sharp crack startled Faye out of her thoughts. She jerked at the second, gasping at the touch of friction against her own vampire.

"Do as she commanded and hold your purr," Kayla ordered.

Faye's breaths drew short as she gazed at the red mark left on the man's shoulder. Faye could hear the difference in the male's purr once he corrected it, but she didn't notice it before. How many times had Rune felt that sting while he was a novice?

Faye dragged her bottom lip through her teeth. "Is being commanded part of the training?" She could hear his deep purring voice from their dreams. It felt like a lifetime ago. She'd held his throat not knowing what to do and he'd crooned, *Command me.*

"It is a sentiment of devotion." Rune kept his hand on her knee and swept her hair behind her shoulder.

Eyeing my throat, vampire? Faye dropped her shoulder and turned in his direction but not enough to look at him. "Like love?"

Rune laughed softly behind her, and Faye bristled. "Love is a mortal word. They fall into love and fall out of love a few decades later. Grow apart. Immortals feel deeper. Our devotion is eternal. The sentiment, I am yours to command, means to be an extension of the other's will."

Faye knew those words. He'd spoken them to her during their dreams. He loved her? Her chest tightened with hope before the reality of their situation tore it from her. She was mortal and he'd dismissed their fated tie, claim it to be a spell. Faye buried her hurt, focusing on the couple before her.

Kayla traced the riding crop down the male's spine. "Is she wet, vampire?"

Faye shifted her hips, leaning forward. Rune's thigh was taut beneath her. She moaned quietly, watching the couple before them with hooded eyes. The muscles in the vampire's back rippled as he touched her, pressing a finger in. Erin's breaths grew ragged as she tangled her hands through his copper hair. She pulled him closer, grinding against his mouth.

"You are permitted to get closer if you wish." Rune's voice held a roughened edge, his accent thicker.

Did he like to watch too? Moving closer would mean leaving this perfect friction of his thigh. She was slick, aching for him.

Erin came with a cry, panting for breath.

Faye leaned forward, pressing harder against Rune. "I thought he was a novice."

Thirty-Six

"The caliber of men you associate with is appalling. Bringing a
woman to orgasm is the beginning." Rune ran the back of his
fingers up her spine.

Ask to tend to her.

The Ra'Voshnik prowled his mind, urging him to lay her naked
on his bed. Where he would alternate between worshiping at her altar
and stroking her with his hands while he drank from her inner thigh.

Rune breathed in her scent, laced with her arousal. Darkness, his
fangs throbbed. Aching to sink into the slender column of her throat.
He leaned closer to say at her ear, "The training dark-blooded males
receive is holding a woman's release." He flexed his leg each time she
shifted on him. "Stretching it." Rune stroked Faye's flowing black
hair. The silky texture ran through his fingers. "Overlapping them."

Faye watched the couple, and Rune couldn't help but watch her.

Her subtle movements, the catches of breath. The feel of her rocking against him. The way the beat of her heart picked up when he spoke, all of it enticed him. His gaze fell to the flutter of her pulse.

It was too easy to get lost in her. Rune inwardly shook himself. He should be searching her mind, looking for the spell tying her mortality to him. But he couldn't break free of her pull. Fantasizing even now about holding her close while he thrust into her. The way she would turn up her chin and offer him her throat.

Faye jerked in his lap the same moment Kayla brought the riding crop down on the male's back. He listened to the beat of her heart racing. She liked this. The corner of his mouth lifted. The minx had to control every aspect of her life; it was fitting she would prefer to be in control in the bedroom. She'd taken him by the throat. He grinned at the memory and found himself curious to what other predilections she possessed.

Tend to our queen. Pin her and make her writhe beneath our mouth.

He ignored the Ra'Voshnik's frantic demands, too focused on her. Taking in every reaction. Rune watched as Faye grew still, the tension in her muscles building. Darkness, she was close. He shifted his leg beneath her, needing to ease her ache. "Is my thigh to your liking?"

"Why did she hit him after he made her come?"

Ignoring my question? Rune leaned closer to her, his chest brushing her arm. "Because he failed to hold her release. A less experienced male would press on, pushing harder, attempting to make her come again. We are taught to read her body. Keep the rhythm she sets and know when to push her."

She glanced back at him, her gaze lowering to note the shadows he knew swayed beneath his eyes. "You've done this training," she asked.

"I have."

She leaned forward pressing into his thigh. "How many times did a riding crop meet your back?" Interesting. The minx wanted him under the crop. When it became evident he was not going to answer, she turned back to the couple. "How do they graduate from being a novice?"

"Make her come for ten minutes."

She stiffened for the briefest moment. Then turned so he viewed a teasing profile of her nose and lips. "Ten minutes? That's a novice."

Rune fanned his breath over the shell of her ear and rasped, "A male is fully trained when he can hold her for thirty." He stifled a groan eager to hear the sounds he could elicit from her lips while he worked her body to his satisfaction. The Ra'Voshnik circled just beneath the surface, agreeing with his notion.

She looked back at him fully and rolled her hips. Darkness, he wanted to pin her to him and make her come while he rocked against her.

"You want me."

Take what is offered, the Ra'Voshnik roared as Rune countered, "You are just as affected." He shifted beneath her to prove his point and was rewarded by her breathy sigh.

"You can have me if you take me through my Ceremony of Blood."

The Ra'Voshnik purred through his mind, bringing each position it wanted her in to the front of Rune's thoughts. Rune took hold of the bothersome creature, dragging it to the depths of his mind.

There were so many ways he could please her and leave her virginity intact. "Performing your ceremony is unnecessary, I would use my hands and mouth." A different kind of tension filled her at his words. Rune lifted his chin breathing in her scent. "You ache for me. I could ease you with a bite."

Touch me, he silently pleaded. His night breeze stripped him of reason. His attraction to her a spell holding power over him. But in this moment, he didn't care. He wanted her naked and pinned beneath him. Wanted to taste her desire as she came apart under his mouth.

She met his heated gaze as her full lips curled in a smile. He sucked in a breath when she ran her hand over his chest to his shoulder. "My ceremony is the necessity. Your touch is not." She took a strand of his hair twirling it around her finger. "Aren't you supposed to be looking through my mind for the spell that makes you hard for an unsophisticated peasant?" Her gaze dipped to his straining erection. "Or are you too distracted?"

You've angered our queen again. Let me mend things with her, polished fool. You turn her from us.

Be silent! Rune glared at the minx poised in his lap. "I have not been led by my cock in thirty centuries. I have no intention of start-ing now." Rune gazed past her to the couple. "I am still recovering my strength, my hold over the Ra'Voshnik is tenuous."

"He's the only part of you I like." Faye flicked his strand of hair away, turning away from him, her focus centered on Erin and her vampire.

Let me rise. She prefers me to you! Rune clenched his teeth, grating, "You believe the Ra'Voshnik that resides within me fancies you?"

She lifted her chin in that defiant way he favored and despised in equal portion. "I know he does. I feel him when you search my mind."

"It does not want you."

She ran her hand down the lapel of his jacket, straightening his pristine suit. "Weren't you the one that said, *What good would a lie do between us?*"

Thirty-Seven

Faye pushed off his chest and returned her attention to Erin and her vampire. She kept her back to Rune, who remained silent, withdrawing his touch. His rejection hurt, carving into something deep inside her. Faye reached for her anger, clinging to it desperately.

She glanced at the brunette as she arched her back. Her vampire purred between her thighs, worshiping at her altar as he stroked his fingers into her.

How did she do it? Let these men touch her and not grow attached. Did she miss them when they left? Faye clenched her jaw. Being blinded wouldn't save her. Rune already inhabited all her fantasies. "I've seen enough of your dark court sex games. If you're not going to poke around my head, I'd rather soak in a bath and read."

"You will need to remove yourself from my lap if you wish to return to Hell."

Faye stood and glanced over him. He rose without a word, not looking at her as he held his hand palm up. She placed her hand in his and their surroundings changed, snapping to his study. Rune dropped her hand and went to his desk.

Pain stung her heart. He dismissed her. Like the high bitch queen. Like every other dark-blood. Faye covered the hurt with the only emotion that worked to sooth her. Fiery anger. "Is our meeting concluded for the day?"

"Yes." He didn't look at her, flipping through loose pages on his desk and began reading.

Fuck this guy. She turned, leaving his study. She went to her room, leaving her door to the hall open as she started a hot bath. She opened various oils smelling them, hoping the scent would carry to Rune and his bloodlust would chew on his brain. She selected one that smelled like roses and poured the contents of the bottle into her bath.

She tossed in some mineral salts and a floral bubble bath before she retrieved her book.

Faye sat on the bathroom counter, leaving her door open while she waited for her bath to fill. She shifted, pressing her thighs together. Taking a deep calming breath, Faye rationalized she was sexually frustrated because of what she saw. Simple easy explanation. This was a completely natural reaction and didn't mean she longed for that arrogant dick.

Faye closed the door and locked it. Knowing it wouldn't keep him out since he was a magic wielding, pompous ass who could just poof into places. Still seething, Faye stripped and set her book on the ground near the tub. She stepped into the hot water and moaned as she sank down into it.

She leaned back, closing her eyes. She ran her hand from her throat down her body. Trailing between her breasts to her hip. Sliding lower to the ache between her legs. Her fingers slipped along her wetness. Faye's lips parted as she circled her clit, palming her breast.

She thought of the couple, imagining herself in Erin's place. But the vampire between her thighs didn't have copper colored hair. Long white-blonde hair spilled forward, brushing her inner thighs as his mouth worked her.

Faye moaned quietly, touching herself with both hands. Imagining his tongue on her clit. That it was his fingers that stroked into her.

Her pace increased, imagining Kayla standing behind Rune. Her riding crop struck his shoulder. Faye's lips parted.

Her lids slid closed as she whispered, "Harder."

Her imaginings changed. She now held the crop. Spurring him to her commands.

"Deeper." The words escaped her as a breathy sigh. She rolled her hips, moving at a frantic pace.

Faye imagined brushing the crop down Rune's shoulder, his side. Using it to push his hair from the side of his face so she could watch him worshiping her.

His name escaped her lips.

Rune stared at the loose pages, the only articles that predated Saith. He kept his gaze lowered, refusing to look at Faye. She read him too easily. Held too much sway over him.

She'd left his study and he listened as she ran a bath.

It did nothing for his self-control. Her scent lingered on him, the trace of her arousal stole his clarity and reason.

We would have her, in this very moment, if it weren't for your foolish pride. The Ra'Voshnik thrashed from its confines. Rune buried it deeper until its screams were a far-off echo.

A heavy scent of roses wafted into his study. His brow lowered. Was she emptying vials into her bath? He ran the heel of his palm down his erection. He shouldn't have taken her to witness court training. He shouldn't care if she didn't fit into his world. She wasn't his.

He searched her mind several times, unable to find the spell tying him to her. The result of his effort left one explanation. No, he couldn't be fated to a mortal peasant. She was as affected by their tie as he was. Rune sighed, knowing he lied to himself. He was far more affected by her, and she knew it.

He stood with a growl, abandoning his research. He needed to cleanse her scent from him and clear his mind. He phased to his room and undid his cuff links.

He stilled as Faye moaned. He glanced in the direction of her room as the Ra'Voshnik broke free. It raged to the surface, answering her. Rune's fangs lengthened to sharp points.

She needs us.

Rune growled. He needed to clear his head. The minx tied him in knots and the Ra'Voshnik willingly embraced it. Rune exhaled reaching for patience. He'd offered to tend to her. Wanted to touch her so desperately he would see to her pleasure and forgo his own.

He gritted his teeth as he stripped off his shirt and jacket, tossing them aside in his frustration.

He reached for his pants and stilled as another breathy moan carried to his sensitive ears. He imagined the minx in her bath. Eyes closed. Her head tilted back as her moans slipped from her parted lips. Rune cursed under his breath as she moaned words, driving him to the brink of his control.

"Rune." She moaned his name, and he couldn't be certain if she did so out of passion or scheme. Worse he didn't care.

The Ra'Voshnik circled his mind, urging him to her. For the first time in his long life, Rune and the Ra'Voshnik were in agreement. He opened their adjoining door and stalked to her bathroom. He knocked and the minx gasp, splashing water.

"Go away," she yelled.

Ask to tend to her. Tell her she is our queen and we are hers to command.

"May I speak with you," Rune asked through the door.

"No!"

Rune pressed his hand to the door. "Please."

He heard her step out of her bath followed by the rustle of cloth. The door clicked and she stood before him wrapped in a towel. She glared up at him. "What?"

His dark queen stood before him. Radiant and powerful. A purr rumbled from his throat, and he stepped into her, crossing a line he no longer cared about.

Faye's gold-flecked black eyes widened, and she took a retreating step, igniting every vampiric impulse within him.

Our queen longs to be chased. Rune agreed with the sentiment, taking each step she gave until the counter met her back.

Her breaths became shorter as her pulse raced. Rune leaned closer, resting his palms on the counter on either side of her. He brought his lips a moment from hers and waited. *Touch me,* he silently pleaded, awaiting her invitation.

Faye's hands found his waist, her fingers sliding to hook under his belt. She leaned up brushing her lips over his and Rune closed his eyes. He groaned, unable to deny how right and true if felt to have her in his arms.

He touched the side of her face, gliding his fingers over her jaw before sliding into her hair. Gently tilting her chin, patiently awaiting anything she would offer.

She parted her lips, shyly darting her tongue over the seam of his lips. Rune pulled her closer. She consumed his very being. He deepened their kiss, claiming her mouth with slow deliberate strokes.

Faye moaned against him, sliding her hand lower to run her fingers along his cock. She gripped him more forcefully and the Ra'Voshnik raged to the fore. It grabbed the back of her thighs and lifted her high against him, guiding her legs around his ribs. It kissed her throat and phased them to his bed before Rune regained control.

He pulled back to gage her reaction. Faye didn't seem to notice. She lay against his dark sheets, flushed and panting. A hand in his hair and the other setting her nails to his shoulder.

His lips trailed kisses down her throat, to her collarbone. Lower as he untucked the towel wrapped around her. She tensed as he swept her covering to the side.

Rune moved back up her body. His gaze swept over her, taking in every inch of her before losing himself in her lightning-streaked eyes. "You are the most beautiful sight I have ever beheld." He kissed her at a slow, easy pace. Savoring the feel of her as he ran his fingertips over her side, down her belly, following to her hip, and sliding along her thigh before starting again.

He did this until the tension left her and she softened beneath him. Continued until her nails were biting into his back and she rolled her hips for him.

Rune trailed kisses down her body. He teasingly flicked his tongue over her nipple, and she arched up. Her nails scored his back. He licked and sucked, teasing her breasts in an attempt to have her mark him again.

She didn't, still shy, gentle with her touch. Rune pulled her to the end of his bed and knelt before her. He eased her thighs over his shoulders and parted her gently. Groaning before his tongue swept through her slick folds. She tasted like her scent. Subtle, with a hint of sweetness.

The Ra'Voshnik purred through his mind, *She tastes better than I imagined.*

He didn't purr, only pressed his mouth to her to tease, lick, and nibble at her delicate flesh.

Faye arched her back, rocking her hips against him. Rune watched her responses, adjusting his pressure and timing. He took her clit between his lips, teasing her with a gentle suck while his tongue worked.

She tensed, digging her heels into his back as he moved in time with her body. He purred softly. A hint of vibration travelling over her. Faye gave a breathy cry arching her back harder, and he stopped.

"No, please." Faye reached down, touching the side of his face. "I liked it."

Rune began again, and Faye spread her legs further. Her hand tangled in his hair just behind his temple.

"A little harder." Faye panted, pulling his hair as she rocked her hips against his mouth.

She tensed; her body strung tight as she closed her legs over his head. She scratched at the sheets, tightening her hold on his hair.

"Rune." She cried his name as she came.

Rune eased his touch. He pulled back to lick through her folds savoring her taste. He moved lower, pressing his tongue inside her. Reveling in the intimate fluttering he was responsible for. Faye drew a shuttered breath, and he did it again.

"If you told me I would end up in your bed when you first brought me here, I wouldn't have believed you."

Rune froze as her words sank into his desire riddled mind. He pulled away and rose to his feet, wiping his hand over his mouth. *What had he done?*

He brought the minx to his bed. *Pleasured her* in his bed.

Our queen belongs in our bed.

Rune took a step back as a single thought echoed through his mind before he phased out of his room.

She is not mine.

Thirty-Eight

Bliss rained through Faye's body, soft and gentle, echoing a pleasure she'd never experienced alone. She stretched her arms overhead, dragging her legs together. She would need him to show her what he liked so she could return his affection. She knew a lot in theory and eagerly wanted to apply them to Rune.

Faye curled on her side with a lazy smile, still catching her breath. Her brow pinched. He wasn't at the edge of the bed. Faye twisted to glance behind her at the bathroom. The door opened to a darkened room.

"Rune?" Faye called, sitting up. An empty silence rang within her as she stood, covering herself with her towel. Her euphoria faded with each step. Leaning into his bathroom, she found a darkened room staring back at her.

Faye rocked back on her heels as her face fell. He left. Hurt and shame warred within her, colliding so fiercely it eclipsed her anger. She pulled her towel tighter around her. Faye left his room needing to get away. From him. From his scent. From everything that reminded her of him.

She made her way back to the south wing, holding her tears at bay. Not caring who saw her as she walked. She'd been so happy just minutes ago. He'd left without a word, leaving her feeling used and dirty.

Soft light filtered into the room through three tall arched windows. Faye trudged past them, her begrudging steps leading her to the bathroom. Faye closed the door and let her towel drop to the floor.

She turned the shower on and sat in the spray. Hot water sluiced over the back of her neck and shoulders. Faye hugged her shins, lowering her head to her knees. Her tears fell, hot and silent, as she hugged her legs tighter.

"Bitch?"

Faye stared at a tile beside her, letting the tears fall from her unblinking eyes. She didn't fight the misery threatening to consume her. Didn't respond to the knock at the door. Didn't acknowledge her sister as she stepped into the bathroom.

Sparrow opened the glass door and crouched into Faye's vision. "Hey, are you— What happened?"

Faye met her sister's gaze, and her tears somehow came harder.

"It's okay, you're okay," Sparrow said, getting to her feet and awkwardly stepping over her. Her sister sat down and wrapped her in her arms, pulling her close. Sparrow rocked her, resting her cheek on the top of her head as she stroked her back.

"Did he hurt you?" Faye vaguely registered the viciousness in her sister's voice.

Yes! No. She squeezed her eyes shut, clinging to Sparrow's arm. Her voice came out a broken plea, "What's wrong with me?"

"Nothing is wrong with you," Sparrow said against her hair.

"He's fated to me," Faye sobbed. *I feel it.* "Why am I not enough?"

"Oh, honey," Sparrow said, squeezing her tighter. "You are more than enough. This is that shadowy fuck's damage, not yours."

Sparrow held her as she cried. There *was* something wrong with her. Some integral piece she was lacking. Faye knew it. Rune knew it. Even fate knew and carved away so much from her because of it.

"Did he say something to you? I'm about to stab his bitch ass."

Faye took a shuttering breath. "We were intimate," she said blinking through the hot rush of tears. "Then he left."

"You blew him, and he left?" Acid dripped from Sparrow's words, a burning promise of pain.

Faye shook her head. "I didn't touch him," she whispered. She didn't understand. He yearned for her. She saw it stirring in his dark gaze. He came to her. Pleaded at her door. Went to his knees— for her. Then he abandoned her without a word.

"Fuck him. Fate tied you to an idiot. If he doesn't appreciate you, it's his loss, not yours."

Faye leaned on her sister in silence, muttering, "I wish I didn't care." *Or want him. Or see him when I thought about the life I wanted.* Faye exhaled and so much more left her as she said, "He's going to haunt me for the rest of my life."

Sparrow snorted. "No, bitch. I won't let him. I guarantee you his ass is haunted by you." Faye remained silent as her tears slipped down her nose, lost within the misted spray of the shower. The hot water washing over her did not drown out the feel of him. The way his hands carefully left a trail of his embrace. She wanted it gone. Needed it stripped clean. Cast away his touch and abandonment. Her sister squeezed her, holding her through her silence and misery.

"I know he's thinking about you right now. You consume his every waking moment."

Thirty-Nine

Rune materialized in his father's crystalline palace. The vast hall stretching before him, it's arching walls raising into a vaulted ceiling, constructed more like a chapel than a throne room. Large crystals lined either side of the hall, encapsulating the unfortunate beings who garnered his father's wrath.

They stood as eternal sentries, broken in mind and body, condemned as ornaments his father used to decorate his palace. Time stretched past them, holding no meaning. Those encased were unable to die and return to the Darkness.

Rune's image flickered several times, and he bared his fangs. His head whipped to the side as he demanded, "Cease this!"

Return to her! The Ra'Voshnik roared, raising through his mind, fighting for dominion of his body.

Fury roiled through Rune. "You brought her to my bed. Desecrated what I would offer my queen!"

She is our queen.

"She is not my queen!" Rune bellowed as the crystal beneath him cracked, splintering from him in every direction. The cracks deepened, widening as they split the walls of the throne room.

She was not his fate. She couldn't be his. Fate would not condemn him so thoroughly. Not like this.

Chest heaving, Rune surveyed the damage he caused. He mastered his powers millennia ago. He hadn't lost control since his youth. Before he could mend the damage, the Ra'Voshnik sank its claws into his awareness and dragged his consciousness into the depths of his mind.

Rune descended into himself, meeting it. He had enough of the fool creature and its incessant want for the mortal death awaiting him. Desire was as fleeting as pain. Wanting the minx was irrelevant when the cost was his life.

Pain sank into his throat as he stood before the Ra'Voshnik. A replica of himself that could not be more different. It sank its claws deeper into either side of his neck. Pain was a fleeting thing, and the creature finally found the end of Rune's patience.

His will did not bend. Not for a spell. Not for a peasant. And certainly not for the Ra'Voshnik who invited their very death to his bed.

"Your will is already hers. You didn't mind her in your bed when you were feasting between her thighs. She is everything we've dreamed of, *and you left her!*" The Ra'Voshnik's claws connected behind Rune's windpipe as it hissed, "I will return to her and mend things."

Rune seized its wrist and squeezed. Crushing bones until the grip on his throat slacked and fell away. He speared his other hand into the creature's chest in a practiced motion, and tore its heart free. The Ra'Voshnik's dark eyes clouded as it collapsed at his feet.

Rune kicked it onto its back. Pausing for the briefest moment as he gazed down his own dead form.

He'd always imprisoned it in his mind, viewing the bothersome creature as the cost of his power. It would continue to heedlessly court his death. The spell must be tied to the Ra'Voshnik. If he killed it, would he still be a Pure Blood? He would remain a Shadowman like his brothers. Like his father. Become lesser as a turned vampire perhaps?

It mattered not. The consequence was a necessity, this spell had gone on longer than Rune could tolerate. Killing the Ra'Voshnik would sever the tie the minx held over him. The leash she unknowingly held. Yanking him closer with every exchange.

Rune knelt beside the fallen creature taking it by the throat. He took a final breath bracing himself for pain he was sure would follow. With a twist of his wrist its head separated from its shoulders.

He'd expected agony. A tearing of some kind when he ended the creature. But Rune felt nothing. He got to his feet, the Ra'Voshnik's head lie on its side, its long white-blonde hair staining red in the growing pool beneath it.

The Ra'Voshnik blinked before its gaze swept up to meet his.

Rune recoiled as a smirk formed over the creature's mouth. "Did you honestly believe all those centuries you studied under Saith— *Until our body failed you,* I haven't killed you?" It laughed then settled itself with a sigh before saying, "You have died dozens of times, while our body lay unconscious, recovering."

The creature's form dissipated into smoke and shadow, its dark shadowy gaze lingering, being the last to fade. Its disembodied voice echoed around him, travelling upward.

You can't kill me. We are two halves of the same coin. There is no separation for ones like us. We exist in tandem or not at all.

A mental barrier fell over Rune, caging him. *You can wait in the shadows while I return to our queen.*

Rune's power rose, answering his fury. The fool creature sought to trap him and take possession of his body. *Never.* The mental bindings shattered around him as he ascended to his physical body.

"My will is greater than yours. Every deed you commit, every thought that rattles through your fool mind— *Is because I allow it.*" Rune stalked to the edge of the hall, a pillar of shimmering crystal rising to meet him. His realm obeying his will.

Rune touched the pillar, spreading his fingers wide. He summoned the Ra'Voshnik and cast its consciousness into the crystal. The creature did not separate from his mind. Rune tried a second time to no effect.

Frustration mounted in Rune. He dropped his hand, burying the creature within the recesses of his mind until he no longer felt its frantic thrashing. Rune stalked toward his father's throne, while the creature's roar echoed from its confines. *Return to her!*

Rune growled, rubbing his hand over his bare chest. With a flicker of his mind a trunk appeared before him. Rune crouched and opened it, withdrawing a shirt. He stood, roughly pulling it on. He'd finished buttoning it before he recognized the boots trapped within the crystal pillar beside him.

His gaze lifted to a woman. Fiery red hair fanned out around her, still and suspended in her prison. Her chromatic sage gaze met his and a dark smile spread over his lips. She was a broken mind trapped in flesh that would never return to the Darkness. Sadi had broken her mind and shattered her core, centuries ago. Stripping her of the day-blood shard she once carried. Rune sealed what remained of her flesh with his father's other gruesome curiosities.

Forever imprisoned in Standing Shadows.

"Sadira," Rune said, inclining his head, greeting the queen who enslaved him for a hundred and thirty-seven years. Her gaze flicked over him and frantically searched her surroundings. "Lovely to see you as always."

Rune strolled away from her approaching his father's macabre throne. Julian was created with nine other shadowmen as caretakers to Hell and serve Saith.

His father rebelled against Saith, along with the other shadow-men in what would be known as the Great War. After his father's victory, Julian killed each of his brethren. Using their bones to construct a throne Rune never sat in.

He walked passed the grisly chair to the passageway behind it, leading to their family's quarters. Rune climbed the steps needing silence and distance to clear his mind. The minx consumed his thoughts, eroding his will. He would ask Sadi to look into his mind, perhaps she could see the spell binding the minx to the Ra'Voshnik.

Rune's thoughts wandered to Faye. He could still feel her, hear her breathy sighs. Her taste lingering on his tongue making it impossible to center his thoughts. He silently strolled the familiar halls, needing to cleanse Faye's scent from him.

Darkness, let me find the spell tying her to me.

Remaining with her was a death sentence.

Don't let her be mine.

Forty

Faye's days merged together as she stared at the ceiling wide awake, Sparrow snoring sound asleep beside her. Each time her eyes closed, she remembered. His touch. The feel of his mouth. The way his hair slid over her inner thigh while he worshiped at her altar.

The soft light from the twilight sky remained constant, bathing the room in a romantic glow. Rune had carried her to his bed, wrapped up in the way he made her feel. A mistake she wouldn't be repeating. He wanted her enough to taste her but wouldn't perform her ceremony. Faye shifted in the plush bed, pulling the blankets tighter around her.

He avoided her the past two days. Faye searched for him but he was nowhere to be found. The first day she'd wanted his absence, spending the day in bed. Letting her pain consume her. Sifting through the misery he created. The second she went looking for him, determined to corner him and tell him exactly what she thought of his behavior. But their host was absent.

Faye went to his study and reluctantly peeked into his room, retreating when she caught sight of his bed. She went to the hot spring, finding it empty, and in her desperation, she sought out her evil twin. But it seemed she and her male were scarce as well.

Sparrow groaned and pulled the blanket over Faye's face. "Go to sleep," she grumbled.

Faye pulled the blankets down and blew her hair out of her face. "I'm not making any noise, hooker."

"I can hear the gears in your head smoking," Sparrow said, rubbing her eyes. "Did you want to go look for him again?"

Did she? She was so angry with him but a small part of her, a tiny part she hated, missed him.

"Ok let's go hunt down the shadow dick," her sister said, rolling out of bed. She pulled a robe over her nightgown and Faye did the same.

They went to Rune's wing and Faye followed Sparrow as she entered Rune's study. Faye went to his desk. The same papers topped it, in the same small piles. The same books. Everything as it had been yesterday.

Sparrow picked up the pile of yellowed pages closest to her. "I'm in your study, Runey," she said, tossing the pages over her shoulder. The parchment scattered in all directions, coming to rest at the foot of two bookshelves.

"What are you doing?" Faye hissed.

Sparrow waved her off, saying, "I'm getting your man's attention." To the air she yelled, "I know you're here shadow dick." She grabbed another stack of papers and flung them over her shoulder, before knocking the books to the ground.

Faye stared wide eyed with her mouth a gape. "Don't—"

"It's already done. Come on," Sparrow said, grabbing Faye's wrist. She dragged her along to Rune's bedroom and threw the door open. Faye dug in her heels and cringed; afraid he would be in his bed. Or dressing.

Sparrow paid her no mind, shouting, "Runey! It was very rude to go down on my sister and leave. At least wait for her to tell you to go away."

Faye's gaze fell to Rune's four post bed, relieved he wasn't there.

She grabbed Sparrow's wrist with both hands, forcefully pulling the petite blonde away, needing to distance herself from his bed.

Sparrow twisted out of her grasp and sprinted toward the four-post bed draped in dark silk. "Sparrow!" Faye yelled as her sister leaped onto his bed.

"I'm on your bed shadow bitch! Come stop me," Sparrow yelled, jumping up and down on Rune's bed. After a few moments she stilled as her shoulders slumped. "I really thought that would work," she said, bouncing down to sit on his dark sheets.

Faye widened her eyes motioning for Sparrow to join her at the door. "He's probably going to smell you and have a tantrum. Come on."

Sparrow flopped back on his sheets and turned toward the pillows. "Which side does he sleep on?"

"Sparrow," Faye hissed, as her sister snatched the pillow closest to her and laid her head on it. Her brow came down as she sniffed the pillow. "Does he smell like this?" Sparrow asked, taking another deep breath. "What cologne is this. It would smell better on Vash."

Faye stalked to her sister and ripped the pillow away from her, tossing it back on what she imagined would be his side of the bed. "We can't be in here."

Sparrow snorted, making no move to get up. "You've been sleeping like shit. I vote we sleep here until his shadowy highness comes home." Sparrow rolled over to retrieve the pillow Faye threw. "You can curl up to this until he gets back," her sister said, shoving it to Faye's chest.

Faye knocked it away. "I don't want it."

Sparrow eyed her and scooted further in on the bed, getting under his sheets. She fingered the silk. "He's a dick but he likes very nice things. Come on," she said throwing the sheet back in invitation.

"What are you doing?" Vashien's voice startled Faye.

Sparrow flopped down on Rune's bed to peer behind Faye. "Sleeping here with Faye until Runey comes back."

"You are insane," Vashien said, catching Sparrow by the ankle and dragging her to the end of the bed.

Sparrow was dead weight, fisting the dark silk, saying, "I know he'll come back if he senses us in his room."

Vashien took a breath, scrubbing his hand over his face. "Get up."

"It's a good plan," Sparrow whined.

Vashien grabbed Sparrow's arm and bent down to throw her over his shoulder.

"Put me down!" Sparrow squirmed, still holding Rune's sheet that dragged from Rune's bed. Vashien exited the room and Faye followed closing the door.

Sparrow ran her hand along the inside of his wing, near his back and Vashien nearly stumbled. "Don't do that," he said, thumping her with his wing.

"Put. Me. Down." Sparrow said, doing it again.

Her sister and Vashien vanished. Faye stopped in the hall, deciding she didn't want to be in the east wing while they worked out their argument.

Faye glanced into Rune's study and the mess Sparrow left. She rubbed the back of her neck, walking in, refusing to glance at the settee before the fireplace. She gathered the papers, not knowing what piles they were originally in. She made the same neat stacks and arranged them on his desk as they had been.

She picked up the books next, setting them on the corner of his desk. She strolled to his chair running her hand over it. He couldn't stay gone and just leave them in Hell. He had to come back. Didn't he?

Faye's hand dropped as she turned away. She could spend the morning in the gardens. The sunlight would warm her and settle her mind until Rune decided to show his face. She wasn't sure if she wanted to rage at him or demand an explanation. She wanted both.

She smiled to herself. Stabbing him crossed her mind on more than one occasion. Nothing an immortal couldn't heal from. She wasn't sure what vampires viewed as affection, so she stayed her hand. Refusing to offer him something he might find pleasurable.

Forty-One

Rune stood on an open terrace, surveying his realm. The Ra'Voshnik roared from its confines, thrashing against the bindings holding it in place. The creature demanded its freedom, wanting to return to the minx. Relentlessly fighting him for the past three days.

He felt Sadi phase into his realm, arriving behind him.

Why is she here? She offends our queen. Remove her from your presence.

Rune ignored the creature turning to Sadi. She raised a brow, glancing him over. "You don't look well."

Because you are near! The Ra'Voshnik's scream echoed through Rune's mind.

"I need your expertise," Rune said, leaning against a crystal pillar.
Sadi nodded in answer and agreement.

"I need you to search the Ra'Voshnik's mind and locate the spell binding it to the mortal."

"I doubt your overgrown bloodlust will let me near it," she said.

"I will remedy that."

Sadi glanced around her. "We would be more comfortable in Chaos."

Rune infrequently visited the Familiar's home realm. Morbid closed his realm to outsiders and Rune had only been to Morbid's estate. With a sigh, Rune admitted, "I am unable to phase. It is trying to return to Faye as we speak. Stopping it is hindering my ability."

"I can take us," Sadi said, as their images flickered. Her midnight eyes met his gaze as she tensed, trying again. They flickered once more, and she bared her teeth. "Do you want me to seal the creature in its own mind while I'm at it?"

I will kill her before I allow her to touch me, the Ra'Voshnik answered.

"Let us see how difficult it is to locate the spell before we consider other arrangements for it," Rune said, nodding to Sadi before he descended into himself.

She appeared beside him a moment later, standing at a depth within his power comfortable for her. A growl echoed from far below them. Sadi looked down at the black marble at her feet, and said, "He sounds rather upset."

"The fool creature is fixated on Faye. I need the tie to her mortality broken."

Sadi stepped away from him and waved her hand. What looked to be a stone alter large enough to hold a man appeared before them. Large, free standing candelabras were positioned at each corner illuminating the space.

"You can confine him?" She asked. At Rune's nod she patted the stone.

Rune summoned the Ra'Voshnik, binding it to form and mentally restraining it to the stone. It fought him viciously, struggling against the altar.

Sadi's eyes widened, and her jaw slacked for a moment before she recovered her composure. "He looks like you."

"It has since our first meeting," Rune said quietly.

The Ra'Voshnik focused on Sadi. "When I get free, I will bring your head to my queen as a gift."

Sadi stroked the side of its face, not flinching as it snapped its fangs at her. "She is your death, but I will free you of her soon enough," she quieted, standing beside the altar, staring off into nothing.

Moments passed and Sadi pulled back sharply as the Ra'Voshnik laughed. It turned to Rune, "She didn't appreciate me showing her how we worshiped at Faye's altar." It grinned, turning its attention back to Sadi, "We knelt to her for a *very* long time."

Sadi hissed at it, grabbing its face under its chin. Her nails dug into either side of its mouth. It smiled up at her. "You look betrayed," it crooned, then said, "Know I would still be feasting on her if I wasn't bound to a frightened bitch who ran."

It parted its lips, inhaling deeply. "You taste of jealousy, want, and death."

Rune willed it quiet, silencing its lies. He could not taste Sadi or Morbid's emotions, and the creature sought to sow discord. Rune waited patiently, giving Sadi the time she needed to search its mind.

Time passed, stretching as Sadi remained still over the Ra'Voshnik. As Rune began to grow concerned, Sadi shoved away from the creature and left his mind. "What did you do?"

"She doesn't appreciate the desire we have for our queen."

Rune cursed in High Tongue and returned it to its prison before ascending to his body. Sadi stood, waiting for him. "Tell me you weren't kneeling before the mortal."

"Did you find a spell?"

Sadi searched his eyes and turned away. "I combed through its mind twice while it showed me all the things it wanted to do to Faye. You need to distance yourself from her, Rune. She's death. Not just yours. Everyone. Whatever you two are doing will bring down the realms."

"I have it under control."

She stepped toward him. "You don't. I can discern fantasy from memory. He showed me *memories*. You are too tangled in this. Too close to her. There is no spell, Rune."

"You found no spell tied to the Ra'Voshnik?" That couldn't be. Rune stepped away to wipe his hand over his mouth.

Sadi shook her head as the creature's voice echoed from far below him, *She is your fate. Accept it.*

She is not mine! Rune's growl echoed through his mind silencing the Ra'Voshnik.

Rune didn't fear death. He expected to embrace the Darkness in a war or in some other fashion defending his court.

All my efforts on you will be wasted.

His mentor's words echoed through his memory, haunting him for centuries. Had Saith somehow known this would befall him? A mortal would drag him closer to the grave with each passing day.

A muscle ticked in his jaw. His death would be senseless and would leave his court vulnerable. Lyssa would be challenged as High Queen without the strength of her court behind her. Morbid did not participate in wars stating it was fate and it was not his place to interfere. Sadi fought alongside him but would not do so for Lyssa.

The weight of his years bore down on him. Too much rested on his shoulders to accept the fate the Ra'Voshnik embraced too eagerly. Fate could not be this cruel. Ending him, destroying what remained of his court, and his court's legacy in one arcing swing. This could not be fate.

Rune closed his eyes silently pleading, *Don't let her be mine,* while the Ra'Voshnik's laughter echoed far below him.

Forty-Two

Five days came and went since Rune left her in his bed, and he was still nowhere to be found. Vashien tried to phase out of Hell yesterday, and it'd been disastrous. Vashien flickered, and Rune's magic crackled, throwing him into a wall where he fell. Unconscious.

He'd cracked a bone in his wing, and Sparrow was hysterical over his still body. Faye had struggled to pull his arm from beneath him to show her sister his soul shard was still surrounded by dark mist. "He's fine. He's alive." Faye had said, and her sister calmed.

They'd tucked him into bed. His wing hung at an unnatural angle and Sparrow covered it with a blanket. Sparrow decided to let it regenerate naturally, afraid her inexperience in healing might leave his wing damaged.

He'd woken this morning and Sparrow was still doting over him. Faye left the love birds alone, giving them some privacy.

Faye walked through the hall leading to Rune's room and study, ready to peek into his two rooms and spend the rest of the day in the hot spring.

Faye approached Rune's study and glimpsed leather-bound books piled on the floor in high stacks through the door. Her brow knit together as she leaned in. Rune stood among the stacks of books, placing them in his bookshelf.

His empty bookshelf.

Her eyes widened as she glanced over the rest of his study. Every book was turned, their pages facing out instead of their spines. Faye covered her mouth to keep from laughing. Her gaze turned to him. He kept his back to her, ignoring her presence as he continued his work.

Like she didn't exist. Like she was never in his bed. Faye gnashed her teeth and picked the closest book, whipping it at his back. "Where have you been?" She asked, her voice raising with her fury.

"Does it matter?" He answered. "It would seem you and the blonde harpy kept yourselves amused in my absence." He reached down, picking up the book she hurled at him and returned it to its rightful pile.

"You don't get to pretend nothing happened. What the fuck is your problem?"

"My fucking problem? I had a moment of weakness." He peered at her, pinning her with his pale blue gaze. "I recall you enjoying it."

She'd planned what she was going to say to him. She'd seen their whole conversation play out in a number of different ways. This wasn't one of them.

Hurt and pain cut through her, tearing open wounds still raw and aching inside of her. Wounds he inflicted. She stepped closer, suppressing the urge to take the book he shelved and throw it at him. Needing him to hurt the way he hurt her. She tensed, dropping her shoulder back and he spoke, stilling her movements.

Rune spoke in a low tone, glancing down at the book he held. "I am sorry."

Faye's anger choked her. "You don't get to be sorry!" She yelled, shoving him. Her fury mounted twisting into something different. An unfamiliar rage circled for an outlet, demanding to be loosed.

"You came to me," she yelled, hitting him again.

"You pretended to want me."

"You left me!" Faye hit him and her fury found its outlet.

A deafening crack snapped through the space. Faye's shirt pulled tight and gave as her back went rigid at the new weight.

Black curling mist exploded as her hands met Rune's chest. Rune struck the stone wall behind him. Faye jerked at the sickening crack, and he fell to his knees. It was the wall Faye stared at. A deep depression embedded into the stone. Cracks fissuring away from it.

Rune's wet cough dragged her attention lower. His hair was cast forward, the ends sweeping the ground. Smearing red splatter that speckled the stone tiles between his hands.

"I'm sorry," Faye said, rushing beside him, toppling his piles of books with her wings. She pulled his hair to the side. "I'm so sorry," she repeated, smoothing her hand over his back. She yanked her hand away when she touched jagged ridges that didn't belong in a back.

"Sparrow!" She screamed into the hall. To him she muttered, "It's okay. You'll be okay. Sparrow can fix you."

His hand covered hers, and he drew a labored breath. "I am well." He shifted his back and bursts of popping wet sounds filled the space between them until his back smoothed.

Faye stared, unable to look away. "I thought only women could heal."

"Vampire," was all he said, his voice a horse whisper. Rune pulled his shoulder back. Another snap sounded and he stood. Offering her his hand.

"Bitch?" Sparrow held either side of the doorway, leaning into Rune's study. Her sister glared at Rune, her wings, and the damage done to the wall. "Nice wings," she finally said as Vashien came to a halt behind her.

Faye pulled her wings in tighter, knocking over another stack of books in the process while Vashien stared at her.

"Quit eyeballing her," Sparrow said, elbowing Vashien in the side.

"Sorry," Vashien muttered and smiled at Faye.

"You, shadow dick. You're lucky she already beat your ass. I'm watching you." Sparrow held two fingers in a V and lifted her chin. She stabbed them to either side of her windpipe and pointed at Rune before walking out. Vashien in tow behind her.

Faye glanced at Rune's hand and stood without his assistance.

He lowered his hand and stepped around her. Faye turned with him, "We're not done."

"I am sure we are not, however after your outburst I am in need of blood. Unless you are offering, it would be kind of you to continue our discussion at my desk."

Faye followed him, watching as he plucked a wine bottle and glass out of the air. He poured a glass and drank it down faster than Sparrow could. He refilled it and motioned to the seat across his desk.

She stood beside the chair, growing suddenly tired. She stifled a yawn and glanced down at the chair. "You don't have wing friendly furniture," she said, stretching her wings out a little. The motion betrayed her, and Faye arched her wings back, yawning.

"Noted," he said, filling his third glass. He strolled to the settee, and Faye remained where she stood. Her breaths came a little faster. He glanced back at her, sipping his drink. "You can sit with your back to the fire."

That worked when she was curled up to his chest, reading a book. "I'll stand."

Rune silently walked back to her and leaned on his desk. "I should not have left you as I did."

Faye met his gaze. "Why did you leave?"

He took a deep breath and stared toward the door for long moments.

Was he wishing he could leave? Thinking about whatever woman he was with? Faye's thoughts spiraled until she derailed them by saying, "Why are you willing to do that, but not my ceremony?"

He tapped his index finger against his glass once. Twice. "The ceremony puts you in danger, which places my life in jeopardy. My answer is no."

Faye's wings sagged. She glanced up at him even though he wouldn't meet her gaze, and said, "Wouldn't it be safer if I can heal myself. I would be harder to kill. Me alive, equals you alive. Win, win."

He finished his glass and set it on his desk between them. Meeting her pleading gaze, he said, "You have not invoked your blood. The risk outweighs any benefit a Ceremony of Blood could offer. You would be gifted a tendril and left without the shard needed to wield it."

"You need me to cooperate with you because I'm as strong as you are."

"You are stronger." His voice was deadpanned as he watched her.

Faye's brow lowered as she dropped his gaze. She couldn't be stronger than him. Her heart pounded harder as she swayed on her feet. She was getting so tired, her energy slipping from her like water through parted fingers. "Somethings wrong," Faye muttered.

Rune took her arm, steadying her. "Shifting is taxing until you are able to control it."

"I'm not done…" Faye's words slurred as the edges of her vision blackened. The room spun, and Faye was moving. She lifted her feet into her view. Moving but she wasn't walking. She peered up at the underside of Rune's chin. He was carrying her. "I'm not done talking to you," she said, laying her head on his chest.

"I know," he answered.

Faye was nestled into a soft bed as warm blankets were pulled around her. She turned on her side as her mind drifted. "I know I don't end up with you, but I need you for my ceremony. I want a family one day. Is that so hard to understand?"

The weight at her back faded as her consciousness slipped. She vaguely heard him speak as the blankets tucked around her sleeping form.

"I will think on it."

Forty-Three

Faye picked at her dinner. She sat with her sister and Vashien at the table in the den. She'd woken up a short while ago tucked into bed in the room adjacent to Rune's, starving. Now that she was fully awake, replaying her conversation with Rune, she quickly lost her appetite.

Sparrow poured herself a shot, swinging her leg under the table. "Did you two make up and he's going to do your ceremony now?"

Faye swallowed, putting her fork down. "He said no."

Still holding the neck of the bottle, her sister wrinkled her nose. "What do you mean he said no?"

"I asked him, and he said no," Faye said flatly, not wanting to talk about it. Anger and hurt simmered in her, leaving a bitter taste in her mouth. Faye couldn't grasp how he could want her, take her to his bed, make her finish harder than she ever had in her life. But performing her ceremony? Out of the question.

My answer is no.

She tightened her grip around her glass and a sudden urge filled her with an alarming intensity. She imagined crawling into his lap, yanking his hair back to expose his neck, and biting the base of his throat. Faye ran her hand through her hair dismissing the impulse. She spent too much time with the vampire. She was starting to think like him.

Sparrow snorted pulling her attention back to the table. "Does the guy only fuck vampires? Tell him you'll bite him. I'll glamour you up with fangs and everything."

Vashien shook his head finishing his wine a little too quickly. He set his glass down and said to Faye, "Don't feel bad. He's performed one ceremony."

Sparrow coughed, "What? Top shelf, trained male, and he did one?"

Vash nodded. "He did the High Queen's ceremony."

"And he was that bitch's consort," Sparrow added. "Maybe he only likes stuck up bitches. Tell him you'll wear designer heels and step on his neck."

Faye's mood soured with each syllable that passed her sister's lips, distilling her anger into a bitter rage. She couldn't help but wonder if Rune left the High Queen just as quickly. But she and Rune were the same. Perfect. Polished. Royal.

"He was her consort much later. He was with her for a century and relinquished the title," Vashien clarified.

Sparrow laughed before taking another bite of steak. "He left the High Queen. Maybe he prefers males." Her eyes widened. "Or he's impotent. I have a gold mark that says he can't get it up. There are rumors you know. I didn't believe them but maybe."

"He's not impotent," Faye muttered.

The table fell silent as Vashien, and Sparrow looked at her like she'd grown horns. "Bitch have you seen his," Sparrow asked, waving two fingers.

"No," she answered. Quieter she added, "I felt it."

Some part of him wanted her. She had no issues getting his attention. It was the man who chose to ignore her. His deep accented voice crept through her mind.

I have not been led by my cock in thirty centuries. I have no intention of starting now.

He desired her but she wasn't good enough. Darkness, did she tell him she wanted a family one day when he carried her to bed. The memory was a fuzzy half dream. She hoped she'd been dreaming and didn't blurt that out to him. She sped past his study wanting to avoid him until she worked up the nerve to know for sure.

Sparrow slapped the table in front of her, pulling her from her thoughts. Faye glanced up at her sister. "What kind of handful did you get?" Her sister asked as Vashien groaned, scrubbing his hand over his face.

"Stop groaning, this is important," Sparrow said to Vashien over her shoulder since she was standing on her knees in her chair, leaning over the table to Faye. "What kind of 'C' are we talking?" Sparrow held her hand in front of her, squeezing her fingers together to mimic something Faye wasn't interested in reliving.

"We're not discussing this," she said.

"Fine," Sparrow huffed, going back to her seat. Her eyes lit and it was Faye's turn to groan. "Tell me how you slammed him into the wall. And those wings. They're shimmery like the Hell crystals. If that's not enough to show his shadowy highness your fated, I don't know what is. We need to get you a whole new wardrobe. You should be wearing those bitches out all the time."

Faye pushed the food around her plate. "I don't know how to make them come out. Or stay."

"You slept most of the day. You should be eating," Vashien said, sliding Faye's plate closer to her.

"Did you see the dent in the wall she knocked Runey into?" Sparrow asked Vashien.

"Darkness, woman. Let your sister eat."

"Fine."

Forty-Four

The Ra'Voshnik circled his mind, furious to be out of Faye's company the past two days. *Go to her,* it growled, stalking the edges of his mind.

She is avoiding us. Give her time.

Rune leaned back on his heels surveying the chaos the blonde harpy reduced his study to. The bookshelves were half emptied, the volumes stacked according to subject. It would take him another week to right his library.

Footsteps carried to him. Faye walking up the hall, her stride distinctively longer than her sister's when she walked alone. The Ra'Voshnik perked up immediately. *Tell her we miss her,* it purred through his mind.

The creature was not helping his situation. Rune paused, glancing over the tomes, realizing he'd shelved the last three books incorrectly.

He rearranged the volumes and spoke into his mind.

Give her space. She will see us when she is ready.

The creature growled its disagreement and attempted to phase them into the hallway.

Calm yourself or I will bury you.

The Ra'Voshnik circled his mind, running its claws over Rune's awareness. *She needs us. Comfort her. She wants young. She is nervous because you left her unanswered. Your missteps are turning her from us.*

Be silent.

I will give her the young she desires if you will not. The Ra'Voshnik snickered as Faye's footsteps stopped in the doorway. Rune tensed, holding the leather-bound book in his hands so tight he was leaving indentions in its cover. *You're nervous.*

Rune ignored the creature, turning toward Faye. "Good morning," he said. His words felt stiff. He wasn't certain what to say to her. It would be best to let her lead.

She tucked her hair behind her ear and said, "Good morning." She glanced past him at the travesty that befell his library. She grimaced and said, "I'm sorry. I didn't know she did this."

Tell her it's fine. Tell her she can have your dusty library if it pleases her.

Faye stepped into his study and the Ra'Voshnik purred tracking her movements as she maneuvered around the piles of books. She stopped at the first bookshelf still containing tomes. "I can help you flip your books around."

Rune watched her pull the tome free and said, "Your sister did more than flip the books." She turned toward him and he continued with a grin, "She shuffled them. All of them."

Her lips parted as she looked at the book in her hands and the stacks surrounding them. Her cheeks pinkened as her gaze rose to meet his. "Can I help you put them back?"

"I'm afraid my books are in High Tongue," Rune said, setting his volume on a pile beside him.

She did the same and looked up at him. "Can we talk?"

Yes! The Ra'Voshnik cried frantically for her.

"Of course," he said. Faye continued to watch him, and Rune swallowed, reaching for something to add.

"Would you like to sit?" Rune asked as he dragged the creature into the depths of his mind. Silencing its prattle.

Rune's mind blanked as she walked to the settee instead of his desk and his thoughts ran to the last time they'd sat there. She took a seat on one end with a knee tucked under her and examined her nails in an effort not to look at him.

"I thought you would need space before we started our meetings again," Rune lied as he took a seat on the opposite end. The meetings were pointless. He was searching for a spell that didn't exist. He would need to come up with another solution once he settled her to the idea.

"It's not that." She took a deep breath and her hands fell in her lap as she met his gaze. "Did you have a thing with Sadi? Is that why you don't want to do my ceremony? It's weird?"

Rune blinked, struck mute. Caught off guard by questions he wasn't expecting.

Answer her! Your hesitation looks like admittance. Let me rise if you can't speak to her, the Ra'Voshnik's voice echoed from far below him.

He swallowed and said, "No. I have never been intimate with Sadi."

Tell her we desire her.

Faye studied her nails again and said without looking at him, "I'm not as practiced, or as polished as your other lovers." Her cheeks flushed and she glanced up at him. She swallowed but didn't look away. "If you showed me what to do, my ceremony could be pleasant for both of us."

For the first time in Rune's long life, his face heated.

"That— It…" Rune's words failed him as the Ra'Voshnik roared. Thrashing against the bonds imprisoning it.

He exhaled, "Pleasure is not the reason I refused your ceremony."

Her eyes hardened as tension set in her shoulders. "What other reason do you have to deny me," Faye demanded, anger dripping from her every word.

Matching her venom wouldn't serve either of them. Rune kept his tone even, attempting to reason with the spitting minx. "The ceremony is inherently dangerous. You are stronger than I am."

She scoffed at him, looking him up and down. "I can't be stronger than you. If you want to be cruel, then own it. Tell me the real reason."

"Faye," he said gently.

She leaned forward baring her teeth. "Does it infuriate you that you, the great Shadow Prince could want an unsophisticated peasant?"

Tension set in Rune's jaw as he said, "I—"

"Don't lie to me we passed that a long time ago!"

"You do not understand what you are requesting!"

"I understand I want a life! A full life and you can't be bothered to—"

"I curse fate for saddling me with such a stubborn creature." At Faye's stunned look, Rune realized his words.

Faye's lips parted as he stood to his full height. *He does think I'm his. And he looked furious for it.*

"You think I'm so lowly. Let me tell you, Shadow Prince, you are no joy to be fated to either." Faye crossed her arms waiting for a blistering insult.

"I do not think you lowly." His voice was hollow as he stared into the blue flames.

Faye's anger ebbed, cooling with her growing insecurities. "What is your hang up if I'm not lowly? Do I not measure up to the list of women before me?"

He gave a low laugh and took a deep breath before turning toward her. "I do not have a list of lovers."

Faye glared up at him. "I need you to try a little harder if you're going to lie to me."

Rune returned to his seat at the end of the settee. "I am not lying to you."

Faye drew her legs up, studying him. He had to be lying. He was three thousand years old. "I prefer honesty to flattery, or whatever it is you think you're doing." Rune exhaled and scrubbed his hand over his face. "Fine, you've taken no lovers. What would you call what we did?"

"Tending," he answered flatly, before adding, "I tended to you."

Dark courts and their bullshit sex games. "And how many women have you tended?"

"Excluding my training and including you?" He asked with a raise brow, setting his ankle over his knee.

This dick was not allowed to be upset with her. "Yeah, I don't need an exact number. Round to the nearest hundred."

He didn't smile, held up his fingers, and answered, "Two. You met Lyssa. You are the second."

Faye could only tilt her head at him and blink. "You were her consort."

His smile was humorless as he gazed at the fire. "And I never hardened for her. I would not recommend you mention it. She would likely attempt to have you killed."

He spent more than a hundred years with her. "You did her Ceremony of Blood."

"A potion I took for her ritual forced my body to comply. I brought her across whole and did not linger in her bed."

Darkness, this man, left her conflicted. If she wasn't the issue, then it had to lie with him. "Are you worried I won't like it?"

He gave her a contrary glance. "I can hear and scent the body's responses. It is not a difficult read."

The most conceited answer she'd ever heard in her life. But it left only one option. He found her lacking somehow. Faye's shoulders slumped. "What's wrong with me? I'm one of two women you've been with. You want me on some level."

"You do not understand what you are asking for. I am no turned vampire with a previous life to temper my vampiric urges. Pure Bloods have the Ra'Voshnik. It is a predator in its purest form living within me."

Faye rested her arms on her knees, glancing at the fire. Needing to see anything but him. "I prefer that side of you."

"You would not if you truly knew it," Rune said quietly.

He would believe her if he paid attention when he poked around her head. She leaned into the aggressive presence that longed for her. If he cared to look, he would have noticed it. Faye sometimes wished she could take that part of him and leave the man.

She leveled her gaze to his. "We both know we're not right for each other. You don't have to add me to your list of lovers. I'm asking for my ritual. Close your eyes if you like, just hold me above the Darkness."

"It is not that simple," he countered.

Faye sighed, looking up. Here we go. "It is. Breach me and get off me. That's all I'm asking you to do."

"You are stronger than me. We will require the assistance of others."

Every argument Faye prepared blanked from her mind. He wanted to bring others to perform her rite. She paled, pulling her legs in tighter.

"Not in the bed," Rune said as though he could hear her thoughts. "This is the cost of power. When the woman is stronger than the man, others are needed to hold her mind and keep her from plummeting into the Darkness."

Faye's level of comfort began and ended with Rune. She didn't anticipate having an audience. She's never heard of a Ceremony of Blood being done this way. "Can they see or feel what we're doing?"

Rune canted his head at her like she was the one introducing nonsense into their conversation. "No. A mental tether is created through the minds. Sadi will—"

"She hates me," Faye said without thinking. Her evil twin was definately not invited.

"She does not hate you."

"Oh really? If I wasn't fated to you, she would throw my ass into the Darkness herself."

The corner of Rune's mouth lifted into a ghost of the smirk he typically wore. "She is my oldest and most loyal friend."

"Friend?" Faye asked. The dark courts defined that as loosely as they did kidnapping.

Rune exhaled, leaning back in his seat. "Familiar call to predetermined mates. Familiar are fated to other Familiar. She came to court after she invoked her blood. I have known her, her entire life and never pursued her. I trust her. She has saved my life many times over. She is strong and will do as I ask."

Faye knew Sadi's loyalty ended with Rune. She would protect him and protect her through proxy. "I'm fine with your conditions."

"Are you fine with death?" He asked.

"I think you and my evil twin will be able to hold me above the Darkness."

Rune thinned his lips. "You are risking more than your life. We will both survive your rite, or we will both perish."

"Aren't you being a little dramatic, big guy?"

"My death will have consequences. My court has survived for more than five thousand years, it will fall with me. Lyssa will be challenged for her seat as High Queen and likely overthrown. My brothers are considerably weaker than I am. My younger brother Jareth will be forced to maintain Hell's floor. Is your rite worth that risk?"

Was Faye willing to have some half measure of life because she was unlucky enough to be fated to a broody vampire? The outcome he sought to escape was inevitable and Faye wasn't willing to sacrifice for a thing that would come to pass anyway. "You can't untie yourself from me, and I don't think fate would tie you to me just to kill you. If I plummet, let me fall."

"Spoken like a true Familiar."

"I don't turn into a cat. I don't think I'm Familiar."

Rune rubbed his hand over the back of his neck. "I suppose if it happens now or within the century, it makes no difference." He stood and said, "I will make the arrangements. You will be meeting my court soon." He turned and silently strolled toward the hall.

"Rune," Faye called. He turned to glance at her over his shoulder.

"Thank you."

Forty-Five

M orbid laughed, leaning his chair onto its two back legs. He rested his booted feet on Rune's desk, crossing his ankles. The laces of his tall leather boots mostly untied, spilling heedlessly onto Rune's documents.

His study remained cluttered with piles of books. Rune exhaled and swirled the crimson wine in his glass, surveying the other shelves he had yet to fill. The blonde harpy must have spent hours shuffling books between shelves until nothing was where he'd arranged it.

Why are you thinking of books when we could have our queen in our bed?

If all goes well her ritual will take place tomorrow night, Rune said to the Ra'Voshnik as his gaze returned to the Familiar King.

"Would it pain you terribly to stop laughing and answer my request?" Rune asked.

There is much we could do before her ceremony. We could learn her. The ceremony will go smoother if she's acquainted with us. Draw our queen a bath. She's always soaking in the hot spring.

The Ra'Voshnik droned on and Rune tuned it out in favor of listening to Morbid finally speak. "How did she convince you to do this?"

Rune remained silent because he honestly didn't know. Perhaps he was a fool to agree. A fool to give in to the deep-seated want to touch her and learn all the different ways he could coax her into screaming his name.

We could take her until the young she wishes for... takes root.

Be silent, Rune growled. His indulgence in her was enough of a danger. Immortals did not beget young with mortals.

Do you intend to sit by and allow another male to sire her young? The Ra'Voshnik offered him a scene of Faye beneath the copper-haired vampire they'd seen at the brothel. The male's fingers digging into her hip and tangled in her hair. The cries he wrang from her when she'd allowed him to tend to her, echoing through his mind.

Rune's fangs lengthened. A growl slipped from his lips as he banished the sight of his queen with another male.

The Ra'Voshnik laughed, circling his mind. *Our queen,* it purred. A muscle ticked in Rune's jaw as he dragged it so far beneath the surface he no longer heard its taunting laugh.

Rune swallowed the contents of his glass and set it on his desk. He'd been fighting an unavoidable fate. One he would come face to face with shortly.

Morbid folded his hands in his lap and smiled at Rune. "I will help anchor your woman. Have you asked Sadi?"

"I intend to."

"Asking Lyssa to serve as a well?"

Rune cursed in High Tongue. Lyssa became murderously jealous anytime a female was within his proximity. Her behavior worsened after he relinquished the position of her consort. Rune narrowed his eyes at the Familiar King. He would not be requesting Lyssa's assistance but asked, "And how do you see that ending?"

Morbid looked up for a moment. His brow drew together, and he jerked his head back as though something was thrown at him. "Not as much blood as I thought there would be. More tears, though."

"Do you truly foresee these events, or is it all Familiar bullshit?"

Morbid looked him up and down then broke into a wide grin. "Ask Lyssa and find out."

Rune raised his brow and looked away. "I am not that curious."

"Coward," Morbid laughed.

He turned his attention back to Morbid and asked, "Will you tell me what she is?"

The Familiar King winked at him and answered, "Your queen."

Forty-Six

Faye held the crimson silk robe up in the mirror, smoothing the material over her hip.

"Wow, you're getting the full experience." Sparrow whistled low as Faye turned to her with a questioning glance. Her sister twirled a finger at the robe, and said, "Ceremony of Blood robe. Runey will be wearing a matching one."

She imagined Rune dressed in the same red silk. The front of it hanging open to reveal the hard planes of his chest. She dismissed the thought. She would see him soon enough. His court arrived this evening. Sadi included.

Faye wondered if the High Queen would be there. If she had to pick between her evil twin or the high bitch, she would go with evil twin. Hissing bitch trumped the High Queen asking Rune if she spread her legs for him.

She folded the robe over her arm and turned toward her sister. Faye took a deep breath willing the tension from her body. Her action did the opposite, and Faye bit the inside of her lip.

She glanced at her sister, asking, "Do you have any more collars that..."

Faye bit the inside of her lip and waved her hand over her body.

Sparrow's brow lowered for a moment before her eyes widened. "Yeah, I have a ton of them."

"Ones you haven't worn," Faye clarified, the last thing Faye wanted was Rune smelling her sister on her.

Sparrow snorted and leaned her head into the hallway. "Babe."

Vashien appeared next to her a moment later. He glanced between the two of them and leaned in the doorway. "Don't do whatever she's telling you to."

Sparrow slapped his arm. "She is asking, thank you very much," she said, holding her hand out. "I know you stockpile the lingerie collars, give."

Vashien's cheeks tinged pink as he glanced Faye's way.

"Hey," Sparrow said, jabbing him in the arm. "She's not going to save you, she's the one asking. She needs one I haven't worn for Runey."

"You want to wear lingerie to your Ceremony of Blood."

Faye found the stone squares making up the floor riveting as her face heated. She thought Sparrow would have a cache of them, not mortify her in front of Vashien. How was she supposed to look him in the eye tomorrow at breakfast?

"Stop embarrassing her. You're always pulling them out. I know you're hiding a bunch of them. Give me the shoe box you hide them in or whatever so Faye can pick one."

Faye ignored the sound of shuffling and glanced up when the door closed.

"He's gone. It's so cute how your blushing minutes before you're going to fuck the Shadow Prince."

Faye's flush deepened. "It's a ceremony."

Sparrow quirked her lip and nodded at her. "You keep telling yourself that," she said as she dumped the contents of a wooden box over the bed. "I thought he would have five or six," Sparrow said, grabbing a handful of collars and letting them fall.

Faye glanced over the scraps of different material. There were dozens of them. Faye held up one made of leather with metal studs in it. "These are the ones you haven't worn?"

Sparrow gave her a toothy grin and shimmied her hips. "He likes to play dress up."

"Darkness, save me," Faye muttered picking through the collars. "How do you know what they look like."

"Easy," her sister said, spreading the chokers out. Dark mist coated her hand and she waved it over the bed, as her dark mist rolled over them, they changed.

Faye swallowed. Maybe she shouldn't have asked what they looked like. Some of them were straps and ribbons, others were made of studded leather. Faye picked up a piece that was underwire with thin chains draped over the front of it and held it out toward her sister. "Vash likes this?"

"Oh, you have no idea," Sparrow said, taking the lingerie. It transformed back into a leather choker, and she dropped it back in the box.

Faye stared at the assortment of lingerie, not sure what to pick. She didn't want her ceremony to be one-sided. They could both have a pleasant evening before completing her ceremony. She wanted something for him but wasn't sure what direction his tastes ran. She'd never imagine Vashien would like some of these, maybe the same could be said for Rune.

Sparrow snorted at her indecision. "You're taking too long. Stop thinking so hard. They're men. Wrap your tits in some lace and their happy."

Faye's shoulders slumped. "What if he doesn't like it?" What if she just made her ceremony awkward trying to give him something he didn't want.

"Darkness, you are the most over thinking bitch in all the realms." Sparrow waved her hand again, reverting the lingerie into strips of material. She outstretched her fingers, curling them in a rolling wave as she peered over the assortment. She picked up one made of grey and pink lace, and another made of red leather.

"Pick one," Sparrow ordered.

Faye took the lace choker and her sister snickered, "Pussy."

"I'm not wearing red leather to our first..."

"Date?" Her sister finished for her.

"It's not a date," Faye argued, sliding the collar in her pocket.

Sparrow linked arms with her and started toward the door. "Come on. We can't be late for your date."

"It's a ceremony," Faye hissed as they met Vashien in the hall.

They made their way to Rune's study where they would meet other members from his court. Faye silently prayed that the high bitch didn't come to assist him.

Rune claimed she was stronger than him and Faye wasn't sure she believed him. It had to be true, or he wouldn't involve his court. What reason did he have to lie when he was performing her ceremony?

That needed other people, Faye reminded herself. She'd thought her ritual would be a private thing between her and a blood priest. Fate had other plans. At least the extra attendees would stay in his study and not join them in the bedroom.

Sparrow hugged her arm. "My baby bird is finally getting laid."

"I'm not getting laid," Faye countered.

"You totally are, by his shadowy highness," Sparrow squealed, squeezing her tighter.

Faye stepped into Rune's study and froze. There were more people here than she expected. They sat in various chairs around the tall piles of books and empty bookshelves. She struggled to swallow as the reason they were all here weighed down on her, feeling all too real suddenly.

Her heart pounded as she glanced to Rune who stood beside the floor to ceiling window gazing out over his realm. A man with long dark hair and dramatic sweeps of color around his midnight eyes sat in Rune's usual place behind his desk. He rocked Rune's chair, balancing it on its two back legs, while his booted feet rested on the desk.

To Faye's left was another man, sitting with his legs crossed, reading a book with a martini glass on the small table beside him. Faye blinked. His features followed Rune's beyond a normal family relation. His white-blonde hair was short, tousled to look like he hadn't spent much time on it, but Faye was sure he had.

He looked so much like Rune but so different. There was no underlining tension in his expression. The corners of his mouth tilted up in a relaxed smile as he turned a page in his book. This would be

Rune— *If the Shadow Prince was normal,* Faye thought as her gaze fell to the weaker, dark misted shard he wore. He dressed in the fashions of Necromia. A fitted white dress shirt tucked cleanly into his slacks, forgoing the tailored suit Rune always wore.

He turned toward them, and his smile widened, reaching his pale blue eyes. Faye noted his lack of fangs as the man said, "You must be my brother's guests." He stood, laying his book next to his drink and walked over to them. "My name's Jareth. You must be Faye, Sparrow, and Vashien." He looked at each of them as he said their names.

"Runey didn't tell you my name was blonde harpy," Sparrow said with exaggerated excitement. She glanced past Jareth at Rune and said, "Admit it, you're starting to like me."

Jareth laughed and stood beside Sparrow, leaning to the side until his arm brushed hers. He tilted his head toward her, pointing as he spoke. "You've met Sadi and her mate Damian. That's Morbid and you already know my brother."

Damian laid his arm over the back of the settee as he looked back at them. Faye didn't see Sadi but recognized her tuffs of black lace and belted, heeled boots hanging over the armrest.

Damian's silver eyes gleamed as he met Faye's gaze. A feline smile spread over his mouth. "Evening, delicate."

Rune cut off Faye's reply. "Call her that again, and I will tear your vulgar tongue from your mouth."

Sadi sat up to glare their way as Faye turned toward Jareth to whisper, "Delicate is vulgar?"

"It's a Familiar term meaning virgin," Sadi answered with a clipped tone.

Damian gripped her throat and pulled her back down to his lap. "It means fine meal, don't lie to the girl."

A growl emanated from Rune and Damian turned his head. "I didn't say she was *my* fine meal." Sadi's mate turned his attention back to Faye. "The Shadow Prince will certainly feast on you though."

"Don't mind him, sex and violence are all he's capable of," Jareth said, waving a dismissive hand at Damian.

Sadi's booted foot snapped up, aiming for Damian's head. He caught her ankle and pressed his lips to the side of her calf. "Occasionally at the same time," Damian purred, glancing down at his lap.

Faye wasn't sure what occurred since the settee faced the fireplace, but Damian bared his teeth as he winced and Sadi shot up to stare daggers at her.

Damian slung his arm over Sadi's shoulder and down between her breasts, dragging her to sit against him. He kissed her hair and growled, "Bite me again and I will fuck that attitude right out of you."

Faye looked away and Sparrow snickered as Jareth led them to a bar cart.

"Are you Rune's twin?" Sparrow asked.

"No, I'm his younger brother. We all bare our father's stamp. Some better than others," Jareth said the last to Rune, with a laugh. The corners of his eyes crinkling.

His attention returned to them as he wiggled a glass. "Drink?"

"No thank you," Faye answered as she rubbed the side of her neck, glancing over the full room. "Why are there so many people here?"

"Rune is performing your rite. Sadi and Morbid will help him hold you over the Darkness. The rest of us are here to serve as a well. If Sadi needs to siphon more power, she'll take it from us."

"Don't you think this is overkill?" Faye asked the back of Rune's head.

He turned around meeting her gaze. "It is a precaution. There is a contraceptive brew in your room. Open our adjoining door when you are ready." Rune strolled past them, inclining his head to Faye as he left his study.

Faye exchanged a look with her sister, her nerves freezing her in place. Sparrow smiled brightly, oblivious to the tension thrumming through Faye's body, and nudged her toward the door.

Forty-Seven

Faye stood before her full-length mirror, the pink and gray lace choker around her neck. She scrutinized her nude form, crimson silk flowing down either side of her. She should have asked Sparrow how to get the collar to work.

She let her mind drift, remembering how she sat with Rune on the settee. Running her fingers lightly over his index finger. Pausing to brush his shard. She'd looked up at his mouth wanting to feel them. Fantasizing about what it would be like to be desired by a man like him.

Wanting him to need her and pull her into his arms.

Faye jerked as a light constriction closed over her body. She was now dressed in gray lace with pink accents. She turned from side to side wondering if this was too much. The bra and thong hid nothing beneath the intricate lace pattern. A garter belt of the same material held up sheer gray thigh high stockings.

She closed her robe and tied it. If he didn't like it, she could take the collar off. Faye flushed, imagining him untying her robe and gazing at her beneath it. Faye glanced at the door in the mirror's reflection, and her heart pounded in her ears.

Ceremony, this is a ceremony, she chanted to herself as she moved to the door. She stared at the door handle. Her lips parted as she took hold of it, turning the knob. It clicked and Faye shyly pushed it before pulling her hand away.

The door opened into his room a few inches. She didn't see movement through the sliver into Rune's room.

She stepped back when the door opened. Rune stood in the doorway wrapped in a matching crimson silk robe. He stepped into her room, and she took another step back.

Veined misted shadows crept from beneath his eyes, mesmerizing her in place. He stepped closer and Faye's breaths turned shallow. She lost herself in his pale blue gaze. The backs of his fingers smoothed under her jaw, tracing to her hair. He pulled a length of her black hair forward, letting it slip through his hold.

"Be easy. Your heart is racing," he said, walking past her to the table. He adjusted his robe and took a seat, holding his hand out to her.

Faye hesitated before taking his hand. He pulled her closer, his lips brushing softly over the back of her hand. She was close enough to perceive his scent of sandalwood and amber. He pulled her hand down, guiding her to take a seat on his thigh. Faye glanced at his mouth, remembering the last time she was in his lap.

They would be doing much more than they'd done at the brothel.

He stroked her hair and picked up an untouched cup from the table and held it between them. She'd been so preoccupied with her choker, she forgot to drink the tea left out for her.

"Sorry," she muttered taking the small glass.

Faye drank the contents as he caressed her back. It was warm, with a hint of bitterness. Like a tea she let steep too long. Faye leaned forward setting the glass at the edge of the table, freezing when Rune stopped to trace the strap running across her back.

Faye forced herself to straighten as his hand glided down to her waist, delicately hovering over the straps beneath the silk. Maybe she shouldn't have worn this. He didn't look happy as he followed her garter belt. The shadows intensified reaching lower.

She fingered the edge of his robe, gazing down at her tantalizing view. Faye wanted to drag her teeth over the spot where his neck met his shoulder. Her gaze lowered to his collar bone, ending at the hint of the hard plains of his chest beneath the red silk.

Faye knew this was what she wanted, but her confidence rapidly depleted as he gazed at her intently. "Do I touch you to start?"

Rune brushed her hair over her shoulder, slipping his fingers over the back of her neck. He leaned closer. His lips a moment from hers. "The door serves as invitation to your bed. However, I think it best if you lead."

She would control their evening. The thought appealed to her as she imagined him worshiping at her altar, then bound with his wrists overhead while she ran her nails over his chest.

Faye mentally shook herself. Nothing would start if she didn't touch him. She leaned in and kissed him. His lips parted and she deepened the kiss, her tongue stroking into his mouth. Taking from him.

His surrender set her blood aflame, coursing through her as she tangled her hands in his hair. Her nipples hardened into tight peaks when he pulled her closer, molding her against his chest. Heat pooled at her center when the proof of his desire ground against her thigh.

"Kiss me," Faye moaned against his mouth in a desperate plea.

Rune held her tighter. One hand splayed over her ribs and the other in her hair. He gave no quarter, possessing her mouth. He ravaged her, slow and deliberate, opening her wider for him.

She licked his fang and a metallic taste bloomed on her tongue. Rune groaned as he captured the back of her hair, slowly using his other hand to tug at the sash of her silk robe.

Faye wasn't thinking as he pulled her robe open. His hand caressed down her side as he pulled back, breaking their kiss. Faye panted as she gazed up at him, her mind a fog of wanton need. His downcast eyes gazed at her, awestruck as his hand slid down the lace trim of her garter belt. "You are the most beautiful sight I have ever beheld."

His words doused her passion. The stinging memory of sitting up alone in his bed filled her with tension. "I heard that line before. Are you planning on running off again?"

"Forgive me," he murmured, drawing her closer. He kissed the underside of her jaw. The corner of her mouth. "I acted in haste. If you allow it, I will stay until morning."

Faye brought her lips to his, their kiss sweet and savoring. She didn't want the hope, or believe he would want more with her. They weren't right for each other. She wasn't the queen raised in a dark court who would command and possess him, and he wasn't the simple, kind man she envisioned sharing her life with.

But Darkness, he felt right. Being in his arms, touching him— Felt like home. Faye steeled herself. This was a ritual, and the rose-colored dreams of a future with him would shatter in the morning when he left her bed.

His memory would haunt her, but she could make the memory worth the pain.

She smoothed her hand over his chest. "I'm ready."

Rune stood, cradling her against him without breaking their kiss. He laid her on the ivory sheets.

"Take off your robe," he crooned as he hooked his finger under the strap of her thong. He met her gaze, waiting. Faye nodded, slipping her arms out of the robe while Rune slid the bit of lace down her legs and knelt before her.

He set her leg over his shoulder, and Faye dragged her heel up his back. "You don't have to do that."

He gave a low laugh, pressing his lips to the inside of her thigh near her knee, and moved lower. He looked up at her from beneath his dark lashes and smirked.

"I do this for me, not you."

Forty-Eight

Faye panted, soft sounds escaping her lips as Rune devoured and worshiped her. He parted her gently and kissed her clit before drawing it between his lips. She squirmed, fisting his hair as his tongue worked her. She twitched with each flutter passing over her sex, echoing her pleasure through her body.

The tension coiled in her again as he teased her with a firmer pressure. Building that rise of pleasure until it snapped. It'd snapped so many times, and he'd just started.

"Rune, please. I can't."

He eased his touch and pressed his tongue into her. Faye cried out, pulling his hair as she rocked her hips. Fucking herself on his tongue.

He pulled back to kiss and tease her slick flesh. "You can," he breathed, moving higher to where she was most sensitive. "Would you like a demonstration?"

He purred against her mercilessly. Faye screamed, her back bowing as ecstasy crashed over her. Through her. Permeating into her, to her very soul.

"Please," Faye begged without realizing it. She repeated her plea again and again as Rune pinned her waist, drowning her in a pleasure so intense stars glimmered in her vision. "Please," she whispered.

Not knowing if she was begging for mercy or demanding more of him.

Rune relented and groaned against her. His tongue swept through her folds as his eyes slid closed. The veined shadows swaying beneath his eyes as he reverently tasted her. As though he truly worshiped her and needed to etch this moment into his being.

Faye curled onto her side when he finally released her. Panting and short of breath. She stared up at him as he let his robe fall to his feet.

Faye's gaze swept down his perfectly chiseled body and her expression faltered when she caught sight of his erection. He was much too large to take into her body.

Faye sat up, glancing down at her hand, pressing three fingers together on her ivory sheets. She thought her sister was joking about a three-finger killer. Faye turned her attention back to Rune, keeping her gaze above his waist.

He glanced down at himself and turned back to her with an arrogant grin. "Having second thoughts?"

The flush from the orgasms he wrang from her covered the self-conscious heat spreading over her cheeks.

"No," she answered, wondering how he intended to wedge that into her.

He returned to her, kissing her as his hand smoothed down the front of her throat, to the front of her chest, and cupped her breast. He moved the pad of his thumb over her nipple in torturous circles and Faye moaned into his mouth.

Rune teased her, toying with her body until her nails bit into his shoulder and back. His hands slipped lower, under her, palming her ass as he easily picked her up. Faye stiffened; his fingers too close to her slick heat.

Rune moved them further onto the bed, nipping at her earlobe. "Calm yourself," his accented voice was filled with dark promises, "I will be easy with you."

Faye gasped when he touched her, teasing her opening but not pressing into her. She felt exposed. Spread wide and at his mercy with her legs around his waist like this.

She moaned as he slid two fingers through her folds and clung to him when they found her too sensitive clit. He made her body sing, alternating his touch until Faye was sure she would break.

She leaned back when he gave her a reprieve, catching her breath. She cupped her hand to the side of his face, brushing her thumb through the misted shadows that swayed beneath his pale blue gaze. They shifted, swirling in different directions as her thumb passed through them, then dissipated to nothing. "What are these?"

"The Ra'Voshnik rising in me."

The part of him that clung to her when he was in her mind. Faye smiled and asked, "Can I see it?"

Rune kissed her, laying her on her back, before saying, "It would be best if I remained in control." He shifted his hips and his considerable length moved over where she ached for him.

Faye reached between them, her fingers curling around the tip of his cock as he thrust over her. His shadows intensify and Faye reached for more of him. Rune groaned as black flooded through his gaze and dissipated. "You are making it difficult to hold my focus."

She leaned up kissing his throat. "I want tonight to be pleasant for both of us," she said before biting the base of his throat, holding him with her teeth.

Vibrations whispered under Faye's mouth as a low growl sounded above her.

He dragged her against him, hooking his arm under her leg. Faye let go when he shoved her leg against her side. Pinning her beneath him, exposing more of her sensitive flesh as he thrust over her harder. Her breath caught when he gripped her tighter, his claws prickling but not breaking her skin.

Rune fisted her hair, rocking against her harder with a low growl. She was too sensitive. It was too much. Faye's hand shot to his throat, squeezing until he slowed his onslaught. "Be nice," she grated before pressing a kiss to his hair and releasing her hold.

He moved over her in slow rhythmic strokes, releasing her leg and met her gaze.

His eyes were entirely black. Faye's eyes widened and he purred, holding her tighter. His dark gaze filled with the yearning she saw in their shared dreams.

Faye brought her fingers to the side of his face, and his eyes slid closed as he leaned into her touch.

It is a predator in its purest form living within me.

Faye thought Rune spoke of an aspect of himself. Urges and instincts.

She glanced up at the man who wasn't Rune. He gazed at her with a drowning need Rune never gave into. Desperation, longing, and desire rolled into a single expression reflected in the dark pools of his shadowed eyes.

"You're the Ra'Vo…"

"Ra'Voshnik." He answered, holding her closer as he rubbed the side of his face against hers in an animalistic display of affection. "You are my queen."

He kissed her, nipping her bottom lip while circling her nipple with the back of his curved claw. Pinching and teasing the peaks of her breasts until she arched her back for his touch. His thrusts moved in time with the pressure she needed, until her nails dug into his back.

He purred softly, nuzzling her throat. "Not tonight, but soon. You will submit to my fangs, my cock, and my will."

His heated words sent her to the very edge as she imagined herself beneath him as he drove into her. His mouth pressed to her neck. Her nails bit deeper as she cried, "Please."

The feel of a tongue at her entrance startled her. The Ra'Voshnik smirked at her, possessiveness dripping from him. "My will," he said simply, before leaning closer to croon against her lips, "Take it for me."

The phantom mouth pressed against her and thrusted its tongue into her in time with his cock sliding over her clit.

Faye's head fell back, and her lips parted. She clung to him, taking what he gave her. Rolling her hips as she spread her legs wider, wanting more of him. Needing more.

"Offer me your throat," the Ra'Voshnik purred as his claws sliced through the choker leaving Faye completely bared to him

Faye didn't hesitate, lifting her chin and turning her head to the side. Exposing the slender column of her neck.

He bit down, and Faye screamed, not from pain but pleasure.

His fangs sank deep, and pleasure jolted through her sex, deeper than his tongue could reach. When he withdrew his bite, the pleasure receded only to return when he drank from her. Each pull sent the pleasure deeper into her.

She came hard, imagining it was his cock thrusting into her as he took her again and again. He was hers. This was the man fated to her. She cried the name of the man who cherished and yearned for her. The man who didn't question their tie or see her as lacking. Her perfect dark-blooded man.

"Voshki."

Forty-Nine

Rune's eyes cleared as he dragged the Ra'Voshnik beneath the surface. It didn't fight him, floating through his mind content. Rune gazed down at Faye, her skin gleamed with a sheen of perspiration. A strand of dark hair clung to her face. She panted through parted lips, flush spread down her throat, between her breasts.

That is how you should always leave our queen. Take her to our bed and we will finish her rite, the Ra'Voshnik said, thoroughly satisfied with itself.

Jealousy clawed at Rune. Faye had writhed for the creature, let it take her throat. Called it Voshki.

And worse it obeyed her.

If you won't share her, I'll have to take her from you.

Be silent, Rune grated.

Faye gazed up at him and her smile faded. Was she disappointed he was at the fore instead of the Ra'Voshnik?

I told you she preferred me to you, the creature brushed the surface of his mind wanting to return to Faye.

This does not matter, it is ritual, Rune told himself. He dragged the Ra'Voshnik to the recesses of his mind and asked, "Do you wish to proceed with your rite?"

She nodded and touched his face, gazing past his eyes as though she were looking into him. "You're two men in one body."

Rune took her hand and pressed his lips to her palm. "I am sorry it was rough with you."

"He's not an *it*," Faye scowled at him as the Ra'Voshnik cackled far below him. "Be nice to Voshki."

Tension riddled every muscle in Rune's body. "That is not its name."

"Then what is it?" She asked, wiping the strand of hair out of her face.

"The Ra'Voshnik does not have a name," Rune grated.

Faye lifted her chin in that defiant way that drove him to madness. "I named him. His name is Voshki."

Rune looked away and then returned to her. "Do you want your rite completed or did you want to spend the rest of the evening discussing the finer intricacies of my vampiric nature?"

"I knew part of you liked me," Faye said, reaching between them to stroke his cock. Rune groaned, feeling the veined shadows slipping from beneath his gaze. She leaned up, kissing him before laying back on her sheets. "I just wasn't aware it was a separate part."

Rune growled and Faye giggled at him. Giggled. Beneath a Pure Blood. Wanting him to let the Ra'Voshnik rise. Armies fled at the first sight of the creature, but not the young mortal. She beckoned it.

And it bowed to her will.

Jealousy looks terrible on you. Rune ignored the Ra'Voshnik's remark and brushed his mind over Faye's. "I need you to relax so I might hold your mind."

Faye closed her eyes, her lips upturned in a triumphant smile.

Rune withdrew into himself and stood at the edge of her mind. Flattening his hand against her mental shield, he focused his power to pierce it. Creating a doorway for himself. Her shielding eased back, allowing him entry

Rune took hold of her mind and pulled her into his. Faye's brow drew together.

"Be easy." Rune crooned, brushing the back of his fingers over her cheek. "You need to be in my mind so I can hold you above the Darkness. If we stay in yours, you are likely to slam your shields on me and plummet alone."

He kissed the corner of her mouth and divided his focus between his body and the intangible ravine that cradled the Darkness. Faye materialized before him and wrapped her arms around his neck when she looked down.

"Why are we up so high? Where are we?" Faye squeezed her eyes shut clutching to him desperately.

"Above the Darkness," Rune answered.

Faye's eyes widened as the Ra'Voshnik snaked its arm around her waist, pulling her into it.

Rune bared his fangs, "Do not frighten her."

The Ra'Voshnik held his gaze and pressed a kiss to her hair. It muttered, "We have you," and released her.

Faye twisted in his arms to glance at the creature. She turned back to him. "Can Voshki hold me above the Darkness?"

Hurt twisted in his chest and the creature spoke before he could. "You're safer in his hands. The Shadow Prince has a disciplined mind." It ran its fingers through her hair and Rune fought the urge to eviscerate the creature. It turned to him and said, "I know my limitations."

They growled at each other, and Faye slapped his chest. Him. He gazed down at her, canting his head.

"I'll stay with you. Be nice," she said.

The Ra'Voshnik laughed and Rune exhaled.

"Your instinct will be to dive. I need you to fight it and stay with me." He gazed down at her and asked, "Ready?"

Faye nodded.

"I have you," he promised. Rune angled his hips, pressing into her. Working her in slow shallow movements.

He held her in his mind, prepared for the start of her descent. Rune stifled a groan as her soft flesh gave and she took him into her. Faye took a sudden sharp breath, her eyes wide. She arched her back away from him. To Rune's horror her eyes slid closed and she dove through the psychic chasm. Plummeting toward the Darkness far below them.

"Faye!" Rune screamed, unable to pull her out of her freefall.

Her body hung limp in his arms. Her long black hair whipped around them as they fell.

He channeled all his strength into slowing her descent, barely perceiving the skin under his ring as it blackened and charred on his physical hand.

"Rune!" Sadi's voice screamed from far above him.

"Cut the tether!" Morbid's voice thundered.

"NO!" Sadi's panicked screams lanced his ears. An influx of power surged through the tether connecting his mind to Sadi's, replenishing him.

The Darkness, raw raging power, coiled and crashed beneath him. Fear took hold of Rune, its icy fingers sinking deep. Reaching through his being. They weren't collectively strong enough to pull Faye out of her dive.

If I plummet, let me fall.

No! Rune clutched her tight, tucking her to his chest. He couldn't let her go. Rune cleared his mind, losing precious seconds as he devised a solution. He routinely walked into The Crumbling. Could withstand ten to fifteen minutes in it. He could shield them through the Darkness and pull them out when her dive eased.

Rune wove the shields to regenerate from him. Pain was fleeting, he could focus through this and keep her safe.

He tightened his hold over Faye, keeping her close. He rolled them so his back would hit first. Making it easier to focus on ascending in the right direction.

The first touch of the Darkness burned through his shield, searing his mind with pain that electrified every nerve ending in his body.

He'd misjudged this. The Darkness was exponentially stronger and far more destructive than The Crumbling. It consumed his power in an instant. A drop of water absorbed into a vast ocean. Pain beyond his comprehension racked his body.

The last thing he heard was Sadi screaming his name.

Fifty

The taste of blood, rich and exquisite, coated Rune's tongue. He swallowed instinctively and groaned. Every part of him hurt. He opened his eyes, recognizing his bed. But it felt wrong. He drew his power from his reserves below him, always aware of it. His power wasn't below him here. It was above him.

Far above him.

"I have you."

Rune turned toward Faye's voice. Memories rushed back followed by alarm. He fell into the Darkness.

Lips were on his before he could speak. A hand gripped his throat, claws digging in, stinging as they drew blood. Legs straddled him, wet heat sliding against his hardening cock. Rune groaned as he closed his eyes. Her scent enveloped him. His night breeze through plumb blossoms intoxicating his senses.

Rune pulled back. The points of Faye's iridescent wings arching behind her, framing her face. She smiled at him, desire clear in her eyes.

Rune thinned his lips, she would look at the Ra'Voshnik this way. Not him. "I fell into the Darkness." Was he dead? Alarm filled him as he realized his mind was quiet. Where was the Ra'Voshnik?

"I have you." This winged Faye repeated his words. She pulled him close by his throat and affectionately brushed the side of her face against his. This wasn't Faye.

"How?" Rune stroked her hand, slipping a finger between her palm and his throat, coaxing her into loosening her grip.

"You live because you are mine. I caught you." Faye's winged double tightened her hold, pulling him into a kiss. "I have you," she said at his lips.

Rune broke the kiss and eased her claws out of his throat. The winged-double straightened her back, her shoulders tensing.

Was she like him and this creature was paired to her, slumbering dormant?

He glanced over his surroundings, recognizing the hollow in the Darkness where he first met Faye. She possessed wings then too.

"Tell me what you are." Rune brought her dainty claws to his lips, pressing a kiss to them.

"Want you," the winged Faye growled, rising to her knees.

"No," Rune said gently, shifting her hips as he held her against his thigh. "Where is Faye?"

She glared at him. Her lightning-streaked midnight eyes glittered with malicious intent, as her wings tightened to her body. "She sleeps," the winged double answered, looking over her shoulder.

Rune followed her gaze, shocked to see Faye curled on her side, sleeping. Beside her was the Ra'Voshnik. He was certain when he woke he'd been alone.

"I saw you falling." She leaned forward, kissing him gently. "You belong to me." Another kiss. "I have you. My beautiful hunter."

Darkness, being with her felt so right. It would be so easy to lose himself in the soft feel of her lips. To think of nothing else but the feel of her in his arms. He pulled her closer, and her wings dragged along his forearm.

This wasn't Faye.

"Where is your body?" Rune asked between her light kisses.

"Resting," she answered. Aggravation coated her voice. She seized his throat, glowering at him, before saying, "Above."

She kissed him harder, demanding more, and Rune pulled away. She rose and he pinned her waist down. Darkness, she was harder to corral than the Ra'Voshnik. "I cannot use Faye's body while she sleeps."

"We are the same," she insisted.

Rune's jaw went slack as she fisted his cock, stroking him.

He drew a ragged breath trapping her wrists in one hand, holding them away from him. "You are different," Rune said, lifting his chin at Faye's sleeping body.

The winged double turned. "She is the vessel."

Her attention returned to Rune, holding his gaze. "I am the power. You woke me. You're mine."

"I am," Rune agreed, pressing his lips to her fingertips. "How did I wake you?" *Give me a hint as to what you are.*

"I slept," Faye's double absently touched his lips. "Waiting." Her hand traced down his throat to his collarbone. "I felt you." She brushed the back of her fingers over his chest. "Always crashing near my shores."

She spoke in more riddles than Morbid. He needed to coax more information from her. "I do not understand your meaning."

"I am trapped in the Darkness until you make us whole. But I *felt* you. Crashing near my shores. For centuries."

Crashing? She felt his backlash when he failed to unravel The Crumbling. "How can you feel me for centuries? Faye is only twenty-five." Sadi mentioned previous lives, was this part of her constant?

"I am eternal, sewn into the Darkness itself."

Hope dug into his chest. It wasn't ideal, but it would be a type of immortality. Rune's breath left him. Was he truly gifted with his dark queen? He was left with more questions than answers.

"Where are we?" Rune asked.

"In the portion of the Darkness that is mine. My power grew until I woke. I watched you at my shores. Your blood sings for me." She leaned forward, kissing Rune.

Her lips moved over his, but Rune remained still. She pulled back with a scowl. "Why do you hold back? You want me."

Trying to reason with her was like trying to explain patience to the Ra'Voshnik. "I want you whole. What are you? Where is your altar? Tell me anything."

The winged Faye made a noise that could have been a growl. "Invoke the blood, join the vessel and the power. You talk too much."

She ran her claw along the length of her collarbone. His fangs lengthened as he breathed in the scent of her dark exquisite blood. It flowed over her breasts, trailing onto her legs and between them.

Rune clenched his jaw, beating down the urge to fuck her while he licked her blood off her body. She collected some of it on her finger. Rune stared transfixed as she brought it to his mouth. He groaned, parting his lips for her.

She pressed her finger into his mouth, his lips closing around it. Darkness save him, he sucked, licking off the blood. The winged double pulled her hand back, laying down as she spread her legs wide for him.

Rune closed his eyes as urges and instincts he'd thought were the Ra'Voshnik's raged in his mind. He wanted to pin her and stroke into her wet heat as he licked the blood from her body. With great effort he pulled it back, settling himself.

Panting from his efforts he gazed at her. "I cannot use your vessel while she sleeps."

"Then wake her." The winged Faye rolled onto her side and drew her foot back. She struck in a motion so fast it blurred, kicking him in the chest.

Rune slammed back into his physical body with enough force to jar his teeth. He and Faye were now in his bed, in his room.

He shut his eyes and grimaced against the screaming and sizzle of magic hitting the shields outside his room.

Stop! Rune growled over a broad mental sending that anyone within the vicinity would hear.

"Rune!" Sadi's panicked scream sounded from the other side of the door.

He turned his attention to Faye. She slept curled on her side, just as he'd seen her in that place in the Darkness. He brushed her hair away from her face. Her lids fluttered. With a sigh she rolled over to face him and curled into his arm.

He winced as he pulled his sheet up to cover her. Rune stood, his body in fine disagreement. He called a pair of pants, and his magic didn't answer. Faye's rite sapped him of every ounce of power he held.

Rune retrieved a robe from his closet. Each step shot searing pain through his chest and back. He sucked a breath and pulled the robe on before slowly making his way to the door. Rune pressed his hand to the wall, opened the door, and stood dumbstruck.

Tears ran down Sadi's face. The smell of burnt flesh assaulted his senses next. He glanced down at her hands. "What did you—"

"I saw you fall into the Darkness." Sadi leaped toward him, hugging him tightly. Rune hissed in pain, the only thing saving him from being taken to the ground was his hold on the doorframe.

Rune lightly wrapped an arm around her. Her tears fell on his shoulder. In all the centuries he'd known her he'd never seen her cry.

"Are you injured?" Sadi released him, stepping back as she wiped her tears away.

"How did you burn your hands?" Rune turned his back to Sadi, pulling his hair over his shoulder so she could inspect him for damage. She ran her hand down the length of his spine.

Sadi assessed the court each time they returned from battle. Where he'd been was no different.

"She was fighting with your shields like a newborn kitten," Morbid answered. "I told her she needed to worry if the shields suddenly dropped. If they are regenerating, they must be pulling power from a source that lives."

"Where are the others?" Rune asked.

"They're still recovering." She tapped his shoulder indicating for him to turn around so she could finish her inspection.

"I am well." Rune met her gaze, nodding at her.

Sadi narrowed her eyes at him before continuing her task. "You were missing for more than an hour. I couldn't reach you. I couldn't feel you." Sadi's gaze flitted over his body. Assessing, tallying, then her gaze rose back to his chest. She pressed two fingers to his sternum.

Pain wracked Rune and he growled.

"How did you fracture your ribcage in so many places?" Sadi rubbed her eyes, beginning to look more like herself. She raised her hand over his chest. "I don't have the strength to heal you completely," she said as heat seeped through his chest, into his back.

"Come now. The Shadow Prince needs to rest and recuperate." Morbid took his daughter by the elbow, leading her away before she could finish, and said over his shoulder, "We'll be in the north wing."

We have much to discuss. Rune sent the thought to Morbid as he closed his bedroom door.

He glanced down at the sleeping woman in his bed. His queen.

Would she want to wake in his bed? Perhaps he should join her in the adjoining room, and she could decide for herself in the morning.

Rune gathered her in his arms, collecting his sheet with her. With a hiss he lifted her and carried her to her bed. She grumbled in her sleep, clinging to him. Her nails biting into his back. Every step was agony, but he was too drained to use his power.

He cursed in High Tongue and lowered her onto her ivory sheets. Faye closed her arms around his neck holding him tighter. With a sigh Rune took her hand in an attempt to untangle himself from her. Her nails dug into his back again, sharper.

Claws Rune realized.

"Come now, vsenia." The High Tongue term of endearments slipped from his lips before Rune realized. He pried a hand free, and Faye twisted in his arms. *So stubborn, even in your sleep.* He held her hand away as she fought to keep him in her embrace.

She made an exasperated sound and wings burst from her back, shredding the mattress and blankets under her. Faye pulled at her wrist and her wings flared, cutting forward, encircling them both.

Rune exhaled as she relaxed in his arms, apparently happy to have him captive. He surveyed the damage she'd done and glanced at the woman curled up to him. "Must you ruin all my things?"

Rune bared his teeth adjusting his hold on the sleeping minx. Her wings loosened when he allowed her to wrap her arms around his neck once more.

Wrapping his sheet around her nude form as best he could. Faye stirred as he settled him into his dark sheets. She draped a wing over him and she curled closer. Rune tensed as she rested her head on his chest. She paid him no mind, using him for her comfort and slung her leg over his thigh.

It was strange to be alone with his thoughts. Stranger still to have the queen he wished for his entire life sleeping beside him. He'd been unkind to her. There was much he needed to mend between them.

The Ra'Voshnik, even silenced, disturbed his thoughts. Faye wanted the creature. Preferred her Voshki to him. Rune closed his eyes. They had a great deal to speak on. He and the Ra'Voshnik could not be separated.

Jealousy was an unfamiliar emotion for him, and Rune found he hated it. Immortals often invited others to their beds. *Typically after being together for centuries,* Rune thought bitterly. His lips thinned as he ran his fingers through Faye's hair, staring up at the ceiling.

What would he do if Faye wasn't willing to have them both? She could only desire the Ra'Voshnik. But she'd kissed him after she'd been with the creature.

Rune's thoughts circled back on each other in his mind. Nothing could be done until he spoke with her. He pulled his fingers through her hair a last time letting it slip through his hold. He closed his eyes and surrendered to the exhaustion racking his body, falling into a deep sleep beside his fated queen.

Fifty-One

Faye woke slowly to a view of Hell's twilight sky through tall narrow windows. A low vibration lulled her with its gentle constant purr. Her brow came down as she realized exactly what room she was in and who she was curled up against.

If you allow it, I will stay until morning.

Her heart constricted. He would leave soon. Faye shifted beside him, finding a more comfortable spot on his chest. Wanting to savor their final moments. Rune drew a sharp breath beneath her, and the room filled with silence.

She upturned her head to glance at him and he tensed further. Did he regret what they'd done? What she let him do. Faye sat up, pulling the sheets around herself, and stilled.

The front of his black robe hung open revealing heavy bruising over his chest. Disjointed memories drifted up in her mind, and she glanced away as they slowly pieced together.

"How did you get hurt?" She asked.

"I am drained and mending, a moment," Rune's voice was deeper, he sounded exhausted. The effortless predatorial grace he possessed was gone, replaced with slow, stiff movements. His long white-blonde hair fell forward in vivid contrast to the ugly bruises marring his pale skin.

Scenes stitched together in her mind, filling her with false recollections, but she remembered them as though she'd committed these acts herself. Faye flushed deeply as the memories took shape fully. She'd straddled him. Moaned as his hard length slid against her while she rocked her hips. Darkness, she leaned back and spread her legs for him.

Worse than her blatant offering was the rage that filled her when he refused. "I hurt you," Faye whispered. She'd truly viewed him as a possession and wanted to punish him for daring to disobey her.

Bile rose in her throat. These emotions weren't hers. This wasn't her. They were sick and Faye couldn't separate herself from them. *This wasn't her. Wasn't her.*

Faye backed away in a panic, stumbling off the end of the bed. She hit the stone floor, tangled in his sheet. Her stomach revolted as Faye rolled onto her hands and knees before dashing to his bathroom.

The lid clanked as Faye violently shoved it up and emptied the contents of her stomach into the toilet. She coughed on her knees in front of the bowl.

Tears pricked Faye's eyes, she couldn't dislodge her unwanted memories from her mind. She didn't do these things. Wouldn't do them. She would never feel like this.

A sheet fell over her, warming as it slid across her shoulders. Hands gathered her hair, holding it away from her face. Faye turned to find Rune kneeling beside her. He twisted her hair into a bun, and it somehow stayed in place when he let go.

"I am sorry I failed to hold you above the Darkness," he said, offering her a towel. Faye took it and the talisman he'd given Sparrow appeared on the ground next to them. He touched it and said, "Water and bread— Simple bread."

"I remember..." *Hurting you. Expecting you to obey me without question.* A pleasant chime interrupted Faye's thoughts. A silver tray appeared with four glasses and a pitcher of water beside a plate of small rolls.

Rune poured a glass, holding it out for her while he smoothed his hand over her back.

Faye took the glass, her breaths finally slowing. The nightmarish scene faded to settle in her mind. She rinsed her mouth and set the glass on the tray, drying her face with the towel. She closed the lid and sat back, sitting sideways between Rune's legs.

He pulled her closer, stretching his legs out on either side of her with his back to the tub that matched the one in her room. She stared dumbly at his bare foot poking out of the bottom of his dress slacks.

Her double called her a vessel. "Am I a body? Is she the dark queen you've been waiting for? When I invoke my blood does she take over?"

"No, vsenia," he answered, pulling her to his chest. "I am certain she is part of you. The only race I know of that can take a vessel are Pure Bloods." Rune reached out, taking the plate of rolls, and held it in front of her.

Faye took one, tearing off a small piece of it. Rune's words were no comfort as her breaths came faster. "What if she's like them, and I'm the vessel she plans to take?"

Rune rubbed his hand over her back in soothing strokes. 'Your heart is racing. Breathe in," he said, tracing his fingertips up her spine. When he reached the top, he said, "Breathe out," and followed her spine down.

Faye breathed with his strokes, hugging his other arm to her as she nibbled on bites of bread. "What do I do if I'm a vessel. How do you fight that?"

"You are not," Rune said, in a calm even tone. "My mother and Lyssa's mother were used as vessels for the original Pure Blood sisters. My mother killed the being that would have taken her body and became a Pure Blood. Lyssa's mother succumbed to it."

"How will I know the difference? "

"Tell me what you remember."

Faye concentrated on his touch and her breathing. The last thing she remembered as her was a burning sting when her body yielded to Rune's. Then she saw herself falling with Rune and reached for them.

She swallowed and said, "I remember everything."

"As you?" Rune asked.

Faye nodded.

"When the Ra'Voshnik—"

"Voshki," Faye said weakly.

Rune exhaled. "When you were with Voshki, I witnessed it. I feel what the creature does because we share a body. But the memories and thoughts are not mine. It has its own mind and speaks to me too often.

"I suspect your winged double is somehow your power running off instinct and base needs. The same instincts your Anarian upbringing suppressed."

Rune's words sickened her. She wasn't like that crazed bitch. Everything about her felt foreign and wrong. Faye's gaze met Rune's. He didn't seem overly upset by his treatment. Did all dark-blooded women act this way?

Faye muttered, "She thinks she owns you."

The corner of his mouth lifted. "Ownership is how a dark-blooded female shows affection to their male."

Faye laid her head on his arm. "I don't want to own you." Rune stiffened. "No I don't…" Faye hugged his arm tighter. "Your customs are strange to me."

He pulled her hair loose now that she was calmer and said, "They are customs you should have been raised in."

Faye remained silent. She didn't want to be raised in a dark court. She wanted a partner, not a possession to be commanded when the urge struck her and shelved when she was bored with it.

"Are you in any pain?" He asked.

"You're the one injured," Faye muttered. She leaned away to glance at his chest over her shoulder and asked, "Why is this still here when you healed up after I knocked you into the wall?"

"I have been preoccupied and need blood."

She hurt him, the least she could do was offer him the blood he needed to heal. "You… can take it from me."

He pressed a kiss to her hair. "I appreciate the offer, but bites are sexual. You are still adjusting, and I would be taking advantage of the situation."

A wine bottle appeared next to the silver tray. Rune poured the dark red liquid into a glass.

"Is that blood?"

"Yes, it is called crimson wine," Rune said before he drained the glass and poured a second.

Rune reached behind him and opened the faucet. Steaming water was poured into the tub. He ran his hand through her hair, and Faye couldn't help but remember how he touched her last night. It felt like he cared, and it was more than a ritual between them.

Faye smiled to herself. It was more than a ritual for Voshki. He called her his queen. He cherished her. And because he did, she gave him everything, took his bite while she screamed for him. Faye froze.

Everyone was in the study when she was—

Faye flushed. "Did they hear me last night?"

Rune chuckled.

"I'm serious."

"It is customary to shield the room when performing such duties."

Fifty-Two

Faye sat with Rune, silently taking comfort in his embrace. She closed her eyes, listening to the sound of water flowing behind her. His fingertips slid gently over her back as she rested against him.

He reached to shut the faucet off, and said, "A moment while I get your bath ready."

Faye sat up as he stood, going to his white marble counter. A dark wooden box appeared. Rune opened it and gathered a few thin vials of clear liquid and two pouches made of sheer white material.

Faye sat on the edge of the tub, absently gliding her fingers over the water's surface, letting the steam warm her. Rune poured the vials into her bath, and Faye leaned closer. Earthy smells reminded her of her walks in the forest bordering her home after a storm. The two oversized perforated pouches were added last, floating half submerged in the steaming water.

"Would you like me to stay and wash your hair?" He asked quietly, stroking her hair tentatively before caressing the back of her neck.

Did she? Faye stared at her bath water as a bag floated towards her. She made pouches like these along with other ointments for her village. Healing the sick and injured took longer without magic, but Faye did what she could to help.

She reached for it, curious which herbs would be in them. Faye squeezed it, disturbing its contents, and paused. She didn't recognize any of them. Her questions stilled as the water began to cloud until it turned milky white.

Faye glanced up at Rune. "Is it supposed to do that?"

"I thought you would prefer privacy," he said.

"You've already seen everything."

"It does not mean I am entitled to continue doing so."

Faye stood and said, "I would like it if you washed my hair."

Rune leaned in the doorway and turned his head to face into his room. He didn't look like the Shadow Prince, standing before her barefoot, wearing a robe over his slacks. He was Rune, the man beneath his title and power.

She turned her back to him, and his dark sheet slipped down her body and gathered around her feet. Faye stepped into his bath, lowering herself. The hot water soaked into her. Easing her muscle aches and leaving a tingling sensation on her skin, her head rested on the lip of the tub.

"You can turn around now," Faye said, not sure what to make of the man she woke next to. Was his kindness charity because he hadn't been able to hold her over the Darkness? When he deemed them even, would they return to what they were before?

Their strange truce left them both tense and frustrated.

Something clicked behind her, and Faye glanced up. He sat at the head of the tub and stretched his arm out, neatly rolling the sleeve of the robe. Muscles and tendons shifted along his forearm as he worked his sleeves into a cuff near his elbows.

His fingers threaded through the back of her thick black hair, reminding her of the way he'd kissed her and pulled the sash of her robe open last night. Faye closed her eyes as he guided her down, lowering her into the bath. He caressed the nape of her neck and Faye's lips parted.

Rune wet her hair, his thumb brushing over her temple to trace her hairline before smoothing behind her ear. She leaned back when he guided her up, and said, "Thank you for this."

"I will endeavor to be kinder with you," he said as a sweet floral scent washed over her. Faye sighed as his hands glided through her hair. Rune brushed his thumbs over her temples and added, "I recall promising to be better behaved in person."

Faye kept her expression relaxed. He'd never spoken of the dreams they shared. The way she leaned on him, reading her books. Safe and warm in his arms. Her mind wandered to their last dream, where he kissed her. Touched her like something he treasured.

And she'd sank her claws into his neck.

"I'm sorry I dug my claws in your neck," Faye said, glancing up at him.

He chuckled above her, flashing her a glimpse of fang. "Your temperament is suited for my kind."

Faye mulled over his words. Was he flirting with her? Faye had trouble holding her thoughts. Darkness, his fingers were bliss on her scalp. Rune lowered her into the water again, rinsing her hair.

She stared up at him, lazy and content. Whatever he put in this bath was better than the hot spring. Nothing hurt, and her skin hummed with pleasure. Rune met her gaze and she asked, "What are we doing?"

He canted his head and lowered his brow for a moment then answered, "Whatever you wish," and lifted her head up.

"Is this because we fell? You're working off some guilt?"

"No," he said quietly. Veined shadows crept from the corners of his eyes. "I wish to pursue you romantically."

Faye froze, her mind blanking. She hadn't dared to think he would want anything deeper with her. She was sure he would leave her bed when morning came but woke in his instead. She grasped for a subject to fill the silence she let grow between them and eyed the swaying misted shadows beneath his eyes. "Is Voshki awake?"

He was silent for a beat, then said, "There are few moments when it is not." Faye brightened, and Rune thinned his lips. "It would seem I am ill-suited to compete with the creature."

Faye looked away, feeling guilty for wanting the Ra'Voshnik inside him. Taking the parts she wanted and discarding the rest. The very reason she despised dark-bloods who would do the same to her.

"I treated you ill and have much to mend between us," Rune said, caressing the side of her neck. "I shall if you would allow me to."

Hope and hesitation filled her in the same instance. Faye hadn't allowed men to engage her. Choosing to abstain rather than hurt, Voshki wouldn't hurt her. Faye was sure he loved her. This kind and considerate side of Rune made him nearly irresistible, but could she trust him? "How does this work with... both of you?"

Rune's jaw tensed. "I am untried in these situations. In private, I could allow your Voshki to rise. I will warn you. The creature speaks too often and is quite opinionated."

Faye giggled. "I would like that."

He gave her a curious glance and said, "If this suits you, are you willing to accept my advances?"

"If I do, will we be equals?"

Rune laughed softly. "No. You are a woman."

Seething rage filled her, and Faye sat up, glaring at him over her shoulder. She was going to show him how suited her temperament really was.

Rune held his hands up in a peaceful gesture. "You misunderstand my words. We are not equals because I am an extension of your will. You are the queen I will serve before all others."

Faye's fury cooled, and she settled against the tub below him once more. She glared up at him, her anger lingered. Simmering. If Rune sensed it he paid it no heed and leaned over her, bringing his lips a moment from hers. "I am yours to command," he rasped.

Faye wanted to kiss him. Wanted to let him take her back to his bed. But more than desire, she wanted acceptance. Love.

What he offered was obedience.

"You don't even know me," she whispered at his lips.

"I know you," he crooned. "You are the minx that upended my orderly life. You are fierce and loyal. Cunning. I was a fool to ignore what the Ra'Voshnik recognized in you from the start. Accept me, and I will spend the rest of my days making it up to you."

If they could meet each other halfway, make room for the other. It might be enough.

With that hope Faye leaned up and touched her lips to his in a soft kiss.

Fifty-Three

Faye's lips whispered over his, a feather-light caress. Tentative. Hesitant. Rune smoothed the back of his fingers over her cheek and pulled back. He'd caused her reluctance through his misdeeds. Knowing he was responsible was a knife twisting in his chest.

The Ra'Voshnik slowly circled the edges of his mind, sluggish as he was. *Ask her forgiveness,* it grumbled.

Faye would need actions, not words. Rune gazed down at his queen and said, "Allow me to court you and begin anew."

She sank deeper into her bath. "If you want to court me, I don't want to be trapped here." She upturned her face and said, "I want to go home. I want my freedom back."

Build her an estate. The Ra'Voshnik purred through his mind, eager to curry Faye's favor. Urging him to return with her to her home.

Rune held no desire to reside in Anaria, and arguing with her would prove pointless. His queen desired control, needing things done on her terms. Proceeding by her decision. Perhaps he could offer her something she might prefer more than returning to Anaria. She'd grown aroused with the male beneath Kayla's crop. What other proclivities did his queen possess?

Rune leaned closer to say, "And if I were to request you remain with me until I find your altar?" The minx stilled, gazing up at him.

"If I pleaded…" Rune purred softly as her pulse quickened.

Faye parted her lips as his breath fanned over her ear. She exhaled slowly, and her lids slid closed.

"Begged," Rune rasped.

Pink tinged her cheeks, and she turned toward him. Her gaze fell to his mouth for a moment before returning to him. "The proud Shadow Prince would beg an Anarian peasant?"

"Would you want me to?"

Faye blinked, the flush crossing her cheeks had nothing to do with the bath she soaked in. Rune wanted to lift the corner of his mouth but refrained. He'd pushed far enough. Faye would mull over his words and cultivate the ideas he planted.

Rune pulled back slightly, running his fingers through her hair. Giving her time to collect herself.

After a while, she said, "I'm due back in my village."

"I will happily escort you anywhere you wish. Your village. A bookstore in Necromia."

Faye's smile lit her gold arced eyes, and an unfamiliar tightness took hold of Rune's chest. His queen's happiness oddly filled him with the same emotion.

Finally learning to enjoy life? The Ra'Voshnik snickered.

The creature was right. Rune looked forward to the moments he could spend with Faye. Longed for them.

Faye leaned into his hand. "Can we go to my village tomorrow?"

"Of course," Rune said, brushing his fingertips along her scalp. Faye leaned further into his hand and closed her eyes. He was certain if she were able, she would be purring for him at this very moment. "Tell me when you wish to go."

Faye sighed her agreement as Morbid's voice filled his mind.

If you wish to speak with me, Prince, I suggest you do so now. Angelique grows restless and is demanding we return to Chaos. She will require my attention for the next few days.

I will arrive in a moment, Rune said to Morbid's mind and snapped the connection.

We will remain with our queen, the Ra'Voshnik growled, prowling his mind.

We will return. Be silent. Rune grated as he glanced down at Faye. "I have some matters that require my attention. You should soak a while. The herbs help with discomfort and assist in healing."

"Thank you." Faye nuzzled his hand and moved away, sinking into the milky bath to her chin.

Rune stood and phased to the north wing. The creature growled, pulling back before bashing itself against the surface of his mind. It fought him viciously for dominance of his body. Desperate to return to Faye. Rune sank his claws into it, dragging it down.

If you cannot conduct yourself in a civilized manner, I will treat you as an animal.

Return to her, the creature yelled from its confines.

Be silent, Rune grated. There was more to be done than laying at her feet. The fool creature had a singular mind.

Rune followed Morbid's mental tug to the third bedroom. The Familiar King stood near the fire, cradling a sleek white cat. Morbid's wife rarely accompanied him to court before she was poisoned and remained solely in Chaos after. This was the first time he'd seen her since the assassination attempt.

Angelique twisted her head, biting the leather trench covering his forearm while kicking his hand with her hind legs. Morbid turned toward him, meeting his gaze.

"Is the Lady well?" Rune asked.

Morbid pet her affectionately, indifferent to her teeth and claws. "Being away from Chaos unsettles her mind."

Rune nodded. "I will be brief. Tell me what she is."

"I have told you time and again Prince, she is your queen."

Tension lined his shoulders. "You know well that is not my question. What race is she?"

Morbid shrugged. "Can't say. Does it matter?"

"She needs her shard to defend herself," Rune pleaded.

Morbid leaned back and raised his brow. "From what Prince?"

Those that would harm her to strike at me, Rune thought bitterly. Morbid clasped his hand over Rune's shoulder and met his gaze. "Every answer you seek lies directly in front of you."

The Familiar King vanished before Rune could reply. He glanced up and exhaled. Familiar riddles were of no use to him. He reached for Sadi's mind.

I require your assistance on a matter.

Sadi appeared next to him. Disheveled, and covered in Damian's scent. She was wrapped in a robe made of layers of lace. "It's early," she growled.

It most certainly was not, but from the look of her, Damian woke her at a dreadful hour and had not allowed her a moments rest.

"Apologies," Rune said. "I need to witness the fall. Understand how I survived."

Skilled Familiar were able to step into a point in time during an individual's life and watch the events unfold. This type of viewing was known as witnessing. Rune understood his ask was taxing, but it was necessary.

Sadi took a deep breath, rolling her shoulders. "You need to tread carefully with her. My visions say she's death."

Sadi stepped into his mind and carried his consciousness with her. They appeared at the top of the psychic ravine cradling the Darkness. A few feet away Rune saw himself holding Faye while the Ra'Voshnik lingered nearby.

Sadi held up her hand and twisted it as she curled her fingers down.

The scene played as Rune remembered. They plummeted. Sadi screamed above them.

Just as Rune hit the Darkness it formed a hollow, encasing them. He'd never seen the Darkness behave this way. It churned and curled in on itself, but this. The winged Faye had said a part of the Darkness was hers.

Had Faye's survival instinct saved him because he refused to let her go?

Rune glanced at Sadi as the vision pulled them *through* the Darkness. Dragging them deeper. Sadi tensed and muttered, "I don't like this."

Neither did he. Rune reminded himself witnessing events in this matter couldn't hurt them. He endured the uncomfortable moments and the Darkness opened into a circular room Rune recognized. Fine white sand covered the ground. His bed arranged at the center of this circular hollow cut into the Darkness.

Faye's winged double stood near the bed floating a few inches off the ground. Her hair and lace gown drifting around her as though she were submerged in deep water.

The telltale signs of Familiar magic.

She outstretched her hand, carefully guiding their limp bodies onto the bed.

The scene froze and Sadi turned toward him. "She's not Familiar. How does she have our magic? How are there two of her?"

"Can you look into her double? Does she have her own line separate from Faye?"

Sadi quieted for a while and frowned. "I've never seen anything like this. They are the same line. You thought the lives I saw were a spell being perfected. What if this part of her is what carries through her lives."

Sadi waved her hand and the scene dissipated, melting away. She paced the room, hugging her arms to her sides. "I feel death in my vision. I can't see it clearly, but I feel it."

"I am quite difficult to kill," Rune reassured her. "I need to locate her altar so I can make her whole."

Sadi paused before the window, glancing through it to Hell's ever-twilight sky. She quietly murmured, "Like calls to like."

Fifty-Four

Faye had been soaking long enough for the water to have cooled by now. A smile spread over her lips, maybe magic was good for something. A soft chime sounded. The silver tray holding the water and bread vanished. The small black stone forgotten on the floor.

Faye's stomach angrily gnawed at her. Would Rune join her for breakfast? Did he even eat? Faye's eyes fell back to the obsidian talisman. Sparrow definitely ate and was probably pulling her hair out looking for the black stone.

Vash couldn't phase out of Hell but could he phase food from his tavern in. She would kill for some chicken fingers right now. Something normal instead of the fancy meals they'd been having. Faye flipped the lever to drain the bath and got out, retrieving Rune's talisman.

She shut the door and dried off, glancing over towards the dark wooden box he left open. Vials, bottles, and various pouches of herbs were neatly arranged in their individual compartments. His soaps and cleansing oils were arranged with the same organized care in neat low lipped containers along the edge of the mirror.

She wrapped the towel around herself, resisting the urge to shift his things a few inches. Faye walked through Rune's room, returning to hers. Her steps faltered at the sight of her mangled bed. Deep gouges tore through the blankets and mattress. Stuffing and torn material spilled out on to the floor. Did he do that?

Faye walked past it and dressed quickly, heading back to the south wing. She slowed her pace walking past Rune's study hoping to find him behind his desk. She wondered what matters he was seeing to when she realized the space was empty.

She found her sister in the den, squinting as she picked over yesterday's platter of dried meat, cheese, and crackers.

"Hit Rune's bar cart too hard?" Faye asked.

Sparrow sat with a huff. "Your evil twin started screaming and she hit me with her black tentacle."

Faye tensed. "She did what?"

Sparrow waved her off. "Tendril," she corrected. "She drained us."

Faye's gaze swept over her sister. "Did she hurt you? Do you need a healer?"

"It feels like a bad hangover," Sparrow said, scrubbing her hand over her nose. "Did Runey take care of you?"

Faye surveyed the room. Her sister noted her reaction and said, "Vash isn't here, he's sparring with Damian in the courtyard."

"Sadi didn't drain him?"

"No, I think she drained us all. I woke up to a cute love note from Morbid saying not to disturb you and his shadowy highness. He gave us tea bags for this shit to recover." Sparrow pushed a tall glass of dark liquid further away from her. "Vash choked it down. I can't."

Sparrow slapped the table and winced at the sound. "I forgot. Runey came in here looking for your magic vagina."

A parchment folded into thirds appeared in Sparrow's hand. Faye took it and arched her brow at her sister when she glimpsed the wax seal was already cracked.

"What," Sparrow exclaimed. "I stopped. Your dealings with him are private." Her sister rolled her eyes. "You never kept secrets from me until him."

"They aren't secrets. They're private," Faye said opening the letter. She read it and read it again. It was a sentence written in smooth masculine script.

Sparrow held her hand out, grasping her fingers at the letter. Faye handed it over and set the obsidian talisman on the table. She touched it and said, "Eggs and toast please." Faye turned toward Sparrow expecting her sister to have an order at the ready, but she remained silent, tilting her head at Rune's letter.

"Why is he so boring?" She finally said, before reading the letter in a deeper voice, poorly imitating Rune's accent. "Rune Sacarlay, the Shadow Prince, of the Court of the Black Rose requests permission to court Faye Alexander of an undetermined court."

Sparrow sighed letting the letter fall to the table. "Tell me he wasn't that boring in bed." Her sister brightened. "Did you make him purr and ride his face?"

Faye flushed at the memory of Rune holding her down while he purred against her. Sparrow gasped at her reaction and clasped her hands together. "You did! I didn't think you had it in you. Tell me everything." She leaned forward thrumming with excitement.

Faye looked down at her hands. She couldn't describe the rush of feelings that washed through her when she thought of Voshki and Rune. It all seemed so simple when it was just them while she soaked. Apprehension laced with guilt choked her. Was she allowed to want them both?

"There's two of him," Faye spoke in a hushed whisper, studying her hands.

"What?" Her sister bit out and poked her knee when she took too long to answer.

Faye glanced up, and her sister quirked her lip, widening her eyes at her. Faye took a steading breath. "There's another part of him, his bloodlust."

Sparrow's eyebrows lifted and she nodded appreciatively as she leaned back in her chair. "Are we talking about how he gets a little wild when he's got the bad eyeliner?"

A pleasant chime sounded, and Faye glanced at the breakfast she was no longer hungry for. Faye looked away and answered quietly, "He brought me into his mind. There's two of them, I saw them both."

Sparrow wrinkled her nose as she crossed her legs under her and asked, "How does that work. Do they take turns?" Faye flushed deeply. She supposed they had. Her sister snorted and shook her head. "You have two trained males. Darkness, I hate you. Everyone, everyone has a bad fuck before you find someone who knows what they're doing. But not this bitch. Not Faye."

"Stop yelling so loud," Faye hissed.

Sparrow's shoulders slumped. "He must have showed you a really good time if you're too shy to talk about it, so why do you look like I trampled your garden?"

Faye closed her eyes and pressed her hands together. She brought the tips of her index fingers to her lips and glared at her sister. "There are *two* men in him," Faye said, opening her hands as she enunciated each word.

"And?"

Darkness, why did she want to talk to Sparrow about this. Of course, this would be her answer. "What do you mean, and? Am I supposed to pretend it's fine and date both of them?"

Sparrow stared at her wide-eyed. "You want him to be your boyfriend."

Faye shoved her sister's leg. "What do I do?"

Sparrow sighed dramatically. "As far as anyone can tell, he's the Shadow Prince. It doesn't matter if there are two of him. It's private," her sister said the last with a toothy grin.

"But I know there are two of him."

Her sister blew a blonde curl out of her face. "You are so worried about the wrong shit. You like him, right? I know you like him."

Faye nodded.

"Then ask him to bring you into his mind and fuck them both," her sister said as she pulled Faye's plate in front of her. "We're staying, right? Runey added Vash to his wards so he can come and go and not get blasted."

"He's searching for my altar."

"I'd say he found it."

Faye kicked Sparrow under the table.

"Not so hard bitch," Sparrow complained rubbing her shin. "What are you upset about? You have a man that gives you orgasms and is tracking down your shard. Do you want him to buy you a puppy too?"

Faye exhaled, stealing a slice of toast from Sparrow's plate. On the surface being with Rune looked perfect. He was wealthy, handsome, and powerful. But Faye saw deeper aspects that cast their relationship in an unfavorable light. He was an immortal dark-blood and Faye wasn't. She didn't fit into his world. She didn't want his obedience or to join his dark court of luxury and wealth. How could she live in this knowing her village suffered?

She needed Rune to see her. Choose her.

Sparrow crossed her arms. "I can see the smoke coming out of your ears. Stop overthinking and just fuck him. Preferably both of them."

"What does that make me?"

"A lucky bitch?" At Faye's scowl, her sister apologized. "I'm sorry but who's going to know? They're in the same body, you can't really avoid it. They're a package deal. Lots of dark-blooded queens have multiple lovers. You're just starting your," her sister wrinkled her nose. "There's a fucking word for it, I don't remember."

"I don't want a multiple lovers," Faye bit out.

Sparrow rolled her eyes and threw her hand up, leaning forward. "Well, you don't get anything if you don't make a decision. You're allowed to fuck him. You're allowed to not fuck him. You just have to pick one."

Her sister was always too quick to leap into things blind. *The consequences will be worth the memory.* Sparrow would have pounced on Rune at her first opportunity. Faye chewed her toast, staring into the fireplace. Getting close to him left her open for heartache. "What if I invoke my blood and I still age, or if he never finds my altar?"

What if he leaves me?

"Honey, you're worried about the wrong questions."

Faye eyed her sister. "What question should I be worried about then?"

"What makes you happy?" Sparrow hooked her foot behind Faye's ankle and gently swung her foot. "That's the only question that matters in the end."

"It's not that simple," Faye answered.

Sparrow snorted in response. "It is, you're just a control freak." She leaned an elbow on the table and gazed past Faye. "Your boyfriend is here."

Faye elbowed Sparrow before turning toward Rune.

Her sister stood and flicked a length of Faye's hair. "I'm going to watch Vash and Damian be all sweaty." She pointed at Rune as she passed and said, "Be nice to her, fangs."

The corner of his mouth lifted as he took a seat beside Faye. "Is fangs my name or the Ra'Voshnik's?"

Faye laughed. "You're fangs, he's Voshki."

Rune nodded with a smile. "I wanted to speak to you about your line."

Faye brightened. "Did you find something?"

"I am still researching your altar. Sadi looked into your line."

Faye's expression instantly soured, and Rune brushed the backs of his fingers down her arm.

Rune's look softened. "I understand you have your differences. I am not asking you to like her. She is the darkest and most skilled Familiar aside from Morbid and the Familiar King never gives a straight answer. I have known her for seventeen centuries. She has saved my life on more than one occasion."

"She's still a bitch," Faye added.

Rune nodded, momentarily arching a brow. "I can agree with your sentiment."

"Am I related to her?"

"No, and I am unsure why the two of you hold such a likeness. Your line is not Familiar. You are tethered in the Darkness."

My shores, her winged double's words echoed through her mind.

"You have lived many lives, they have run concurrently the past eight centuries," Rune explained.

The information settled heavily on Faye. "Am I immortal then. Can I be immortal." Faye didn't dare to hope. Afraid to want things that could be taken from her.

Rune brushed his fingers over the back of her hand. "I do not know for certain. I will continue searching for your altar. Darkness willing, your immortality will set when you invoke your blood."

A hope Faye coveted desperately but feared wanting.

Fifty-Five

Faye studied her reflection. It had been weeks since she wore her own clothes. They seemed out of place on her and the lack of familiarity with her own belongings left her feeling unsettled. She'd unknowingly grown accustomed to dressing in what Rune gifted her.

In comparison her black trousers and gray sweater seemed simple and plain.

Faye set her winter coat on her bed and finished packing her vials and ointments. A knock pulled her attention away from her task.

Rune stood in the doorway, the glow of hellfire flickering over him. "May I come in?"

Faye nodded as she cinched her pack closed. She shouldered her pack, looking him over. Nothing about this man was inconspicuous. "Can you take me home? I'll return around sundown."

"I will accompany you."

"You'll terrify the whole village."

The corner of his mouth lifted. "Prey will always flee a predator."

Faye glared at him, anger whispering through her veins. "They aren't animals." He wanted to court her but continued to look down at her kind. "Maybe it would be better if I went alone," she said.

A muscle ticked in Rune's jaw. He took a deep breath and exhaled slowly through his nose. "I would ask you allow me to accompany you."

Faye smoothed over her temper. He was making an effort and she could do the same. "You'll need to invisible yourself." Faye couldn't have him spooking the whole village.

"You take too much care with these mortals."

Faye clenched her jaw. "I'm one of those mortals."

With a pointed look, he said, "You are *not* one of them."

His disdain for Anarians shoved a wedge deeper between them.

Rune's look softened in response to her anger. "It pains me beyond words that you were subjected to Anaria. You are dark-blooded, meant for so much more than your meager beginnings."

Faye took a step toward him and hissed, "My meager beginnings shaped who I am."

He exhaled, searching her gaze. "It is your old life. You belong in dark-blooded society. They are a liability to you at best."

"I don't care about dark-bloods or their archaic courts."

"You *are* a dark-blood. It matters not if you care."

Faye seethed. "Invisible yourself and take me to my village!"

Rune's shoulders stiffened. He held his hand out to her, biting out the words, "As you command."

Rune phased them inside her cottage in Anaria. The Ra'Voshnik prowled his mind. *Stop angering our queen,* it grated.

Rune ignored the creature, glancing over the simple dwelling as his night breeze rushed away from him, into her room. He took a breath, fighting for patience. How she could hold on to this place— This village, with all he could offer? She clung to her old life with such desperation, unable to see how ill-suited it was for her.

It is her preference, we bow to her will, the Ra'Voshnik purred.

She preferred this hovel because it was all she knew. *She deserves more than this.*

It is not our place to question her.

Rune tuned out the Ra'Voshnik as Faye returned to him. Anger simmering in her gaze. "Are you invisible?"

"I will not be detected by your Anarians," he answered.

Faye exited her home and Rune followed, closing the door behind him. He walked beside her in silence. He resented the rags she dressed in but held his tongue, knowing she would only dig her heels in. He appreciated her fiery nature but couldn't fathom why she held so tightly to this miserable life.

The unpaved road they walked dusted his shoes. Rune turned toward her. Her long silken black hair fell in a glossy sheet down her back, shining in the afternoon sun. She was lovely to behold even in her subpar garments. His night breeze was an enigma. A beautiful puzzle he was eager to solve.

"I would like to understand you," Rune began. Faye gave him a sideward glance and he continued, "Why do you cling to this?"

The Ra'Voshnik clawed at his awareness. *Stop talking.*

She rolled her eyes at him and looked forward. "Why do you?"

"I would not cling to this," Rune paused, looking for a term that would cause the least amount of offense to his queen as the creature ordered him to remain silent. "Lifestyle," Rune said after a time.

"Why do I have to change for you? You could just as easily live in Anaria." She shot him a pointed look. "Join my circles."

Revulsion filled Rune, surely, she jested. "*We* are dark-blooded, as far removed from the Anarians as they are from the animals they herd."

Rune realized he'd misspoke as Faye's eyes blazed with fury. "They are not fucking animals."

"Apologies, I did not mean to offend you."

She grew more flustered with every word he spoke.

Shut up. You are turning her from us.

Rune fell silent as her village came into view. How could she prefer this? Rune scented livestock and unwashed bodies. The odor grew thicker as they entered the meager village. Rune tensed expecting the Ra'Voshnik to seize on what it would consider prey. To his surprise, it ignored the villagers and remained focused on Faye.

Rune's gaze fell to a small altar burning at the center of the open square. He stepped away from Faye to glance at the offerings and his brow lowered. These mortals burned offerings to The Creator, Saith.

His mentor's voice dragged through his mind. *All my efforts on you will be wasted.*

Their efforts were wasted. Saith would never lower himself to acknowledge an Anarian and his one-time mentor was long dead.

Rune turned back to Faye, watching as she smiled warmly, speaking to several of the villagers. Darkness, he would commit atrocities for her to look at him with that same affection and acceptance.

Bow to her will and she shall.

Be silent.

Rune stepped around a young girl leading a goat as he made his way back to her. He surveyed the handful of shops and homes, attempting to find anything here he would prefer.

He found nothing redeemable.

Faye continued on her way, ignoring him entirely. She entered a store where she traded her potions for a miniscule amount of coin. He wanted to set up an account for her but worried his hot-tempered minx would take offense.

She entered a store that sold remedial confections next and the confection clerk's pulse increased. Rune stepped into the shop and parted his lips, taking a slow inhalation. The male's want crossed his tongue and Rune tensed.

Kill him! Tear his head from his shoulders!

Rune dragged the Ra'Voshnik below the surface as the clerk smiled at Faye, leaning his hip on the counter. He filled her order and brushed his fingertips over hers as he collected her payment.

Rune left the shop, stifling a growl. He was not jealous of an Anarian candy merchant.

Faye met his gaze for a moment before brushing past him. In a hushed whisper, she asked, "Why is your eyeliner showing?"

Rune didn't answer, following her along a dirt path north. It led out of the village and ended as they reached the top of the hill. She turned to him wide-eyed. "You did this?"

Faye could only stare at aunty Clara's house. The lawn was covered with thick grass, the gate rebuilt. The large house was repaired and repainted, white with red trim. It looked better than it did when she was a child. It looked... new.

Rune returned her look with one of confusion. He canted his head and said, "I kept my terms of our bargain. Is this not what you required?"

Faye threw her arms around him, pulling away before anyone saw her hugging nothing. She couldn't find the words to express her gratitude. "Thank you," stumbled from her lips.

She turned from him and hurried to the gate. The children all wore matching uniforms. Adults with the same outfits walked the grounds with the children. The little ones squealed her name as they ran to her. Faye needed to talk to Aunty Clara. She spotted one of the older girls and stood on her toes to wave. "Kimber!"

The tall brunette smiled and walked over to Faye. She turned sixteen this year and had an interest in making potions like Faye to support herself when she outgrew aunty Clara's house.

"Kimber will give you your treats, guys," Faye informed the children, dropping an arm around the younger ones that hugged her waist.

Kimber took the package and beamed. "Can you believe it? Aunty Clara has workers, and we have teachers. We even have horses."

"How did this happen?" Faye could hardly believe all the changes.

"The High Queen. She rebuilt the orphan homes in five villages."

Faye smiled as she grappled with the new details. The High Queen? That bitch didn't do this. Faye's temper flared, thinking of the High Queen's parting words to her.

Feel free to call your court to war against the Shadow Prince.

Faye turned back to Rune, his expression revealing nothing as he trailed behind her.

"Darkness, look at all the candy Faye gave me!" Kimber clutched the bag to her chest.

"It's not only for you."

"Hey, that's for all of us."

The small children gave chase as Kimber ran off to the new swing set and slides.

Faye stood overwhelmed for a moment. Rune came up beside her, his expression concerned. She smiled up at him. "You got them teachers and a staff."

"This is how orphans are cared for. Did they require something additional?"

This was not how orphans were cared for. Was this normal in Necromia? "You gave the High Queen credit and did this in five villages."

"It would be suspicious if I only rebuilt this orphanage and claimed credit. Lyssa rules this land. The people should look to her."

The high bitch didn't deserve credit for Rune's kindness. *Kindness you blackmailed him into,* she couldn't help but remind herself. Faye pushed the thought aside. She didn't care how it happened. The home she loved was restored.

Aunty Clara came out to the porch, and Faye waved, rushing to the old woman to hug her in greeting. Faye went about restocking the supplies and found every drawer full. All her tonics and ointments were stocked, and there were other jars and vials she didn't recognize.

The old woman swatted her bottom as she entered the kitchen. "The High Queen set up accounts to Necromia for all that. You don't need to worry about us."

Faye sat with the old woman, conflicted. She was glad they had supplies, and the repairs were made. What would Faye do now that she didn't need to help out around here?

Movement caught her eye as Rune glided past the doorway. Faye guessed he took a seat on one of the chairs outside.

Aunty Clara made tea as they sat. They talked for hours, gossiping and eating pastries. The elderly woman recounted all the mischief the children were getting into and went on to explain all the renovations and her small staff.

"I sent one of the boys to your place to have you come to dinner, but they said you weren't home." Aunty Clara's day-blood shard glimmered as it swirled into itself.

"Sparrow and I are spending some time in Necromia." Faye lied.

The old woman's eyes lit as she smiled. "You finally find a boy to settle down with?"

Faye looked down at her tea. "Not yet."

"You're so hardheaded."

Faye heard Rune chuckle and found him standing in the doorway. She tucked her hair behind her ear, casting him a discrete rude gesture.

Aunty Clara stood up to peer out the kitchen window. "You should go before it gets dark. It's no good to walk in the dark."

Faye stood up and hugged the old woman goodbye. When she turned, the doorway was empty. Faye stepped outside and caught sight of Rune's long white-blonde hair. He stood on the other side of the gate, waiting for her.

Faye hugged the children on her way out. As she crossed the gate, Rune held his hand out to her. "Shall we?"

"They can't see me disappear." Faye motioned for him to follow her as she headed up the road.

Faye cut across a field to the road that would lead back to her home instead of walking through the village again. She glanced at Rune. The setting sun cast hues of red and orange over him, lighting the edge of his hair.

Handsome wasn't a fitting enough description for him. This man was otherworldly. They couldn't be more different. He seemingly didn't comprehend why his repairs would surprise her. And he did this in four other villages. He had to be obscenely rich to afford and maintain all of this.

Rune's voice drew her from her thoughts. "I would like you to accompany me to the Artithian princess's wedding."

Faye's mind blanked, and she blinked at him. "You want to bring me? In front of all the realms."

He smiled, arching a brow at her as they walked. "That is the intent."

"Take someone else," Faye muttered, glancing down at her bare index finger. Being surrounded by dark-bloods was uncomfortable enough, being surrounded by royal dark-bloods sounded like a nightmare.

"I am pursuing you. There is no one else." Faye gave him a sidelong glance. Longing filled his gaze. "How can I prove my intentions to you?"

By choosing me and not trying to discard the parts you don't like. "When is it?"

"A month's time."

Faye stopped on the road. They were far enough from the village now. "Then you have a month to win my affection. Shall we?" She held her hand out to him.

Fifty-Six

A week passed since Faye's visit to Anaria. Rune routinely sought her out during the day. Asking her to share a meal, where he drank blood while she ate or he simply remained in her company as he read documents.

When Rune was away from her, he scoured documents looking for leads that would shed light on what she was or her altar.

Today Rune read brittle, yellowed pages as she arranged her herbs on drying racks.

"How do you…" Faye bit the inside of her lip when Rune glanced up from his research. Under his gaze her nerve quickly left her. She focused on the leaves on her drying rack, and said in a rush, "How are you so sure I'm your queen?"

"You consume my every thought. I long to be near you." He spoke with such calm conviction, guilt nipped at her for questioning him. Faye tentatively glanced up and the corner of his mouth lifted. "I have tried to stay away. I managed five miserable days. My blood sings for you."

A romantic notion because she was young. "It'll stop singing as I age," Faye said flatly. He would remain the same as she withered with time. He would leave.

Rune pushed his chair away from the table and extended his hand. "Come here."

Faye came to stand between his knees. She placed her hand in his, not meeting his gaze.

His lips brushed the back of her hand and he glanced up at her from beneath his thick dark lashes. "Sit with me."

Faye lowered herself to his thigh, desperately wanting to believe his words. Needing to believe fate superseded circumstance. The part of her that guarded her heart said it wasn't enough. Urged her to run before she fell any deeper. Cut her losses or hurt forever.

Rune's hand closed over hers as he stroked her back. Faye's tension fell away and he said, "I will never turn from you. I do hope you become immortal when you invoke your blood. But if that is not our fate, I will cherish the time I have with you and wait for your return."

Faye leaned forward to rest her forehead against his. His words touched her, soothing the scars she carried on her heart. She wrapped her arms around him, tangling her hands in his white-blonde hair. He pulled her closer, his lips a moment from hers. She closed her eyes letting his words resonate in her. Humming along the connection she felt between them.

She leaned forward touching her lips to his.

It was a soft, chaste kiss. He didn't take or demand more. His longing and reverie evident in every touch. Being in his arms felt so right, it scared her.

The part of her mind that protected her heart for so many years screamed his words were honeyed lies. That she should run before he could hurt her. Faye pushed it away, silencing the protesting voice. Concentrating on his touch. How she felt when he held her close.

Faye pulled back, breaking their kiss. She was met with a soul deep yearning reflected in his pale blue gaze. His veined misted shadows swayed, brushing over the tops of his cheekbones. She swept her thumb through the shadows.

"Would you like me to let Voshki rise?"

"No," she breathed as she brushed her fingertips over the side of his face. "Can I touch you?"

He smiled up at her, giving her a flash of his fangs. "You may do anything that pleases you."

She stood to retrieve a length of uncut ribbon Rune gave her to bind the herbs together.

The corner of his mouth lifted as he glanced up from her ribbon to meet her gaze. "You wish to be restrained?"

Faye ran the length of the silk between her fingers. "Oh, this isn't for me." He arched his brow and she giggled. "You're the one who couldn't control himself and ripped up my bed."

He canted his head at her. "Always blaming me for your actions. *Your* wings shredded *your* bed when I attempted to untangle myself from *your* hold. I did however enjoy the way you clung to me in your sleep. An experience I would not mind repeating."

Faye wet her lips. She couldn't tell him, but she missed the dreams where she slept in his arms while he stroked her hair. She curled her finger at him as she sauntered over.

Rune obeyed, gazing down at her. "What game did my minx have in mind?"

"One where you don't get to touch me." Faye waved her finger in a circle indicating for him to turn around. He turned as she bid. Faye pulled his arms behind his back crossing his wrists before binding them with her ribbon.

Rune twisted to glance down at her. "You realize I can break this."

She met his gaze with one of mischief. "But you won't."

"And what would my queen command of me?"

"Sit."

Rune turned and took his seat. Faye bit the inside of her lip as her toes curled. With all his power, he would choose to submit to her. The control she wielded over him intoxicated her, making her bold.

Faye stroked the front of his throat and Rune lifted his chin, giving her more access. A low rumble emanated from him, vibrating beneath her touch.

"Are you purring?" She teasingly ran her thumb over his bottom lip. Rune answered in a low groan.

Faye crawled onto his lap, straddling his hips. Rune stared up at her, his gaze predatory. "I'm going to touch you and you will not move."

He smiled up at her, male desire blatant in his eyes. His deep, accented voice caressed her as he purred, "Yes, my queen."

Faye stood on her knees and gripped the front of his throat. She was a little taller than him in this position. Her heart pounded wildly as her gaze lingered on his lips. She wet her own and bent to brush her lips against his.

The touch of his lips thrilled her. His mouth began to move with hers, kissing her gently. Faye fisted his hair, tugging back until he hissed a breath.

"You don't get to move," she whispered against his lips. Faye kissed him again and he remained still, keeping his lips parted for her. She loosened her grip on his hair and sighed, "Good."

She breathed in his scent of amber and sandalwood, giving herself over to the feel of him. She licked his fangs and teasingly nibbled on his bottom lip. Her hands explored the hard planes of his body.

His surrender affected some primal, visceral part of her. She wanted to take everything he had to give. To let her want devour him whole. Her nipples tightened, pressing against the thin fabric of her shirt. Rune closed his eyes as Faye tightened her grip on his throat, dragging his bottom lip through her teeth.

She flattened her hand over his chest moving lower. His muscles tensed, flexing beneath her touch. His groans made her desperate for more of him. Faye's nails dragged over the material of his fine shirt. She kissed him harder, needing more.

Faye seized the front of his throat, pressing him back against the chair. "Kiss me."

In a blur, he leaned up, his tongue stroking against hers. His fang nicked her lip.

Rune pulled back, but Faye moved with him, too caught up in the moment to care. Her hands tangled in his hair, pulling him in. He groaned as she rolled her hips, moving over his hard length. She moaned into his mouth, pressing harder. Her heart thundered in her ears as her body tensed. Faster. Harder. Darkness, she could come just by doing this.

"Bitch, I'm ordering lunch."

Faye froze, her gaze snapping to the door.

It clicked open as Faye scrambled off Rune.

Sparrow stood wide eyed in the doorway for a moment before she gave them both a toothy grin. "Are you finally going to fuck him?" Then she gave a pointed look at Rune. "Go easy on her." She shut the door, yelling through it, "I'll just order extra food. Don't forget to hydrate!"

Mortified, Faye turned back to Rune. "I'm so sorry."

The corner of his mouth lifted into a sexy smirk and Faye didn't find it intolerable. The sight made her ache for him all over again.

"I believe Sparrow ruined your game. May I free myself from your bonds now?" He asked.

Faye's eyes widened, she forgot she tied his wrists. "Stand up, I'll untie you."

Rune stood, bringing his arms in front of him and held her knotted ribbon out to her.

"How'd you do that?" Faye asked as she took the ribbon and began the work of untying it.

Rune rolled his shoulders. "Phasing through material is a simple task."

He could have gotten out of her hold at any time, but he stayed to please her. A smile tugged on her lips.

"I could tend to you if you wish." He lifted his chin and inhaled, closing his eyes. He met her gaze again, a dark hunger flickering in his stare. "Ease your ache."

"And who would tend to you?"

"I can slake myself. You could watch if you wish." He teased.

Faye's gaze lowered to his straining erection. The thought of him stroking himself excited her. Darkness, he was too tempting. She wanted him, and it frightened her. Her fear didn't lie with him. She feared he would realize fate wasn't enough to bridge their worlds and leave her.

She forced herself to take a step back. "I think I've had enough excitement for the day."

"Should I procure a riding crop for you?" He asked.

Faye stood frozen as flush spread over her cheeks.

He raised his brow at her reaction. "Unless you prefer something else. I could ask Kayla to arrange a merchant. I am sure she would be more than happy to show you her arsenal. You could pick and choose what strikes you."

Faye turned her back to him, wishing she could phase and hide.

Rune stepped toward her, the backs of his fingers grazing down her arm. "You have nothing to feel shame for. We all have our own desires." His hand slid to hers and brought the back of her hand to his lips. "I prefer the riding crop to a candle holder if I have a say in the matter."

Faye laughed and leaned into him. Curiosity tugged at her imagination as she relaxed against him. "Can we look together?"

He stroked her hair. "I will have it arranged."

"Are you sure this is okay?"

Rune smiled down at her and pressed a kiss to her hair. "You crave control, and if this is what you need, I give it freely."

Fifty-Seven

The time worn pages crinkled as Rune carefully opened the ancient tome. Soft light from Hell's ever-twilight sky streamed in from the floor to ceiling window behind him. He rubbed his fingers over the center of his forehead. He'd combed through every book and scrap of parchment that predated Saith and found nothing to bring him closer to Faye's race or altar.

We should seek our queen, the Ra'Voshnik said, impatiently prowling the edges of his mind.

Rune's thoughts wandered to his night breeze. How she bound his wrists and climbed onto his lap. The memory of her soft lips lingered with him. She focused his attention to a razor's edge and in those moments all he could see was her. Rune smiled, recalling the feel of her nails scoring his chest. He would lean into her proclivities, explore her desires. A pleasant experience she would associate him with.

The creature purred its agreement. *Bring her into your mind, we could both tend to our queen.*

Do not frighten her.

She won't be screaming with fright.

Do not press the issue, we see to her desire. Not yours.

Sadi appeared beside his desk, wearing typical Familiar fashion. A tight corset over a shirt with billowing sleeves, paired with a skirt with slits that ran the length of her legs. Her thigh-high, belted boots completed her outfit. She took a seat on his desk and rested her feet on the arm of his chair. The panel of her skirt falling between her thighs.

Get her legs away from us, or I will present her head to our queen as a gift.

She leaned forward to rest her forearms against her knees and said, "You're courting her."

"I am," Rune answered, getting to his feet to shelf books he had yet to read.

"Have you forgotten your blood debt? Alister will come for her." Sadi said, pivoting on her desk to watch him at his bookshelf.

He never imagined the cost of his arrogance would extract so deep a price.

The frail-blood will die before we surrender our queen, the Ra'Voshnik growled.

Be silent, Rune grated as he slid a book into place.

The unofficial title he bestowed upon his day-blood brother ushered in a tide of pained memories. The wounds he hid didn't scar with the passage of time. They festered, guilt feeding off his every misdeed.

"Should I collect his head?" Sadi dragged the metal tipped claw of her ring over her bottom lip, excitement lighting her eyes.

"No." Alister's path hadn't crossed Rune's in eight centuries. Alister was no threat, his older brother didn't have the strength to challenge him. Faye would remain safely at his side, under his protection.

The light faded from Sadi's eyes as she let out a long breath. "I looked into her line. She's ancient, her line is tethered *in* the Darkness."

Faye's winged double told him as much. "Will she be immortal when she invokes her blood?"

"You need to tread lightly with her. She's death. I can't see it, but I can *feel* it."

His night breeze was on her ninth life, her previous deaths didn't drag him to the Darkness. Rune suspected the eternal part of her safeguarded his life. "I am quite difficult to kill. Did you find anything useful in her line?"

"Her line is strange. It took me days to walk it. During the past eight centuries her lives have been constant. When she dies, she's immediately reborn, the magic takes root in an Anarian woman near birth. It seats in the child and kills the mother."

"That cannot be shared with her." Knowing she caused her mother's death would cripple Faye.

"She looks like me during her repeating lives. Then her line goes dormant. It's quiet during Saith's life and the Great War. Then her lives are peppered along her line again. There's no pattern to it. She's always a woman but her appearance varies in her older lives." Sadi's throat worked. "She dies young Rune. In every life."

Rune turned toward Sadi as worry and protectiveness clawed through him. "How does she die?"

Sadi shook her head. "I can't witness it. A blinding light and pain are all I see."

Dread crept up Rune's spine. "How old is she when this happens?"

"Twenty-five years to the day."

Rune cursed in High Tongue. "Faye is in her twenty-fifth year." His night breeze was young and fragile. He would protect her. His gaze met Sadi's. "Thank you."

She tapped her nails on his desk and stood with feline grace. "Be careful with her. If she escorts you to the Darkness I'll find her in each life. Her death will be a drawn-out thing of beauty."

The Ra'Voshnik's roar echoed through his mind the same moment Rune caught her wrist as she turned to leave. He bit out, "You will not touch her."

Kill her! The Ra'Voshnik's fury roiled through him, bleeding into him.

Sadi's gaze lowered to his hold, then flicked back up to him. "My loyalty runs to you, not her. You want her safe? Stay alive."

He allowed her to pull her wrist free and vanish from his study.

She threatens our queen, and you let her live? The Ra'Voshnik bellowed.

Calm yourself. She's Familiar. She believes her vision to be true and moves with our interests in mind.

The Ra'Voshnik growled but ceased its argument. Rune collected the books he'd been reading and returned to his desk. Faye's line disturbed him and weighed heavily on his mind. He craved her presence, needing to remind himself she was under his care and safe.

The creature purred, agreeing with his sentiment.

Rune pushed his senses over his estate searching for her. He phased into the outer gardens in the event she was soaking in what she deemed, Hell's hot spring. Faye was on her knees, collecting leaves from her garden. She spent so much of her time on these concoctions for little return.

Rune silently strolled to her. "Good afternoon."

She jumped at his voice and jerked in his direction, her expression promising violence.

The Ra'Voshnik raged to the surface wanting to clash with her, excited by her temper. Rough play was common among vampires. Had she stabbed him with the letter opener under different circumstances he would have pinned her and made her lick the blood from her weapon. Then taken other things to those lush lips.

Rune dragged the creature beneath the surface. Imaginings were pleasant enough, but his night breeze was no vampire. She needed to be comfortable with herself before he could introduce his darker impulses.

Faye pointed her little garden knife at him. "I'm going to tie bells to your shoes so you stop sneaking up on me."

He glanced at the knife, then back at her. "Apologies." She turned her back to him, continuing her collection. Rune canted his head. "How long have you sold your potions?"

"Nine years. I started before I moved out with Sparrow."

So much of her young life wasted on this tedium. He wanted to provide her with whatever she desired, but he needed to word it in a way Faye wouldn't take offense to. "I could inquire about a storefront in Necromia to sell your potions if you wish."

She turned toward him. Her brows drawn down, as she said, "I don't want a store."

He spoke a dozen languages fluently yet could never speak the right words to her.

Take her to buy more plants for her garden. Or books! Rune silenced the Ra'Voshnik and asked, "Why do you sell your wares each month?"

She shook her head and returned to her gardening.

Rune sat beside her, resting an arm over his bent knee. "I am making an effort to understand you so I may court you with some degree of success."

Faye gave him a sidelong glance and said, "I can't explain something you have no concept of."

"Then teach me."

She set down her basket and knife and looked him up and down. "You're too old to learn new tricks."

The corner of his mouth lifted into a smirk. "I would be willing to learn a trick or two if you were to instruct me."

Faye crossed her legs and faced him, her expression solemn. "Our village has an Anarian healer, but without magic there is only so much she can do. I do what I can to help my village."

His night breeze carried responsibilities for a village she should have never belonged to. Responsibilities, he realized, she would never relinquish. "I could hire a healer for the village. Perhaps some other vendors and rebuild some of the homes."

Faye's gaze softened and Rune's heart leapt into his throat. Darkness, did he finally find the right path with her?

"You would do that for me?"

"I would do a great many things for you."

Faye took his hand, brushing her thumb over his knuckles. "Thank you."

Her small gesture moved him so deeply. Rune gave her hand a light squeeze. "I will arrange for the village to be cared for, and we could perhaps use your newly found free time to learn court protocol."

Faye's mouth went slack as she pulled her hand away. Her slight frame going rigid. "I will still visit my village every month."

"Vsenia, dark-bloods do not belong in Anaria."

Faye pulled further away from him, bringing her knees up. "I'm not a dark-blood. Anaria is my home."

Rune exhaled and spoke gently, willing her to understand. "You are dark-blooded and you should never have been abandoned to that village." Rune couldn't understand why Faye would choose a dirt road village over what he offered. She should be glad she wasn't one of them.

She stood, taking her basket.

"Faye."

She ignored him, marching out of the gardens.

How could she be so stupid? Faye clenched her jaw. She thought he finally understood her. That his geriatric brain finally clicked, and he could see why she was loyal to her people.

No, she was an idiot, and he was trying to buy her.

Rune materialized in front of her, catching her against him. She pulled away, shoving at his chest. "Don't magic in front of me."

"Tell me what I've done to anger you," he said too gently. His pale blue gaze was pleading.

Faye made an exasperated noise. "That I have to tell you is the issue."

Rune exhaled, stepping closer to her. "That you refuse to speak to me is the issue. I cannot learn if you never offer the context of your mind."

"You want me to abandon my village!" Faye screamed.

He took her hand, giving her a gentle squeeze. "You are not one of them. You do not belong there."

"Why am I the only one that has to change? Why don't you give up your life?" *Why can't you accept me?*

"I am where I belong. Where you belong."

Tears pricked her eyes. "I don't want to belong here."

Rune stabbed his fingers through his hair. "You will never let go of that village."

"You don't want me." He would never accept her.

Rune looked at her like she'd struck him. "You are the only woman I will ever want."

Faye pulled her hand away, embracing her fury to keep her tears at bay. "You want the idea of your dark-blooded queen. Not the minx who wears rags and won't abandon her village." Rune reached for her, and she took a retreating step. "I'm not one of you. If you want me, you need to start with accepting me as I am. Not what you think I should be."

Rune nodded at her, taking a slow step toward her. "I am sorry."

He slowly took her in his arms, holding her close. Faye slipped her arm under his jacket clinging to him. She didn't want to cry. Didn't want to miss him when he realized what she already knew. They were too different, and fate wasn't enough.

But it was too late for her. When he did finally leave, his memory would haunt her for the rest of her life.

"I am sorry." He stroked her hair. "I will see that your village never suffers, and we will visit each month, or as often as you wish."

Faye squeezed him tighter in answer, not trusting her voice. If he could accept her, really accept her as she was, they might have a chance.

Fifty-Eight

Faye tied her hair half up as she walked along the hall in the east wing. Her vampire sat at his desk, pouring over aged documents. His gaze lifted to meet hers as she strolled into his study. Her fingertips skimmed along the top of the settee as she made her way to his desk. She smiled as those lovely shadows swayed beneath his eyes.

"You don't hide your eyeliner half as much as you used to." Faye feigned a look of innocence as she dragged her finger over his desk. Her skin heated as he tracked her movements. The predatory glint in his eyes was at odds with the playful smile across his lips.

He stood as she reached his chair. "Your Voshki is less of a nuisance if I share time with it." Rune leaned closer to her, bringing his lips a moment from hers.

"Sharing time with him," Faye corrected, straightened the perfectly arranged lapel of his jacket. "We have an appointment with Kayla."

Rune subtly shifted his position, backing her into his desk. Faye's pulse quickened as she glanced up. A crimson so dark it looked black covered his gaze. Those lovely veined misted shadows were swaying over the tops of his cheekbones. The low rumble of his purr filled the space between them.

"She can wait," Voshki purred, leaning closer. Placing his hands on either side of her.

She swallowed. They were too tempting. She ran her nails down the center of his chest before flattening her hand and pushing him back. "You're a terrible influence."

He straightened and gave her a cocky grin. "I am aware," he said as the shadows receded from his gaze to reveal pale blue eyes.

Rune extended a hand to her. "Shall we?"

Faye placed her hand in his, and her surroundings faded, replaced with a lavish room decorated in every shade of red.

Rune inclined his head. "Kayla."

Faye smiled at her. She wore a strapless corseted gown in the same antique gold she'd worn the last time Faye saw her.

"Shadow Prince. Lady Faye. Lovely to see you again so soon." Kayla curtsied. Her gold dusted brown skin gleaming in the soft candlelight.

"Thank you for doing this for me." Faye beamed.

Kayla took her arm, leading her away from Rune. "Of course. We do this for many of the noble ladies," she said as she led Faye to three red tables and turned back to Rune. "Are you coming or just going to be surprised by what the Lady selects?"

Rune took a seat on one of the high-backed chairs near the refreshments table and met Faye's gaze. "You should make your selections without my influence. We can revisit this together at a later time."

Kayla smiled, pressing her hands together. "You've found yourself a gentleman."

"He's not," Faye said in a hushed tone.

Kayla leaned toward her saying in an equally soft tone, "None of them are."

They shared a laugh as they came to the first table. Riding crops, sticks, paddles, and something with several leather straps attached to a handle were evenly spaced over the table. Faye glanced back at Rune, who now sat with his ankle over his knee, reading documents. This man told on her and didn't have the decency to look her in the eye.

"Did he tell you to show me the riding crops first?" Faye asked in a hushed whisper.

Kayla waved her hand. "These are very popular among many ladies."

Faye listened as Kayla explained each tool and selected the riding crop Kayla used during their previous visit. A smile played on her lips as she swatted the palm of her hand with it. She imagined running it under Rune's jaw as he knelt before her. Faye pushed the fantasy away. The man would set her blood on fire if she let him.

"If you want to purchase any items, just lay them horizontally in the gold marking." Kayla tapped the rectangular engraving.

Faye selected two riding crops and placed them in the marker.

The next table held restraints and blindfolds. Some of the lengths of cord were smooth, others were coarse. Faye took a length of red silk, running it through her fingers.

Kayla picked up the matching purple silk. "These also come reinforced with magic, but they don't make anything dark enough to hold the Shadow Prince. You'll just have to rely on him behaving," Kayla said with a wink as she wound the purple silk, setting it back on the table. She picked up a length of smooth cord next. "We also offer classes on shibari here." Kayla looped the rope on her bicep and continued to loop and pull the rope further down her arm creating a beautiful design. "Or private individualized classes at your home if you'd like."

Faye glanced back at Rune, wondering if she would be able to sweet talk him into a class or two. She set the pink and black cord in the golden marker. Her gaze flitted between the red and purple silk before she selected them both. Her last pick was a black blindfold lined with soft fur.

Kayla led her to the third table. A small black chest rested at its center. Kayla opened the lid and Faye leaned forward to peek into it. The items she placed on the markers rested on the bottom of the chest.

"I will leave you two to it. If you would like anything else just place it in the marker." Kayla curtsied and vanished.

Black flickered over the room and faded. Faye turned toward

Rune. The corner of his mouth lifted. "I would prefer not to be interrupted a second time."

"And what did you imagine happening?" Faye teased.

Rune vanished his documents and strode to her carrying a small plate of candied fruits. Selecting a berry skewered with a metal pick, he stepped into her, bringing the berry to her lips.

Faye smiled as the veined shadows crept out from beneath his eyes. "Your eyeliner is showing." She leaned forward and closed her lips over the berry, pulling it free in a slow, sensual motion.

Rune pulled the box closer and lifted a length of red silk. "Am I to be restrained again?"

"They have rope classes too." Faye smiled up at her vampire.

"I would request that you allow private lessons. I would appreciate keeping my private life, private."

Faye giggled and he leaned closer, his lips a moment from hers. Faye ran her hands under his jacket, over his sides. His muscles corded and flexed at her touch. "Were you hoping I'd tie you up and kiss you again?"

He stroked her hair, touching his forehead against hers. "Perhaps. A small price for the feel of your lips."

Faye ran her palms to his broad chest. "We can't do this here."

"We most certainly can." Rune swept his thumb along her jaw. "I reserved the room for the rest of the day."

"Presumptuous of you." Faye breathed.

"Your sister is not able to interrupt us here."

"Can we witness more training while I have you bound?" Faye asked leaning into his hand.

Rune brushed his thumb along her throat as he threaded his fingers through her hair. "My minx is a voyeur."

Faye laughed as her cheeks heated. "Maybe I should have you massage my back instead."

Rune's voice dropped an octave, his accent thick. "My hands on your body is still a reward."

"Then I'll have to tie your hands." Faye kissed him softly and smiled when he remained still. "He learns."

Rune purred, leaning closer. "I have a high intellectual agility."

"Good," Faye took the length of red silk from him and said, "Take off your shirt."

Faye looked over the room as Rune removed his jacket.

"What are you searching for?"

Faye smiled up at him and answered, "A place to tie your arms over your head."

Rune raised a brow, continuing to unbutton his shirt. "The top of the bed posts will have what you seek."

Faye stepped up on the bed and flattened her fingers over the top of the post. She felt a metal loop embedded there. She slipped the silk through it and curled a beckoning finger at Rune.

He stripped off his shirt and silently strolled to her. Faye couldn't help but admire how the candlelight reflected off the hard planes of his sculpted body. Her vampire was the most handsome man she'd ever seen. Rune turned his back to the post and lifted his wrists over his head.

Faye quirked her lip when he gripped the top of the post and leaned forward to stare down at him. "Why are you so tall?"

He smirked at her and answered, "Fate did not grant you a small male."

Faye bent his arms until Rune clasped his elbows. She smiled, taking her time to lace the silk over and around his forearms. Binding them together.

She got down and stood in front of him, admiring her handiwork. Faye slid her fingers under his belt and stood up on her toes. Rune leaned forward, lowering his head. Her lips met his. Feather-light and gentle as she ran her nails down his torso.

He groaned against her mouth and Faye finally pulled away. Black swept through his gaze and dissipated. "Perhaps a chair would be better suited for your games," he said, leaning toward her.

"Not for this one." Faye left him and went to the box. She returned with the blindfold. The corner of Rune's mouth lifted as Faye stood on the bed once more and secured the blindfold over his eyes.

Faye came down, stepping in front of Rune. She frowned as Rune tracked her movements and tugged the blindfold lower.

"I do not need to see you to know where you are. I can scent you. I hear your heart beating," he said, leaning closer.

Faye smoothed her hands over his chest and ran her nails lower before stopping at his pants. Pressing a kiss to the center of his chest as she unfastened his belt.

Fifty-Nine

Rune's mind blanked as she pulled his belt open and unfastened his pants. The minx blindfolded him. He wanted to see her, watch her reactions. His fangs lengthened at the scent of her arousal. He wanted her pinned beneath him, his tongue coated in the taste of her.

Pin her, demand her submission, the Ra'Voshnik growled through his mind.

This is what she craves—

Rune's breath caught as she pulled his length free. Darkness, he ached for her.

"What did you say earlier?" She asked. "Being tied was a small price to feel my lips."

Rune's head fell back as she cupped him while stroking his length. Her touch was so different from his own. She was gentle, torturous. Too light. He felt her go to her knees and canted his head.

Her tongue dabbed the tip of his cock and Rune went rigid. The minx did it again and he hissed.

"Tell me what you like." She stroked him, licking him in longer swipes.

Tell her you would like to fuck her mouth, the Ra'Voshnik grated.

Rune tensed as she took him past her lips. The warmth of her mouth surrounded him and Rune couldn't think. He'd expected the creature to overtake him while his focus was in shambles. It remained present but made no move to strip him of his body.

I will rise when she releases us. It would upset our queen if I snapped her bindings.

She moved her mouth over him in time with her hand and Rune's knees nearly buckled. "My experience is limited," he rasped. Rune cursed in high tongue, willing his body still. His queen wanted him bound and he would remain so. Rune's back tensed as she took him deeper, touching the back of her throat. His breaths became labored as she worked him.

She pulled back and said, "I like the way you taste."

Rune caught his breath looking down. "Keep your pace and you will receive more than a taste."

The minx lightened her touch, running her lips along his length. Offering soft kisses and licks until he was certain he'd be driven mad.

"You said I could watch while you slake yourself."

Rune drew a ragged breath. "Untie me and I will gladly let you watch."

She released him and stood. He listened as she walked to the front of the bed. *Not untying me?* Glass clinked and Faye returned to him. He and the Ra'Voshnik groaned when she grasped him again.

Her hand moving against him, slick with oil.

"Show me how you'd want to take me."

She wanted him to fuck her hand? His lips parted, as his fangs lengthened. Readying to sink into the woman who should be pinned beneath him. He fought the urge to take her throat and hold her legs spread while he fucked her hard. This was what his queen craved and he would give it to her.

"Grip me harder." Rune thrusted into her hand. "Harder with both hands."

He bucked his hips, thrusting into her hold. Pressure built as Rune's fangs throbbed for her.

"Cover the head with your hand." Darkness, he was close. He groaned, feeling his cock twitch. "About to come."

Her grip loosened. She teased his tip with one hand, while the other cupped him.

Rune bared his fangs and thrusted harder, not able to get the friction he needed.

"Is this all you'll give me, a few minutes of thrusting?" Her hand slid down his shaft and back up, twisting her wrist at the tip. Rune cursed under his breath. "You keep saying that. What does it mean?"

"The equivalent of fuck." Rune thrusted lightly in her grasp following her lead. "When you allow me to take you, I am going to edge you for hours."

"Hours?" Her hands twisted over his cock.

He groaned and smiled. "I have a long history of repaying kindness."

"Am I detecting sarcasm?" Faye tightened her grip, stroking him hard.

Rune growled, thrusting with her. The minx released him completely. Rune stilled, his heart thundering. He scented the air and turned toward her. "This arouses you. What game are we playing? Do you want to hear me beg?"

She lightly teased the tip, letting him languidly thrust against her too gentle fingers.

"What would it take to make you sweat?" She asked.

He chuckled, then groaned as she stroked him. "If you wish to see me wet, we can shower together."

Faye gripped him hard and pressed her body against his side. He widened his stance so she could straddle his thigh.

"Kiss me," she commanded.

Rune lowered his head and met her lips. He was easy with her, kissing her gently, waiting for her to demand more. Her tongue glided into his mouth in unhurried strokes.

Faye sighed to him between kisses, "Show me how you would want to take me. But don't come."

"You want me to edge myself?"

She moaned against him, licking his fang. Giving him a teasing taste of her blood.

Rune did as she commanded, losing track of how much time

passed as she kissed him. Riding his thigh.

Her hold loosened as she pulled away from their kiss. "Slake yourself."

Rune phased through the silk binding him and tore off the blindfold. He snaked his arm around her waist, dragging her against him. Darkness, he needed her. He groaned, nuzzling her neck. "Offer me your throat," he grated.

"After I see you finish," she said, smiling up at him.

Tell her she looks beautiful, the Ra'Voshnik insisted. Rune gazed down at her. Her eyes lit with excitement. Her skin was flushed. She was radiant. His.

Ours, the Ra'Voshnik growled.

Rune returned its growl with one of his own and said to Faye, "Then watch me come. Witness what you do to me."

Her gaze lowered to his cock as he took hold of himself.

Rune held her close, brushing the side of his face against her hair. Breathing in her scent as he stroked harder. Falling into the rough rhythm he needed. Rune chased his pleasure. His body stiffened with a growl as he came, spending for her onto the floor.

Faye turned her face up to him and he took her lips, hard and claiming. She pulled back after long moments and Rune jerked as her fingertips teased the wet tip of his cock. He pulsed under her touch, stirring for her once more.

Sixty

Faye watched in fascination as he hardened again. Sparrow told her men went limp after they came. She glanced up at Rune. Black poured through his gaze, spilling like ink through water and dissipated before it covered the entirety of his eye. He didn't have the sleepy, satisfied look her sister told her about.

His focused intent and desire settling squarely on her.

Faye traced her fingers along his length, and he groaned, lightly thrusting into her hand. "You seem insatiable. Is this a vampire trait?" Faye asked.

Rune leaned back on the post, allowing her exploration. "I would not know. I felt nothing until I caught your scent at the Hunter's Moon ball."

Her vampire purred and raised his chin until the back of his head rested against the post. Faye's gaze followed the sharp line of his jaw to his throat, moving lower to the spot his neck met his shoulder.

The sudden urge to bite him while she snared his muscles under her nails rose in her. Faye's lips parted as she noted the slight flush over his cheeks. She stroked him harder, watching his mouth. The glimpse of fang. The way his brow drew together with each breath and groan. A possessiveness swept through her. He came undone for her alone. This powerful male belonged to her, and his surrender curled her toes.

She smoothed her fingers down the underside of his jaw, caressing lower to his throat. His purr vibrated beneath her touch. Faye seized him by the neck and pulled him toward her. She stilled a moment, astounded Rune obeyed her without hesitation. "You're so sure I'm your queen," Faye said before teasingly licking the seam of his lips.

His eyes slid closed as he leaned closer. Against her smile he rasped, "All my desire belongs to the fiery minx I am fated to. I patiently wait for her to accept me."

Faye moaned, pressing her body flush to his. "If you promise not to edge me for hours, you can have me."

She gasped, grabbing his shoulders for balance as he lifted her against him, guiding her legs over his ribs. The heat of his mouth caressed her throat before his fangs grazed her at an agonizing pace.

"It is customary to wait for a lunar cycle to pass before engaging a woman after her Ceremony of Blood," he said at her throat.

Faye squeezed him with her thighs and rolled her hips. "It's been over a week. I feel fine."

Rune gazed up at her, running the bridge of his nose under her chin affectionately. "It does not mean you will be without pleasure."

His fingertips smoothed down the small of her back and two fingers slipped into the waist of her pants and panties. He tugged on the fabric gently. Faye straightened her back, hugging him tighter as he pulled her clothes through her.

Faye stared as Rune tossed her pants over the back of the closest chair and removed her top in the same manner. She gazed down at him and blinked. "That's a trick."

"I have many," he crooned as he eased her onto the perfectly made bed. Faye curled on her side, admiring her perfectly chiseled vampire while he stripped.

Rune joined her, lifting her against him as she wound her legs over his waist. He held her tight, rocking his hips. Faye's eyes squeezed closed as a moan escaped her lips. His cock glided through her folds, pressure meeting over her clit. Faye dug her nails into his shoulder for leverage, moving with him. Chasing the pleasure Rune offered her.

"Tell me how you like to be touched," he said, caressing the underside of her breast. Faye whimpered pressing against him harder. His lips touched hers and he asked, "Do you prefer a gentler touch?"

He lightly outlined her nipple, watching as it hardened to a stiff peak. Rune's gaze lifted to hers, and he asked, "Something harder?" He pinched her, rolling the sensitive tip between his thumb and index finger.

Faye panted, arching her back at his treatment. She raked her nails over his shoulders, down his chest. Rune lowered his head to her other breast. "Or would you prefer my mouth on you?" His tongue swept across her nipple, wetting it. He blew on it, and she gasped. "Teeth?" He asked, carefully capturing the hardened peak before teasing the very tip with his tongue.

Faye trembled, tangling her hands in his hair, pulling him closer. "Rougher."

Rune growled against her, teasing her with his lips and teeth. Pinching her and tugging her nipple, plucking it through his fingers. His teasing pleasure edged in pain coursed through her, taking her to the very edge where Rune held her. Withholding the last stroke or caress that would snap the tension stringing her body tight.

"Please," Faye whispered, grinding over him faster as he mercilessly worked her body.

"Please?" Rune asked, palming her breast, molding her soft flesh to his hand. He pinched the tip until Faye winced. "Were you wanting to come, my queen?" He raised a brow at her, his expression the picture of gentlemanly consideration while he worked her until all she knew was a fevered frenzy beneath his touch.

"Yes," she begged, needing more of him. "Please."

Rune kissed the corner of her mouth, affectionally brushing the side of his face against hers. At her ear he said, "Command me. Demand your desires."

"I need more," Faye whimpered.

"More what? Be specific."

"Please, let me finish." Faye gripped the front of his throat, adding, "Stop teasing me."

He pulled her in tighter, his mouth settling on the side of her neck. "Offer me your throat."

Faye wrapped her arms around him, tangling her hands in his hair as she turned her head to the side. Baring the column of her throat for him. Rune's fangs sank deep as pleasure seared her, snapping the tension he built and strummed. Ecstasy seized her, paralyzing her as wave after wave crashed over her.

When her senses returned to her, she clutched him close. Her long black hair clung to her sweat-slick body. Faye squirmed against him, needing him to fill and stretch her with his cock instead of the feigned sensations his fangs mimicked.

"I want you inside me," Faye breathed, stroking his hair while he drank from her.

The hand on her ass slipped lower until his fingers found her wet folds. Faye arched her back, lifting her hips. Greedy for his touch. He slid two fingers over her opening, applying a slight pressure as he slipped back and forth over top, not entering her.

"Please, you won't hurt me. I need you," Faye cried, desperate to have him inside her.

"My queen is quite impatient," Rune said between slow draws over his bite.

Faye leaned into him, resting her head on his shoulder as he eased a finger into her in short strokes. Withdrawing, then pressing deeper.

"Move against my hand. I fear hurting you." Rune said before drinking from her once more.

His digit was larger than hers, reaching further than his tongue. Faye closed her eyes holding him tighter. Breathing in his scent of amber and sandalwood as she tentatively rolled her hips. His touch sliding in and out of her rekindled her need.

She rocked back on his hand in time with pleasure that seated deep within her and its slow withdraw as Rune drank. Faye surrendered to the feel of him. Quickening her pace, riding his hand with abandon as she ground against his cock.

Faye cried out breathless against Rune's neck as she came. Rune held her through her pleasure, and she collapsed against him. Spent and euphoric.

Rune lowered her onto the bed, trailing kisses down her body. He lingered at her breasts, teasing the hardened tips until she writhed beneath him.

Faye propped herself up on her forearms and glanced down at him as he moved lower. "What are you doing?"

Her vampire gave a low laugh while he settled between her spread legs. "Did you truly think I was done with you?"

Sixty-One

Faye crossed her leg in front of him, running her shin across his chest. Rune kissed her silken flesh a last time, chuckling as she pushed him away. He rose from his knees, wiping his hand over his mouth. His night breeze curled on her side, flushed, and short of breath. Her lightning-streaked midnight eyes glazed with pleasure.

Male pride filled him. He eased her into a handful of gentle orgasms. He craved the sounds of her soft cries and moans, but he'd exhausted his queen. The Ra'Voshnik purred through his mind content. They'd agreed not to disturb the other while they were with their queen.

Until she wants both of us, it reminded him.

Unlikely, though, if his queen desired it, he would bend to her will. Rune collected Faye in his arms and tucked her under the blankets. Her nails bit into his waist as she looked up at him. "Lie down with me."

Rune moved her to the middle of the bed and slipped under the blankets beside her.

She curled up to him as she had during their dreams. Her head resting on his chest, and he absently ran his fingers through her hair.

"I want to ask you a question." Faye didn't look up at him, her fingertips tracing the muscles down his side.

Rune remained silent, listening.

"Why do you let me do these things to you?" Her voice was quieter. Hesitant.

He grinned and pressed a kiss to the top of her head. "You need to become acquainted with yourself before you can learn another. This is what you need, and I am honored to give it to you."

She traced circles over his chest, seemingly mulling over his words. "But you're the Shadow Prince. You rule Hell. It doesn't upset you?"

A chuckle escaped his lips and Faye braced herself up on his chest to glare at him. "I believe you feel more for me than you are willing to admit," he purred

She settled back against his chest with a huff, "Keep dreaming fang face."

Rune couldn't help the smile that pulled at his lips. His minx cared, worrying for him. In a soft tone he said, "You do not offend me, and I rather enjoy your treatment." He pulled his fingers through her black hair, watching the strands fall. "I have found, if you live long enough, there are few roles fate will not assign you. You are not tarnishing my status or title, neither of which mean a great deal to me."

"I'm not going to act like your dark-blooded women. You can tell me no, or you're not in the mood. I don't expect you to serve me."

"I am aware."

Faye jabbed a finger into his side in response and curled closer to him. He stroked her hair, running his fingers down her back as her breaths grew deep and even. Faye dozed off as he lay awake staring at the red tapestry billowing over the ceiling. He felt content. He was still repairing much of the groundwork between them, but he could feel a bond beginning.

She would come to his way of thinking in time. Until then he would shower her with pleasure and let her come to dark-blooded society when she was ready.

Faye woke to a soft rumble, the lulling vibrations keeping her in a half sleep. She was warm, comfortable. The scent of amber and sandalwood mixed with the sweet floral scent of the bedding. Faye sighed as fingers brushed through her hair making her scalp tingle.

She curled closer, her leg draped over his. She took a deep breath, opening her eyes. Would this be what life with him would be like? She gazed over the opulent room. Spoiled in wealth and luxury.

A pang of guilt twinged in her chest as she scratched her nails lightly over his torso. She hadn't abandoned her village or forgotten where she came from. Rune would help her care for her village. Her thoughts wandered to her vampire. Her growing feelings for him frightened her. She had no safeguards to protect her heart from this affectionate side of him.

"Are you well?" He caressed her back.

Faye sighed, snuggling closer to him, and closed her eyes.

"I bought you a gift."

Faye smiled against his chest. "Did you?"

His hand returned to her hair. Twirling strands around his finger before letting them fall. "A gown for the wedding we will attend."

"There's a bunch of dresses in my closet." Along with more clothes she hadn't worn yet.

He chuckled. "This is a formal event. You need a gown, not a dress."

"And where is this gown?" Faye asked, sighing as he stroked the backs of his fingers down the side of her neck.

"It was delivered to your closet."

Faye groaned, "That means I need to get up."

"We can stay as long as you wish. I could tend to you again."

A flutter of memory teased between her legs. She still tingled from his earlier attentions. Could almost feel him licking inside her. "You've tended enough."

He laughed softly and squeezed her to him, and said, "As you command."

Faye lowered her brow at his words. He had strange customs but

340

if he was willing to accept her, she would make the same effort for him. She pushed off his chest, sitting up. "I'm starving. How long was I sleeping?"

"A few hours," Rune answered. "Did you prefer to dine here or return home?"

"They have food here?"

"Kayla's establishment is full service. If you wished, you could witness training while I massaged your back."

His offer was tempting, but Faye scooted closer to him and patted his hip before saying, "We can do that another night."

Rune got to his feet and gathered her clothes, laying them next to her before he began dressing. Faye pulled her shirt over her head and slowed as she pulled on her pants. Her lips parted as his muscles tightened and rippled with his movements. She bit the inside of her lip, and as though he could feel her gaze, Rune glanced at her. She wasn't sure when his arrogant smirk became endearing, but she liked it all the same.

He adjusted his jacket as he walked to her and outstretched his hand. "Shall we."

She took his hand and her surroundings shifted, refocusing until she stood in the hall outside her bedroom. Faye's hand slipped from his as she stepped into her room.

"May I come in?" He asked at her threshold.

She glanced at him over her shoulder. "I think we're past that point in our relationship." When he only canted his head at her, Faye rolled her eyes and said, "Come in."

"Treating you casually is disrespectful."

More of his weird customs. Over her shoulder, she asked, "Can I just tell you it's okay, then you won't be disrespecting me?"

"Leaving the door between our rooms open is how you would tell me you would like me to tend to you." The backs of his fingers caressed the small of her back. "You should, by right, be in the larger room, and I should be in the consort's room."

Faye turned and settled her hand on his waist as she craned her neck up to look at him. "I'm not taking your room," she said, giving him a pat and stepped back. "Why are you in that room if it's a... queen's room. Or something."

Rune thinned his lips and his eyes hardened for a moment before his features relaxed. He met her gaze, and said "I needed a room on an exterior wall. This was the only one available at the time."

Faye smoothed her hand over his side, stopping herself from asking about the strangely specific response. If he wanted to explain it later, she would listen. She opened her closet door, and said, "How about if I have the door open you can come in and I would welcome your company?"

The corner of his mouth lifted as he strolled to her. "And if you want affection you will come to my bed?"

Faye smiled at him. Her vampire compromised with her. They could make this work. Her gaze fell to a large black rectangular box resting on her dresser in the back of the closet. A smaller black box on top of it. She expected a package. How big was this gown that it needed a box that took up the top of her dresser?

Faye walked into her chandelier closet and another black box caught her attention. The one from the brothel she and Rune just left. She pulled her gaze away from it, reaching for the smaller box. She removed its lid and pulled away the black tissue packed inside. Black satin heels nested in the bottom of the box. The front of the open toed shoes were simple, but the heel. Faye took it out of the box.

Glittering dark gems accented with tiny purple jewels covered the heel and faded into the back of the shoe. The swirling, delicate pattern was reminiscent of paintings she'd seen of the Darkness.

"These are beautiful," Faye said, arranging the heel and tissue back into the box before setting it down. She took the lid off the larger box and rested it on the side of her dresser. The box was filled with layers of the same black tissue paper, crinkling as she removed them.

This was a gown? Faye lifted the gray slip out of the box.

"This is really elaborate for lingerie." Faye held the garment away from her with straight arms, studying it. The material was light-weight. The gray fabric glittered as it caught the light. Faye squinted, leaning closer. Tiny gems were sewn into the fabric. Thousands of them.

"You are holding a gown," Rune insisted.

"It's see-through," Faye said, holding the so-called gown between them, meeting his gaze through the sheer fabric.

He chuckled, leaning his shoulder in the doorway of her closet.

"It will not be when you put it on."

Faye reappraised the cut of the gown. It exposed more than it covered. The front of the dress was connected to a beautifully crafted jeweled collar. Faye didn't see how this would stay in place having such a deep V cut while also being backless. The draping of the back of the gown dipped too low to properly cover her ass. At least the long skirt was modest.

Faye arched her eyebrow at the slit that ran high up the front of the dress. She was wrong. There was nothing decent about this dress. She turned, saying, "Rune, I can't wear this. Can you return it?"

"These types of gowns are purchased with blood. I will not return your gift."

"What?" Blood? She must have misheard him.

Rune nodded and said, "Blood is a common commodity among the dark-blooded."

"For what? Your blood wine?"

"I rarely barter my blood. I imagine I would be a very expensive bottle of crimson wine. My blood is more likely to be used in spells or tonics." Rune said, taking the gown and hanging it up. "Come, you are hungry and need to meet with your sister to regale sordid tales."

Sixty-Two

Rune accompanied Faye to the south wing of his estate. The Ra'Voshnik purred as she took his hand, twining her fingers with his. Holding hands was an odd but pleasant experience. Something not practiced within the dark courts. Faye happily leaned into him, so he said nothing as they strolled hand in hand.

As they crossed the threshold into the den, Faye smiled up at him and dropped his hand in favor of the plates of food spread over the table. Sparrow laid sideways in an oversized chair. Her legs and neck resting over each armrest.

She gazed at him, and said, "What'd you do to my sister Runey? You were gone forever."

He arched a brow but didn't respond.

Sparrow snorted, getting up and grumbled, "Tight lipped fucker. She's going to tell me anyway." To Faye she said, "Should we just have an early dinner? Vash should be back in an hour or so."

"Did you want to have dinner with us?" Faye asked him with a smile, he would give anything to continue seeing.

"I have a small detail that needs my attention. I would be delighted to join you within the hour."

"Good, the boys will be back in an hour. We can have girl talk." Sparrow said, taking her seat across from Faye, then turned to Rune to wave her hand dismissively at him. "Begone."

Faye gave him an apologetic look and he smiled. Rune inclined his head before saying, "Ladies," phasing as he straightened.

A light breeze rustled Rune's long white-blonde hair. He stood on the landing of Lyssa's estate. A mirror of his home in Hell.

Why are we here. Return to our queen, the Ra'Voshnik growled, growing more agitated as he approached the large double doors. They opened when he reached the steps. Gabriel smiled in greeting.

Rune liked Lyssa's son, preferring him over his harpy twin Morgan. Both of Lyssa's children inherited their features from their father. A man who helped Lyssa escape his queen and court, paying with his life.

Gabriel's deep red hair glimmered in the waning sunlight. "You don't visit often," he said, opening the door wider.

Rune stepped into the great room and said, "I have come looking for Lyssa."

"She's been in a mood," Gabriel warned. "So good luck and I'll keep Morgan at bay." Gabriel winked and left down the hall to the right.

Rune drove his senses past his body, over the estate identical to his, searching for Lyssa.

Come.

Rune turned, The Ra'Voshnik bristling at her command. He submitted to the will of one woman, and it wasn't Lyssa. Was never, Lyssa.

She was in her study. He walked the familiar path, comparing the differences between their homes attempting to calm himself. Rugs, plants, and portraits decorated much of the space. Fresh cut flowers brightened the rooms and lent their sweet fragrance. Lyssa's home was warmer, more inviting than his.

The Ra'Voshnik's voice filled his mind, *Our queen could warm our home. Creating her own space will incline her to stay.*

Perhaps he should ask if Faye would like to decorate. If she promised not to give the blonde harpy free reign, Rune thought to himself.

Rune knocked, then pushed the door open. Lyssa's study was laid out differently than his. Instead of bookshelves, her walls were open. Portraits of the court and their families hung tastefully. The only similarities her study shared with his was the placement of their desks. They both sat with the spanning window as their backdrop. Where his view was an ever-twilight sky, hers was spelled to allow the sunlight to stream in and not burn her.

Lyssa sat behind her desk. Her hazel gaze met his with a cold expression.

"Business then?" Rune asked, studying her.

Lyssa lifted her head and sniffed. She wrinkled her nose with a look of revulsion. "How dare you come into my home, reeking of *her.*"

"Is this how you want to proceed?" Rune asked. They were Pure Bloods. It would take more than a week of no contact for Faye's scent to fade enough to not be detected.

He rather enjoyed having her scent on him. She marked him, searing his very soul.

"How does your Anarian whore keep up with your stamina?" Lyssa asked sweetly, her jealousy turned her smile ugly.

Take that bitch by the throat and throw her through her window before the sun sets, the Ra'Voshnik growled, urging him to phase her into daylight and hold her until she apologized to their queen.

Rune exhaled for patience and Lyssa continued to glare at him. Calling a flower arrangement he passed in the hall, Rune strolled to her desk. The metal vase rang as he placed it roughly on her desk, before sliding it in front of her. "Do not scent me. Concentrate on your flowers."

Lyssa parted her lips and took a deep breath. "It's been an age since I've tasted your anger," she said, leaning back in her chair. "Is she shy, or does she strip whenever you arrive?"

Rune knew she wouldn't be thrilled to see him in another woman's bed, but this. "I have come to request Saith's journal."

She continued as though he'd never spoken. "Does she spread her legs for you?"

Letting her goad him served no one. "Is it still in the cata-combs?" He asked.

Lyssa tilted her head looking him up and down. "They say you took her to Kayla's brothel. Is she a properly trained whore now or does she whimper for you to worship at her altar with the lights off?" Lyssa's eyes lit. "Or do you turn the lights off and tell her you cannot see in the dark?"

Kill her, the creature grated.

Rune ignored them both. "I will have a copy made and bring it back to you by the end of the day."

"I hope she doesn't mind too terribly," her gazed fell between his legs before meeting his once more. Her expression a mixture of concern and sympathy. "When you can't get it up."

"Give me Saith's journal, and I will leave," Rune said through his teeth.

"Do you feed on her? Careful, or your little pet may die beneath you."

"Enough!" Rune yelled.

"I will tell you when it's enough! You are in my realm, in my home. Fuck you and your whore. I give you nothing! Get out of my realm."

Rune phased as Lyssa stood, picking up the flower arrangement and throwing it at him.

Sixty-Three

"So," Sparrow said, thrumming her nails on the table as Faye remained quiet eating cuts of grilled pear. "You were gone for almost four hours, bitch."

Faye glanced up at her sister. "I fell asleep."

Sparrow's eyes lit up as she sat taller. "You were in bed with him? Did you tie him up again?"

Faye flushed. "No."

Sparrow gasped widening her eyes before saying, "This bitch is lying." She laughed and clapped her hands as Faye's blush deepened. "Darkness, can you set an image crystal because I would love to see that shit. We could sell them and make a fortune."

"No," Faye hissed, glaring at Sparrow as she kicked her under the table. "How do you know everything?"

Sparrow snorted. "I walked in on you, and he was like this." She leaned forward, putting her arms behind her, crossing her wrists over her lower back. "Doesn't take a genius."

Faye stared at her plate, refusing to incriminate herself further.

"Don't be so boring," Sparrow said pouring herself a shot of whiskey. "At least Rune lets you tie him up. Vash was having none of it."

Faye eyed her sister. "You asked to tie Vash up?"

Sparrow threw back her shot and poured a second. She held the glass near her lips, pointing at Faye. "And the fucker said no."

Faye bet her sister went into their bedroom with twenty feet of rope without talking to Vashien beforehand. She giggled thinking of Vashien's reaction, falling out of bed backing away from Sparrow.

"I think Rune will let me take some rope tying lessons they offer at the brothel," Faye said.

"Shibari? He looks kind of boring in his stuck-up suit. I guess he's less boring when he takes it off." Sparrow's mouth widened into a toothy grin. "What do you do to him once he's all tied up?"

Faye shrugged, biting into a piece of fruit.

"I need details," Sparrow whined, laying her head on her arms and looking up at Faye with her best pair of sad eyes.

"Save that shit for Vash." Faye dipped her fingers in her glass of water and flicked it at her sister.

Sparrow hissed, swiping her face with her sleeve. "You can give me details, or I can just start naming things off. When you blush I'll know I hit the right one."

Faye sighed, "You're such a bitch."

"You ride his face yet?" Faye shook her head and Sparrow scrubbed her hands over her nose and mouth. "He's been trained to pleasure women. Trained, bitch. Why are you even tying him up? You should ask him to tie you up and have him show you all his tricks."

Faye imagined him tying her down and Rune purring against her when she couldn't get away. It was too much. Too intense. "I like it better when I'm in control."

Sparrow grinned unhindered. "You step on his neck or spank him?"

Faye's mouth fell open and she could only stare.

"No? Too far?" Sparrow asked. Her shoulders slumped. "Don't tell me you just tie him up and kiss him."

Faye looked down at her plate and muttered, "It's private."

"Fine," Sparrow grumbled.

Faye changed the subject to Aunty Clara's house and how Rune was going to help her take care of the village.

Sparrow blinked at her. "He does all that and you're not fucking him. Teach me your ways."

"He's making an effort so I'm trying to be understanding of the court stuff. It's like they live in a different world."

Sparrow waved her hand, gesturing at their surroundings. "Do you not see this shit? This is another world, with delicious food and top shelf liquor."

"How are my best girls?"

Faye turned toward Vashien's voice. He stepped into the den and Faye glimpsed a dark suit and white-blonde hair gliding silently behind him. The sight of him made Faye's heart beat a little harder. She smiled when Vashien noticed Rune pulling his wings in tight.

Sparrow shot a glance between her and Rune. "Darkness, look at this bitch lighting up and shit."

Vashien inclined his head at Rune. "Shadow Prince."

Rune offered him the same respect, saying, "Rune is adequate. There is no need for titles among our courts."

Sparrow nodded at Vashien as he took his seat next to her. "I call him Runey."

Faye leaned closer as Rune took his seat beside her.

"Do you eat? Or should we order blood?" Faye asked, touching his thigh. Her nails lightly scratching over the dark material.

Rune brushed her hair behind her shoulder, caressing the side of her neck with the backs of his fingers with the motion. "Crimson wine."

Sparrow touched the talisman ordering their dinner, finishing with, "And a glass of crimson wine for the great Shadow Prince."

The corner of Rune's mouth lifted. He took Faye's hand, pressing his lips to the back of it.

Her sister narrowed her eyes at Vashien. Poor guy was so rigid, his wings tucked in close to his body. It would take time for him to get use to Rune. He didn't share Sparrow's ability to embrace every situation with little regard for the outcome.

Sparrow poked his wing and said, "You could stand to be more romantic."

Vashien turned toward Sparrow, some of the tension leaving his body. "I am literally in Hell for you woman. What else do you want?"

Sparrow propped her head up on her hand and said, "Runey lets Faye tie him up because he's not a *chicken*."

Faye's face heated. She widened her eyes at Sparrow and kicked her under the table.

"Ow! That was hard bitch." Sparrow rubbed her shin.

"The Sha— Rune trusts her," Vashien said, pouring himself a stout glass of whiskey and lifting it to his lips.

Sparrow sulked at Vashien, her shoulders slumping. "You don't trust me?"

"In the bedroom, fuck no."

Faye set her elbow on the table, pointing at her sister. "You just lost all your secret privileges."

Sparrow snorted, waving her hand. "It's only us," she said, then turned her gaze to Rune. "Are you going to let Faye take Shibari classes?"

Rune glanced at Faye then Sparrow. "Perhaps."

Faye sighed as her sister lit up and asked, "Can I take them with her?"

Rune exchanged a glance with Vashien before turning back to Sparrow. "The classes are individual. You may not learn on me. Speak with your male."

Sparrow turned, eyes pleading, toward Vashien.

He swallowed the contents of his glass before muttering, "Fuck me."

Sixty-Four

The weeks passed quickly. Rune brought Faye four candidates to choose from who would serve as a healer for her village. It surprised her that he was able to find day-bloods willing to work with Anarians.

He explained the position was within his court, and they would be paid a salary to care for her village. Faye didn't understand it entirely but was grateful her village wouldn't need to scrape and save to have medicinal care.

She began leaving the door open between their rooms, inviting Rune's company during the day. At night she joined him in his bed and was met with either pale blue eyes, or Voshki's dark misted gaze. They talked into the night some nights, others she writhed beneath him, screaming her pleasure. At the end of each evening, she slept curled against him, cherished in his arms.

Faye stood in front of her mirror, studying her reflection. The illusion of what she would have been if she'd been court-born staring back at her.

Rune had been right. When she slipped the sheer dress on it wasn't see-through. It didn't look like a gown a vampire would pick out, the intricate jeweled choker covered most of her neck. She smiled. Or maybe that was the point, Rune didn't want his eyeliner showing at the wedding.

She swayed her hips, the skirt sweeping with her movements. It was beautiful. The gems sewn into it making it appear as though she was stepping out of the Darkness itself as it coiled at her feet.

Her glossy black hair was pulled into a high ponytail and Sparrow helped her with her make-up. Faye didn't recognize the lined, smokey eyes and plum-colored lips that stared back at her. From her face to her satin heels, nothing about her, was her. Faye caught Rune's reflection in the mirror. He came to stand behind her, gazing at her, thunderstruck.

He leaned closer, not touching her as he rasped at her ear, "You leave me without words."

He affected her, striking right to the core of her being. She only wished he would look at her this way when she was herself. She buried the thought behind a smile and slipped her hand into the crook of his arm. They were going to a fancy event. Of course, he would think she was pretty in formal dress.

It didn't mean he wished she was a true court born dark-blood.

They walked together to the great room where Vashien and Sparrow stood, waiting for them. Her sister was breathtaking in her strapless red dress.

Sparrow shrieked when she caught sight of her. "How the fuck did you get her to wear that?" She asked, taking Faye's hands and stealing her from Rune. "Darkness, this dress. Look at you, showing side boob." She turned to Rune. "I could never get her to do that. Good job."

"You look beautiful." Vashien smiled, warmly as Sparrow returned to him.

Rune slipped his hand over Faye's lower back, and she leaned into him.

"Shall we be off?" He asked.

No. Faye glanced down at her bare index finger before dropping her hand and straightened her back. She nodded, dreading the fact she was about to be surrounded by dark-bloods from courts and noble families. Everything she spent her life avoiding.

Rune explained, when they arrived at the Artithian palace they would walk together down the great hall and present their gift to the newly married couple. It sounded simple but set her teeth on edge.

Their surroundings faded and refocused much brighter. Faye shielded her eyes as they adjusted. They stood outside on a stone landing with Sparrow swearing under her breath behind her.

Faye hardly registered the dozens of people bustling about by the palace walls that towered above them. It gleamed in whites and golds, with tall arching windows and shining points.

Hulking armored men with white feathered wings stood at the edges. A pair of them holding open huge double doors.

"Vsenia," Rune smiled down at her, offering his arm.

She walked beside Rune, startled as the crowd parted for him. Faye's heart thundered. All the dark-bloods were staring at them and she stiffened under their gaze. Rune seemed unphased by the attention, strolling to the double doors, ignoring the stares and whispers completely.

Sadi and Damian approached them, adding to the whispering murmurs.

"You look like you belong here, dove," Damian said, regarding her with a feline grin. His arm around Sadi's waist.

Faye smiled at him as she glanced over the crowd. The women dressed in gowns like hers, sheer, skintight, and revealing. Damian and Sadi's attire didn't hold to the formal dress. Damian wore low slung black leather pants with his boots. The deep purple trench he wore accented with a black scarf looped around his neck, resting against his bare chest.

Sadi wore an embroidered corset over a white low-cut shirt with billowing sleeves that barely covered her high breasts. Her black skirt was ruffled, cut nearly indecent in the front, angling to be longer in the back before falling into a small train. Her thigh high belted boots covering her exposed legs.

The Familiar pair strolled into the building in front of her and Rune.

He made eye contact with one of the guards and motioned to Vashien and Sparrow, and said, "Please escort my guests to my seating."

A look of confusion covered the man's features for a moment before he bowed his head, and said, "Of course, Shadow Prince."

Faye's breath caught as they crossed the threshold. The whites and golds continued into the gutted interior. The building was a massive hall, one room that stretched on for what she guessed would be a twenty-minute walk.

Overhead were grand, glittering chandeliers in matching rows. The arching ceilings stretched into a wide swath of intricate stained glass that made up the center of the roof. Light streamed through it lighting a walkway along the white marble floor through the center of the hall.

She walked with Rune down a few stairs to the lower level leading to the white marble floor, doing her best to ignore the dark-bloods surrounding her.

Faye glanced across the space. Rows of seating lined either side of the hall. They rose higher as it moved further back. Above the ground seating along each wall were carved pillars that separated what looked like three floors of box seats. The guests Faye spotted in these upper floors sat with glasses and other refreshments, having the entire box to themselves. Unlike the shoulder-to-shoulder ground seating.

The important dark-bloods, she mused as she stepped forward with Rune. Women in the crowd continued to examine her, looking her up and down before stopping on her bare index finger. Their eyes widened as they quickly turned back to their partners. Faye squeezed Rune's arm as she noticed other people staring and whispering to each other.

Names Faye didn't recognize were called and a pair of women began walking down the stained-glass path.

"Do I look okay?" Faye asked as they moved closer to the walkway.

Rune met her gaze, his look softening as he smiled at her. "You are stunning."

"Then why are they glaring at me?" Faye plastered on her fake smile and glanced out at the crowd.

"The Familiar princess, Sadist Benevolence and Damian De Lor Meire." A brilliant light engulfed Damian, and reformed larger. Faye swore she heard her sister squeal in delight as she struggled to hide her shock at the massive black tiger with red stripes that now occupied the space beside Sadi.

In a sweeping move she tossed her ruffled skirt over Damian's back and sat, crossing her legs. Faye could only stare as Damian prowled down the stained-glass path.

Rune's hand settled over hers as they took another step forward.

The guard who announced the names inclined his head at her, and asked, "Your name, Lady?"

Faye glanced at Rune, and he gave her a gentle nod. Faye turned back answering, "Faye Alexander."

"The Shadow Prince, Rune Sacarlay, and Lady Faye Alexander."

Faye followed Rune's easy pace. An easy pressure brushed her mind, and Faye relaxed, letting him in. *They stare because a woman has never accompanied me.*

She kept her head forward. *Ever?* She asked in her mind, hoping Rune would hear her.

Small things I safeguarded to offer my queen. Things I now surrender to you.

Faye's heart tightened. He was choosing her, in front of all the realms. She wanted to hug him, but it was impossible here. She tilted her head to watch the colored hues light his features as they walked. He was so beautiful and held himself alone for so long. Faye tightened her hold on the inside of his arm.

This could work. She could fit into his world, and he would help with hers. She could be happy, have a family.

Faye glanced up at him again, finally able to admit to herself she was falling for this man.

They followed behind Sadi and Faye watched the rhythmic sway of Damian's tail as they walked. A pair of smaller thrones at the end of the walkway came into view. Stairs rose behind them to the king and queen of Artithia, Jha'ant and Sabadoc. The bride and groom sat in smaller versions of the elaborate thrones, dressed in flowing white and gold robes.

Rune stopped at the end of the stained-glass path and inclined his head. "We offer our blessing."

Our? Faye held her face neutral as an intricate gold box appeared before the bride. She took the box and inclined her head at Rune

"We thank you, Shadow Prince." The princess turned to Faye and inclined her head with a genuine smile. "Lady Faye."

Sixty-Five

R une bowed and phased his offering among the others. He straightened, aware more people watched Faye than him. He thanked the Darkness for the effect Faye had on the Ra'Voshnik. A crowd of this size would have sent it into a tirade otherwise.

He phased them to his reserved seats and thinned his lips when he found only two chairs in it. Vashien sat to his right with Sparrow perched on his lap.

"My apologies. There should have been four chairs here." Rune said, releasing Faye's hand as she smiled up at him. She left him defenseless. His queen belonged in the ravishing gown she was initially reluctant to wear.

Faye's hand slid over his side. "It's okay. I can sit on your lap. They're really big chairs."

"Please sit," Rune said, gesturing to the chair. "Sitting on my lap here would give others the wrong impression." He reached for her mind and her shields eased, allowing him to slip past. *You can sit on anything you wish when we return home.*

The light blush on her cheeks made the corner of his mouth lift. He'd never felt this content in his life. He felt young, eager for his days with her.

"I'm sitting on Vashien's lap. What impression are we sending?" Sparrow asked.

Rune glanced to the table between the chairs finding a single glass and a decanter of red liquid. Crimson wine by the look of it. Apparently, the revisions to his invitation were not received.

"A moment," Rune said, holding up a finger and stepped into the hall to make eye contact with a guard. He established a communication tether to the man advising him of the error in his seating arrangements. The guard apologized and by the look on his face, Rune would wager he was giving someone a blistering tongue lashing.

Rune returned to Faye. "They will bring in more chairs and proper refreshments."

"Was that blood? I knew that was blood. I almost drank that." Sparrow said, leaning forward in Vashien's lap to sneer at the decanter of crimson wine.

Rune chuckled. Faye's harpy sister began growing on him. He liked Vashien, though he pitied the male for choosing Sparrow as a partner.

The blonde harpy wiggled on Vashien's lap and asked, "Impression, I'm setting?"

"If Vashien were court born and you were not formally announced. Sitting on his lap labels you as an unscrupulous woman."

"He means whore." Vashien bounced Sparrow on his knee.

Sparrow wrinkled her nose. "You court fuckers are way too up tight."

"Shadow Prince."

Rune turned toward the male voice. Three men stood in the hall. Two held chairs and the third a tray of refreshments.

"Thank you." Rune turned, taking Faye's hand and guiding her away from the chairs.

The men arranged the additional seats and placed the tray on the table. "Is there anything else you require?"

"No, thank you," Rune said as the men bowed and quickly left.

"You have your own chair now, get off me," Vashien said, bouncing Sparrow more forcefully.

She snorted in response. "I'm sitting by the food. Do you see this?" Sparrow picked up a small cut of meat wrapped in a green leaf.

Vashien stood, forcing Sparrow off his lap and moved to the free chair.

Amused by the exchange, Rune poured Faye a flute of her pomegranate juice and offered her the glass. She took a small sip, her eyes closed as she sighed.

School your expression. Gabriel's voice sounded in Rune's mind. *I brought you grandfather's tome. I'll place it under your chair. Feel for it with your mind and vanish it.*

Sparrow stood up and leaned against the balcony looking down. "Hey, they're dancing now."

"Did you wish to dance?" Rune asked, lifting Faye's hand as he bowed to press his lips to the back of it.

Faye squeezed his hand and he let her go. She rose to join Sparrow on the balcony. Rune did a quick scan, locating and vanishing the book before sending his thanks to Gabriel.

She is far too pretty to be with you.

Rune smiled, taking his place at Faye's side.

"I don't know how to dance like that," Faye said, looking down at the mass of swaying gowns.

Rune absently stroked her back. "I can lead you through it if you wish."

"Just dance like Sadi and Damian, bitch." Sparrow said, pointing.

Rune shook his head. She was Familiar to her very core. Damian went through the steps of the dance, carrying Sadi. Her legs firmly around his waist, holding herself up.

"No," Rune answered.

Faye leaned back against him.

Rune's gaze wandered to the box seats directly across from his. He glanced away, not giving it a second thought.

Lyssa's seats were empty.

Sixty-Six

Rune returned home with Faye after she and her sister tired of watching the festivities. They materialized in her room and Rune stepped back sweeping his gaze over her. Every inch of her the dark queen he'd wished for his entire life.

He followed her as she strolled into his room. Faye came to a stop beside his bed, glancing back at him, her full lips lifting in the smile. "Can you help me take this off?"

Why take it off when we can fuck her in it? The Ra'Voshnik purred through his mind.

Rune grew hard as he grazed his lips over her shoulder. The backs of his fingers skimmed up her bare back in a slow, sensual caress. He unfastened the jeweled choker that held the front of the gown up.

Faye held it, keeping the gown from slipping down her body.

Rune's fangs throbbed, knowing she would soon be standing before him wearing only the lace thong and her heels.

She turned toward him and leaned up, her lips brushing over his. She kissed him as her free hand slid down his chest, trailing lower.

She pulled his belt open and let the jeweled collar fall to the floor. The gown pooled at her feet. "I think you've kept me waiting long enough," she said, running her nails over his hard length.

Rune groaned, staring down at her. Could scarcely believe fate blessed him with such beauty. He lifted her, gripping the back of her thighs as he guided her legs around his waist before lowering her onto his bed.

Runes kisses trailed lower. He pulled the bit of lace she still wore aside and brushed the back of his fingers over her. An appreciative groan escaped him when he found her wet. Faye pulled her legs together as he slipped her lace thong off.

He stood and Faye straightened her leg bringing her heel into his line of vision. "Leaving the heels?"

He brought his lips to her ankle, while holding her gaze. "Yes."

Rune stripped, tearing the clothing from his body. Faye smiled. Someone was in a hurry.

His fingertip traced the outside of her thigh as he said, "Spread your legs for me, vsenia."

Faye sat up and held her legs together, crossing her ankles to cover her sex from his view. "Make me," she said with a playful smile.

Rune arched his brow and hooked the bend of her knee, dragging her to the edge of the bed.

Faye jerked as a tongue glided through the folds of her sex. "Was that you?" She asked.

His grin widened, and black swept through his gaze before dissipating. "Did you wish to have Voshki join us?"

Faye panted as his clever phantom tongue teased her clit. Rune canted his head at her and mouths closed over her breasts. Teeth and tongues teasing her nipples setting her blood aflame.

Faye fell back, arching off the bed. "How are you doing this?"

She asked, overwhelmed by the sensations stringing her body tight.

"Phantom touch," he answered.

Faye screamed as another tongue licked inside her.

"It is actually a combative technique Voshki altered during your ritual. I have a touch more control over my will than he does." Rune said, stretching out next to her. He slid his fingers along her jaw, turning her to look at him. He captured her mouth in a slow kiss. When she was writhing beneath his will and moaning into his mouth, he pulled back with a satisfied grin. "Are you going to spread your legs for me now?"

Rune glanced at the legs she still held closed.

Faye struggled to remember her game, resisting the urge to let her legs fall wide. He turned back to her and cupped between her legs. She felt the touch of his hand, but it did nothing to stop the phantom mouths he conjured on her.

Faye gasped as he slowly eased a finger into her. He pressed in, pulling out to press a little further. Tension coiled in her, her muscles growing taut with it. She kissed him, brushing the side of her face against his. "Please."

"Wanting to come so soon?" Rune brought her right to the edge and eased back.

"Please," Faye repeated in a breathy moan as she rocked her hips, needing his finger inside her. He teased her mercilessly. In her frustration Faye dug her nails into his back.

"Did you learn this during your training?" She asked.

"Among other things." A possessive glint lit his pale blue eyes as he eased another finger into her.

Faye gasped, clinging to him as he pressed firmly into her. She stilled as her pleasure mounted. Building. He curled his fingers inside her.

"Rune." She dug her nails into his shoulder as she came. Waves of pleasure washing over her, through her.

Rune watched her come apart beneath his hand and will, continuing the rhythm she needed. When she came down he withdrew his fingers and stood at the end of the bed. He leaned over her, her legs pressed to his chest.

Spread her legs and make her take your cock, the Ra'Voshnik growled, eager to feel her soft flesh give and take him deep.

Rune pressed two fingers into her. Stroking into her harder, readying her. "I could do this all night, unless you wanted to spread your legs for me, minx."

Faye's knees fell wide and Rune gazed down at her. She was lovely, panting as she stared up at him with passion glazed eyes.

Rune withdrew from her, ceasing his phantom touches. He positioned himself between her legs and lowered himself over her. He angled his arm under her back. "Hold on to me," he said.

When she did, Rune lifted her with him as he sat back on his heels. He held her against him as she wrapped her legs around his waist.

He kissed her and rested his forehead against hers. "I have waited my entire life for you. I am yours to command."

Faye traced her fingers over the side of his face. The tenderness in her gaze made his heart ache. "Did you just say you love me in dark-blood?" She asked.

Rune held her tighter and said, "I will remember to express my devotion in Anarian so my mule-headed minx will understand my meaning."

Faye rocked her hips over him, the tip of his cock teasing her entrance. Against his lips she asked, "And how would I say I love you in dark-blood so Voshki knows I'm fond of him?"

The creature chuckled, purring its contentment. *She prefers me to you.*

"Only the Ra'Voshnik?" Rune asked.

Faye leaned forward, the tip of her tongue flicking over his bottom lip. "I make do with you, my arrogant Shadow Prince."

The corner of Rune's mouth lifted. He rolled his hips forward, pressing into her. His fangs lengthening as he said, "Devotion among immortals is expressed in two parts."

Rune withdrew and pressed further into her. The way her lips parted as she took more of him into her body beckoned his vampiric instincts. The need to take her throat and drive his cock into her wet heat lashed at his control.

Rune grated, "One becomes the will of the other."

She cried out as he thrust deeper, her nails digging into his back.

"While the other takes ownership of the first," Rune said at her ear as he pinned her hips to him. Moving beneath her, possessing more of her with each stroke.

"Ownership?" Faye clung to him, wrapping her arms around his neck as he took her in an easy rhythm.

"Commanding me or telling me I am yours is how we express devotion."

Faye moaned and gripped the front of his throat, crying, "Harder."

Rune purred in unison with the Ra'Voshnik. *She wants us to spread her legs and fuck her hard. Take what is offered.*

He ignored the creature obeying his queen as he seated himself completely.

"Fuck," Faye sighed against his neck, trembling in his arms.

Rune adjusted his hold and said, "Lean back."

Faye rested against his arms. Her breathy moans timed with each surge of his hips. She tightened her hold on his throat as her other hand reached between them. He slowed to watch as she touched herself.

"No, don't stop," she growled.

Rune gave a soft laugh, giving her what she needed. A flush spread between her breasts as he perceived the initial tremors of her orgasm. "Come for me, love."

Her lips parted at his words as she squeezed around his length again and again.

Rune thrusted into her harder, deeper. He grated, "Offer me your throat."

She turned her head to the side, and Rune sank his fangs deep.

"Fuck me. Come for me." She commanded.

Rune groaned, losing himself in her. He came hard, his cock pulsing as he spent deep within her.

Rune pulled her against him, absently thrusting into her as he caught his breath.

She clung to him, rocking her hips. Faye leaned back to look at him as he hardened again while inside her. "My vampire is insatiable."

The corner of his mouth lifted. "I am yours to command, my love."

Sixty-Seven

Faye collapsed breathless against Rune's chest. She straddled his hips as he reclined against the headboard. Her slender arms wrapped around his neck, holding him close. He teasingly shifted his hip to thrust into her, eliciting a moan from her lips. By the Darkness, how was he still hard? He'd kept her up most of the night. The man should be done.

"I'm hungry," Faye said, pressing her hands to his chest as she lifted off him— Surprised she made it off his lap. He'd pinned her to the bed the last time she tried to pull away. A predator intent on keeping his prey.

"You should go while I still have a hold on my instincts." His gaze dipped to her breasts as he licked the point of his fangs. "I have a mind to pin you to this bed until dawn."

Faye watched his mouth, debating if she really needed a break.

Darkness, he was too alluring. So different from the man she hit with a candleholder weeks ago. He looked happy, content. It made her heart tighten.

Rune's words clicked in her mind and Faye glanced over her shoulder at the ever-twilight sky through the narrow windows along the far wall. "It's never dawn here."

A wicked grin crossed his lips.

"No. I am starving and can't be sustained with blood like some people," she said.

He purred, leaning forward. "I will calm myself."

Faye wasn't sure how much she trusted his statement. He canted his head, peering at her with dark misted eyes.

She pointed at him and said, "Give me fifteen minutes before you start hunting me. I might bring food back to bed."

His grin lifted into a smirk. "I would like to feed you a great many things."

Faye imagined him gliding over her lips, remembering the feel of him stroking her mouth. Faye mentally shook herself and gave him a stern look. "Fifteen minutes." She got out of bed and picked the gray gown off the ground, laying it over the rumpled sheets. Then she went to his closet, stealing a robe.

She gave Rune a final look as she slipped into his robe. He tracked her movements but made no move for her. Satisfied she would be able to get something to eat before he came to collect her, she made her way to the kitchen.

Faye quickly collected a plate of cut fruits, eating a few berries.

Soft footfalls penetrated the silence. Faye gazed down the hall holding her plate. Rune stalked toward her. His pale blue eyes were different, his features tense. Anger seething from his gaze. Faye's brow lowered. His clothes were wrong, and his hair was pulled back, tied at the base of his skull.

A metallic sheen reflected over his shoulders. Two swords Faye realized. Floating behind him. She took a step back. "Rune?"

His image flickered and he reappeared in front of her, towering over her. He fisted her hair cruelly, wrenching her neck up as her back met his body. Pain radiated over her scalp and Faye stood on her toes trying to lessen the pressure.

The sword, cold and sharp, wedged under her chin. "Don't call me his name," a gravel filled voice grated against her ear. "Move and I will carve your head from your body."

Terror leached through her mind, giving way to panic, and Faye screamed, "Rune!"

The blade was so sharp she didn't realize it cut her until she felt the thin trail of blood slipping between her breasts.

Rune appeared on the opposite side of the kitchen, the island counter between them, dressed only in unfastened black slacks. He didn't look at her. Only canted his head at the man behind her as though he were inconvenienced.

The man shook her hard. Faye shrieked as the blade jostled against her throat. She grasped at the blade, cutting her hands as she desperately attempted to keep it off her neck.

Rune ignored her cries to fasten his pants. When he finished, he exhaled and said, "Would you be kind enough to refrain from slicing up my whore? I fancy her throat."

Faye froze at his dismissive words as the man tensed behind her. His fist tightened in her hair as he snarled, "Do not lie to me. I saw you with her."

A dark smile painted across Rune's aristocratic features. "And what exactly did you see frail-blood?"

Faye stood on her toes, pulling away from the blade. It lowered a fraction as the man grated, "You took Prinia from me solely because she was an Anarian. And now, you parade one of your own in front of all the realms."

Rune shrugged, "You could have paraded yours. I warned you not to marry her."

"I loved her!"

"Your pet was not fit for our court."

"She wasn't my pet!" The man took a ragged breath. The second came smoother. "You lie to save her. I would have done the same. Brother, I know you," the man said, dragging the blade tight to Faye's throat once more. She sucked a fearful breath, holding as still as she could.

"Then you should know better," Rune spoke casually as he pulled out a stool, dragging it loudly. He leaned over the counter selecting an apple before sitting down. Rune bit into it and gestured toward her. "Tell me she is not the very image of Sadi. Come now frail-blood. We both wanted to fuck her. Now I do." Rune smirked, tapping his temple. "Minus the Familiar madness."

The words hit Faye like a blow. Acute, searing pain tore at her heart as tears welled in her eyes. She was a fool.

"Your scent covers her. She reeks of sex." The angle of the blade curved down, no longer slicing against her skin.

Rune held up his hand, ignoring the man. A woman appeared next to Rune. She was petite, waves of her fawn-colored hair tumbling down her back. Rune's fingers traced past the woman's jaw into her hair. *The same way he touched me,* Faye thought as hot tears spilled down her cheeks.

Rune's indifference was the worst cruelty. He said he loved her. He served her. Rune turned the woman to face them and the blank stare of her vacant eyes jarred Faye from her thoughts.

The woman's irises were cloudy, staring off into the distance. Unaware of her surroundings. She looked empty. A body abandoned by the soul who once inhabited it.

"You confuse devotion with fucking," Rune explained, leaning closer to the woman to inspect her eyes. The corner of his mouth lifted as his eyes gleamed with perverse amusement.

He took a small bite of apple and removed it from his mouth, slipping it between the woman's lips. Her eyes never shifted as she dutifully chewed and swallowed. Rune raised a brow and said, "Have her trained quite well."

He didn't wait for a response, turning his attention back to the woman. Rune jerked her against him as he bit into the pad of his thumb. He gazed into her eyes the same way a lover might, his fingertips stroking behind her ear, following forward along her jaw.

His bloodied thumb brushed across her lips.

Bile rose in Faye's throat. Her mind screamed betrayal at the intimate exchange unfolding before her. The crushing feeling in her chest overwhelmed her, she scarcely felt the blade slack against her skin. Could hardly breathe.

The woman opened her mouth and closed her lips over Rune's thumb. He tilted his head back and groaned.

Hot tears fell from Faye's unblinking eyes. Betrayal and shame burned her. She desperately wanted to look away but found her gaze affixed.

The blade pulled tight to her throat, but Faye couldn't bring herself to care as her tears fell one after the other.

"I saw you," the man's voice waived for a moment before he continued, "You're lying. I know you love her."

"Love?" Rune laughed.

"Have you sunk so low, you now use their words?" Rune asked before hissing as his brow drew together in pleasure. He exhaled, meeting the man's gaze. "Does she suck on anything you put in her mouth?"

"Rune, stop. I'll kill her."

"I have a better suggestion." Rune stood, shoving the woman over the counter between them. Pinning her by the neck. "I shall keep your whore and you can keep mine. Trade for a week." Rune leaned forward looking into the woman's haunting face before lifting his gaze. "Perhaps two. Would you like a demonstration of what you smell on my whore?"

Black swept through his gaze and dissipated, as he gripped the woman's waist. His black-tipped claws piercing the fabric. A cruel smile played on Rune's lips. "Does she make any noise?"

The sword clattered against the floor. "Rune stop."

Faye crashed to her knees, and Rune was on the man the next instant. In a blur of motion Rune seized him by the throat. Faye flinched as his back slammed against the counter, cracking the wooden cabinet beneath it. Rune leapt up and braced a knee on the man's chest, still pinning him by his throat.

Faye retreated to the corner of the kitchen on unsteady feet, sobbing.

The man only narrowed his eyes, stretched over the counter next to the woman, who eerily remained as Rune left her.

They spoke in low tones that didn't carry to Faye.

A gravel filled voice said, "You can't hurt me more than you already have. You can't outrun a blood debt. I'll come for her. But I'll show mercy, I'll just kill her."

Faye jerked when the man spat in Rune's face. He and the woman vanished without a word.

Rune wiped his face, leaping down. His expression changed when he met her gaze. Anguished shadows filled his eyes. He reached for her. "Vsenia."

"Don't fucking touch me," Faye sobbed, slapping his hand away. Her stomach rolled, threatening to empty its contents.

"Alister needed to believe my words to keep you safe. Everything I said was a lie," he said. His expression pleading, begging her to understand. To forgive him.

Rune wanted Sadi. He didn't love her, she was just a body. Faye fled running to her sister's rooms as Rune called her name following her.

Sixty-Eight

Pain sliced through Rune's heart as Faye fled. He followed, calling her name.

What have you done! The Ra'Voshnik roared, bashing itself against his awareness.

"Faye, let me explain," Rune called, ignoring the creature. Agony clawed in his chest with each of her broken sobs. "Vsenia."

"Sparrow." Faye pushed open the door to her sister's room.

Rune stood at the threshold as Faye stumbled blindly into the darkened room. Her sister and Vashien slept as Faye crawled onto the bed feeling for her sister beneath Vashien's wing. "Sparrow."

"Faye? Hey, honey what happened?" Sparrow brushed Faye's hair back and wiped her tears. Hellfire blazed to life, lighting the room.

Rune narrowed his eyes as they adjusted to the light. Sparrow pushed Faye back, her gaze fixed to the blood trickling down her throat.

The little blonde's gaze shifted to Rune, burning with rage and accusation. "Did you fucking cut her?"

Tell them what happened, the Ra'Voshnik roared as Sparrow pressed her hand under Faye's chin.

"Take me home," Faye sobbed. Her words were a knife to his heart.

Vashien's wings pulled tight against his back. He called his sword as he leapt over Sparrow and Faye, taking a defensive stance between them and Rune.

"Faye." Rune pleaded, desperate to explain.

She clutched Sparrow tighter and the little blonde snarled, "You don't get to say her name, asshole."

"Take me home." Faye's broken voice gutted him. "I want to go home."

Vashien never took his eyes off Rune, his sword at the ready as he stepped backwards. "Stand up. I'll phase us home."

Do not let him take her! The Ra'Voshnik screamed as Rune pinned Vashien's mind. "You will not. My brother attacked her." Rune stepped into the room and Faye shrank from him. "Love, I said those things to protect you. Every word was a lie."

Faye met his gaze, her lashes clinging to tears she had yet to spill. Tears he caused. "You told me you never wanted Sadi."

"Vse—"

Faye's fingers dug into her sister's shoulder as she screamed, "You both wanted to fuck her!"

"Faye."

"I am not your cheap whore!"

Rune took a step toward them. Needing to comfort her. To make her understand. "I worship you. Alister would have killed you if he knew how devoted I am to you."

Faye went rigid with tension. She held his gaze grating out a single word. "Why?"

Rune dropped her gaze. There were no explanations for the atrocities he'd committed. His actions were unforgivable. His cruelty and arrogance costed him dearly eight centuries ago. And it would cost him again. Stripping him of his queen.

"You did that to her." Not a question.

Rune swallowed and nodded before meeting her gaze. Her stormy eyes held no warmth. The affection he'd seen minutes ago withered and died before his eyes.

"I did," Rune admitted.

"You're a monster. I never want to see you again."

Rune released Vashien's mind.

What are you doing? The Ra'Voshnik demanded, circling his mind. *Do not let him take her.*

His queen wished to go. It wasn't his place to question her. He served her will.

He couldn't keep her here. Couldn't make her understand.

Rune could only watch as they faded from sight.

Sixty-Nine

Sleep wouldn't come in the days that followed Faye's departure. Her tear-stricken look of betrayal gutted him, leaving him empty. Rune sat in his study, attempting to read a passage for the third time.

He had no interest in reading these documents. His mind wandering to his night breeze. He'd gone to Faye's home more than once asking to explain, to beg her forgiveness. Faye refused to see him while Sparrow and Vashien barred his entry.

The Ra'Voshnik remained deathly quiet, somewhere in his subconscious. The creature raged, fighting him viciously in the hours after Faye left and suddenly stopped. It did nothing as its presence slowly slipped into the recesses of his mind. It was as though the Ra'Voshnik understood they had irrevocably lost her and no longer cared to carry on.

Rune rubbed his chest over his heart, unable to soothe the

ache. He had a mind to tear it out of his chest for a few moments of peace.

He was no stranger to war, torture, even had his flesh carved from his body on occasion. Darkness, he would welcome any of them— All of them to replace the bleeding ache where his heart once was.

Being without his night breeze pained him like nothing else. He'd held a moment of happiness and he'd lost it. Knowing what his life was with her, he could not return to his existence without her.

Sadi brushed his mind before materializing beside him. Rune glanced up at her. Sadi's resemblance to his queen only amplified Faye's absence.

"She's a fool," Sadi said.

"I am the fool." Rune's voice was empty and hollow, echoing his shame. "I was too arrogant. I thought Alister would keep his distance. I should have seen him coming."

He should have explained his blood debt to Faye and let her decide if she would accept his advances. He thought he would have more time. He'd been desperate to show her the man he would be for her rather than what he had been. The actions and choices that ultimately costed him his family.

"I can collect his head." Sadi offered, sweetly.

"No," Saith ordered the same of him once and when he refused, Saith abandoned him.

All my efforts on you will be wasted.

And they were. Rune spent twenty-two centuries becoming a dark weapon for his court. One Saith favored wielding. And Rune never questioned him, desiring his approval above all others.

Until The Creator ordered him to kill his brother, Rune could finally see there was no loyalty in Saith. Family and court meant nothing to him, and Rune would only be favored as long as he was of use.

Exactly as Alister had warned him, all those centuries ago.

"No," Rune repeated more to himself than Sadi. He monitored his brother. Kept a perimeter around Faye's home.

He would keep her safe and continue searching for her altar. Serving her in what little capacity she still tolerated.

These things were all he had left of her.

Seventy

Weeks passed in the blink of an eye. Faye lay in a tangle of sheets, bunched and dragged to the far corner of the bed, under the window. She tucked against the wall cocooned in blankets with a pile of crumpled tissues beside her.

Her sister's voice carried from the living room. "Fuck off. She doesn't want to see you." The sizzle of magic followed, and the door slammed.

Faye closed her eyes as the tears fell. She told Sparrow what happened. How terrified she'd been. It took a little more than two weeks for her to calm enough to see Rune didn't mean the things he'd said.

And that was where her heart warred with her head. Rune hurt the woman his brother loved. Vashien told her the clouded eyes meant her mind was broken. The woman's vacant stare haunted Faye's dreams, and Rune was the cause.

What kind of a person was she if she could dismiss what he'd done? She may as well have broken the woman's mind herself.

Faye's door cracked open with a light knock. "You can't hide in here forever," Sparrow said, hopping onto her bed and wrinkled her nose in disapproval at the pile of crumpled tissues.

Faye tucked deeper in the blankets, wiping them over her swollen eyes. She was so tired of crying.

"Come on. You need to eat something, bitch." Sparrow said, slapping the blankets. When Faye refused to move, Sparrow yanked on them. "Get. Up. You can return to your moping after you eat."

Faye held on while Sparrow pulled. Her voice broke as she asked, "Am I a bad person?" She felt ashamed for missing Rune. Every morning she woke up reaching for him and each morning she reminded herself he was a monster.

"What kind of stupid ass question is that?" Sparrow quirked her lip then vanished the pile of tissues before sitting next to her.

"I miss him," Faye said quietly, wiping away the new tears. "What's wrong with me? Why do I still want him?"

The image of Rune pinning his brother to the counter burned into her memory along with his gravel filled voice.

I'll come for her. But I'll show mercy, I'll just kill her.

"Honey, no." Sparrow ran her hand through her hair, immediately pulling it back. "You *are* showering today. Your hair is disgusting."

Faye pulled the blankets tighter, not caring how oily her hair was. Sparrow would be lucky if she ate more than two bites of the meal she had no appetite for.

"I'm going to get Vash to drag you out of bed and drop your ass in your hot spring." Sparrow pet Faye's hair again. "Nasty ass."

Minutes ticked by in silence and Sparrow sighed. "He was good to you," she said, wiping a tear from her cheek. "You're allowed to feel things, you're grieving."

"I don't want to miss him," Faye said, drawing a ragged breath.

Sparrow snorted. "I'm more worried about shadow fuck's brother. You really think he will stop coming after you? He's not playing a game of tag. This isn't base, bitch."

"I didn't think of that."

"I did." Venom dripped from her sister's voice. "Vash set up a perimeter. Let that motherfucker show up here. I will fuck his world."

Faye swallowed, remembering the feel of his sword at her throat. "He's dangerous."

Sparrow smirked. "He's a day-blood. I'll rock his shit."

Faye didn't respond and Sparrow said, "Come on. You do need to eat, so get that ass out of bed."

Faye groaned as Sparrow exited her room.

Sparrow called over her shoulder as she left. "If you don't eat I'll get Aunty Clara. She'll be mad."

Faye made an exasperated noise. "I hate you," she called.

"You love me," Sparrow called back from the hallway.

Weeks passed but time did little to ease her heart. Faye pushed her breakfast around her plate. She was sure to anyone watching she appeared to have pieced her life back together, when in truth Faye felt hallowed out. Pushing herself through each day hoping the next would be easier.

She'd abandoned her garden in Hell. Sparrow was all too eager to demand her garden be returned, but Faye refused. Sparrow insisted she would do all the talking and she wouldn't have to see Rune at all.

Faye didn't want her garden. It would remind her of the times she spent with him. So many memories of him haunted her, leaving her feeling empty without his presence in her life.

A knock pulled her from her musings. Sparrow put down her cup of coffee and rolled her shoulders. "We're starting early today."

Rune came to see her every day and each time Sparrow sent him away.

"I got it," Faye said, getting up.

Sparrow froze, giving her a suspicious glance. "You sure?"

Faye nodded. "He's just going to keep coming back."

She opened the door.

"Faye." His voice was hushed as though he couldn't believe she stood before him.

She stepped outside, closing the door behind her. Rune looked the way she felt. He still wore a tailored black suit, but he'd lost weight. His features gaunt with dark circles under his eyes.

She took a deep breath not meeting his gaze. "You need to let me go."

"Please speak with me," Rune begged, his voice pleading.

Faye took a deep breath, reminding herself he was a monster. She needed to end things with him. She would not allow herself to love a cruel dark-blood.

"There's nothing left to say."

Seventy-One

Rune's past had come back to haunt him. Costing him what he needed most in this life. He bowed his head and said, "I am sorry I did not tell you of my blood debt."

Faye peered at him, tilting her head as though he spoke madness. "It's not that you didn't tell me. Why did you have to break her mind? Killing your brother's Anarian wasn't enough?"

Rune recoiled. "You think— I did not break her mind maliciously."

"How do you accidently break a mind?" Faye spat.

Rune paused, recalling the moment that changed his life. The cost of his arrogance. "My brother and I had a tenuous relationship. Alister announced Prinia and I challenged his choice. I expected him to stand down, instead Alister initiated a blood debt. *If you take the woman who quickens my heart, I will take the same from you when your heart quickens.*"

Faye's lightning arced eyes lit with fury, promising violence. "Alister loved a woman and wanted to marry her. And you wouldn't let him because she was an Anarian? *Then* you traded the person you may or may not fall in love with, in the future?"

Her pain and anger tore at his heart. If he had understood what he would be offering in trade, Rune would have left his brother to his choices. But he'd trusted in those who didn't deserve it. Nothing more than a pawn, fooled into thinking he pulled his own strings.

"I lived for twenty-two centuries and felt nothing. In my arrogance I cut my hand and spoke the terms of his blood debt."

Faye gazed off into the forest. "That's not an excuse."

Rune swallowed. "The three of us struggled. I pulled away from Alister's blade and she twisted in my grasp, severing her artery. Prinia bled out in The Eyes before Belind could heal her. Alister sealed our blood debt by kissing my blood off her lips. She rose a vampire a few days later. My blood was too dark for her. It broke her mind. I asked Sadi to heal her, but Prinia is beyond her capability." Sadi spent more than a decade exhausting herself, reaching for a ghost. Prinia never answered her calls that would lead her out of Chaos and back to her physical body.

Faye met his gaze and remained silent, searching his eyes. Rune swallowed. Waiting.

"Can I heal her if you find my altar?"

"Healing the mind and core are Familiar magic. I will ask Sadi if she would be willing to teach you. You are stronger than we are."

"I want to heal her," Faye said.

"Familiar are secretive of their magic. I will speak with Sadi." Faye stood before him but remained completely out of reach. "How do I make things right with you?"

Faye looked away and touched the front of her neck. She spoke so softly he scarcely heard her. "I care for you, but we fundamentally don't work."

Rune stepped closer to her, taking her hand in his. "Then teach me. I cannot be without you. I love you."

"I forgive you. I'll help you repair what you did to your brother's wife." Faye squeezed his hand.

Rune's heart leapt as the Ra'Voshnik stirred, listening. Hoping.

Then she let him go. "But you don't love me. If you did, you would be upset with how your queen was treated for the past twenty-five years, not expecting me to shuck off my old life. You don't hear me. You don't value what I value."

Rune's lips parted. She couldn't mean that. He looked down at her, utterly defeated.

She stood on her toes to press her lips to his. Rune closed his eyes, willing her to feel how he'd yearned for her, his entire life. To glimpse the life he envisioned at her side.

Her fingers brushed over the side of his face, as she gazed up at him. She turned from him going back into her cottage, speaking two words over her shoulder before she closed the door.

"Goodbye Rune."

Seventy-Two

Fate was a cruel mistress. Rune leaned back in his chair, his mind wondering to useless ideation. What his life would have looked like if fate gifted him his night breeze during the first few centuries of his life. His path would have differed greatly.

Rune had respected his queen's wishes. He'd given her space, keeping his distance while monitoring her home and Alister's location.

He would protect her even if she no longer wanted him. He mourned his loss, feeling her absence more with each passing moment. He occupied his days with the few things he had left of her. He maintained her herb garden and searched for her altar.

The Ra'Voshnik had been inconsolable in the hours that followed Faye's departure from their lives. It sank silently into the recesses of his mind and had not stirred since.

Rune's fangs lengthened as a sharp pain lanced his mind. A trigger he wove into his realm, announcing anyone who phased in, including Shadowmen. His gaze lifted as his temper edged for violence.

His front door crashed open and angry footsteps stalked toward his study. Rune scented her and exhaled, returning his attention to Saith's journal.

"What did you do to her?"

Rune spared a momentary glance at his uninvited guest before returning to his research. "Lovely to see you, Morgan."

Lyssa's daughter took it the hardest when he relinquished his position as her mother's consort. Rune ignored her, and carefully turned the page. The tome was detailed, providing a wealth of knowledge on Saith's creations. Processes. But he was no closer to finding a line that tied to the Darkness.

Morgan's deep red hair swayed as she stalked to Rune's desk, resting her palms on it. She leaned forward sharply, snapping with her usual charm, "Mother won't drink. What did you do?"

Rune didn't react, didn't look up at her. Partially because the harpy was bothersome. But more so because she inherited features from Sadira. The queen entombed in his father's crystalline palace.

"I have not seen Lyssa in some weeks now. Perhaps you should speak with your mother instead of insisting on interrogating me," he said, before carefully turning the page as he continued reading.

Morgan shrieked, her power scattering everything on his desk.

Rune's hard gaze lifted. "You are in my realm. My home, child. I grow tired of your tantrums. Leave or I will remove you." The only reason Morgan still walked among the living was because she was Lyssa's child.

Morgan shoved his desk, surging it toward him.

Rune caught the desk, stopping its momentum.

The Ra'Voshnik rose in a heated fury needing violence to ease its pained heart. Rune held the creature far beneath the surface. *Calm yourself, maiming her will upset Faye,* Rune grated.

The Ra'Voshnik didn't put up a fight, drifting back to the depths of his mind. Silent.

Morgan narrowed her eyes, holding Rune's gaze as she phased.

He propped his elbow on the desk and rested his forehead against his fingertips. Would Faye agree to a single death if he begged?

He stood, retrieving Saith's tome. He should be grateful Morgan didn't recognize her grandfather's journal. If Morgan collected it even Gabriel wouldn't be able to procure it for him a second time.

Ignoring the rest of the papers and books littering the ground, Rune sat at his desk opening the tome. The pages fell open to the creation of Shadowmen. The stone slabs remained outside his keep. Rune knew the story. Saith took nine Artithian women, the tenth was meant to be his general. His father Julian.

Rune read the entry. Saith went into great detail. How he used the Darkness to fashion full grown men who ripped out of the bodies of these women. None of them survived Saith's dark magic.

Rune found a small notation near his father's name. Saith's flourished, masculine script read like a Familiar riddle.

I will turn this thorn in my side into a weapon I can wield. I've captured the Elysian Queen.

Elysian Queen? The name of her court perhaps. Sadi's words circled him. Like calls to like. Was Faye her descendant?

Rune rose, gazing out at the ever twilight sky. Pages crinkled under his shoes as he strolled to the window. His gaze lowered to the stone slabs arranged in a circle just outside the walls of his keep.

Realization struck him.

Like calls to like.

He'd mistakenly thought Sadi meant for him to find a link between himself and Faye.

Rune phased to his altar. The stone slab his father was created on. The stone he was born on.

Rune opened his wrist letting his blood flow, collecting on the stone.

"Like calls to like," Rune whispered and began his work.

Seventy-Three

Rune spent the past few days perfecting a spell based off his blood's tie to his altar. He isolated the link between the two and created a spell which allowed him to scry for the location of an altar using blood as its beacon.

He would have immediately gone to Faye with the news, but it was a dreadful hour of the night. He thought of her often. His imaginings bittersweet. He'd found the means to give her everything she wanted. She would have her shard, could have the family she wanted. His heart bled knowing it would not be with him.

Rune's hand settled over Saith's journal. He'd finished reading it, finding nothing of use. Only Saith's cruel use of magic. At a loss he'd reached for Morbid's mind, seeing if Morbid was awake. The Familiar King was ancient, there when Saith came to power.

Prince, Morbid's voice purred through his mind.

You are awake.

I waited up for you.

Rune laughed, wondering if there was anything Morbid didn't
see. He phased to the only location he knew in Chaos and stepped
off the landing pad in front of Morbid's home. There were two
constants in the Familiar's realm. The first being the thunder filled
sky that never rained. The second, while the bones changed with each
visit, they always made up the ground.

Today charred bones littered the ground, crumbling beneath
his steps. Flashes of lightning illuminated the sky as lightning arced
within the heavy dark clouds. Morbid's home took the shape of a
multilevel mansion typically found in Necromia for this visit. Turrets
and gables rose from the Familiar King's home.

The large windows unnerved Rune. The home's interior was
pitch black. Not darkened rooms, but voids containing nothing.

A bone popped beneath Rune's shoe, and he grimaced, glancing
down before phasing to the front door that lay open in invitation.
Once inside Rune found himself in a small room without doors or
windows. Only a staircase that led up.

He climbed the steps given no other choice. They led into a wall
with a door flush to the steps. Rune eased the door open, and it led
into a large room that could be used as a study. Empty bookshelves
sporadically lined the walls. Rugs overlapped haphazardly on the
floor. A large fireplace took up the far wall with two chairs angled in
front of it.

"Shadow Prince, how may I be of service?" Morbid sat in one
of the chairs near the fire. He slouched in the corner of the chair
with one leg bent over the armrest at the knee. He wore his customary leather pants, not bothering to wear a shirt. The Familiar King
probably thought the two brightly colored scarves, looped around his
neck to rest against his chest, made up for it.

Rune took a seat in the chair opposite Morbid and glanced at
the fireplace. Hellfire burned blue. The flames burning were pink.
Rune pulled his gaze away, already feeling his head beginning to ache.
Nothing made sense in Chaos.

Rune turned to Morbid and said, "I am finding it difficult to
locate documents that predate Saith."

The Familiar King nodded. "New rulers often eradicate evidence
of the old."

"You were there. Do you remember that time?"

Morbid's lips parted in a wide smile, displaying his less substantial fangs. "I have a long and accurate memory. What are you searching for, Prince?"

Rune took a shallow breath. Each time Faye filled his thoughts, the pain of her absence stripped another piece of him. Hollowing him out further.

He had nothing left to give, but his regret always found more to take.

"I am looking for a race who existed before Saith came to power. Able to resurrect like a Pure Blood, but their life thread is anchored in the Darkness."

Morbid shrugged. "Can't say. We do have a library with the history of the realms before Saith. You're welcome to it."

Not the answer he'd hoped for but Morbid never answered anything outright. Rune inclined his head and said, "That would be most helpful."

"I'll take you to its landing pad." Morbid stood, smoothing his scarves before phasing them deeper into the Familiar's realm.

A decaying version of the Artithian library rose before Rune. Instead of the gleaming whites and golds, this structure was awash in gray. Deeper blacks ran down the corners, staining the walls.

Morbid started for the building, crushing the charred bones beneath his boots as he walked. Rune chose to phase to the doorway, avoiding them.

He followed Morbid into the building. The interior followed the Artithian library, colored in darker tones of gray and maroon. Familiar strolled through the space in various stages of undress. Sounds of coupling came from various locations on different floors.

The musk of bodies joining permeated the air. Rune parted his lips, taking a slow breath. The taste of want should have been thick in the air. No tastes of emotions coated his tongue. Rune originally believed he was unable to taste the emotions of Morbid and Sadi. Perhaps all Familiar were immune— or at least those who served Chaos.

Morbid past a brazen couple on a table, knocking books to the ground in their endeavors. Rune raised a brow at Morbid. They behaved little better than vampires during the Hunter's Moon. "Is this a normal occurrence?"

Morbid paused at a narrow stairway. "My people are hedonistic by nature."

"Will this building change like your home does?"

"No, this library is a temple of sorts. It doesn't change." Morbid stepped into the lower level and outstretched an arm. "The realms before Saith."

Rune glanced over the space. It was as expansive as the upper level, rows of bookshelves filled the space. It would take time for Rune to navigate this, if Familiar organized the books in any meaningful way.

"Will your people allow me entry when I return?"

Morbid smiled, slapping Rune's back. "If you are here, you were invited."

Rune nodded. "Have you heard of an Elysian Queen?"

Morbid scratched the back of his neck and crossed the room before crouching down scanning the books. He selected a leather-bound book and returned to Rune. "She was a goddess worshiped long ago."

Rune took the offered book. It had no title on the cover. He turned it to see its spine was just as blank. He glanced at the books to find all the spines blank. Darkness, his head hurt just looking at it.

"She is the goddess of wheat and harvest," Morbid said.

Rune thinned his lips. Hardly something Saith would view as a thorn in his side. "May I remove books from this library?"

"Of course." Morbid laughed. "I will take my leave. Angelique needs tending."

Rune inclined his head at Morbid and he disappeared. Rune took a seat at the closest table, opening the book.

It contained information on farming. Rune flipped through pages as it described plants and how to best care for them. Illustrations depicted different stages of growth. Just when Rune was going to close the book deeming it useless, he thumbed over a portrait of a woman.

She stood in a wheat field with her face upturned to the sky. Her hair and eyes were both golden, the color of wheat. Her fingers ended in dainty claws and fine boned wings were folded against her back.

Beneath the painting read: THE ELYSIAN QUEEN, GODDESS OF WHEAT AND GOOD HARVEST

Rune flipped the pages finding no other information on the goddess. He glanced at the dozens of bookshelves filled with books of the exact same size and color. Each of them blank. He returned his book and went to the north-facing corner. He walked to the end of the shelf and took the first five books off the top.

He would read through the night here and visit his night breeze at a decent hour of the morning.

Seventy-Four

Faye showered and dressed, making her way into the kitchen. She cut some fruit as Sparrow made eggs and toast.

"I should have stolen that talisman," her sister grumbled.

Faye ate a bite of fruit and kicked her ankle.

"Ow, bitch. You can't say the food wasn't amazing."

Faye didn't respond as she took her seat. Her mind often drifted to Rune. She'd been happy for a time with him. Those weeks seemed like a lifetime ago.

Faye expected her village to go back to what it had been before she met him, but Rune left the healer and staff at aunty Clara's house. With the new homes being built, other Anarians came to settle in Alexander as well.

She was thankful for his assistance but had to remind herself of their differences constantly. It was too easy to fall back into his arms.

I am yours to command, my love. His amended statement, incorporating her world into his. He'd been gentle and considerate with her. *Darkness help her. She missed him.*

A knock sounded at their door, and Faye exchanged a glance with Sparrow.

Her sister shrugged. "It's been over a week. He stayed away longer than I thought he would. Want me to tell him to fuck off?" Sparrow said the last loudly at the door.

Faye nodded. She couldn't face him. Seeing him brought back too many memories.

Sparrow opened the door enough to lean in the doorframe. "She broke up with you. That means she doesn't want to see your vampire face anymore."

"I found a way to locate her altar."

Rune's accented words sent a shock down Faye's spine. He did it? She would have a shard. Faye gazed at Sparrow, who widened her eyes and turned her hand up in silent question.

"Let him in," Faye said.

Sparrow stepped back as Rune entered. Faye bit the inside of her lip. His long white-blonde hair hung loose down his back, in contrast to his tailored black suit.

Rune smiled at her. "You look well."

"No, no." Sparrow moved to stand between them, blocking her view of him. "You're not here to talk to her fang boy. Altar only."

Rune thinned his lips at Sparrow and exhaled. "Business then." He called a circular metal tray with a low lip. "I crafted a spell that can pinpoint an altar using blood. I will need a small amount of hers."

Faye nodded, and he set the tray on the table. She outstretched her hand, looking away when his fingers slid over her arm. His touch was too familiar— And his scent. Faye missed waking in his bed, curled up to him. Amber and sandalwood surrounding her.

Rune positioned her wrist over the tray. Warmth spread over it, crawling up her forearm.

Faye took a breath. "What are you doing?"

"Numbing your wrist." Black bled through Rune's eyes as his nails sharpened into black-tipped claws.

Faye couldn't meet Voshki's yearnful gaze and hide what she felt.

She wanted to lean into him. To give in to the feeling within her that longed for them every moment they were apart.

Pressure on her wrist brought her back to the present, her blood slowly pooled in the metal dish.

Rune closed his eyes, and Faye swallowed as the veined misted shadows beneath his eyes receded. He brushed his thumb across her wrist and silently withdrew his touch.

Faye retreated to the sink, rinsing the smeared blood from her wrist as Rune picked up the dish.

His shard of Darkness glowed, the black mist curling into itself. Her blood boiled and hissed, and Rune set it back on the table. "When the blood stops reacting, I will need to phase you to Necromia. Your altar location will act as a beacon, and I will phase us to it."

Faye's brow lowered. "I don't have soul shards or supplies to invoke my blood."

"I do," Sparrow announced, disappearing down the hall leaving her alone with Rune. Faye studied her dishes, refusing to engage with him and Sparrow returned a short time later with a small white box.

Faye stared blankly. "When did you get this?"

"I had Vash pick it up a while ago."

Faye opened the box and unfolded the raw red silk. A small basket held a curved knife and a handful of soul shards.

Rune's brow lowered as he reached for the tin holding her blood. It was dark now, congealed to the bottom of the dish. He set it back on the table. "Your altar is in Anaria."

Faye shared Rune's baffled look, and Sparrow broke the silence. "Figures, your altar is here. Maybe that's why your stubborn ass would never leave."

The only reason she stayed in Anaria was because she didn't want to be surrounded by dark-bloods who looked down on her.

Sparrow clapped her hands together, startling Faye. "When do we go?"

She couldn't match her sister's excitement. Inadequacy weighed heavily on her even after all these years. The creeping feeling that her real family knew she was lacking. Their abandonment was justified. "I need to go alone."

Sparrow wilted and gave her a wounded look.

"I love you, but I did this in front of people before. I want to be alone when I invoke my blood." In case it fails again.

Sparrow came forward and hugged her tight, whispering, "You were at the wrong altar." Her sister pulled back, taking Faye's hands as she met her gaze. Faye could only manage a weak smile. "Necromia is a peasant altar anyway. Fang boy is taking you somewhere much nicer."

Faye grinned at Sparrow's words and laughed when she glimpsed Rune's unamused expression as he regarded Sparrow. He probably wanted to throttle her.

She stepped closer to Rune, offering her hand. "Shall we."

Seventy-Five

Faye shielded her eyes as a cold gust of wind whipped her hair. She blinked, gazing over her new surroundings. The morning was too new to warm the rocky cliffside. A dense sea of trees stretched over the acres beneath it.

She stood with Rune in an overgrown field, and at the center of it was a simple stone altar. It was familiar, as though she'd been here before, but there was no comfort in the feeling. Faye took a step back. Everything in her urged her to run. Her heart raced as her apprehension steadily grew.

"Are you well?" Rune stood close, not touching her as he studied her face.

Faye nodded, forcing herself to take a step toward the altar. Fear prickled her skin, like she approached some great sleeping beast and expected to be devoured.

"I don't like how this place feels," Faye said, forcing another step toward the altar.

"How do you mean?" Rune moved with her, remaining at her side.

Her breaths came faster as she drew closer. Dread fell over her in a net, suffocating her. She kicked a dead shrub from the altar's base.

A link protruded from the altar's foundation.

"There were chains here." She knew this with certainty, could feel it.

Rune waved his hand, and all at once, the debris and brush were cleared from the altar. There were words carved in it, the deep grooves visible but too worn to read. The stones seemed to hum with energy, and Faye tentatively stretched out her hand, gasping as her fingertips crossed over the foundation's threshold.

For the first time in her life, Faye *felt* power.

There was no strain to feel it, no effort. It was there, and this altar pulsed with it.

Faye perceived the ripples of raw energy as she moved her fingers. She glanced back at Rune and asked, "Did your alter radiate power when you invoked your blood?"

Rune tensed and pulled her hand away. "Altars serve as a gateway for a connection to the Darkness. The altar itself holds no power." He opened his hand as she had, remaining still for several heartbeats. "I do not feel anything. Your strength is immense, you may be feeling the power that awaits you."

"This power is mine, so it can't hurt me," Faye spoke the self-soothing words before glancing up at Rune. "If I summon something, you'll protect me."

"I would burn the realms for you."

Faye turned toward him and was met with a solemn expression. The man was serious. She crinkled her brow and said, "No. We don't burn realms."

The corner of his mouth lifted as he inclined his head. "As you command."

Faye clutched the white box her sister had given her. Moments passed and she couldn't shake the feeling of dread that gnawed at her.

"This does not need to be completed today," Rune said. "I could research the area. Chains at an altar is disconcerting."

This is my power, and it can't hurt me.

With a final deep breath, Faye stepped onto the foundation. Power hummed through the altar and its foundation, licking up her skin.

To welcome or consume her? She didn't know.

Her eyes narrowed with determination. *This is my power, and it can't hurt me.*

Faye poured the soul shards over the altar. Taking the knife, she cut her hand, letting her blood pool at the center of her palm.

It can't hurt me.

This power is mine.

Faye turned her hand. Her blood splashed against the altar, pouring over the shards.

Her blood hissed and boiled.

This was wrong.

Before she could step off the altar, Faye sucked a sharp breath. Her spine bowed, rigid. She couldn't breathe. A rushing force far below her charged upward. It slammed into her body, stealing her breath. Her shirt pulled painfully tight before it gave.

Everything faded to black except the altar. The ground became the Darkness. The black mist churned, coiling into itself, lit by the glow of the purple tendrils. Thunder boomed and in a cascade of lightning the sky opened above her. Red and angry

She perceived something from above. Falling.

Power crashed over her. Pain beyond her imagination wracked her.

Sharp, acute. Tearing.

Something inside her gave, breaking. The sound of shattering glass filled her ears.

A scream ripped from her throat as raw power plummeted, crashing over her.

One after the other.

Then the void came.

Seventy-Six

"Morbid!" Rune bellowed through the Familiar King's twisting mansion.

Panicked fear knifed through Rune's mind as the Ra'Voshnik wailed, forming no intelligible words. He shook uncontrollably, clutching Faye to his chest. Her body hung limp in his arms. Strands of her hair pulled across her too-still face as her head lobbed to one side. The vacant stare of her lightning-streaked midnight eyes threatened to shatter his sanity.

"Morbid!"

An invisible force strangled his yell silent. He was slammed into the wall behind him, knocking the breath from him. The crushing pressure on his throat continued, pinning him a few feet off the ground. Phantom hands held him captive. One gripped across his face, covering his mouth as others held his wrists and pressed his chest to the wall.

Faye floated in place. Her clothing and hair drifted around her as though she were submerged in deep water. Her iridescent wings opened behind her, their clawed tips nearly scraping the floor

Rune turned inward, frantic to well power, intent on breaking whatever kept him from his queen.

Morbid appeared next to Faye. His voice as ominous as the ever-present storm clouds over his realm. "Do not come into my home, raising your voice and frightening my wife."

And do not challenge me, Shadow Prince.

Rune jerked as Morbid brushed against his core, the innermost part of his mind housing his power. Impossible. His shields were intact. But Morbid moved through his mind— Through his mental barriers, before leaving.

"I will overlook your outburst since you're afraid for your woman." Morbid held his hand over Faye's chest. A thick black cord extended out of Morbid's hand.

A tendril. Rune blinked. Only females had tendrils. Morbid was many things, but female was not among them.

The cord unraveled, opening into a multitude of threads, which moved over and passed into Faye's body.

Bring her back to us. Please, the Ra'Voshnik pleaded.

"Are you finished scaring my wife?" Morbid asked as he continued his work.

The moment Rune nodded the hands released him. He approached Faye and Morbid, studying the strands. There were more than a hundred of them, all moving independently. "You have a tendril."

Morbid looked up at Rune and smiled. "I'll just say you were drunk. Who would believe you?"

"How?"

Morbid winked at him and returned his attention to Faye before saying, "You have your secrets, Shadow Prince. I have mine."

Rune caressed Faye's cheek, his hands tremoring with relief. "What happened to her?"

"She fought," Morbid said as he withdrew his tendril, drawing it back into his hand.

"Fought what?" Rune adjusted his stance as Faye's body floated toward him and gently cradled her to his chest.

Morbid turned, walking away. "Ask her when she wakes, Prince."

"What are these?" Rune called after Morbid, floating a folded handkerchief from his pocket.

"Her shards," Morbid answered without turning.

Rune lowered his gaze to the frail beauty in his arms. She leaned into him. Her eyes closed in sleep. They would have much to talk about when she woke. Her strange soul shards being the first subject.

Rune phased back to Anaria, materializing on the road before Faye's cottage. A flicker of his mind opened her front door, and Sparrow met him as he stepped into their home.

"Faye?" Sparrow shook her sister's shoulder.

Rune stepped around the little blonde noting Vashien at the table. "She invoked her blood and was injured. Morbid healed her. She needs rest."

Sparrow trailed behind him as he took Faye to her room. He hesitated at her bed. "Vashien." The large male stepped into the room. "I do not possess wings. Does it pain you to sleep on them?"

"Lay her on her stomach or her side and spread her wings out," Vashien said.

Rune adjusted her in his arms and laid her on her side. Faye's eyebrows came down for a moment, but she didn't wake. He brushed a strand of hair out of her face.

"Get away from her," Sparrow growled, shoving at his side, and stepping in front of him.

Rune relinquished his position and stood at the end of the bed while Sparrow took another pillow. She lifted Faye's arm, tucking it to her chest. His night breeze sighed, clutching it closer in her sleep.

Sparrow pulled the blanket over Faye, covering her to her chin. She turned and stopped short. "You can leave now fang boy."

Rune inclined his head at her. "I would ask to stay and help care for her."

Sparrow's mouth spread in a toothy grin. "She doesn't want you. Go the fuck away."

"Please."

Sparrow narrowed her green eyes at him. "Kneel and ask again."

Cold, furious anger rose in him. Rune choked it back, as the Ra'Voshnik circled his mind, seeking violence. Vicious and brutal. If the blonde harpy wanted him to debase himself, so be it. Holding

Sparrow's gaze, he lowered himself to one knee.

"Stop!" Sparrow held her hands out at him, looking away. Acting as though he did something repulsive. "Darkness, I thought you were going to call me a bitch and go away."

Rune stood once more as Sparrow took a sideward glance at him. The blonde harpy shivered dramatically before turning to face him again.

"You can stay. But if you make her cry again, I swear to the Darkness, I will cut your balls off and feed them to you." Sparrow jabbed him in the chest with two fingers as she walked past him, exiting the room. "And you're not sleeping in her bed," Sparrow called from the hallway.

Rune's gaze fell to Vashien who somehow looked both relieved and terrified. "Is she always like this?"

The large male looked apologetic. "Yeah."

"Harpy," Rune called into the hall.

"Did this motherfucker just call me—"

Sparrow fell silent, her eyes locked on the talisman Rune held out. Her gaze lifted to his as she swiped the obsidian talisman from his palm. She pointed at him. "I'm amending my statement, shadow dick. You make her cry, and I'm still chopping off your nuts. Then I'm going to have the chefs at Obsidian cook them before I shove them down your throat." She wiggled the talisman between her fingers before ducking out of his view.

Rune glanced at Vashien once more. "She has a colorful way of speaking."

Seventy-Seven

A steady pounding interrupted Faye's sleep. She frowned. The rhythmic sound came from her. Her heart beating in her ears.

Closing her eyes tighter, she rolled on her side. She pulled the blankets closer, growing frustrated when the fabric clung to her fingertips. Her breaths deepened with exhaustion. She stopped fighting with the blanket and her body went limp, waiting for sleep to pull her under.

A new awareness took hold in her mind. A connection to a reservoir of power. More than that she perceived others, could feel their strength and location in relation to hers. One stood close to her. Focusing on it she felt him. The familiarity of his mind. The scent of amber and sandalwood.

He was weaker than her.

Faye fought to open her eyes. "Rune?" She winced, the words

burning her throat.

The bed sank near her, and fingertips brushed over her hair. Faye heard the murmuring of his voice but couldn't discern his words. She managed to open her eyes for a moment, catching a glimpse of white-blonde hair trailing over black material.

Her hand lifted, increasing the tightness over her nails. Her eyes blinked open again. Rune unhooked the sheets from her claws, easing the pressure.

A feather light touch brushed her cheek as her consciousness slipped to darkness.

Seventy-Eight

Exhaustion continued to wrack Faye's body. Rune or Sparrow routinely woke her with meals she had no appetite for. It didn't matter how long she slept, she woke drained and fatigued. A deep slumber beckoned her and falling into it was effortless.

Faye woke some days later to find Rune seated next to her in a fine leather chair he must have brought from his home. His arms were folded. His legs set apart, stretching before him. A thin strip of light streamed into her room through a crack in the curtains covering her window, illuminating the strands of white-blonde hair that fell over the side of his face.

He looked peaceful with his head tipped back, resting against the chair. His eyes closed.

An ocean of memories swept through her at once, filling her consciousness as she gazed at him. Faye winced against the onslaught, shutting her eyes. Flickering images and emotions consumed her. Memory after memory piled into her too-full mind.

Faye squinted, her gaze rising to him once more. Rune stood at the heart of each new memory. Always standing at a place she knew as her shores, gazing into her Darkness. She drew a shaking breath as her mind settled. The last memory clicked into place.

His voice. A distant memory, wrapping around her.

I wish for an equal.

Her memories seemed to go on forever, eclipsing the length of her own. Making her twenty-five years seem like a fleeting moment.

Faye's vision cleared as a possessiveness slid its claws into her mind. The certainty of it more intense than anything she'd felt before. This male belonged to her.

Mine.

Rune unfolded his arms, sitting up straighter. Did he hear her?

Her brow lowered as she began noticing other new and strange things. She perceived the depth of his power and realized he was much weaker than her. Faye's gaze shifted to her door. She sensed Sparrow and Vashien in her sister's room as well. Was this what it felt like to have magic?

A deep reservoir of power connected to her, stemming from far below her. The added layers of sensations were foreign, disorienting.

"Good morning." Rune's voice was deeper, taking a raspier tone when he first woke. Reminding her of all the mornings she woke in his arms. Faye shoved the memories aside.

She sat up and winced. Darkness, she was stiff. "How long have I been asleep?"

"A little more than a week. Are you hungry? Can I get you anything?" Rune asked.

Faye looked away, fighting the feeling of yearning that overcame her, drawing her to him. She felt too much. Too deep with him this close. "I'm thankful you were here to take care of me." She met his gaze, and her heart ached. "This doesn't change anything. We don't work."

Rune leaned forward. "I love you. I know you care for me."

Faye pulled away, needing the distance between them. "It's not enough. We're fundamentally different."

"This past week has given me much time to reflect. I have

thought at length on your parting words. I listen when you speak. I will protect the things you value."

His beseeching gaze stung her heart. "Rune."

"Speak with me for a moment." He reached for her hand and exhaled when she didn't take it. "You want to protect your people. We will form a court. Invite every Anarian you wish to protect, and the same retribution system that stops the dark courts from attacking each other will protect them."

Faye's brow lowered. "I don't understand."

"Your court will be made up of your people. They will not be attacked or mistreated because I will be the consequence for striking against our court. We will protect Anaria."

Faye's lips parted, and tears pricked her eyes. She grasped for words as her mind blanked. "You would do that for me?"

"I would do anything for you." Rune stood, stepping closer to her.

Faye looked at his hand and all it offered. He saw her. Finally understood her. Her hand closed over his, and Rune helped her to her feet. Faye leaned into him, breathing in his scent. Clinging to the man she'd missed and longed for. Her eyes slid closed as his arms encircled her.

He embraced her lightly, stroking her hair as he whispered, "I will be a better man for you."

Tears pricking her eyes as she nodded against his chest. Leaning into the connection that ran between them, binding them to one another.

They stood together for long moments before he muttered, "You need to eat."

Faye reluctantly stepped back, letting him go. "What I need is a shower and some clean clothes."

"Would you like me to get Sparrow?" The back of his fingers slipped down her arm in a gentle caress.

"No. I'm okay." Faye collected her robe and opened her door, crossing the hall to the bathroom.

She showered quickly, scrubbing what felt like a week of grime off her face. Faye stilled when Sparrow's power moved, heading toward the kitchen. Vashien followed soon after.

Faye dried off and stood in front of the mirror. She didn't look different. Envisioning her wings, Faye stared at her reflection, concentrating.

Nothing happened.

Faye pushed harder and hopped in place. Still nothing. Faye dropped her hands to her side. Her gaze fell to her bare index finger, and for the first time, the sight sent a thrill of excitement through her. She had a shard. Somewhere.

Faye dressed quickly, pulling on beige trousers and a gray sweater. She stepped into the hall and found Sparrow, Vashien, and Rune sitting at the small wooden table. Platters covered the tabletop with cubed meats, cheeses, and sliced fruit. Her gaze lifted to Rune as she tilted her head in question.

"Your sister is tolerable when she is fed." Rune grinned as Sparrow snorted at him.

Faye joined them making a plate. "Do you have my shard?"

Rune's lips thinned in response. "You should see it in private."

"I've seen her naked more times than you have. Whip it out." Sparrow said, patting the table between her and Faye.

At Faye's nod, Rune removed a folded cloth out of the inside pocket of his jacket, handing the neatly folded square to her. She took it, gingerly holding the cloth to squeeze the contents. They shifted, clicking together.

"I have never seen the shards you carry," Rune said, concern lacing his voice.

Sparrow rolled her eyes, announcing, "You carry the Darkness. Nobody cares."

Faye unfolded the cloth to find a mass of swirling black mist. She couldn't tell how many were there, the mist obscured the shard within it. But these weren't shards of Darkness. They both had the swirling black mist, but the edges of each curling tendril lit with a glowing purple light. They looked like pieces of the Darkness itself.

Her shores.

These shards were more than just hers. They were a part of her. "I can feel them," Faye said, floating her shards around her as she turned to glance at Rune.

Sparrow's brow furrowed together as she studied Faye's strange shards. "You couldn't just be normal. Had to make up all your own new shit," Sparrow said, glancing from shard to shard, nodding to herself.

Counting, Faye realized.

"Ten," Sparrow said, glancing at Rune. She looked him up and down with a smirk. "You have no chance when she wants to tie you up now."

Faye kicked her under the table. "Sparrow."

"Bitch that hurt." Sparrow bent forward rubbing her shin. "Acting like we don't already know what you do to him."

Faye flushed as Vashien choked. She narrowed her eyes, debating kicking her sister a second time.

Rune thankfully came to her rescue, saying, "I can arrange a jeweler to fit a ring for you. How many of your shards did you wish to display?"

Faye upturned her hand, and the shards collected in her palm. "Just one. I think the coloring will draw enough attention."

"Fuck that. Slap those bitches in a tiara." Sparrow said. Her lips parted in a toothy grin.

Faye giggled, folding her shards back into their handkerchief.

Sparrow's gaze flicked between her and Rune. "Since he's still here, did you take him back?"

"We're starting over." Faye met Rune's gaze. "Without the kidnapping."

Sparrow clapped. "We can do Shibari classes together if we both learn on Vashien."

"No," Vashien hissed, paling as Rune glowered at Sparrow.

Her sister fluttered her hand at Rune. "Calm down fang boy, he'll have clothes on."

"No!" Vashien repeated louder.

Rune turned his attention to Faye. "Did you want to return to Hell with me, or should I have some of the forest cleared and have an estate built here in Anaria?"

"Why are we moving? Did you break her bed?" Sparrow asked around a mouthful of food.

Faye rolled her eyes at her sister. "Rune is going to form a court with me." She explained how they would protect the Anarians.

Sparrow snorted, pointing her fork at Rune. "I'm already in a court with her so you're joining our court."

"We're only four people. Who's your fifth?" Vashien asked.

"Sadi and her mate Damian," Rune answered, pouring a glass of crimson wine.

Faye rested her hand on his thigh. "We can go back to Hell until we pick out a home in Anaria."

"And we can take phasing lessons together," Sparrow squealed.

"You sure you're ready for a life with this?" Vashien lifted his chin at Sparrow as he sipped his coffee.

The corner of Rune's mouth lifted. "I have her out of proxy. You willingly selected her."

Sparrow scowled at them both as Faye giggled behind her glass.

"I am a pleasure to be around. Fuck both of you."

Seventy-Nine

Returning to Hell with Rune was surprisingly natural. Sparrow moved back into her same rooms as Vashien unpacked their things. Faye sat in the oversized room, glancing over the stone walls and artisan furnishings. Rune would help her create a dark court that would protect the weakest among them, what every dark court should have been doing instead of turning a blind eye and hiding in their pampered luxury.

"I'm going to check on my garden," Faye announced, getting to her feet.

"It's been weeks. That shit is dead." Sparrow flopped gracelessly on her bed and upturned her face to peer at her upside down.

Most of it, probably. She hoped she could salvage a plant or two. Guilt ate at her for leaving them to wilt and suffer. Faye made her way to the courtyard, stepping into the gardens. The midday sun beamed down on her. The warmth welcomed her back like an old friend.

Bracing for the worst, she stepped through the second archway. Faye's lips parted as her heart lit. She hurried to her garden unable to believe her eyes. Her plants were alive. More than that, they were thriving.

Faye shifted the plump leaves inspecting the stems and soil. She sat back in disbelief. They were pristine. Rune must have tied the magic that cared for the black roses to maintain her herb garden. She couldn't imagine him watering her plants while she was gone.

But her oversize watering can wasn't in its usual place. Someone set it near the fountain. Faye smiled, brushing her fingers over the leafy plants. Maybe the Shadow Prince did care for her plants in her absence.

Faye left the gardens, biting the inside of her lip. Rune would probably be in his study. She'd missed him. The connection she felt when she was near him. Darkness, she needed to learn to phase. Walking seemed so much longer when teleportation was an option.

She strolled up the hall and peered into Rune's study. He sat behind his desk reviewing aged documents. Books piled in short stacks on either side of him. His gaze lifted to meet hers as she moved across his study. "You kept my garden for me."

Rune canted his head as his brow pinched. "Why would I not?"

"Thank you." Faye smoothed the perfectly arranged lapel of his jacket and took a seat on his thigh.

A whisper of the veined misted shadows crept from beneath his eyes as he lightly held her. "You are most welcome."

This close she could feel his warmth. Perceive his decadent scent of amber and sandalwood. Being with him felt like home. Faye leaned forward, their lips meeting in a soft kiss. "I've missed you," she whispered.

Rune rested his forehead against hers, wrapping her in his arms. A low purr reverberated through him, filling the room. "Every moment away from you has been agony."

Her arms circled his neck. The feeling of possession humming through her. Burning slow and bright. Consuming her thoughts until all she saw was him.

This man belonged to her. To protect and cherish. To honor and love.

And she was his.

She leaned into him. Her lips meeting his in a slow, searing kiss. He pulled her against him, molding her to the hard planes of his body. His tongue stroked into her mouth as his fingers grazed the small of her back beneath her shirt

His touch made her blood sing. Her skin heating in response as she moaned, needing more of him.

She pulled back and a dark, predatory gaze met hers. Faye smiled, her heart softening for the sweet viciousness that lived within Rune. Faye cupped the side of his face, and Voshki leaned into her touch. He took a slow, deep inhalation as his lids slid closed. When he opened them, his eyes were pale blue once more.

Faye lowered her gaze fiddling with the edge of Rune's jacket. "I feel like I'm always ignoring one of you."

"You are not. The Ra'Voshnik and I are always present."

"Can you let Voshki into my mind, like in our meetings?"

The familiar brush against her senses soothed her before a wild aggression edged in sexual heat filled her mind. Voshki's presence enveloped her, covering her with his longing and desire.

"We share an awareness. We each know the other's thoughts and words."

"There's no privacy between the two of you."

The Shadow Prince knows you prefer me. It's no secret, Voshki purred through her mind as a disembodied hand caressed her neck, sweeping her hair behind her shoulder.

Faye's vision blurred for a moment, and she swayed. She pressed a hand to Rune's chest to steady herself as the dizziness passed. A soft rumble sounded behind her as a hand slipped into her hair. She turned to find Voshki leaning on Rune's desk.

"You can visit us both in our mind," Voshki said, leaning forward as his hand tangled in the back of her hair.

Faye's breath caught as Voshki's grip tightened, pulling her hair taut to her scalp. He angled her head up, and Rune's hand tightened over her hip. Faye flushed, caught between them.

Voshki leaned close bringing his lips a moment from hers, releasing his grip.

"We both belong to you," Voshki rasped, lingering. Waiting.

He slid his index and middle finger up her neck. The backs of his black tipped claws gliding upward, sending a tremor of pleasure through her. Her breaths turned shallow as her nipples hardened.

Faye's eyes slid closed as she rocked on Rune's thigh, snaring the hard muscles of his chest under her nails.

"You could have us both," Voshki whispered.

Could she? Faye had been with them. They were both present when they made love to her long into the night. Faye's flush deepened as her blood heated, pooling between her legs. It would be like the phantom touch they'd both used on her.

"Would you want us to worship you?" Voshki asked.

She straightened, meeting Rune's gaze. He watched her, neither giving nor demanding. Voshki was obviously willing, while Rune seemed undecided.

"Are you ok with this?" She asked.

His hand slid down her thigh. "I would give you anything you desire, as long as it is your desire and not the creature's," Rune said the last arching a brow as he glanced over her head.

Faye leaned forward, bringing her lips a moment from his. "He's not a creature," she whispered. "You both belong to me."

Rune's lips met hers. A brief touch, slow and inviting, before he pulled back. Faye followed him, sighing as her lips met his. He caressed her jaw, his fingers trailing into her hair. He pulled her in, tilting her head up. He kissed her with a possessive hunger. Claiming her mouth with each stroke of his tongue.

Faye's nails bit into his chest, scraping over the dark material of his shirt. She moaned into Rune's kiss. His hands held her close while others caressed her.

She rocked against Rune's thigh as a gentle touch slid up the nape of her neck, tangling in her hair. The hand pulled Faye's hair tight, and her breath caught, breaking her kiss. Faye let him guide her head back, staring into Voshki's dark gaze.

Rune nipped and licked down the length of her exposed throat. Faye's lips parted as her breath shallowed. More intense than when they teased her with a phantom touch. She could feel their heat. Their longing. Hear their breaths and groans as they touched her.

Voshki licked her bottom lip, and a breathy sigh escaped Faye. She arched her back as he kissed her deeply. Rune's hand glided over her side, and Faye leaned up wanting his hands on her breasts. His touch brushed over her ribs instead.

Faye grasped his hand, dragging it to her breast. He molded her soft flesh to his palm, circling her nipple with his thumb before pinching the sensitive peak until she cried out.

Their touch overwhelmed her, but Faye craved more. Desperate to be trapped between them, at their mercy. She flattened her hand on Voshki's chest, reveling in the feel of the hard planes of his body. She moved lower, and Voshki groaned.

He broke their kiss as she stroked his cock through his slacks. His brow pinched as his breaths grew ragged. A growl slipped from his lips as he thrusted with her strokes.

Faye kissed Rune playfully before reaching between them to stroke him as well. He moved with her, claiming her mouth. Timing the strokes of his tongue to her touch. Faye rocked on Rune's thigh, giving herself over to the feel of them. She rocked harder, driving her pleasure.

She gasped when Rune stood suddenly, taking her with him. He laid her on his desk and Faye blinked, panting. The haze of passion cleared from her mind. Voshki smiled down at her standing on one end of the desk while Rune stood at the other and spread her legs. Her pulse raced as Voshki leaned over her. Upside down. He kissed her, nipping at her bottom lip before moving lower.

Faye lifted her chin, offering him her throat while Rune stripped off her pants.

"So eager," Voshki rasped, skimming his fangs along her throat, withholding his bite.

Faye sucked a breath when he tore her shirt open. Voshki lingered, teasing her nipple with his lips and teeth. She moaned when Rune's hands gripped the tops of her thighs, his hair falling forward to brush her inner thigh. The heat of his mouth met the side of her knee and moved lower.

Voshki took her wrists and pulled them over her head. He smoothed her hands over the edge of the desk. "Hold tight," he said. His mouth widening into a wicked grin. "When you want us to fuck you, let go."

His words intensified the throbbing between her legs. An ache she desperately needed filled. Faye glanced down at Rune. He held her gaze as he licked through her center. Slow and deliberate.

Her head fell back as she rolled her hips, needing more of him. "Rune, please."

His tongue glided over her as he teased and worked her slick flesh. Voshki's black tipped claws whispered over Faye's breasts. Pain and pleasure shot through her as he pinched her nipples. Tugging them until they plucked through his fingers before beginning again.

Faye dug her nails into the desk. Frustrated with their sweet torture. She needed Rune hard and claiming. She set her legs over his shoulders, driving her heels into his back. "Harder," she commanded, pulling him closer.

His lips closed over her clit, purring as he lashed her with his tongue.

Faye panted, rolling her hips against his mouth. "I need to feel you inside me," she cried out, and Rune obliged her, stroking a finger in. Faye tossed her head, rocking against him as Voshki licked and sucked at her breast. "More. Make it feel like your cock," she cried.

She spread her legs wide as Rune thrusted a second finger into her. Faye pulled her lower lip through her teeth, so close.

Voshki stopped his attentions to lean closer to Faye. He kissed the corner of her mouth and rasped, "Take it for him."

The sound of his deep, accented voice snapped the tension building in her. Her thighs closed over Rune's head as she came. Her inner walls clutching his fingers as he pressed into her further, demanding her surrender.

As he wrung the last bit of pleasure from her, he drove into her harder in deliberate, measured strokes. Roughening his purr against her sensitive clit.

"Spread your legs and take it for him," Voshki purred.

"Rune." Short breaths whispered past Faye's parted lips. She eased her legs apart, her feet coming to rest on the armrests on either side of his chair.

Tension coiled in her body, building quickly. It crested over her and broke, Voshki lifted her shoulders off his desk as waves of pleasure washed through her. Rune eased his touch as she came down euphoric. She glanced up, catching her breath but Voshki was gone. Rune stood, wiping his hand over his mouth. Her brow lowered in confusion.

They weren't holding her up.

Faye turned to see the top of her wing arching past her shoulder. They were tucked tight to her back, holding her off his desk. Faye had returned to her physical body.

"I believe this is my new favorite game." Rune smiled as he gazed on either side of her. "But I will have to shield my furniture."

Faye glanced at the desk. Deep gouges tore through it. His books and papers scattered across the floor. She turned back to him, an apology forming on her lips.

The words froze as black flooded his gaze, swirling over his pale blue eyes before covering them completely. The veined, misted shadows poured from beneath his eyes, swaying over the tops of his cheekbones.

Faye gazed up at him. Wanting to surrender. To bare her throat and spread her legs for the beautiful hunter before her. The corner of his mouth lifted as he leaned closer. His lips brushing the shell of her ear.

"You let go."

Eighty

"Hold on to me," the Ra'Voshnik rasped before receding, returning Rune's body to him. He slid his arm across the small of her back as he guided her legs around his waist. Faye sighed leaning into him, arching her wings forward to wrap around him, and Rune couldn't help but smile.

Bring her back into our mind, the Ra'Voshnik purred.

Rune phased them into his room, lifting her higher as he trailed feather-light kisses along her collarbone. He nipped at her and asked, "Were you satisfied, or did you wish to return to my mind?"

Faye tightened her thighs over his waist. In a breathy sigh, she whispered, "More."

Rune reached for her consciousness and brought her into his mind. The Ra'Voshnik waited on his bed, nude, sitting back on its heels.

He lowered Faye onto their bed, her wings dragging over her as she folded them beneath her. She glanced up at the Ra'Voshnik and smiled, rolling over to crawl to him. Rune groaned at the view of her ass while he stripped. Their physical bodies mirroring their movements.

Faye stood on her knees as the Ra'Voshnik slid its fingers through her hair, drawing her closer. The creature kissed her then brushed the side of its face against Faye's.

It met his gaze and rasped at her ear. "Do you want to please us, my queen?"

Faye sighed as her wings shifted.

The Ra'Voshnik pulled back to gaze at her. "Would it please you to have your lips on my cock while the Shadow Prince fucks you?"

Faye turned back to glance at him over her shoulder. "Please," she moaned, blinking slowly at him. Flushed. Out of breath.

Beautiful.

Rune leaned onto the bed, snaking an arm around her waist, and dragging her back, against him. "Whatever you wish, vsenia."

Faye kissed him, reaching behind to tangle her hand in his hair. Rune groaned, gripping her waist as he ground his length against the soft curve of her ass.

She broke away from him to lean forward, kissing the Ra'Voshnik. She moved lower, arching her back for him as she widened her knees. Rune ran his palm down the back of her thigh, leaning back to admire her delicate flesh. Watched as the Ra'Voshnik gathered her dark hair. Holding it away from her face, he thrust upward.

"Be easy with her," Rune warned.

A muscled ticked in the creature's jaw but he didn't slow his pace. He caressed the side of Faye's face. "You like the way I feel in your mouth, don't you?"

Faye moaned her agreement, arching her back harder to lift her hips for Rune.

He didn't think he would find sharing Faye pleasing but watching the Ra'Voshnik take Faye's mouth— Knowing this excited his queen. Darkness, it made him ache.

Rune took himself in hand, sliding the head of his cock through her sex. Wetting himself with her desire. Faye whimpered rolling her hips in invitation. Rune pressed down on the small of her back and eased himself into her.

Faye moaned, and the Ra'Voshnik's head fell back. Her claws dug into the creature's waist as she took more of Rune's considerable length.

"This isn't going to last very long if you keep moaning around my cock." The Ra'Voshnik grated.

The corner of Rune's mouth lifted as he leaned back, watching his length slide into her. He growled, driving into her harder. Needing to possess her, to hear her scream his name.

Faye cried out and the Ra'Voshnik clenched his jaw, his muscles going tense. A look Rune knew well. Keeping his rhythm Rune leaned over Faye, brushing his lips over the nape of her neck.

"Swallow your Voshki's spend for me," Rune purred at her ear.

Faye moaned, her little claws drawing blood as she tightened her grip.

The Ra'Voshnik drew a ragged breath as it tensed, going still. The creature's brow lowered as it bared its fangs. Faye worked him, moving in time with Rune.

Faye lifted her head, pushing herself up from the Ra'Voshnik's lap. Faye kissed the creature, wrapping her arms around its neck.

"Thank you," the Ra'Voshnik said as Faye lay her head on its shoulder. "Are your wings sensitive?" It brushed the back of its finger down the outer membrane. Then the next. She cried out when he stroked the innermost part of her wing where it connected to her back.

"Here?" The Ra'Voshnik traced soft circles until she trembled.

"Please," Faye sighed, reaching back. Her dainty claws sank into Rune's thigh. She pulled him forward urging him to increase his pace.

Rune followed her lead, taking her harder. His fangs lengthened, sharpening for her. He was a fool to ever have thought her ill-suited. Fate could not have given him a better match.

"Do you like spreading your legs for the Shadow Prince? Having his cock so deep inside you."

Rune groaned at the intimate fluttering around his length as Faye moaned at the Ra'Voshnik's heated words. She was close.

"Have you missed us, love?" The Ra'Voshnik asked. She made an appreciative sound, and it said, "Offer us your throat."

Faye leaned back against Rune, sweeping her hair back as she lifted her chin. The Ra'Voshnik took her throat. Faye cried out, tensing as she came around his cock. She panted, stroking the Ra'Voshnik's hair as it drank from her.

His night breeze reached back cupping the back of Rune's neck. She pulled him closer, bringing his mouth to her throat.

Rune's fangs sharpened, aching for her. He brushed his lips over her pulse. Feeling the hypnotic beat beneath his kiss. His lids slid closed as he opened his mouth wide. The tips of his fangs piercing her flesh.

She submitted to his bite, the length of his fangs sinking into her.

Faye moaned as his arms tightened around her. She clung to the Ra'Voshnik as she came again. The intimate fluttering around his cock he would feel several more times before the night was out.

Rune bit down, sinking his fangs a fraction deeper. Smiling as his night breeze screamed her pleasure. Her wings shot forward, whipping their hair as they folded around the Ra'Voshnik. Encircling it in a tight hold.

Rune withdrew his fangs, pressing his mouth to his bite. Her dark rich blood wet his tongue, and his mind blanked. She was the desire he imagined feeling beneath the Hunter's Moon.

His brow drew down as his tongue slid over his bite. Her power flickered through him, lighting a fire across each of his nerve endings.

Rune cursed in High Tongue as he savored her, knowing full well her decadent blood ruined him. He would crave this for the remainder of his days. Crave her.

Only her.

He groaned, drinking lightly as he chased his own release. Pinning her waist to him. Thrusting faster. Harder.

Rune came with a growl, his body going rigid as he spent deep inside her.

He spent long moments, euphoric and lightheaded. Slowly coming down, he realized Faye stroked his hair as he languidly thrusted into her. His mouth still at her neck.

Her blood on his tongue.

"I love you," Faye sighed, leaning up to nuzzle the Ra'Voshnik. "Both of you."

Rune licked his bite a final time before healing it. He gazed down at the woman fate gifted him. The queen he chose and served. Who embraced every part of him without fear or hesitation. "Everything I am is yours, my love."

"Until our last breath," the Ra'Voshnik promised, shifting her consciousness back into her physical body.

Faye blinked and turned in his arms. He bent to kiss her and stopped. Touching his forehead to hers instead. Vampires shared blood kisses. His night breeze wasn't one of his kind.

Faye lifted her mouth to his as her wings curved around him. Rune groaned as her tongue stroked into his mouth. He'd expected her to pull away at the taste. She leaned into him, deepening the kiss instead.

Perfectly suited.

The warmth from her wings faded around him. Rune pulled back as her wings darkened, becoming swirling black mist holding the shape of wings. It thinned and dissipated, fading from sight entirely.

"I don't know how to keep them out," Faye said.

Rune brought her hand to his mouth, kissing her fingertips. "It takes time." He pressed his lips to her index finger. "We do have to do something about your naked finger," he said and was rewarded by her soft laugh. Rune pulled her in, kissing her softly as he held her close. "I have a jeweler coming this evening. Let me draw you a bath." He gently laid her down and rose.

Faye turned her head, watching Rune walk into the bathroom. She finally understood Sparrow's obsession with ogling Vashien. Faye sighed still tingling from Rune and Voshki's attentions.

Rune returned a short time later. He leaned over her, kissing her as he lifted her into his arms. Faye laughed, breaking their kiss. "I can walk."

"And I can carry you," Rune answered, lowering her into the oversized tub.

Faye sighed as the heat of the water seeped into her. She glanced up at Rune, sinking lower into the steam. "There's room for us both."

The corner of Rune's mouth lifted into that cocky smirk she

grew to love. "I will join you in a moment. I have been neglecting my correspondence with the High Council."

Then he vanished. Naked.

"This man," Faye laughed to herself. She sank lower letting the water come up to her chin. Her black hair drifting around her. Rune materialized a moment later holding a stack of documents. Faye sat up, making room for him behind her. "You just phase around na-ked?"

Rune arched a brow at her as he got in the tub and pulled her back to rest against his chest. "I am in my home."

"Sparrow is nosey. What if she saw you?"

Rune rested his arms in front of her, opening expensive looking letters written in aggressive script she couldn't read. "Some find my coloring unagreeable. I may apologize."

Faye giggled, flicking water over her shoulder at him. He kissed the back of her head and continued opening the letters. On the third Rune cursed in High Tongue.

Faye turned her head in his direction. When he didn't answer she said, "You taught me what that means. What's the matter?"

"Alister."

His brother's name chilled her. The memory of his cold steel at her throat too fresh. Faye sat forward turning to Rune, unnerved by his grave expression.

"He's requesting your formal acknowledgement."

Eighty-One

R une leaned in the doorway separating their rooms, dressed in his customary tailored black suit. Hellfire flickered over him, lighting the edge of his white-blonde hair with a soft blue light.

Darkness, he was gorgeous, and he belonged to her. She bit the inside of her lip, wondering if the possessive desire was something she inherited with her powers, or if it would ease back into the attraction she felt for him in the beginning.

Dismissing her thoughts, Faye slipped into a black dress, pocketing the single shard she would display. There would be time to think about her newly acquired quirks later. There were more pressing details needing her attention. Namely Rune's older brother. "Alister wants you to formally acknowledge me in front of the High Council so he can attack me. What happens if we don't?"

Rune's expression fell. His gaze lowered as he entered her room to stand before her. His hands slid down her arm in a feather light caress.

"If I denounce you," Rune stepped closer, taking her face between his hands. Yearning and sorrow filled his gaze. "Denouncing you would label you as my whore, and you are not." He rested his forehead against hers, closing his eyes. "You are everything to me, and I will never speak the words."

Faye's heart twisted. She leaned up kissing him softly. He held her close, encircling her in his strong arms. Rune brushed against her mind, and she let him in. Voshki reached her first, his compulsive, aggressive affection focusing on her. Enveloping her.

Then she felt him, Rune laid his emotions bare. His love warmed her. His devotion a shield he would use to protect her. Even at the cost of himself.

Rune met her gaze. His pale blue eyes haunted. "I am aware you desire young."

Faye's eyes grew wide as tension set in her shoulders. Her lips parted but no words formed. The heat of embarrassment flushing across her cheeks as she lowered her gaze. She wanted a family but planned to have these talks after things settled. Waiting until she survived his brother to broach the subject.

Rune pulled her closer, stroking her hair. "I love you. Would be honored if you blessed me with young," he said before kissing her, the meeting of their lips soft and tender. "I will find a way around my blood debt."

Around what he'd done. The stain of it still hung between them. Faye wanted to wipe it clean and heal Prinia. "Could you arrange a meeting with Alister? Hopefully he won't want to kill me if he knows I want to help his wife."

"I am sorry my actions have placed you in harm's way."

Faye frowned. At his heart he was still a dark-blood. He'd once asked for the context of her mind to understand things from her point of view. They could make a world they could both live in, but only if they did so together. "You're supposed to feel bad for the action, not the consequence."

Rune lowered his gaze and nodded. "I regret allowing Saith to shape me. For following blindly. I should have taken better care of my family. Protected them." He stepped back, lightly grasping her hand. "I was conflicted over what I had done to my brother. I went to Saith for council." His smile was bitter, distant. "His answer? An order to kill my brother."

His words filled her with revulsion. Her village burned offerings for The Creator. Saith was thought of as kind and fair. Yet this same man that mentored Rune— Shaped the Shadow Prince, ordered him to kill his own brother. Faye squeezed his hand, and he met her gaze. Different shadows haunting them.

"I refused, and Saith raged at my disobedience." He exhaled a shaking breath. "The last words he spoke to me were, *All my efforts on you will be wasted.* He left to pick a fight with my father in Hell, leaving me at the court's estate in Necromia. I should have stopped him or stood at my father's side." He glanced off into the distance, as though he watched the events unfolding. His expression grew taut. Pained. "Saith and my father fought so viciously I felt the snap of power ripple through the realms. I phased to Hell to end their quarrel.

"When I arrived, half the realm was leveled. I reached for their minds and felt nothing. They destroyed each other and the backlash of that power claimed their wives as well. I lost my mentor, my family, and my court that day because I was too proud to let my brother have an Anarian."

Faye squeezed his arm, stepping closer to him. After a while Rune met her gaze. "You couldn't have stopped it. You would have died with them."

Rune exhaled. "You wish for me to sire your young. I want you to understand what I am. What may pass to our offspring. The depth of my strength runs deeper than my father and Saith combined. Though nothing compared to you." A ghost of a smile touched his lips. "I was gifted three shards of Darkness."

A small wooden box appeared in his hand. Rune slid the top off and two unmounted shards floated between them.

"How did you keep them secret?" The blood priests and priestesses would have seen him invoke his blood at the very least.

The black misted shards returned to their resting place. Rune slid the lid closed and the box vanished. "My altar is in Hell. I feared Saith would abandon me if I did not come back with the Darkness. I cloaked myself and invoked my blood alone when I was fifteen."

Faye's chest went tight. He carried that power as a boy. Was

mentored by a monster. She thanked the Darkness he didn't continue down the path Saith set for him. "We'll make things right." She
slipped her arms under his jacket, leaning against him. The steady
beat of his heart soothed her. She glanced up at him, poking his side.
"We don't kill."

He smirked. "I will do as you command with a single caveat. If
you are threatened, their lives are forfeit." His look softened as he
brushed her dark hair behind her ear. He stilled and glanced down
the hall. "The jeweler is here. We should meet the others before I
take you back to our bed."

Faye leaned back, her hands falling to his waist. "You'll have to
move my clothes into your closet."

The corner of his mouth lifted, and Faye heard a faint sound of
metal scraping. "There are two closets in *our* room." He turned in a
smooth motion, offering her his arm. "Shall we."

Faye tucked her hand into the bend of his arm, and they made
their way down the hall. She halted her steps as the great room came
into view. "This is a lot."

Rows of tables covered in black velvet filled the great room.
Boxes were arranged to hold rings, while larger pieces were displayed
against the black cloth. Sadi perused the tables, setting small red
markers near the pieces Faye guessed she wanted.

"There are several rings and other jewelry here. If these are not
to your liking, Frances would be happy to create a custom piece for
you." Rune nodded and Faye followed his gaze.

A man approached them. He wore a blue leather trench without
a shirt. Low-slung pants with knee-high boots, and a scarf coiled
around his neck. His golden eyes dusted with minimal makeup.

An intricate ring that looked more like armor covered his right
index finger. His dark gray soul shard embedded in the first joint.
Faye took note of its design and its similarities to Sadi's articulated
ring.

Frances inclined his head at Rune. "Shadow Prince." Then
turned to her and inclined his head. "His mysterious, yet beautiful
chosen."

"My name is Faye, it's nice to meet you."

Rune made his way to Vashien and Damian. The men congre-
gating near the refreshment table.

Faye let Frances lead her through the tables, offering her displays of rings and the finger gauntlets typically worn by Familiar women. The rings were stunning, but nothing spoke to her.

"Would it be okay if I looked around myself?" Faye asked in a soft tone, worried she would offend the Familiar. His designs were breathtaking, but she needed to find something that was her.

"Of course. If you find aspects of rings you like, pick them up. I can sketch out something new, and we can see about creating a design for you." He took a step back and bowed before he turned, leaving her to browse.

Faye glanced over a table with rings that had diamonds in the band. She picked one up, turning the ring over. Diamonds spanned the whole band. *That's unnecessary.* Faye returned the ring and moved to the next table.

Sparrow sauntered up beside her. Faye glanced from her sister to the fluted glass of champagne. "Really?"

Sparrow rolled her eyes. "It's already poured. What do you think they do if no one drinks it, put it back in the bottle?"

"It doesn't mean you have to drink all of them," Faye said as her gaze wandered over the rings. None of them felt right. Sparrow plucked a ring from the next table bringing it to her.

"This looks like you." Sparrow held the ring out while guzzling her champagne.

Faye took the ring and Sparrow wandered off to get another drink. Faye examined the elegant setting. Hooker picked a good one. It was white gold, simple, clean lines. It would balance well with her unique soul shard.

Faye brought the ring to Frances and said, "I like this one."

He took the ring and slipped it onto the index finger of her right hand, and Faye tensed. She could hardly breathe as she gazed at her ringed index finger. The walls seemed to close in. It felt real now. The band around her finger would soon hold her shard and irrevocably reshape her life. This bit of jewelry reflected her power, marking her a dark-blood.

Francis's hand settled over her own, covering her ring. He rubbed her hand and said, "Breathe. It's not uncommon to feel overwhelmed with your first ring." Faye nodded, taking a deep breath.

The Familiar lifted her hand by the curve of her fingers. "Size needs to be adjusted a touch." At his words the band shrank until it fit her perfectly. Frances held out his hand. "If I may borrow your soul shard, my Lady."

Faye hesitated for a moment, then reached into her pocket to retrieve her shard. She placed it on Frances's palm and braced herself for his reaction.

The Familiar tilted his head, pinching the shard between his thumb and forefinger. He held it to the light as though he inspected a gem. "It looks like you carved a piece of the Darkness free." Frances gazed at her and smiled. "This will make a splendid ring." He set the shard in the ring's setting, and the prongs closed over the shard, anchoring it in place. Frances tapped his nail against it, making minute adjustments. "There," he said, releasing her hand before meeting her gaze. "How do you like her?"

Faye held her hand out admiring the ring. Excitement thrumming through her. She wanted to jump in place. To scream. This bit of metal completed her.

Her ring. Displaying *her* shard.

"It's beautiful, thank you." She beamed, turning the back of her hand toward Rune.

His deep, accented voice spoke in her mind.

You look radiant, my queen.

Eighty-Two

The great room transformed before Faye's eyes as Frances phased away. His tables and rows of jewelry vanished with him. An elegant dark wood dining table appeared near the far wall between the grand staircases.

Damian snaked his arm around Sadi's waist as they strolled to their seats. He turned back to Faye, his movements lazy and arrogant. "You've stolen the High Queen's consort and most of what remained of her—" He sucked a breath when Sadi elbowed him in the ribs.

Damian threaded his fingers through her thick black hair and pressed a rough kiss to her temple. "Playing a bit rough, kitten."

Rune fell into step beside Faye, replying, "We have five members. If you are concerned for Lyssa, you are welcome to remain with her."

Damian pulled Sadi's chair out, letting her take her seat. He smirked at Faye as he took his own, holding her gaze across the table. Gaging the queen of the court, he would soon join.

Faye smiled and glanced up at Rune, brushing her hand over the side of his throat. Turning back to Damian, she said, "I can't steal what belongs to me."

The Familiar's metallic silver eyes gleamed. He turned to Sadi with a broad smile. "Bit of spine in this one. I like her."

Sparrow snorted. "I can pull a bit of your spine out if you keep talking shit."

His smile shifted into a smirk. "You, I already like."

An array of dishes appeared on the table, and Faye's mouth watered over the spread. Rune poured her tea, then a glass of crimson wine for himself.

Faye glanced over her strange group as dishes passed between them. People who would soon make up her court, Faye realized.

"You two birds need to train. Be able to defend yourselves when your court is tested." Damian glanced between Faye and Sparrow. "At the very least, learn to shield until he can get to you." He gestured to Rune with his knife. "I would say dawn in the courtyard, but the sky here doesn't move."

Faye fought the urge to roll her eyes. They wouldn't be tested. Their court wasn't going to war. She only wanted to protect her people from those who would mistreat them.

Faye took the plate Sparrow handed her, selecting a few cuts of herb crusted chicken. "Vash can show us what we need."

Damian scoffed. "When was the last time you trained?"

"It's been some time." Vashien angled his wing past Sparrow and thumped Faye's back. "You're about to have the darkest court in recent history. You'll need to train."

Faye glanced over her sister's head at Vashien. With a sigh she raised her brow, her expression saying, *Do I have to?*

Vashien nodded.

"So, dove." Damian's voice called her attention. He pointed at Rune when she glanced his way. "Learn your shielding from him. Your combat from me." He gave the Shadow Prince an appraising glance. "I've never tangled with a Pure Blood. Care for a dance?"

Sadi laughed, her fingers clasping under Damian's jaw, squeezing either side of his mouth. "He would kill you with half a thought."

She kissed him, going back to her meal.

"What makes you so special?" Sparrow asked, pouring a shot of whiskey.

Damian flashed her a feral grin. "I'm from the Order, dove. Took twenty generations to get to the likes of me."

Sparrow's shoulders sagged. "That's how you got to be a tiger."

Damian nodded. "The Order assigns us to wealthy nobles usually. We serve as bodyguards and bed warmers."

Her sister snickered, "Are you assigned to Sadist?"

Faye nearly choked as Sadi arched a brow, glaring at her sister as Damian laughed. "No, I parted ways with the Order. Artistic differences."

"My visions led me to him." Sadi blinked, Sparrow's words forgotten as she gazed up at her mate. She purred, "I need him to survive what's coming."

Faye exchanged a glance with Rune, before asking, "What's coming?"

Sadi turned toward her startled. Her gaze took them in as though she'd forgotten she was sharing an evening meal with them.

The twin Faye never wanted studied her before uttering a single word.

"Death."

A chill slipped down Faye's spine. Familiar could see the future, and Sadi saw death on the horizon. Before she could ask who's, Damian pointed the tip of his knife at Rune. "These two look similar enough. Glamor her eyes and let my sweet kitten take care of big brother Alister."

"We don't want to kill him," Faye said. Alister was immortal. He'd recover from his injuries if his head remained on his shoulders, but Faye was too strong. She worried if she used magic against him, she would channel too much power through him and break his shard.

Rune's brother lost enough; she wouldn't take more.

"It's not to the death, dove. He just needs to yield or lose consciousness," Damian explained.

Sadi stabbed a cut of meat, lifting the morsel skewered at the end of her knife. "Alister is dangerous."

Sparrow snorted. "He's a day-blood."

"That day-blood has more dark blood on his hands than you

have in your entire body." Sadi's midnight gaze met Faye's. The rage flickering in their depths, unsettled her. "Rune saved you that night, and you abandoned him. Over words."

The table fell silent, everyone tensing as Sadi held Faye's gaze in challenge. A dare to deny her accusation. Anger flushed Faye's cheeks, her power climbing with the emotion.

"Enough." Rune broke the silence, his deep voice taking a hard edge.

"No. She wants a court." To Faye, Sadi hissed, "Understand this. You either have blood on your hands, or you are the blood on someone else's. Those who are clean are untested, young, or cowards."

Faye's back went rigid. She would crush this dark-blooded way of thinking. Beginning with her court. "If you believe mercy and compassion are weaknesses, you're the coward."

"Words of the young and untested." Sadi looked her up and down, then licked her knife.

The casual way she spoke, so certain she was right, scraped Faye's long-standing hatred for dark-bloods. Their arrogance.

"Why are you joining our court?" Sparrow shrugged off Vashien's hand when he tried to quiet her. Licking her teeth, the petite blonde glared. Propping her elbow on the table and opening her hand, silently demanding a reply.

Sadi's power curled within her in response, rising. Without thinking, a flicker of Faye's dark power swept through the Familiar. Faye wouldn't allow her to wield her strength at her sister. Her magic enveloped Sadi's, choking it, forbidding the Familiar access to her reserve.

Sadi's attention snapped to Faye, her teeth bared. "How are you doing that?"

A tendril of power wove itself up Faye's, blending into her own. It climbed steadily as Faye tried and failed to stop its ascent. It reared back just before touching her mind, and claws sliced through her connection, severing her hold on the Familiar's power.

"How did you do that?" Faye leveled her gaze at Sadi.

Sparrow leaned forward, her gaze flicking from Sadi to Faye. "Do what? What are you two doing?"

Sadi glanced down at her meal, stabbing another cut of meat. "Do you feel the depth of their power?"

Faye nodded.

"It seems you have Familiar magic." Sadi bit the cut of beef off her knife tip. "Teaching you will be interesting if you survive Alister."

Memories of his sword at her throat spoiled Faye's appetite. She rested her hand on Rune's thigh, the simple touch comforting her. His hand covered hers, his fingers curling around her palm.

She would need to train to stand a chance against Alister. She met Damian's gaze. "Can we start tomorrow?"

He lifted his brow in agreement as he finished his wine.

Dinner remained tense but uneventful for the rest of the evening. Rune rose with Faye as the others paired off, retiring for the evening.

Faye entwined her fingers with his as they made their way to their rooms.

"You will need to learn to shield yourself if you intend to train with Damian."

Faye smiled up at him. "Are you going to wake up early to teach me?"

He lifted her hand to his mouth, his lips meting the back of it. "Shielding is simple. I can show you before we retire for the night."

She followed him into his room. *Our room.* Faye smiled at the thought. Rune sat at the end of the large bed, guiding her to stand between his legs. He leaned forward, so close she felt his breath on the hollow of her collar bone. He glanced up at her, waiting.

"We're together. You're allowed to touch me."

His blue eyes glinted as he smiled. "You will have to forgive me. I am old fashioned."

"Aren't you supposed to listen to your queen?" Even with her teasing tone, she stumbled over the title. Wondered if she'd ever get used to it.

Rune wrapped his arms around her pulling her closer and kissed the bottom of her throat. "It feels strange, touching you without invitation." His lips grazed along her neck as he spoke.

Faye ran her fingers through his hair. "It doesn't feel strange to me."

His soft laughter glided over her skin as he leaned back. "Lesson first."

Faye reluctantly released him and nodded.

"Shielding yourself is simple. I will teach you different shields and how to apply them to others or spaces at a later time." Faye nodded and Rune continued. "Draw your power to you and let it overflow, spilling past you."

Faye concentrated, studying his shoulder. Her power loomed far beneath her, but like her shards it felt like a piece of her. She took a breath summoning it. Her magic curled slowly, lifting higher, rising to her body. Cold pinpricks covered her as it flowed past, coating her. A black mist edged in purple tendrils flashed over her then faded.

A flick of dark power sizzled at her arm. Her misted shield set aglow where Rune's magic touched her shield.

"It looks like the Darkness itself." He lowered his hand, running a finger along her arm. Her shield glowing to life and fading away in the wake of his touch.

"How do I drop the shield?"

He smirked. "Relax. Let it fall from you."

Faye closed her eyes. Her magic felt fluid and malleable. Eager to obey her will. A breath passed through her lips as she let her shield slip away. It dissipated fading the same way Rune's veined, misted shadows slipped to nothing as they swayed over the tops of his cheekbones.

Strong hands closed over Faye's hips, pulling her closer. Faye sighed, lifting her chin as Rune's lips met the hollow of her throat, giving him more access.

"I worried it would take you hours to relax enough to drop your shield." Another kiss under her jaw. "Or did you hold the shields around your mind to torment me?"

Faye gazed down at him. "You deserved it. So upset to be paired with a mortal peasant."

He held her closer, brushing his fingertips over her back in long soothing strokes. "I regret tarnishing our beginning. I should have recognized the gift fate placed before me."

He gazed up at her. His yearning evident in his pale blue gaze. Darkness, she loved this man. Faye ran her hands through his hair and rested her forehead against his. "You can spend the rest of my life making up for it."

Rune shifted, gently laying her on their bed. He leaned over her, his lips settling over hers in a soft kiss. When he pulled back Faye didn't see hunger or need in his expression. Reverence filled his gaze, and Faye's chest tightened at his words.

"I will worship you for the rest of mine."

Faye groaned when Rune slipped from the bed, taking his warmth with him. Morning came entirely too quickly. She glared in the silent-walker's direction when the water spray in the shower started. Rolling over she clutched Rune's pillow close, breathing in his scent of amber and sandalwood. She closed her eyes letting the fall of water fade to the background.

Fingers brushed through her hair, and she pulled the blankets tighter around her, needing a few more hours. She cracked her lids begrudgingly and gazed up.

Rune smiled down at her; a towel wrapped around his lean waist. "Damian is in the courtyard if you were meaning to join him this morning."

"You kept me up too late," Faye grumbled.

Rune laughed softly, "At someone's insistence."

"Did he ask you to get me?"

"No, I hear him every morning."

Every morning he and Sadi stayed in the north wing. "Sadi's a bitch."

"She's protective of her court."

"Of you, more like. I didn't see her coming to Lyssa's defense." Faye glanced away remembering Rune's words. *Tell me she is not the very image of Sadi.* The wounds she received that night were still raw, and Sadi's behavior did nothing to soothe that pain. "She acts like you were *romantically involved.*"

"Vsenia." Rune lifted her in his arms, pulling her and the blankets onto his lap. He held her close, stroking her hair. "Sadi came to court after she invoked her blood. In the seventeen centuries I have known her, I have never touched her in that way." Rune kissed her brow. "You are the only one I desire."

Faye leaned against Rune's chest, pulling the blanket tighter around her. "You were the High Queen's consort, and you didn't desire her either."

"Lyssa was not the High Queen when I served as her consort. It was... complicated." Rune leaned back, searching her eyes. "You told me once you preferred honesty to flattery. Does that still hold true?" At Faye's nod he continued. "Lyssa's mother Belind ruled our court. Lyssa made a formal petition to Belind requesting I serve as her consort. This type of request is done publicly. I was quite surprised when I was summoned before the court."

Faye's expression contorted in revulsion. "She forced you to be her consort?"

"No." Rune shook his head. "I could have declined her petition. I could have declined her every time she left the door open between our rooms."

"Then why?" Why would he agree to be with someone he didn't want?

He absently stroked her hair. Saying nothing as long moments passed between them. When Faye thought he wouldn't answer, he spoke.

"I felt nothing. My existence was methodical and cold before you. I mistakenly thought desire was a thing to be coaxed and mastered." Rune laughed softly. The sound was joyless. "I regarded the world the same way I regarded my power. I hoped with time and patience, I would feel something for her. Lyssa made no secret of desiring me, so I agreed."

"The High Queen knew."

"Lyssa was aware of my lack of response. I typically remained dressed when I tended to her. We did not share a bed, and I kept my own quarters. I relinquished the position after a little more than a century."

He spent over a hundred years with the high bitch. "How long ago was this?"

"Over a dozen centuries. She continued to ask me to see her. I did so infrequently. The last time I saw to her was more than a decade ago.

"Lyssa invited me to her bed this past Hunter's Moon ball. I declined and told her she should find a male who feels the same way about her that she feels about him." Rune gazed down at her as he ran the backs of his fingers over her cheek, his eyes lit with amusement. "She dismissed me, and I phased to the food station thinking no one would be there that late in the night. A clumsy minx fell into me and ran."

Faye supposed she had Sparrow to thank for this man. She teasingly smiled up at her beautiful hunter. "And was it a bolt of lightning? You instantly knew you were mine without even seeing me?"

Rune laughed as his expression warmed. "The Ra'Voshnik knew immediately. I was not fond of the loss of control."

Faye pouted at him. "Poor Shadow Prince. Is your will still stronger than your flesh, big guy?"

A crimson so dark it looked black bled through his gaze and dissipated. Those beautiful veined misted shadows remained, forking from beneath his eyes, swaying over the tops of his cheekbones. Faye brought her hand to the side of his face. Rune purred, leaning into her touch before he gazed down at her with a soul-deep yearning.

"I am defenseless against you, vsenia. My will, my strength, my life are yours. Command me as you will."

Eighty-Three

Damian was in the courtyard, just as Rune said. He went through a series of precise movements, dressed in low-slung pants and boots. Faye wondered how long he'd been out here. Strips of his red striped hair clung to his sweat-slick body. The hellfire cast bronze highlights onto his brown skin.

He stopped suddenly when Faye stepped onto Hell's landscape, the loose crystals grinding under her steps.

"Was starting to wonder if you'd show." He looked her up and down with a smirk as he flipped a blade the length of his forearm between his deft fingers. "Late night, dove?"

"How are you up so early?"

Damian shrugged. "Haven't been to sleep yet. The Shadow Prince teach you to shield?" At Faye's nod, he moved to a clear area in the courtyard and gestured for her to join him.

"Thank you for this and the court," Faye said.

Damian laughed as his blade vanished, replaced with a slightly shorter one. "You'll be cussing me soon enough." He jabbed her shoulder with two fingers, tsking at her when he made contact. "Shield yourself, always. Enemies can phase behind you and slip a knife between your ribs." He sniffed loudly. "You don't smell immortal. Be hard pressed to recover from a wound like that."

His words left her uneasy. She didn't expect anyone besides Alister to come for her. Faye called her power to her, pulling it up from its depths. Cold momentarily covered her as she shielded herself. Damian arched a brow and touched the tip of his knife to her shield, watching it light and sway around her.

Faye stepped away from his weapon. "Can you not point sharp objects at me?"

"It's a training weapon. Won't cut you." He dragged the blade over his forearm, proving his point. "Alister won't attack you with magic. He'll use steel, temper, and cunning. The man's brilliant."

"You know him?"

"No, but my order adopted many of his strategies. Darkness knows how Michelle and Julian produced a day-blood, but he holds his own against dark-bloods. Even crafted a spell that used blood as a conduit to break shields."

Faye's heart froze as cold slipped down her back. "He can break shields?"

Damian nodded. "He binds the blood of a dark-blood to his blades. As long as the blood is darker than the person holding the shield, Alister's swords cut through them. Sure as a bolt of power would." Faye paled, and Damian smiled, waving a hand at her. "You won't have to worry about that, dove. Even if he still had a cache of the Shadow Prince's blood, you're far darker. He won't be able to break your shield."

"First rule." Damian stepped forward and jabbed her shoulder. The hit jarred Faye's teeth, forcing her to take a step back. "You'll feel the force that hits your shields."

Faye shifted her shoulder. "Have you trained anyone before?" Faye thought being thrown in a pool to learn to swim was traumatic. This was worse.

He gave her a feral grin. "Many, and they didn't whine as much as you."

"Did you teach Sadi?" Faye turned as Damian circled her.

"My kitten deals in an entirely different kind of warfare."

Whatever that meant. Faye sighed, "Do I get a weapon?"

He tossed her his knife and called an identical one. "Second rule," Damian lunged forward, arcing his knife at her face.

Faye reacted out of instinct. She gasped, bringing her arms up and stepping back. A wide band of power lashed from her. A sizzling crack filled the courtyard as Damian was hurled across it. His back met the stone wall with a sickening crack, and he dropped to the ground.

"Damian!" Faye rushed forward, stopping when Damian held a hand up at her, getting to his feet.

Rune appeared next to her, looking her over, then Damian. "Are you well?" He asked Faye.

"Yes, Rune, I'm fine. The one thrown across the courtyard," Damian answered, dusting himself off.

"He just scared me," Faye said to Rune, then turned to Damian. "Are you okay?"

Damian shook the crystal fragments out of his hair before he glanced at Rune. "She hits a bit hard." A dark gray light flashed over Damian several times as he strolled back to her. He looked Rune up and down. "You're in the way, friend." Damian flattened his hand to the middle of Rune's chest and pushed.

Rune didn't budge.

With a sigh, Damian addressed Faye. "Second rule. You need to be desensitized to having weapons swung in your direction. If you are afraid of the blow, you can never counter it. Sometimes you need to take a hit to land one."

He lunged at her, and Rune caught his wrist with a growl. "This is not training."

Ignoring Rune, Damian continued, "Third rule. Having a shield doesn't mean you're suddenly invulnerable." He hooked his foot behind Faye's ankle and shoved her to demonstrate his point.

Faye gracelessly fell on her ass and stared up to find Rune holding Damian by the throat.

The Familiar stood on his toes. "It's the best way to teach a lesson, Shadow Prince. Your dove is a tiny thing. Any male can pick her up with muscle and temper." He turned his head, unable to break free of Rune's grasp. "Now, I don't mind a hand on my throat if it's done in the right spirit. But I would ask you to romance me a little." To Faye, he winked. "He's not this rough with you, is he?"

Rune thinned his lips as Faye got to her feet.

"Alister is a master swordsman. He wields a sword and controls another two by his will. Do you want your mate to learn here or when your brother and his blades are trying to filet her?"

Rune reluctantly released Damian. "If you injure her, I will repay your kindness."

"Were you leaving, or did you want to go a few rounds Pure Blood?"

Faye took Rune's hand in hers. "I'm fine. I threw him across the courtyard. He's careful, and the weapons are fake." Faye poked him in the side with her blade.

"I'll take good care of your dove. Make sure when the queen of our court is tested, her enemies regret the notion."

Eighty-Four

Alister dismissed every attempt of diplomacy they sent. Faye had hoped to resolve this peacefully, but Rune's brother was set on vengeance. Faye tried to see the situation through his eyes. She didn't pretend to understand what he'd been through. The depth of his grief. She couldn't imagine a vacant-eyed Rune or caring for the shadow of the person she loved for eight hundred years.

Faye leaned her hip on Rune's desk, peering through the intricately designed wrought iron glass. Her mind wandered as she gazed at Hell's ever-twilight sky. "I think you should formally acknowledge me."

Rune set his documents down, offering her his undivided attention. "Vsenia, we have been over this."

They had. The past three weeks had been busy, the days bleeding together. Rune taught her to manipulate shields around herself and others. She could throw arcs and bolts of power. Her most recent lesson— Communicating telepathically.

She trained with Damian each morning. Learning combative techniques and how to maintain a shield while being attacked.

In the end, it felt pointless. Alister was thousands of years older than her. A master swordsman.

Faye frowned. "Your brother won't stop."

"I will find another way. One that will safeguard you, and the family you want." He took her hand, brushing his thumb over her knuckles. "The family *we* will have."

He always asked for time. Being immortal, the man had an endless quantity of it. Faye didn't have that luxury. "We need to put an end to the blood debt. Help me find a way to incapacitate him."

Rune squeezed her hand as his lips thinned. "Vsenia."

"He will attack me. If not in The Eyes, then later when I don't expect it."

"There are dozens of combative techniques I could teach you." He spoke in a gentle tone, leaning forward. "They take time to master. Even mastered, you are expecting to be able to manifest your will when you are being attacked. Learning to focus in such a way takes years."

Faye clenched her jaw, turning her attention to Hell's landscape. She had less than a week before Alister forced Rune to name her a whore or acknowledge her.

"Give me two more days to search for an alternative, and I will begin teaching you combative spells tonight. You will need to learn to tear down mental barriers." Rune lifted his chin, glancing at the door. He inhaled and turned his attention back to her. "Dinner is ready. You need to eat. You have been pushing yourself."

"You need to eat too." She smiled up at him as he stood.

Rune followed her lead, pressing his lips to the back of her hand. "What I sip from you each night is more than enough to sustain me."

Faye blushed at the memories of his lips at her throat as they strolled to the great room, hand in hand.

The evening meal had started without them. Faye and Rune took their usual seats. She made a plate, joining in with the laughter and chatter.

"Vash was explaining your idiotic, royal dating system," Sparrow informed Rune despite having a mouthful of food.

Vashien mouthed, *I'm sorry,* to Rune, and Faye took the opportunity to send a thought to Sadi.

I have an idea to stop Alister.

Faye waited, keeping her attention on Sparrow as she ate. Sadi was loyal to Rune, but she was willing to bet she would help if it freed Rune of his blood debt.

"Want to know a really easy fix for all this?" Sparrow dangled the question, entirely too pleased with herself.

Sadi's response was taking too long. Faye began doubting if she sent her thought correctly and turned to glance at the Familiar.

Sadi's sculpted eyebrow momentarily raised as their gazes met, then she bit a cut of meat off her knife paying attention to the conversation between Rune and Sparrow.

Faye explained her plan along her communication thread with Sadi as Rune chuckled, "I have the distinct feeling you are going to tell me."

"If you formally acknowledge her, your shit brother gets to attack her. If you don't, then Faye becomes the slut mistress of Hell. There's a third option you royals are just too stuck up to see." Sparrow beamed.

"I await your invaluable insight." Rune leaned back in his chair. Idly brushing his fingertips over Faye's thigh.

"My invaluable insight won't affect any cute babies you two have either." Faye choked on her drink, coughing into her glass. Scowling at her, Sparrow added, "Bitch don't try to lie. I know you, and you want his babies."

Faye wheezed into her napkin, trying to catch her breath as Rune rubbed her back. Thankfully she'd finished explaining her plan to Sadi before her sister ambushed her.

Sparrow clapped, unable to contain her I'm-a-genius grin. "Announce yourself as Faye's whore. Problem solved."

Leave it to her sister to find a loophole. One Faye didn't want. Questions rose in her mind all at once. If he announced himself as her whore was that all he could ever be? He would have to sacrifice being her husband and consort.

"No." The word slipped from her lips. Faye glanced at Rune and shook her head. "No."

Sparrow's shoulders dropped. "Bitch, you're ruining my perfect plan."

This wasn't perfect. One look at Rune and she knew he would accept it happily, sacrificing his title and social standing for her. He belonged to her, was hers to protect. From himself if need be. No matter how brilliant her sister thought she was, a technicality wouldn't stop Alister. Sparrow said so herself all those weeks ago.

This isn't base, bitch.

Sadi clasped Faye's shoulder drawing her from her thoughts. The Familiar smiled at her. "This can work. Come to the north wing after dinner, we'll iron out the details."

Faye admired the billowing lengths of fabric and colorful tapestries decorating Sadi's den. The Familiar stood at the fireplace turning a short white vase stuffed with fresh cut flowers. She tapped the clawed tip of her ring on her bottom lip before shifting the vase a few inches and scrutinizing it again.

Black light flashed over the walls and faded. "The Shadow Prince has sensitive ears," Sadi said absently without looking at her.

"Yeah," Faye muttered, walking to the chairs before the fireplace.

"You're asking me to go behind Rune's back," Sadi said, adjusting a black rose. "And defy his wishes."

Faye's cheeks heated. She didn't want to lie to him, but Rune wouldn't address his brother. He always asked for time. Immortality gifting him an endless number of days to scheme and plan.

She wasn't blessed with the same luxury.

"Do you really want Rune to announce himself as my whore?" Faye asked.

Sadi adjusted the vase a final time and turned toward her, folding her arms. Faye's brow pinched faintly as she realized it wasn't a vase at all. The flowers protruded from the eye sockets and jaw of an upturned skull.

Faye swallowed, returning her attention to Sadi. "We're both loyal to Ru—"

"I don't see loyalty," Sadi said flatly.

Faye tensed as her magic surged, answering her anger. "Do you think I like lying to him? Alister is coming for me. He is not going to care if Rune declares himself my whore. I want to call in the blood debt and finish this. Is there a way for me to formally acknowledge Rune?"

"You have no noble blood," Sadi said, as she went to the table and poured a glass of wine. "The only avenue you have to lay claim to the Shadow Prince is to form your court and announce him as your consort."

Faye's shoulders dropped as she joined Sadi. Initiating the blood debt would mean ambushing him. Like the High Queen did.

No, Rune loved her. She was nothing like the high bitch. "The High Queen won't sign the petition to form my court."

"There are other rulers, Morbid among them," Sadi said before sipping her wine. "If you witnessed Alister on the battlefield, you wouldn't be so anxious to face him."

"Damian told me he can break shields. He doesn't have blood dark enough to break mine."

Sadi laughed. "That will be the least of your problems. He's a day-blood that consistently killed dark-bloods. His favored move was to phase his opponent into open sky. Dispatch them when the freefall broke their concentration and behead them."

Faye's stomach knotted. As formidable as Alister was, it was safer to face him on her terms than wait for him to attack on his. "Rune's magic has no effect on me. Alister's won't either."

"Your life is tied to Rune's. I will take Alister's mind and kill him before it comes to that," Sadi said with a wave of her hand.

Dark-bloods and their violence. "No, I don't want him hurt. Make me a Familiar binding to put Alister to sleep."

"Bindings are initiated with blood. I can spell a dagger, but you'll have to dirty your hands," Sadi said, lifting her glass to point at her.

"I need to stab him?"

"Did you think Alister would offer up his blood if you asked nicely?"

It was a means to an end. Alister was immortal. A knife wound wouldn't kill him. "We're going to be part of the same court. You don't have to be such a bitch."

Sadi smiled, pouring a second glass of wine. She offered it to Faye as she said, "Then be a queen worthy of him."

Eighty-Five

The course of Rune's life changed in this open, airy building eight centuries ago. It would change once more this day. A token price to pay for his queen. Faye sat beside him before The Eyes and the High Council. Sparrow and Vashien were seated behind them alongside Sadi and Damian.

"The first order of business will be the petition for the formal acknowledgement of Faye Alexander. Shadow Prince, stand before us."

Rune stood, tension lacing each of his muscles. Murmuring whispers scattered over the crowd. Their voices overlapped into a constant unintelligible sound that filled the building. Every seat was accounted for, yet more people filed in, wanting to bear witness. They stood in the stairways, along the walkways. Pressed shoulder to shoulder, each hoping to catch a glimpse of the woman capable of taming the Shadow Prince.

He turned to Faye offering his hand. The Ra'Voshnik purred through his mind, admiring their queen. She wore dark pants with a satin backless shirt with flowing sleeves. Beautiful and fierce. Fate could not grant them a better queen.

Her hand slipped into his as they stepped into The Eyes. Faye held herself well, not letting her emotions show over her delicate features.

Rune stood next to her as pride and apprehension warred in him.

Alister sat in the front row to his right, and Rune noted Prinia's absence. His brother held a tactician's mind, learning from his missteps. Rune wouldn't be able to use Prinia as leverage a second time.

He knelt as they reached the center of The Eyes. Faye followed protocol perfectly, keeping her face neutral and placing her left hand on his right shoulder.

"What is that on your ring?" Lyssa's usual lyrical voice was overshadowed by her cold, condescending tone.

"My Lady's soul shard," Rune replied in kind as the Ra'Voshnik urged him to take Lyssa's head as payment for disrespecting his queen.

Lyssa clicked her tongue at him. "Truly Rune, your vanity astounds even me."

"Shadow Prince." Jha'ant adjusted his glasses, peering at the shard Faye displayed as the crowd quieted. He cleared his throat, turning his attention back to Rune. "Have you come to answer the petition?"

"I have come to inform the High Council of a mistake in circumstance." Rune stood, keeping his gaze on Jha'ant as the rustling and murmurs began anew. Louder.

"There is no mistake. You are court born. You rule a realm. You must answer. Refusal of response is to denounce her." Jha'ant's gaze fell to Faye and softened. The bird king raised a few notches in Rune's eyes. Perhaps he didn't want to see Faye labeled as a whore.

"I am unable to answer on behalf of this petition for the simple reason being, that I am Faye Alexander's whore." Rune expected the gasps, followed by the rustling and chatter of the audience. One voice yelled over them he did not.

"No!" Morgan screamed, silencing the crowd.

I should have announced her, Rune thought dryly.

Kill her so we can finish this and return home with our queen, the Ra'Voshnik growled, prowling his mind.

Calm yourself. This will be over soon. Rune turned to address Lyssa's daughter, who leaned forward as she grasped the railing of her family's box seating, high above the crowd.

Rune glowered at her, his voice menacing. "Do you challenge my choice?"

"No! Rune, she does not," Lyssa yelled. "Rune. Look at me, Shadow Prince." A growl vibrated in her words as she gritted out, "Child, sit."

Gabriel leaned forward, whispering to his sister. When he took her arm Morgan flung her brother off her with a burst of power. Gabriel struck the wall at the other end of their seat area and dropped.

Morgan stared at Rune for long moments. Tension building between them. Hatred burned in her eyes. She bared her teeth before looking away and taking her seat.

Rune's attention returned to the High Council. He would carry this label for her. Keep Faye safe. Protect her from Alister. His brother would renounce the blood debt when he learned Faye could heal Prin. Rune bowed his head, waiting for the words of protocol that would cripple his social standing.

In truth he cared little for his name, less of what others thought.

All he needed was her.

"Wait." Faye touched his arm. "Kneel."

Rune obeyed, sending her a thought. *What are you doing?*

She placed her hand on his shoulder and her voice filled his mind. *You make all the wrong moves for all the right reasons.*

Faye turned to Jha'ant. "I announce Rune Sacarlay, the Shadow Prince, Ruler of Hell, as my consort."

Panic skid down Rune's spine. Faye spoke words of protocol she couldn't know. Spoken here in The Eyes meant this was no court position. When a queen announced a consort within The Eyes, it was a tie between the two, what Faye would call a marriage. Her words claimed him as her own.

And allowed for Alister's vengeance.

Lyssa laughed. "You have no court. What you announce is utterly ridiculous. You are a meager peasant that needs to learn her place."

"Only they do," Morbid said as both Rune and the Ra'Voshnik growled, fixing their attention to Lyssa.

Prey, Voshki purred, eyeing Lyssa's throat. The Familiar King slid a document to Jareth, who read it and then handed it to Jha'ant.

Lyssa stood, snatching the document from the Artithian King.

What have you done? Rune spoke in Faye's mind

Sadi helped me with it. We must face this. Alister won't stop because of a technicality. Trust me to finish this.

This was not their plan. *This is a mistake.*

I'm asking you to trust me. We must finish this.

"Do you accept, Shadow Prince?" Morbid's voice pulled him from his private conversation.

Rune squared his gaze on Morbid. He and the Familiar King would have a long discussion in the near future since he was certain Morbid's signature approved the formation of Faye's court.

He gazed up at his queen. The stubborn minx who didn't fear his nature or the shards he carried. The queen he ached for his entire life. She was nothing he expected but had become everything he needed. "I accept and bow to the will of my queen," Rune spoke the words of protocol and rose.

Faye's breaths grew shorter as her gaze locked with Rune's brother. A vengeful rage hard set in his pale blue eyes. Faye drew her power, letting it flow over her to form multiple shields. This wasn't a sparring match with Damian. This man meant to kill her.

Alister please, I want to help your wife, Faye spoke directly to Alister's mind.

He didn't respond, drawing his sword as he ran his palm over its gleaming edge. Alister stepped into The Eyes, marring the pristine white marble with droplets of red. His dual blades hovering omi- nously over each shoulder.

"I invoke my blood debt," Alister said. His voice was a hollow, gravel-filled grave.

"Denounce it. Now. Brother," Rune demanded, stepping between them.

Faye perceived Rune's magic swiftly rising to meet his will. She choked his strength, unleashing a wide arc of dark power, knocking Rune out of The Eyes.

A dome of churning black mist flashed over the circular platform. Faye's shield kept Sadi and Rune out but also caged her in alone with Alister.

"Alister! Touch her, and I will kill you!" Rune raged. The foundation shook with each devastating blow. Cracks fissured from him, forking across the ground before climbing up the walls of white and gold.

Faye ignored the overlapping screams and shouts as the audience fell into chaos and took a cautious step toward him. "I know you're angry. I'm stronger than Rune. Let me help Prinia."

She tensed as Alister raised his sword. The two floating behind him moved in either direction, menacingly surrounding her—A pack of wolves cornering their prey.

"I see you're made for each other," Alister said coldly before flicking his sword between Rune and herself with effortless grace. "Both of you have such a flair for the dramatic."

"Faye, drop the shield!" Rune roared, eyes gone black.

It sliced her heart to hear Rune desperate and fearful. She'd tried reasoning with Alister and planned for his dismissal. It was time to end the debt between Rune and his brother. Faye lifted her hand, making a fist. Her magic coiled, constricting around him. Alister's body went rigid, his back bowing taut. A small cut was all it would take. A nick and this would be over.

Faye shrieked the next instant, pulled off her feet by a fistful of hair. Alister stood behind her, his image across The Eyes dissolving.

Time slowed as a flash of silver dragged across her throat. She didn't fear his weapon, expecting it. It was the pain she hadn't anticipated. Couldn't focus through it to summon her dagger.

"I expected you to shield her," Alister said coldly.

Faye closed her eyes, letting the pain bite. She welled her power and closed her hand imagining the feel of the metal hilt on her palm, but her dagger didn't answer.

Alister's magic surged, and Faye's eyes snapped open. He summoned a large narrow box. Water sloshing over its wooden sides. Cold panic tore through her mind.

Not a box, Faye realized. A coffin.

Alister took her by the throat, turning her to face him. He turned to Rune and said, "You shield her brother. But did you teach her to breathe underwater?"

Faye's heart hammered in her ears as terror stole her focus. She kicked and thrashed, frantically grabbing at Alister's hold. She'd trained and prepared for a fight. To clash with his swords. She never imagined he would drown her.

Alister met her fearful gaze with a smile. "I would have just taken your pretty head. It's Rune's fault you die hard now."

"Wait—"

The next instant, she was submerged. Ice-cold water ripped the breath from her lungs. The hand at her throat held her in its frigid depths. Faye twisted and kicked her legs, grasping for purchase. Her nails tearing as they raked across the roughened wood.

Her lungs burned, demanding air. She clawed at the arm holding her to her death, reaching higher, shredding fabric.

Faye gasped for air only to be choked with water. This wasn't happening. She couldn't die here. Wouldn't die here. Not after she found the love and acceptance, she craved all her life. Not when Rune would give her the little boy and girl she longed for. Not when she could protect Anarians from vicious dark-bloods.

Her magic rose with her mental cadence as she gazed up at the distorted whites and golds through the water's surface.

Death will come for me, but not today.

Faye's strength flared, power arcing off her back and a crash followed. Her wings freeing her from her watery prison. She sucked greedy breaths of air and closed her hand. The hilt of her dagger answering her summons.

"Death will come for me, but not today!" She screamed, baring her teeth as she plunged the dagger into Alister's side.

He hissed a breath, releasing her to pull the dagger free. A gray mist curved from the bloodied blade, continuing to enter his wound. Alister threw the blade, sending it clattering over the marble. It skid to a stop at the emptied chairs surrounding them.

Even distanced, the mist continued its work.

Alister choked. The veins in his neck straining as he struggled to breathe.

Faye rushed to him, still struggling with her own choking breaths. She took his face in her hands and leaned close. The wet strands of her black hair fell over Alister's face, as she whispered to him before he went still.

She gazed at him; his expression slackened as he rested in a spelled sleep that would heal the injuries she'd inflicted.

Faye got to her feet and dropped her shields. Rune phased to her side as she floated Alister's body to the table, laying him before Jareth. "If you would please see that he is taken home. He will wake in a few hours."

"Of course," Jareth answered with a solemn nod.

Rune's arms encircled her, pulling her against him. Her wings squeezed tight to his chest. "You are reckless," he murmured at her ear.

"I didn't expect him to try to drown me." Faye took a deep breath, clearing her throat. "Sometimes you have to take a blow to deliver one."

She shifted in his arms, and he answered with a low growl before tightening his hold. Faye shoved him harder, whispering, "I'm getting you wet."

"This charade grows tiresome. How dare you not only display a fictitious shard, but have the audacity to display ten of them." The High Queen leaned back in her chair.

Faye glanced up at the unmounted shards floating around her, not realizing she'd summoned them.

Rune's chest vibrated as he growled, "Lyssa."

"Everyone is gifted one shard." The High Queen leaned forward, getting to her feet while laying her palms on the table. "The Creator had one shard. The Shadow Prince has one shard. This." The High Queen sneered, waving at Faye. "This monstrous bitch is a mockery."

Rune released Faye and took a threatening step toward the High Queen. A small carved box appeared in his hand. Opening it, he floated his two unmounted shards of Darkness for the High Council to see. "I carry three shards of Darkness. If you believe this to be but my vanity, by all means, draw power from them."

The color drained from Lyssa's face as she stepped away from the table. Her eyes fixed on his shards as silence dragged between them.

"Since it appears our commitments have cleared," Morbid dramatically motioned to the now empty seats surrounding The Eyes. "I shall also take my leave." He bowed to Faye and said with a feline grin, "Your court is formed, my Lady."

Morbid vanished. The other council members quickly followed. Leaving only Faye and her newly formed court.

Rune stepped behind her, snaking his arm around her waist before pulling her against him. He smoothed his lips over the side of her neck, his teeth scraping her skin. "What is the name of your new court, my queen?" He rasped.

Faye leaned into him, caressing the side of his face, and answered, "The Court of Chaos and Darkness."

Epilogue

Alister jerked awake. He scanned his surroundings, assessing his situation. He expected to be imprisoned in Standing Shadows, his father's crystalline palace. Or tied to a torturer's wrack with Rune waiting for him to wake before he went to work on him.

Instead Alister was in his home. His own bed.

He gingerly touched his side, feeling for the wound Rune's chosen left him. There was no pain. Alister pulled up his shirt. His mouth went slack as he stared. His alabaster skin was untouched. There was no wound.

Rune's chosen had the opportunity to kill him, and she'd chosen mercy.

"Jareth," Alister called for his brother, getting out of bed.

"On the front porch with Prin." His brother answered.

Alister stepped onto his porch. Prinia had chosen this cottage so long ago. A place Alister expected to spend a quiet life with the woman he loved. Jareth and Prinia sat in rocking chairs overlooking the flower fields she once loved.

"He didn't come for her." Alister smoothed his fingertips over the side of Prinia's face, tucking a strand of her hair behind her ear before taking his seat next to her. His mind reeled.

"Time has changed both of you."

Alister didn't respond.

"You live. Proof his queen is gentle," Jareth said.

Alister nodded, taking Prinia's hand. "Rune somehow found a kind queen." Her words circled his mind.

Rune has gravely wronged you. I will make it right.

Alister no longer remembered the sound of Prinia's voice. How she would laugh as he slowly exhaled when she picked these ugly flowers every day.

Hope became a bitter thing to him. He hoped she would return to him. Hoped each morning when he woke, he would see recognition in her eyes. He held onto that hope for decades. The centuries that followed without his kind, gentle Prinia, petrified his heart. His bitterness twisted him.

But Rune's queen sought to save her. Bring his Prin back to him.

For the first time in centuries, Alister let himself hope.

Acknowledgments

I have no words to express my tremendous gratitude for the people in my life.

To my family, thank you for listening to my ramblings and encouraging my nonsense. For decades.

To my editor, Hina at Faemance. The amount of knowledge I've garnered from you continues to astound me. I would not have the story I do without your guidance and insight. Thank you from the bottom of my black heart.

To my chaos demon, Jada. I would not have this story without you. Thank you for the countless hours and beautiful words. I can't express my gratitude for your brilliant feedback and the way you put your whole ass jadussy into helping me polish my story.

To BookTok and my wing woman. Thank you for the encouragement and laugher. Taking this journey with all of you is a privilege I am enormously grateful for.

And finally to my war horse. You've been beside me through every wild notion, every strange endeavor, and every new path I've deemed needs discovering. There's no one I would rather walk this path with. Til death baby.

About the Author

Kalista Neith is a dark fantasy author who writes about love. What people are willing to endure to obtain it, and what they will sacrifice to keep it.

When she's not writing Kalista can typically be found huddled with blankets, eating too many chocolate panda cookies, thinking up new ways to torture her imaginary friends.

Kalista Neith can be found online at:

KalistaNeith.com
Linktr.ee/KalistaNeith

CPSIA information can be obtained
at www.ICGtesting.com
Printed in the USA
JSHW031508050822
28882JS00002B/3/J